THE BIG K

PART ONE

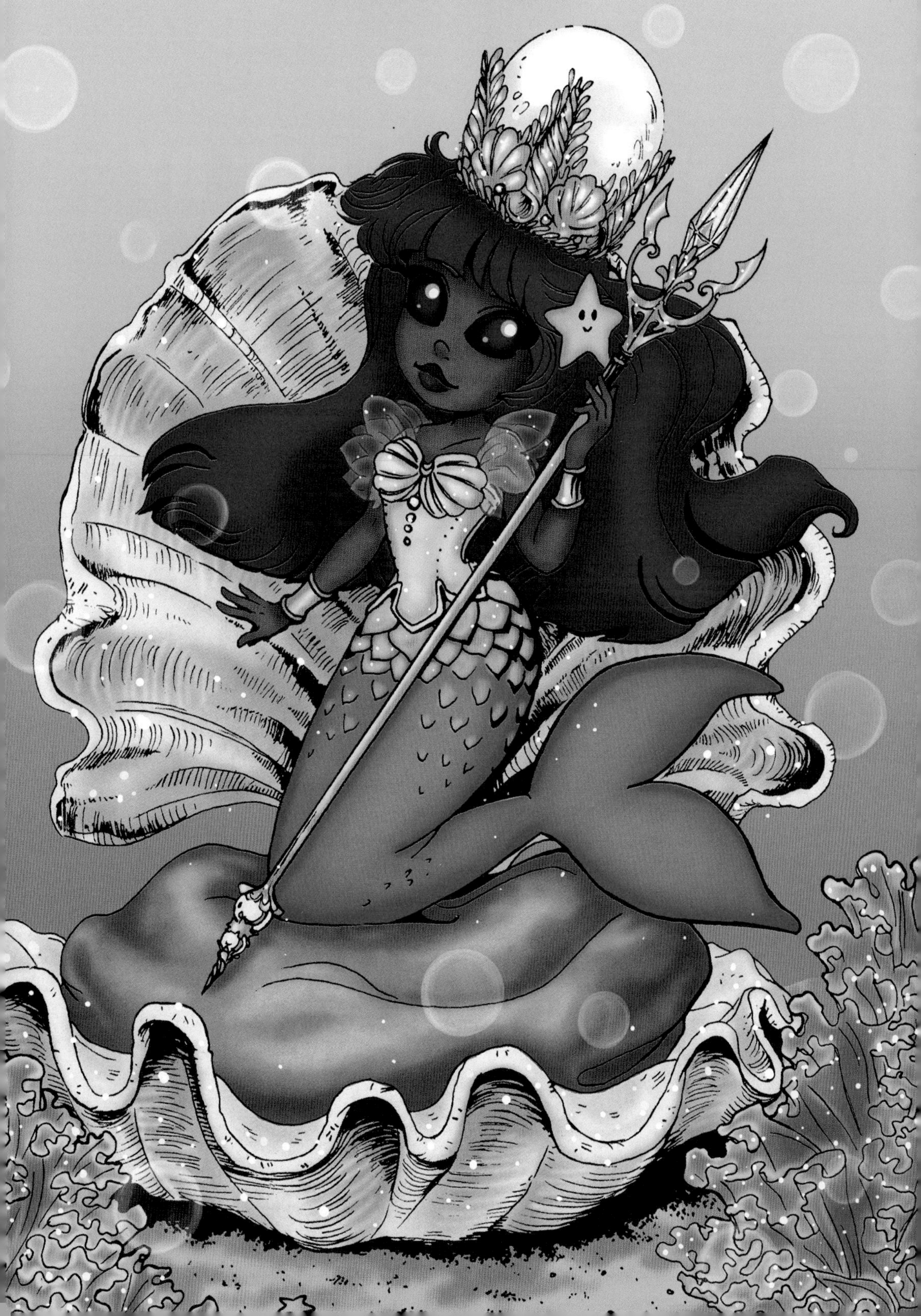

TOYETICA 1

STORY AND ART BY MARTY LEGROW

LETTERING
Justin Birch

COLORS
Mindy Indy

MISS BADLUCK BY
Rebecca Hawk

Bryan Seaton: Publisher/ CEO • Shawn Gabborin: Editor In Chief • Jason Martin: Publisher-Danger Zone • Nicole D'Andria: Marketing Director/Editor
Jim Dietz: Social Media Manager • Danielle Davison: Executive Administrator • Chad Cicconi: Action Lawyer • Shawn Pryor: President of Creator Relatio

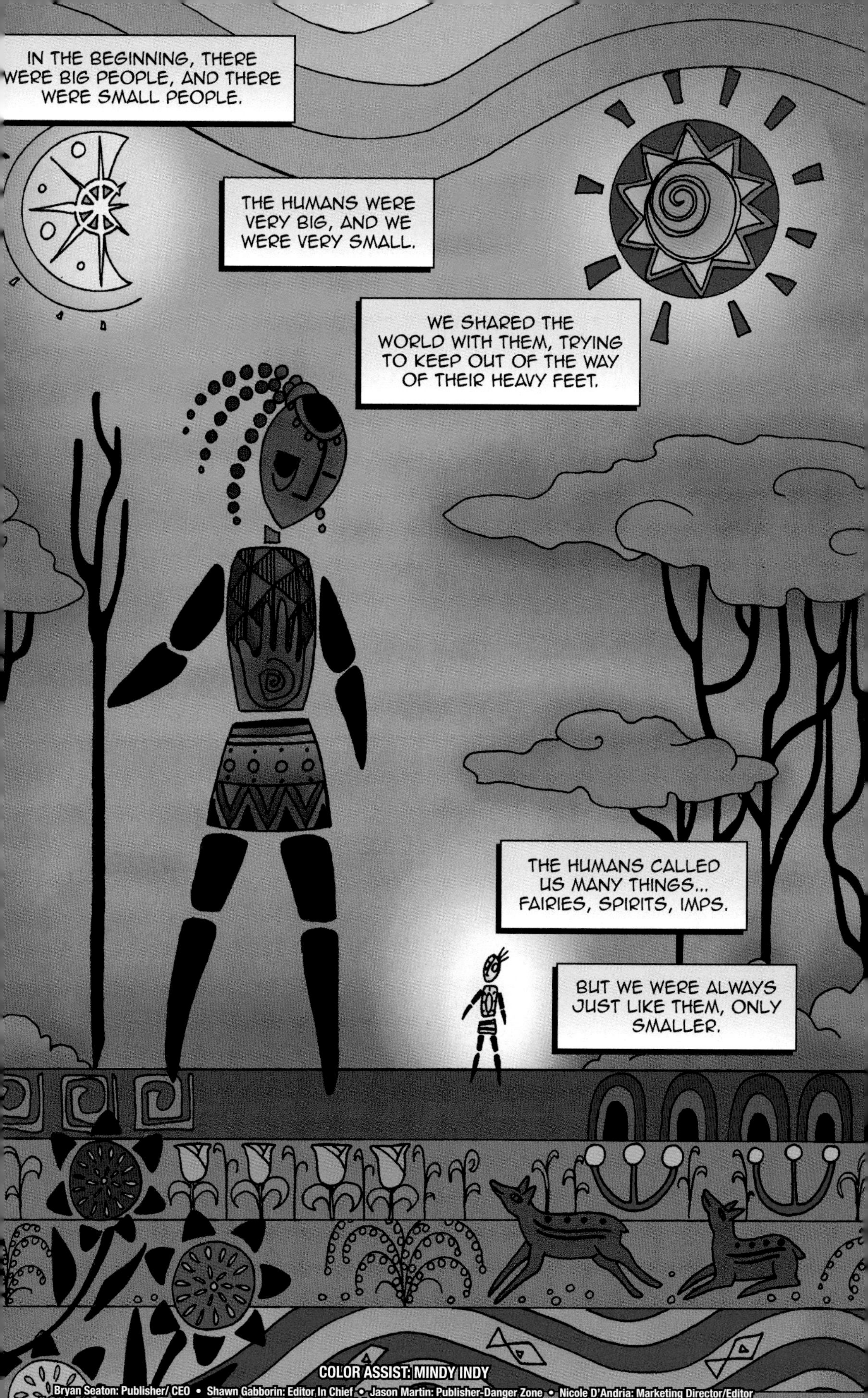
IN THE BEGINNING, THERE WERE BIG PEOPLE, AND THERE WERE SMALL PEOPLE.
THE HUMANS WERE VERY BIG, AND WE WERE VERY SMALL.
WE SHARED THE WORLD WITH THEM, TRYING TO KEEP OUT OF THE WAY OF THEIR HEAVY FEET.
THE HUMANS CALLED US MANY THINGS... FAIRIES, SPIRITS, IMPS.
BUT WE WERE ALWAYS JUST LIKE THEM, ONLY SMALLER.

COLOR ASSIST: MINDY INDY

Bryan Seaton: Publisher/ CEO • Shawn Gabborin: Editor In Chief • Jason Martin: Publisher-Danger Zone • Nicole D'Andria: Marketing Director/Editor
Jim Dietz: Social Media Manager • Danielle Davison: Executive Administrator • Chad Cicconi: Inaction Figure • Shawn Pryor: President of Creator Relations

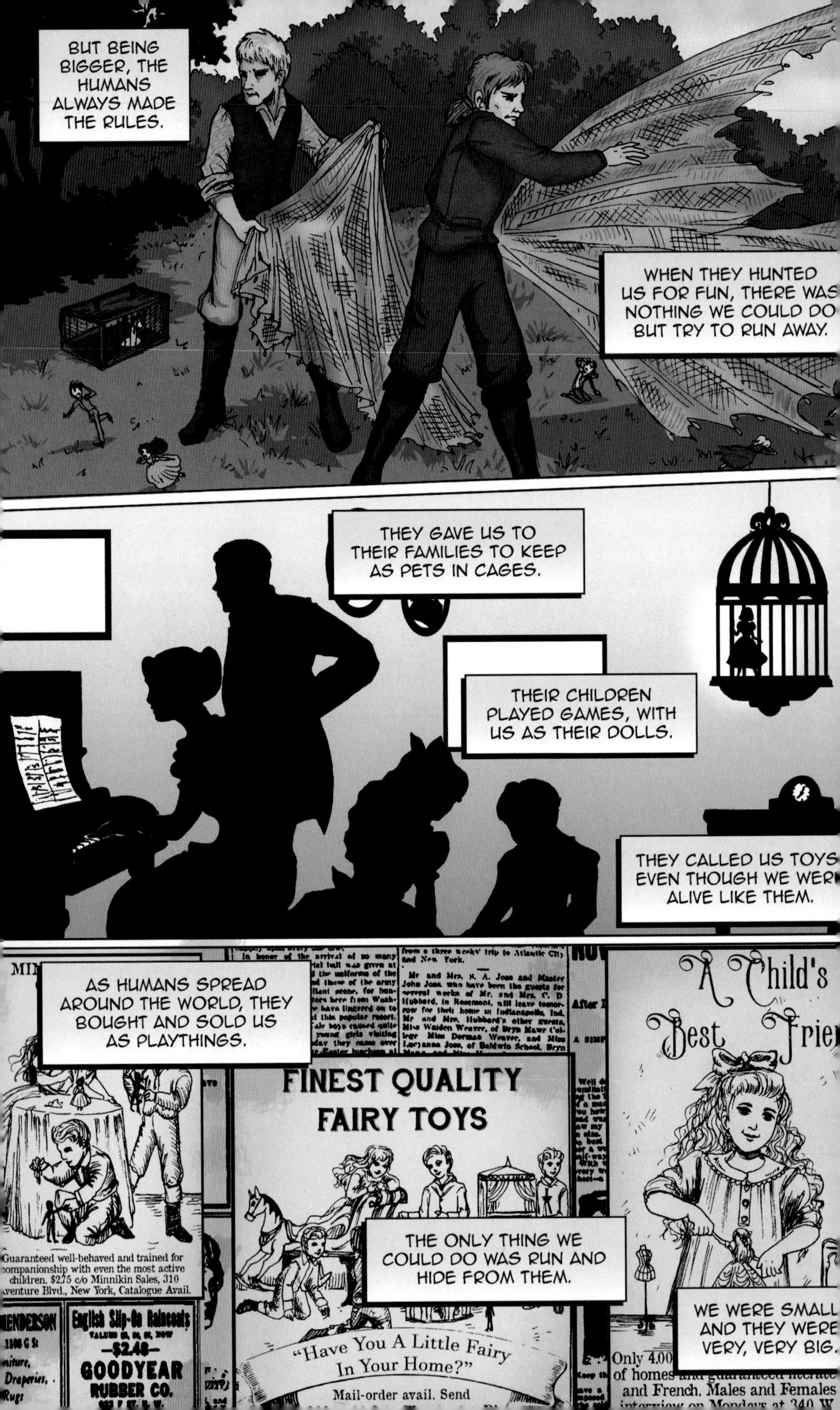
BUT BEING BIGGER, THE HUMANS ALWAYS MADE THE RULES.
WHEN THEY HUNTED US FOR FUN, THERE WAS NOTHING WE COULD DO BUT TRY TO RUN AWAY.
THEY GAVE US TO THEIR FAMILIES TO KEEP AS PETS IN CAGES.
THEIR CHILDREN PLAYED GAMES, WITH US AS THEIR DOLLS.
THEY CALLED US TOYS EVEN THOUGH WE WERE ALIVE LIKE THEM.
AS HUMANS SPREAD AROUND THE WORLD, THEY BOUGHT AND SOLD US AS PLAYTHINGS.
Guaranteed well-behaved and trained for companionship with even the most active children. $2.75 c/o Minnikin Sales, 310 Adventure Blvd., New York, Catalogue Avail.
FINEST QUALITY FAIRY TOYS
THE ONLY THING WE COULD DO WAS RUN AND HIDE FROM THEM.
“Have You A Little Fairy In Your Home?”
Mail-order avail. Send
English Slip-On Raincoats
—$2.48—
GOODYEAR RUBBER CO.
A Child's Best Friend
WE WERE SMALL AND THEY WERE VERY, VERY BIG.
and French. Males and Females

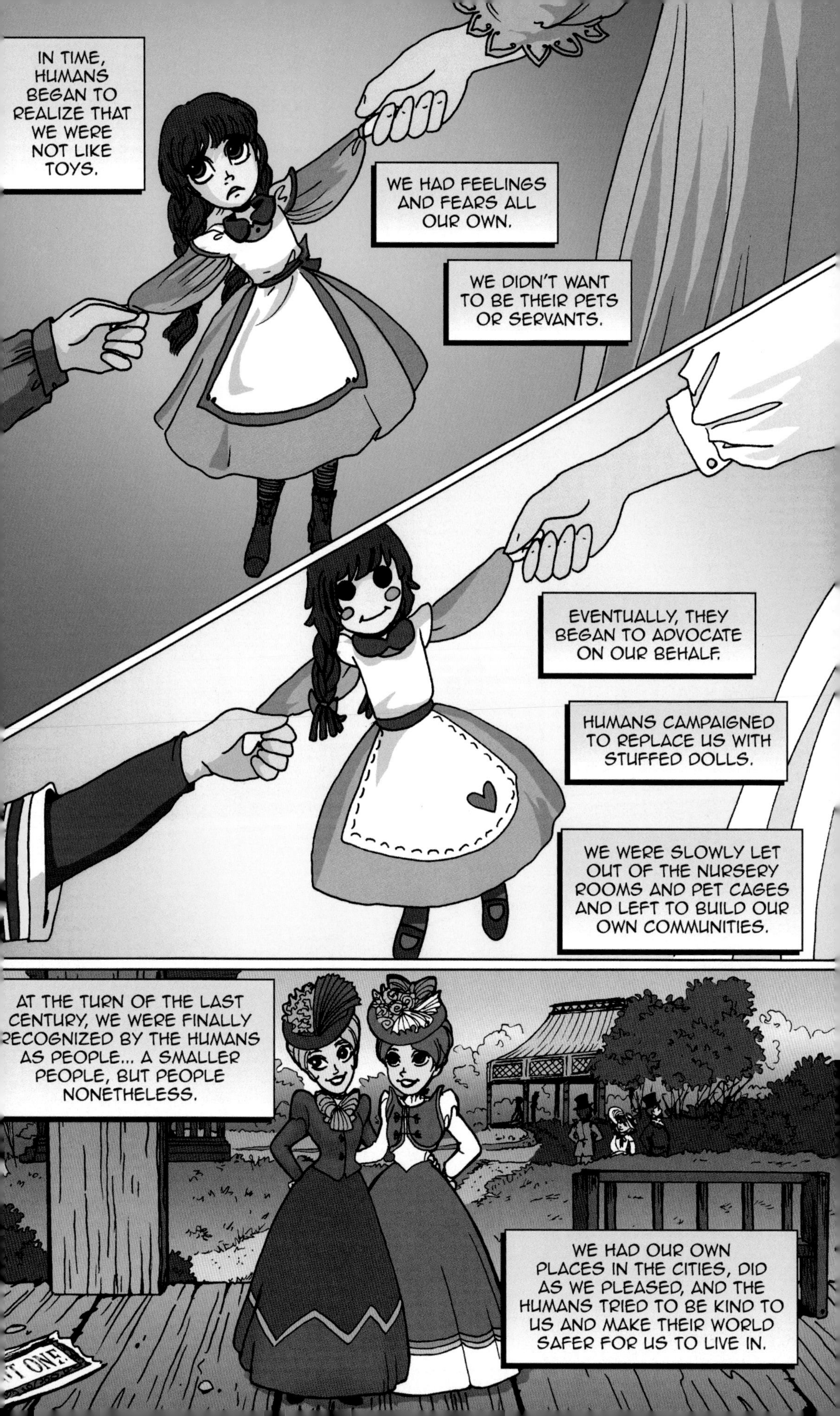

IN TIME, HUMANS BEGAN TO REALIZE THAT WE WERE NOT LIKE TOYS.
WE HAD FEELINGS AND FEARS ALL OUR OWN.
WE DIDN'T WANT TO BE THEIR PETS OR SERVANTS.
EVENTUALLY, THEY BEGAN TO ADVOCATE ON OUR BEHALF.
HUMANS CAMPAIGNED TO REPLACE US WITH STUFFED DOLLS.
WE WERE SLOWLY LET OUT OF THE NURSERY ROOMS AND PET CAGES AND LEFT TO BUILD OUR OWN COMMUNITIES.
AT THE TURN OF THE LAST CENTURY, WE WERE FINALLY RECOGNIZED BY THE HUMANS AS PEOPLE... A SMALLER PEOPLE, BUT PEOPLE NONETHELESS.
WE HAD OUR OWN PLACES IN THE CITIES, DID AS WE PLEASED, AND THE HUMANS TRIED TO BE KIND TO US AND MAKE THEIR WORLD SAFER FOR US TO LIVE IN.

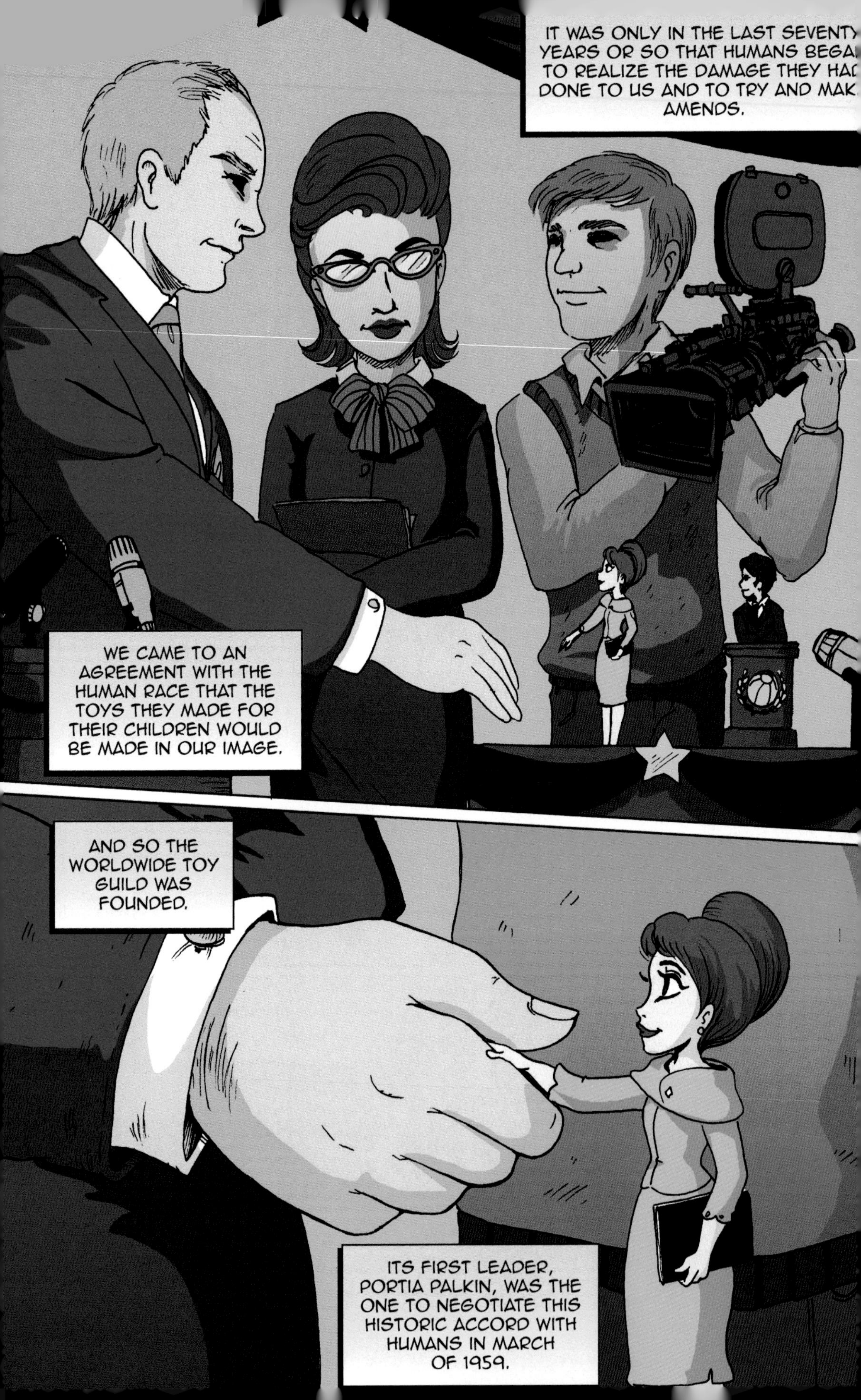
IT WAS ONLY IN THE LAST SEVENTY YEARS OR SO THAT HUMANS BEGA TO REALIZE THE DAMAGE THEY HAD DONE TO US AND TO TRY AND MAK AMENDS.
WE CAME TO AN AGREEMENT WITH THE HUMAN RACE THAT THE TOYS THEY MADE FOR THEIR CHILDREN WOULD BE MADE IN OUR IMAGE.
AND SO THE WORLDWIDE TOY GUILD WAS FOUNDED.
ITS FIRST LEADER, PORTIA PALKIN, WAS THE ONE TO NEGOTIATE THIS HISTORIC ACCORD WITH HUMANS IN MARCH OF 1959.

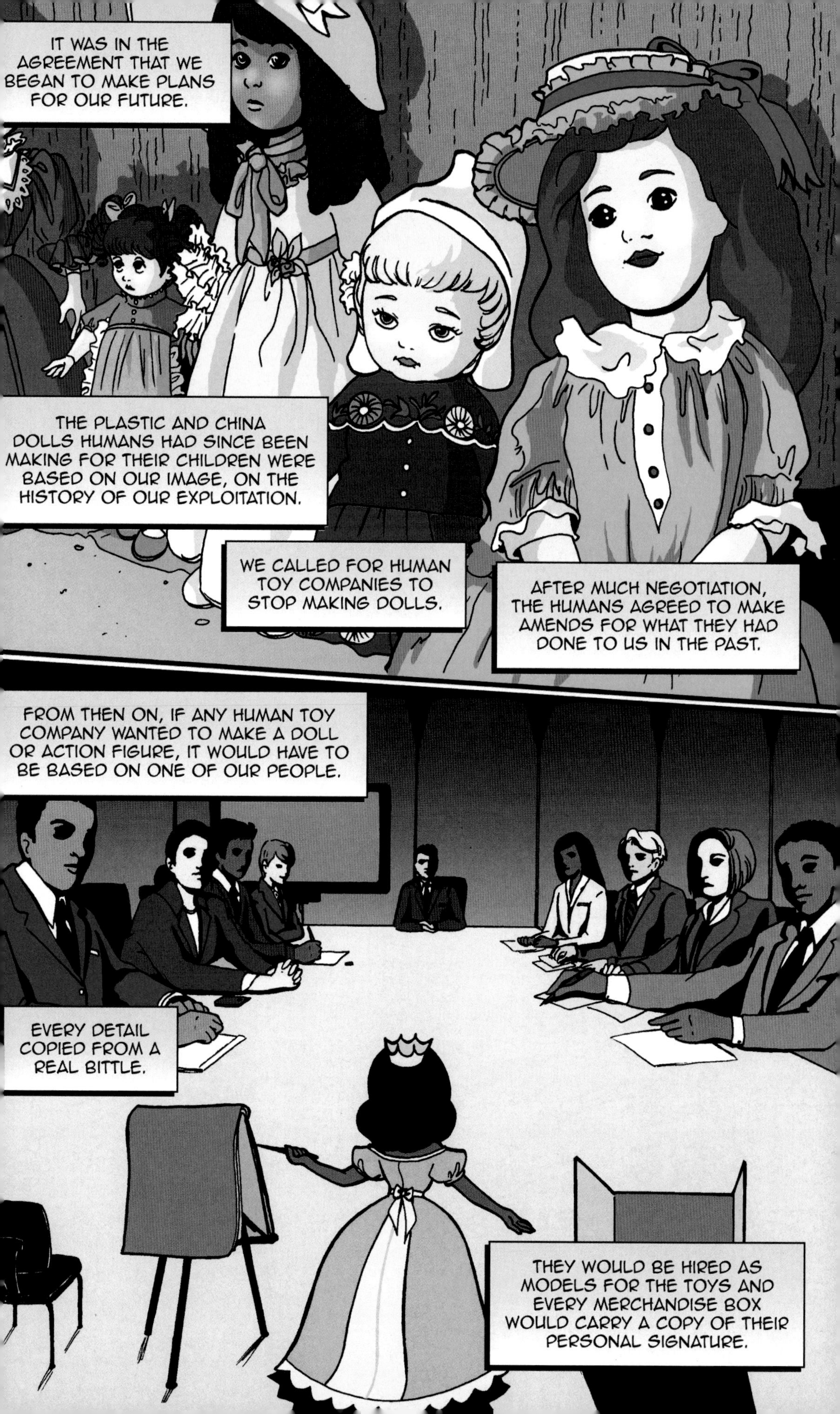
IT WAS IN THE AGREEMENT THAT WE BEGAN TO MAKE PLANS FOR OUR FUTURE.
THE PLASTIC AND CHINA DOLLS HUMANS HAD SINCE BEEN MAKING FOR THEIR CHILDREN WERE BASED ON OUR IMAGE, ON THE HISTORY OF OUR EXPLOITATION.
WE CALLED FOR HUMAN TOY COMPANIES TO STOP MAKING DOLLS.
AFTER MUCH NEGOTIATION, THE HUMANS AGREED TO MAKE AMENDS FOR WHAT THEY HAD DONE TO US IN THE PAST.
FROM THEN ON, IF ANY HUMAN TOY COMPANY WANTED TO MAKE A DOLL OR ACTION FIGURE, IT WOULD HAVE TO BE BASED ON ONE OF OUR PEOPLE.
EVERY DETAIL COPIED FROM A REAL BITTLE.
THEY WOULD BE HIRED AS MODELS FOR THE TOYS AND EVERY MERCHANDISE BOX WOULD CARRY A COPY OF THEIR PERSONAL SIGNATURE.

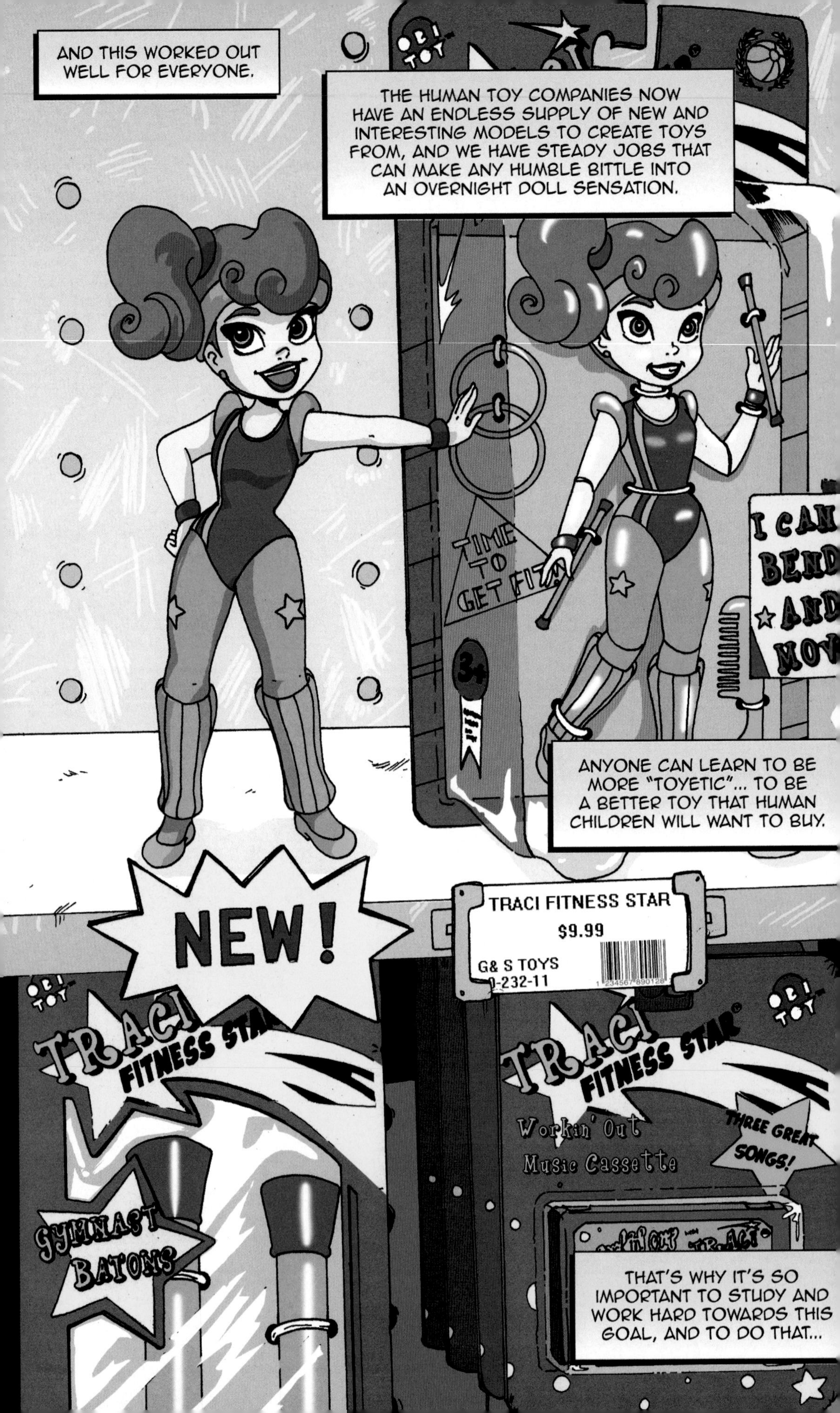
AND THIS WORKED OUT WELL FOR EVERYONE.
THE HUMAN TOY COMPANIES NOW HAVE AN ENDLESS SUPPLY OF NEW AND INTERESTING MODELS TO CREATE TOYS FROM, AND WE HAVE STEADY JOBS THAT CAN MAKE ANY HUMBLE BITTLE INTO AN OVERNIGHT DOLL SENSATION.
TIME TO GET FIT!
I CAN BEND AND MOV
ANYONE CAN LEARN TO BE MORE "TOYETIC"... TO BE A BETTER TOY THAT HUMAN CHILDREN WILL WANT TO BUY.
NEW!
TRACI FITNESS STAR
$9.99
G& S TOYS
0-232-11
TRACI FITNESS STAR
GYMNAST BATONS
TRACI FITNESS STAR
Workin' Out Music Cassette
THREE GREAT SONGS!
THAT'S WHY IT'S SO IMPORTANT TO STUDY AND WORK HARD TOWARDS THIS GOAL, AND TO DO THAT...

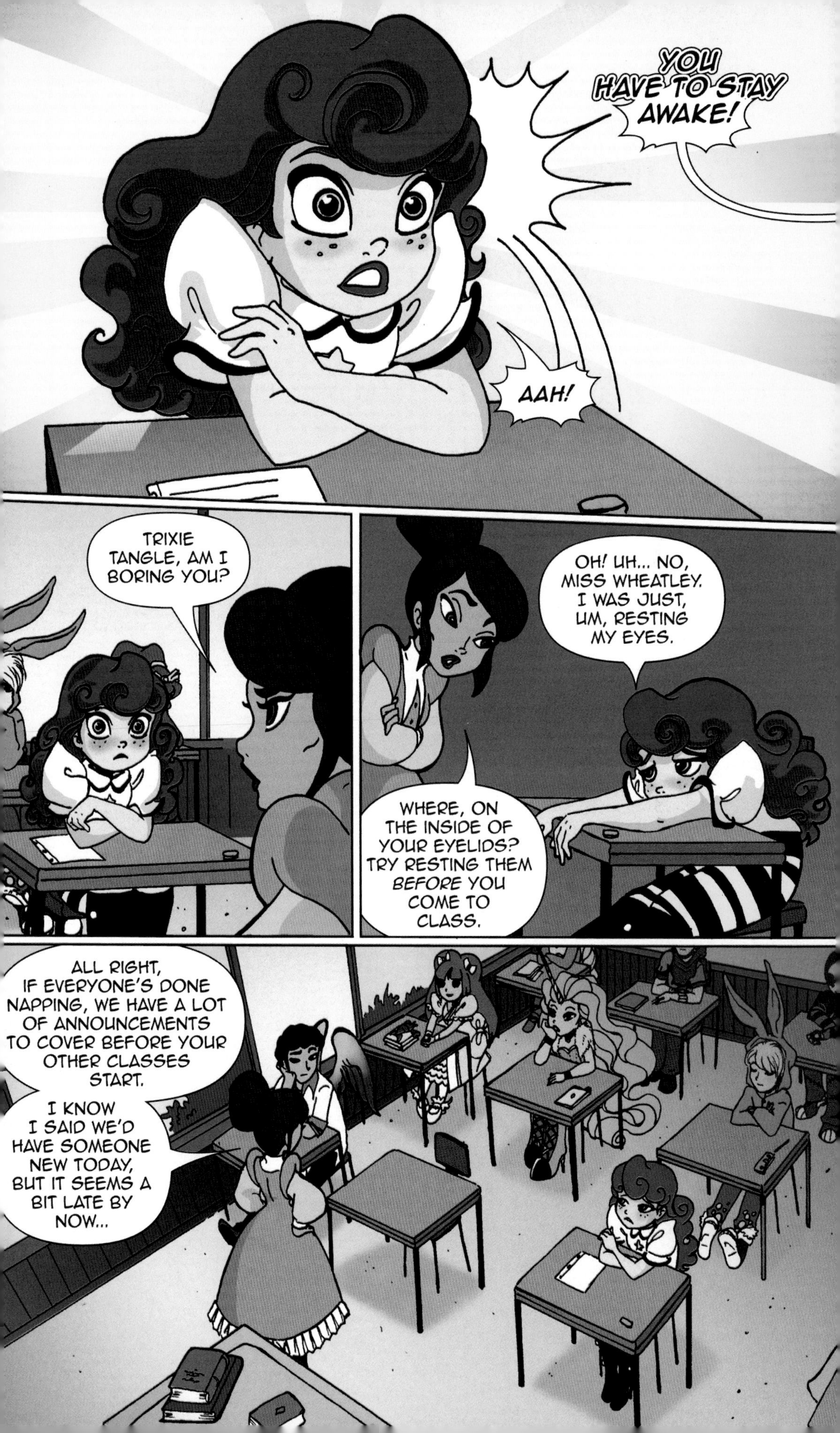
YOU HAVE TO STAY AWAKE!
AAH!
TRIXIE TANGLE, AM I BORING YOU?
OH! UH... NO, MISS WHEATLEY. I WAS JUST, UM, RESTING MY EYES.
WHERE, ON THE INSIDE OF YOUR EYELIDS? TRY RESTING THEM BEFORE YOU COME TO CLASS.
ALL RIGHT, IF EVERYONE'S DONE NAPPING, WE HAVE A LOT OF ANNOUNCEMENTS TO COVER BEFORE YOUR OTHER CLASSES START.
I KNOW I SAID WE'D HAVE SOMEONE NEW TODAY, BUT IT SEEMS A BIT LATE BY NOW...

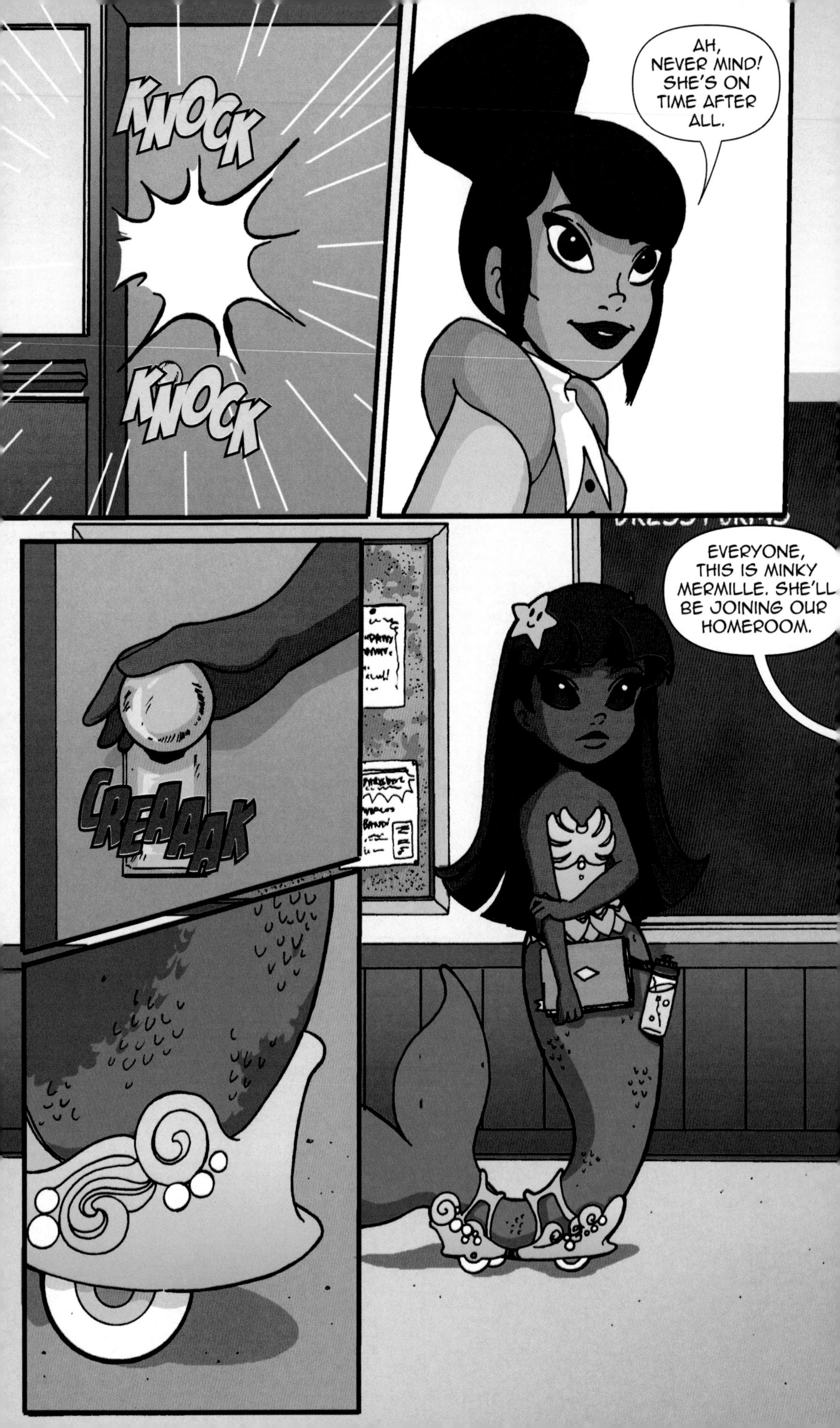
KNOCK
KNOCK
AH, NEVER MIND! SHE'S ON TIME AFTER ALL.
CREAAAAK
EVERYONE, THIS IS MINKY MERMILLE. SHE'LL BE JOINING OUR HOMEROOM.

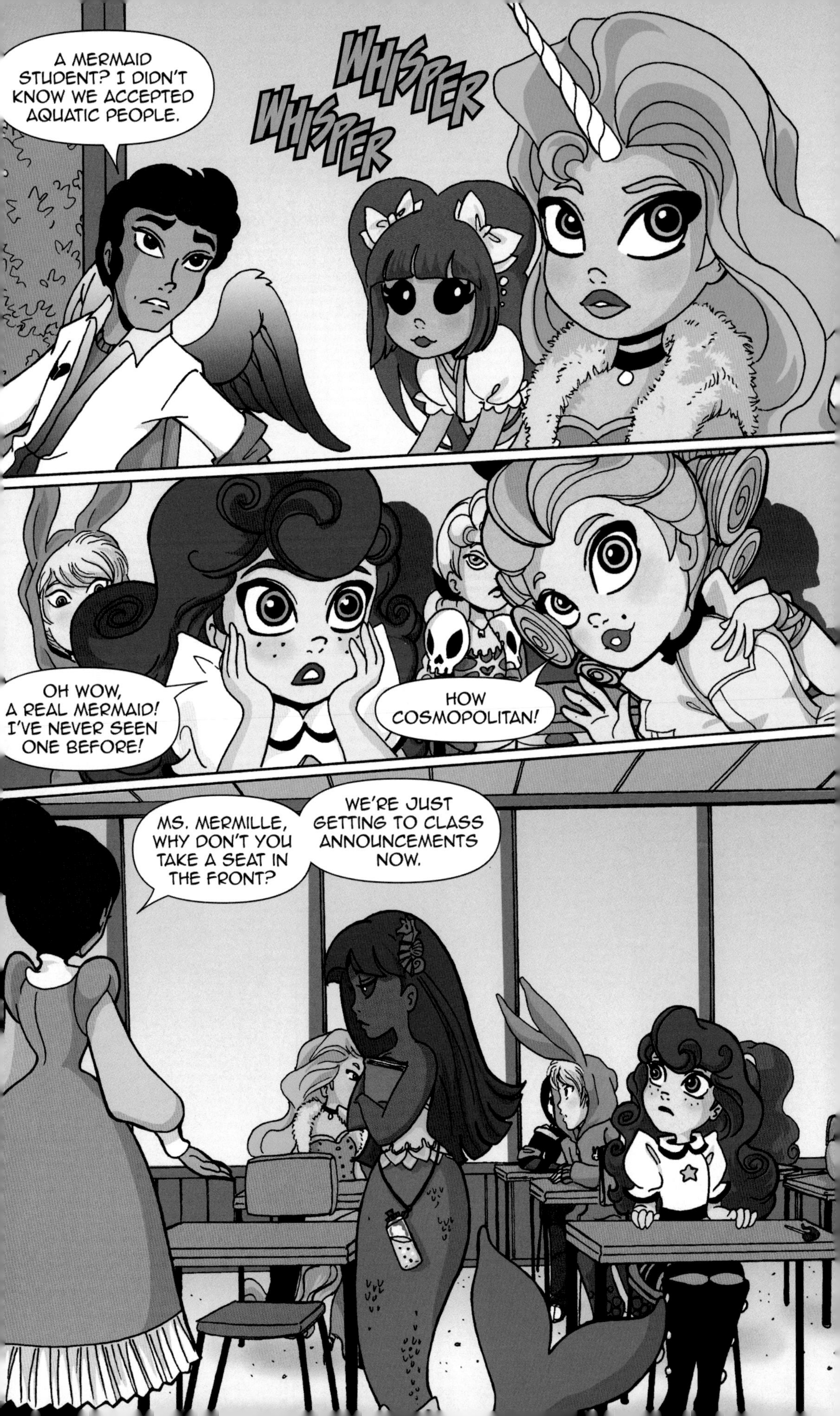
A MERMAID STUDENT? I DIDN'T KNOW WE ACCEPTED AQUATIC PEOPLE.
WHISPER WHISPER
OH WOW, A REAL MERMAID! I'VE NEVER SEEN ONE BEFORE!
HOW COSMOPOLITAN!
MS. MERMILLE, WHY DON'T YOU TAKE A SEAT IN THE FRONT?
WE'RE JUST GETTING TO CLASS ANNOUNCEMENTS NOW.

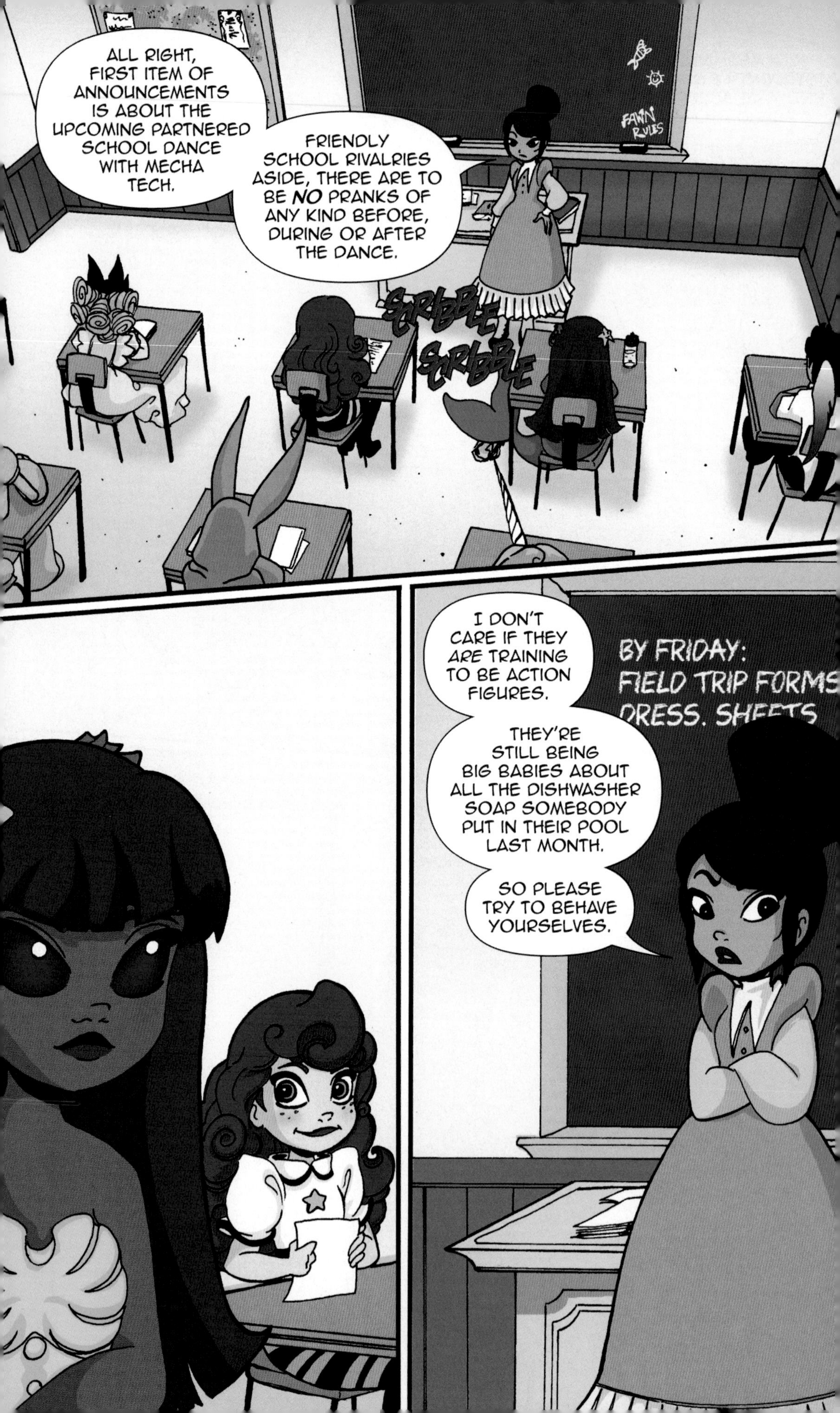
ALL RIGHT, FIRST ITEM OF ANNOUNCEMENTS IS ABOUT THE UPCOMING PARTNERED SCHOOL DANCE WITH MECHA TECH.
FRIENDLY SCHOOL RIVALRIES ASIDE, THERE ARE TO BE *NO* PRANKS OF ANY KIND BEFORE, DURING OR AFTER THE DANCE.
FAWN RULES
SCRIBBLE
SCRIBBLE
I DON'T CARE IF THEY *ARE* TRAINING TO BE ACTION FIGURES.
BY FRIDAY:
FIELD TRIP FORMS
THEY'RE STILL BEING BIG BABIES ABOUT ALL THE DISHWASHER SOAP SOMEBODY PUT IN THEIR POOL LAST MONTH.
SO PLEASE TRY TO BEHAVE YOURSELVES.

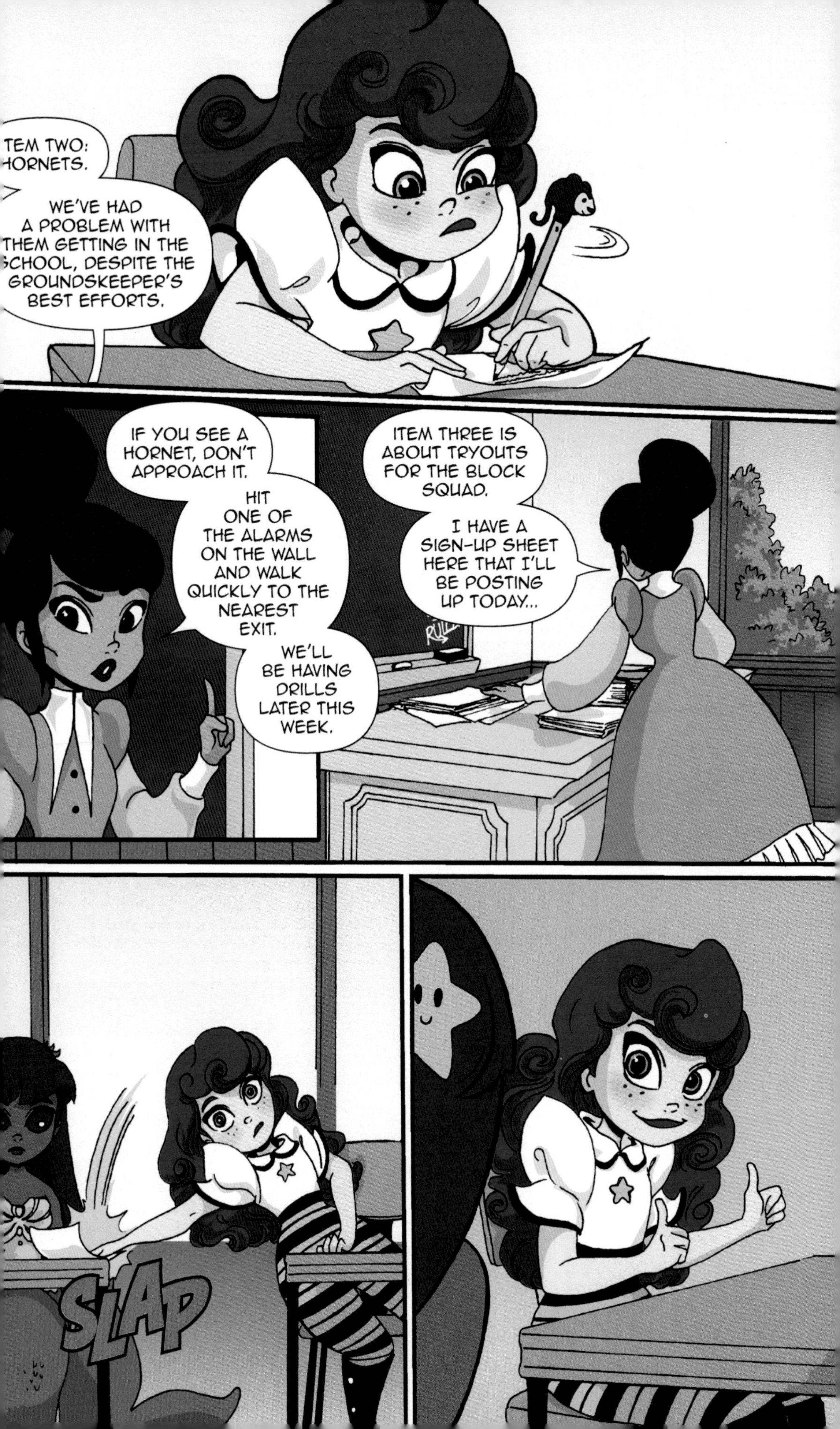

TEM TWO: HORNETS.
WE'VE HAD A PROBLEM WITH THEM GETTING IN THE SCHOOL, DESPITE THE GROUNDSKEEPER'S BEST EFFORTS.
IF YOU SEE A HORNET, DON'T APPROACH IT.
HIT ONE OF THE ALARMS ON THE WALL AND WALK QUICKLY TO THE NEAREST EXIT.
WE'LL BE HAVING DRILLS LATER THIS WEEK.
ITEM THREE IS ABOUT TRYOUTS FOR THE BLOCK SQUAD.
I HAVE A SIGN-UP SHEET HERE THAT I'LL BE POSTING UP TODAY...
SLAP

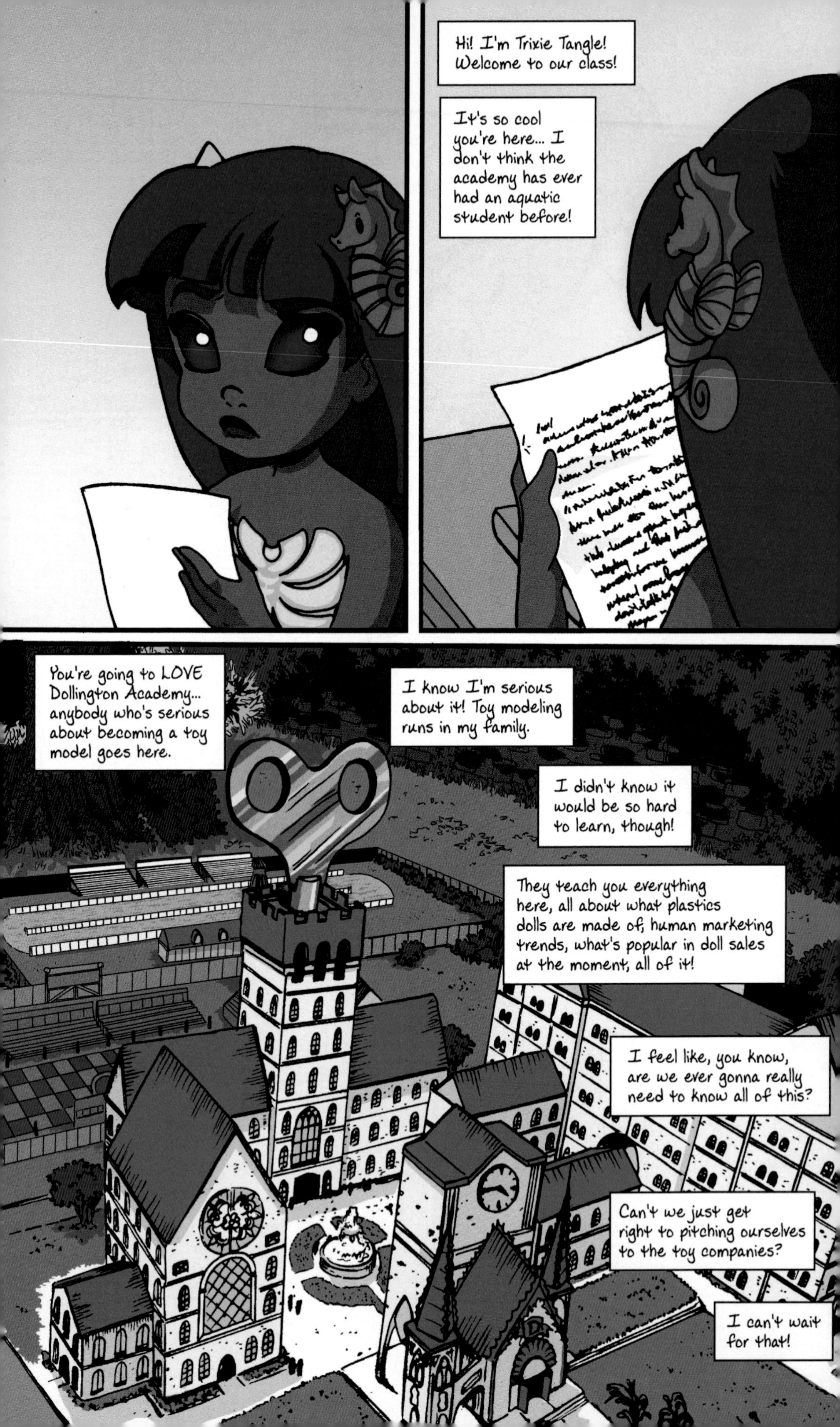
Hi! I'm Trixie Tangle! Welcome to our class!
It's so cool you're here... I don't think the academy has ever had an aquatic student before!
You're going to LOVE Dollington Academy... anybody who's serious about becoming a toy model goes here.
I know I'm serious about it! Toy modeling runs in my family.
I didn't know it would be so hard to learn, though!
They teach you everything here, all about what plastics dolls are made of, human marketing trends, what's popular in doll sales at the moment, all of it!
I feel like, you know, are we ever gonna really need to know all of this?
Can't we just get right to pitching ourselves to the toy companies?
I can't wait for that!

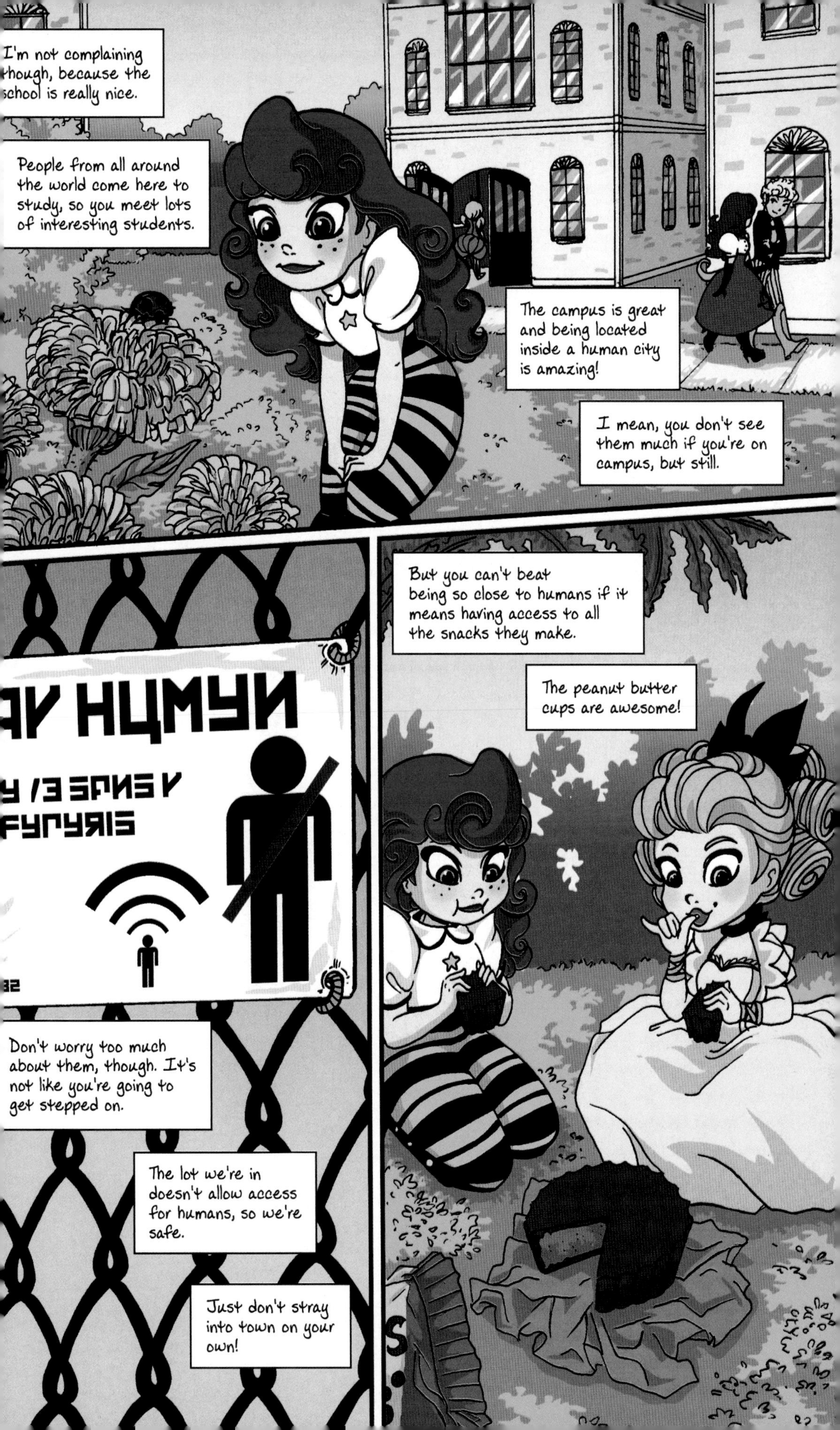

I'm not complaining though, because the school is really nice.
People from all around the world come here to study, so you meet lots of interesting students.
The campus is great and being located inside a human city is amazing!
I mean, you don't see them much if you're on campus, but still.
Don't worry too much about them, though. It's not like you're going to get stepped on.
The lot we're in doesn't allow access for humans, so we're safe.
Just don't stray into town on your own!
But you can't beat being so close to humans if it means having access to all the snacks they make.
The peanut butter cups are awesome!

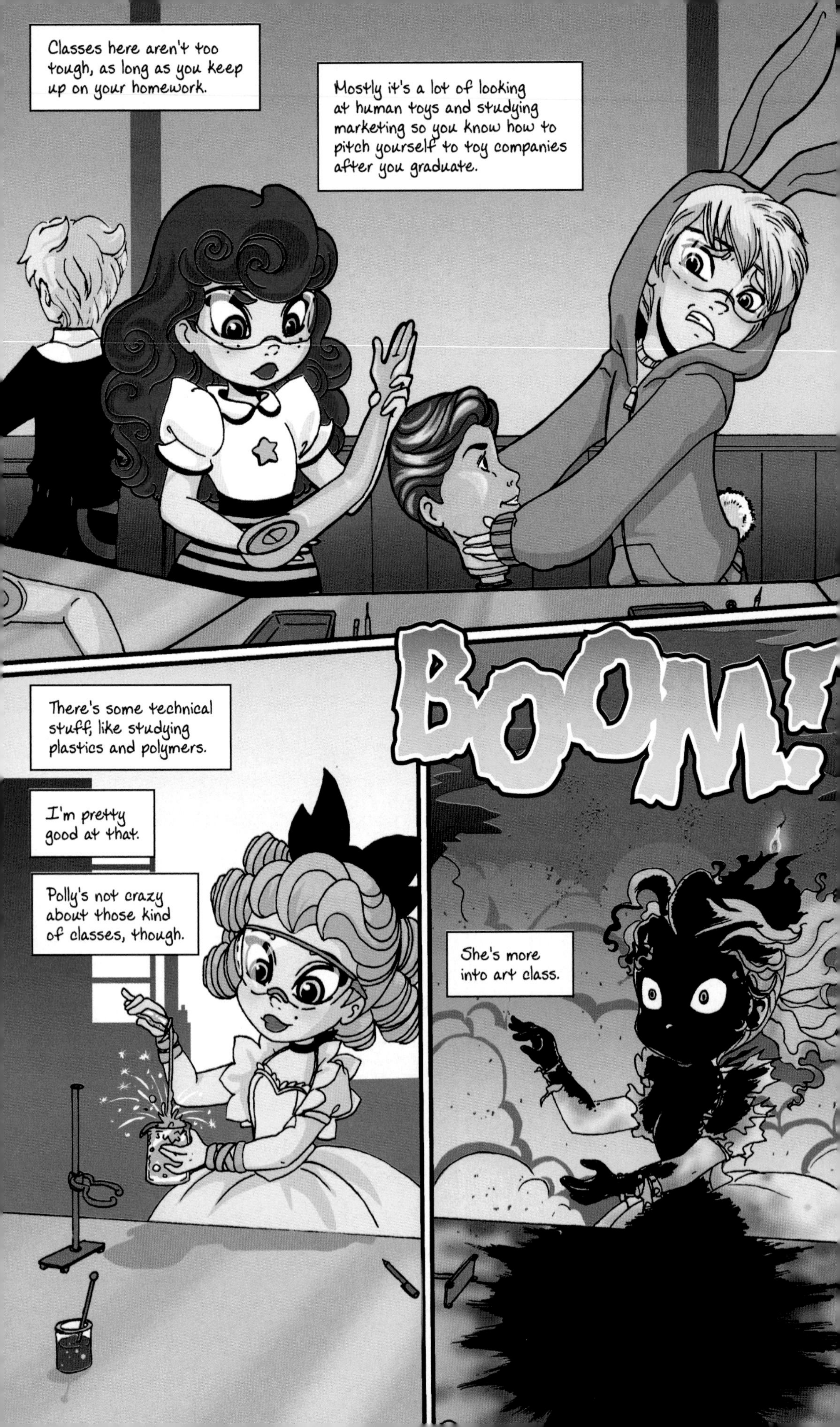
Classes here aren't too tough, as long as you keep up on your homework.
Mostly it's a lot of looking at human toys and studying marketing so you know how to pitch yourself to toy companies after you graduate.
There's some technical stuff, like studying plastics and polymers.
I'm pretty good at that.
Polly's not crazy about those kind of classes, though.
BOOM!
She's more into art class.

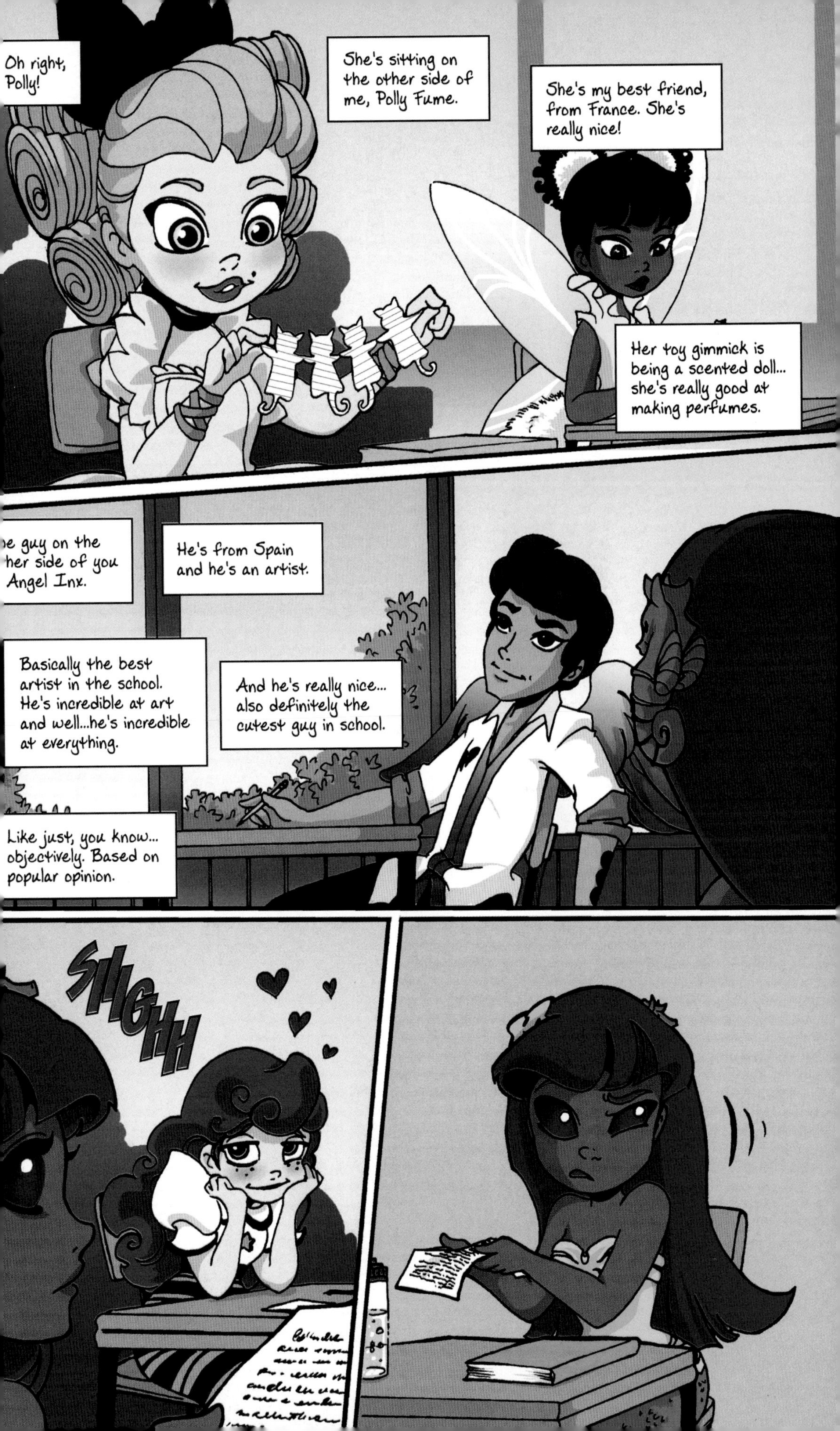
Oh right, Polly!
She's sitting on the other side of me, Polly Fume.
She's my best friend, from France. She's really nice!
Her toy gimmick is being a scented doll... she's really good at making perfumes.
e guy on the her side of you Angel Inx.
He's from Spain and he's an artist.
Basically the best artist in the school. He's incredible at art and well...he's incredible at everything.
And he's really nice... also definitely the cutest guy in school.
Like just, you know... objectively. Based on popular opinion.
SIIIGHH

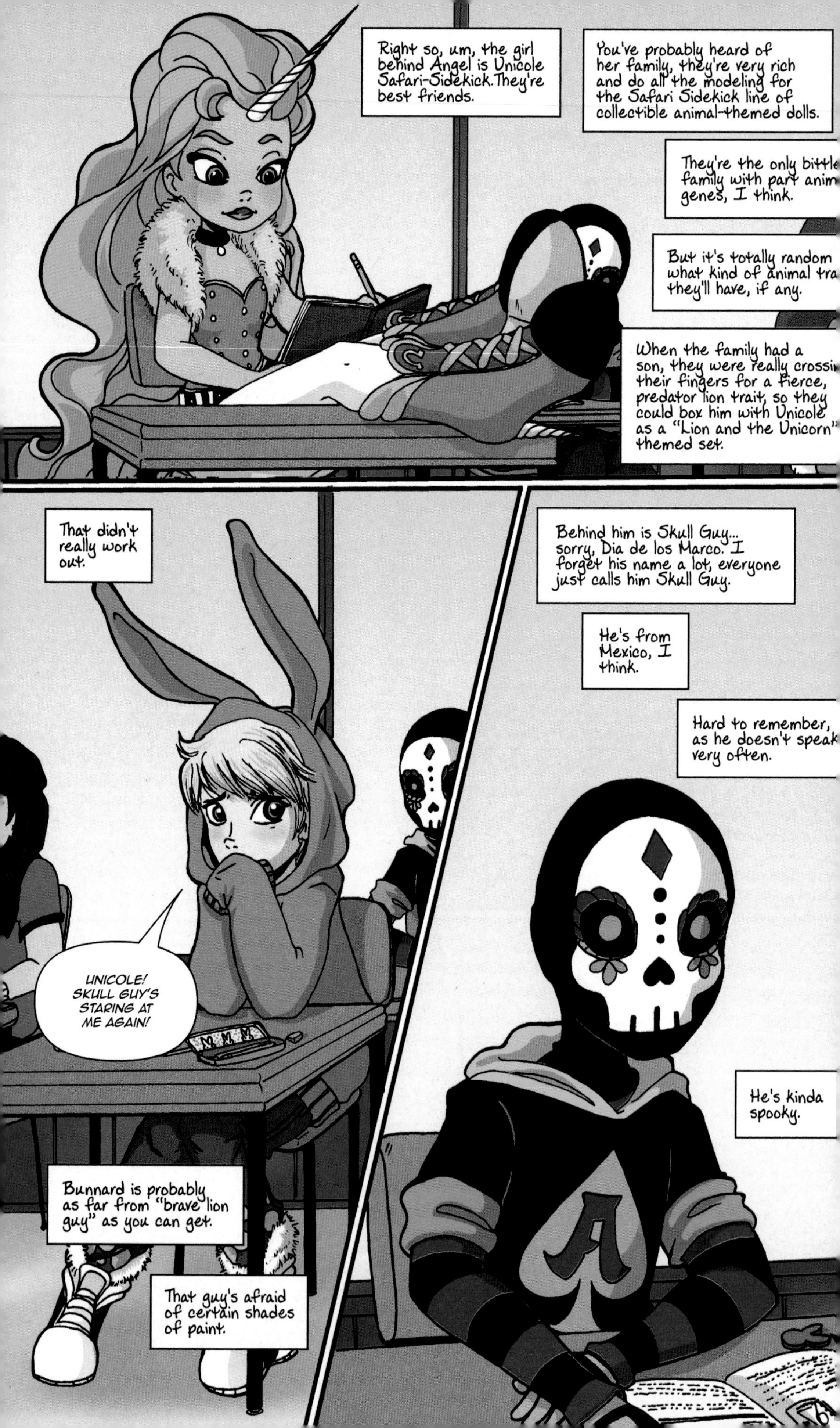
Right so, um, the girl behind Angel is Unicole Safari-Sidekick. They're best friends.
You've probably heard of her family, they're very rich and do all the modeling for the Safari Sidekick line of collectible animal-themed dolls.
They're the only bittl family with part anim genes, I think.
But it's totally random what kind of animal tra they'll have, if any.
When the family had a son, they were really crossi their fingers for a fierce, predator lion trait, so they could box him with Unicole as a "Lion and the Unicorn" themed set.
That didn't really work out.
UNICOLE! SKULL GUY'S STARING AT ME AGAIN!
Bunnard is probably as far from "brave lion guy" as you can get.
That guy's afraid of certain shades of paint.
Behind him is Skull Guy... sorry, Dia de los Marco. I forget his name a lot, everyone just calls him Skull Guy.
He's from Mexico, I think.
Hard to remember, as he doesn't speak very often.
He's kinda spooky.

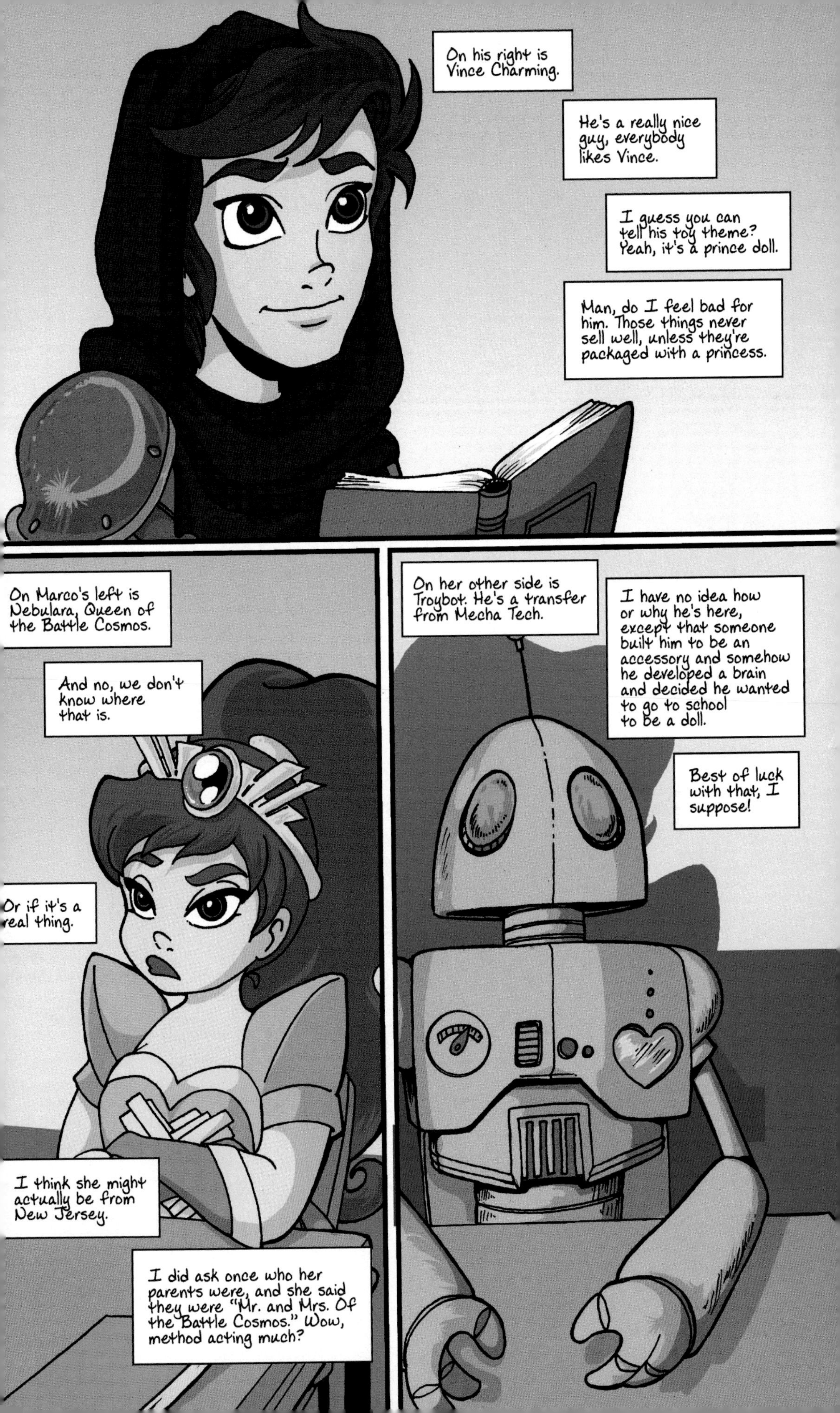
On his right is Vince Charming.
He's a really nice guy, everybody likes Vince.
I guess you can tell his toy theme? Yeah, it's a prince doll.
Man, do I feel bad for him. Those things never sell well, unless they're packaged with a princess.
On Marco's left is Nebulara, Queen of the Battle Cosmos.
And no, we don't know where that is.
Or if it's a real thing.
I think she might actually be from New Jersey.
I did ask once who her parents were, and she said they were "Mr. and Mrs. Of the Battle Cosmos." Wow, method acting much?
On her other side is Troybot. He's a transfer from Mecha Tech.
I have no idea how or why he's here, except that someone built him to be an accessory and somehow he developed a brain and decided he wanted to go to school to be a doll.
Best of luck with that, I suppose!

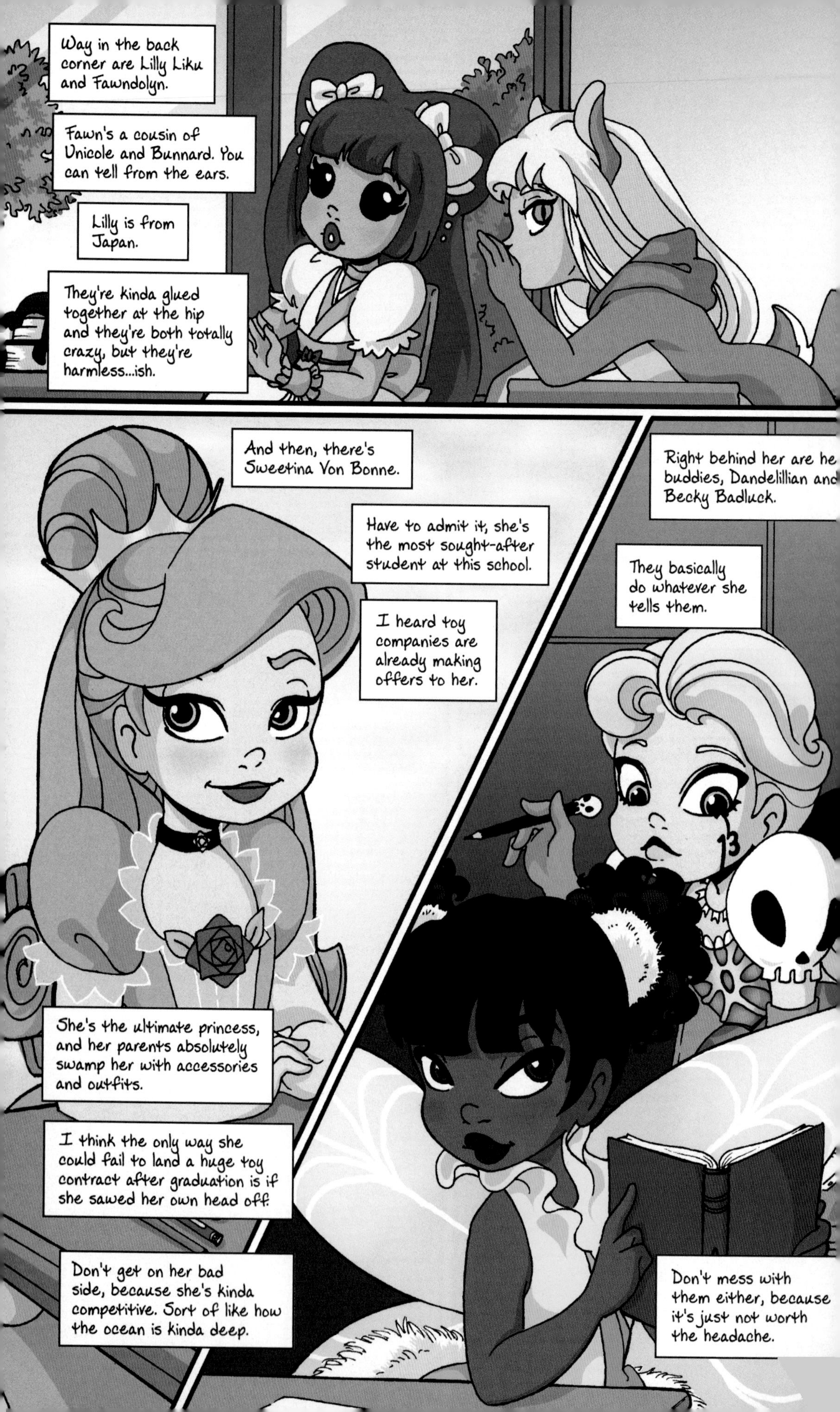
Way in the back corner are Lilly Liku and Fawndolyn.
Fawn's a cousin of Unicole and Bunnard. You can tell from the ears.
Lilly is from Japan.
They're kinda glued together at the hip and they're both totally crazy, but they're harmless...ish.
And then, there's Sweetina Von Bonne.
Have to admit it, she's the most sought-after student at this school.
I heard toy companies are already making offers to her.
She's the ultimate princess, and her parents absolutely swamp her with accessories and outfits.
I think the only way she could fail to land a huge toy contract after graduation is if she sawed her own head off.
Don't get on her bad side, because she's kinda competitive. Sort of like how the ocean is kinda deep.
Right behind her are he buddies, Dandelillian and Becky Badluck.
They basically do whatever she tells them.
13
Don't mess with them either, because it's just not worth the headache.

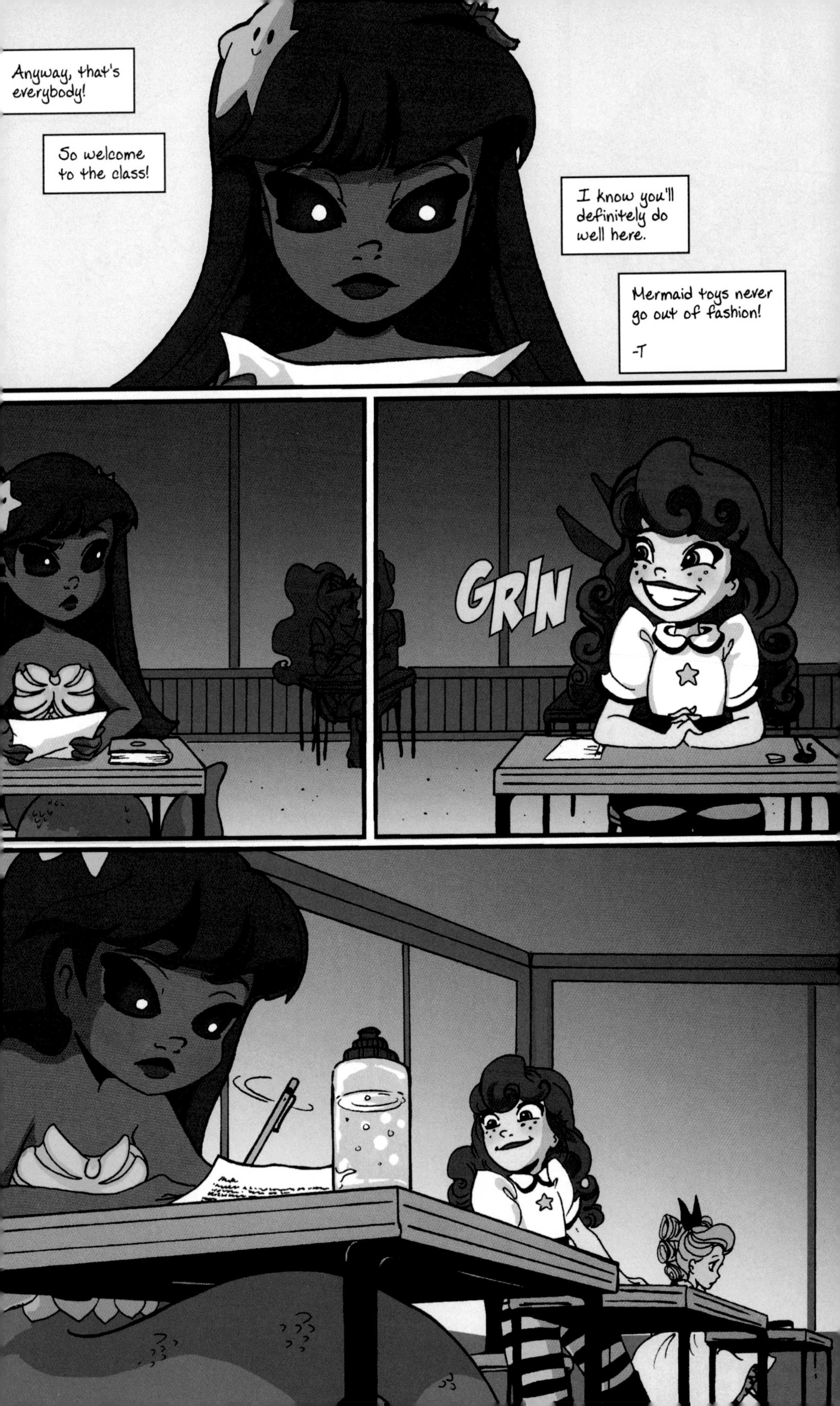
Anyway, that's everybody!
So welcome to the class!
I know you'll definitely do well here.
Mermaid toys never go out of fashion!
-T
GRIN

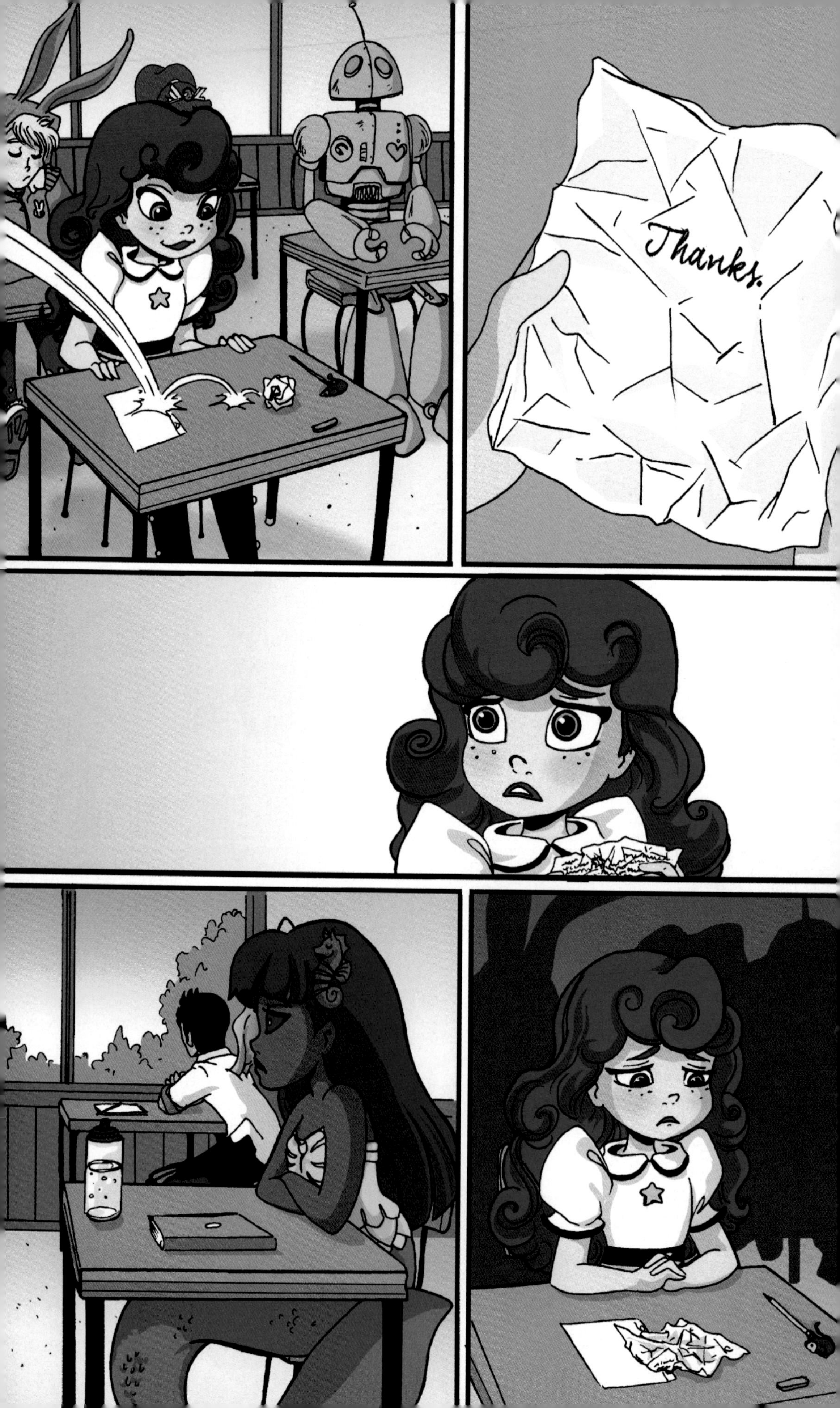

Thanks.

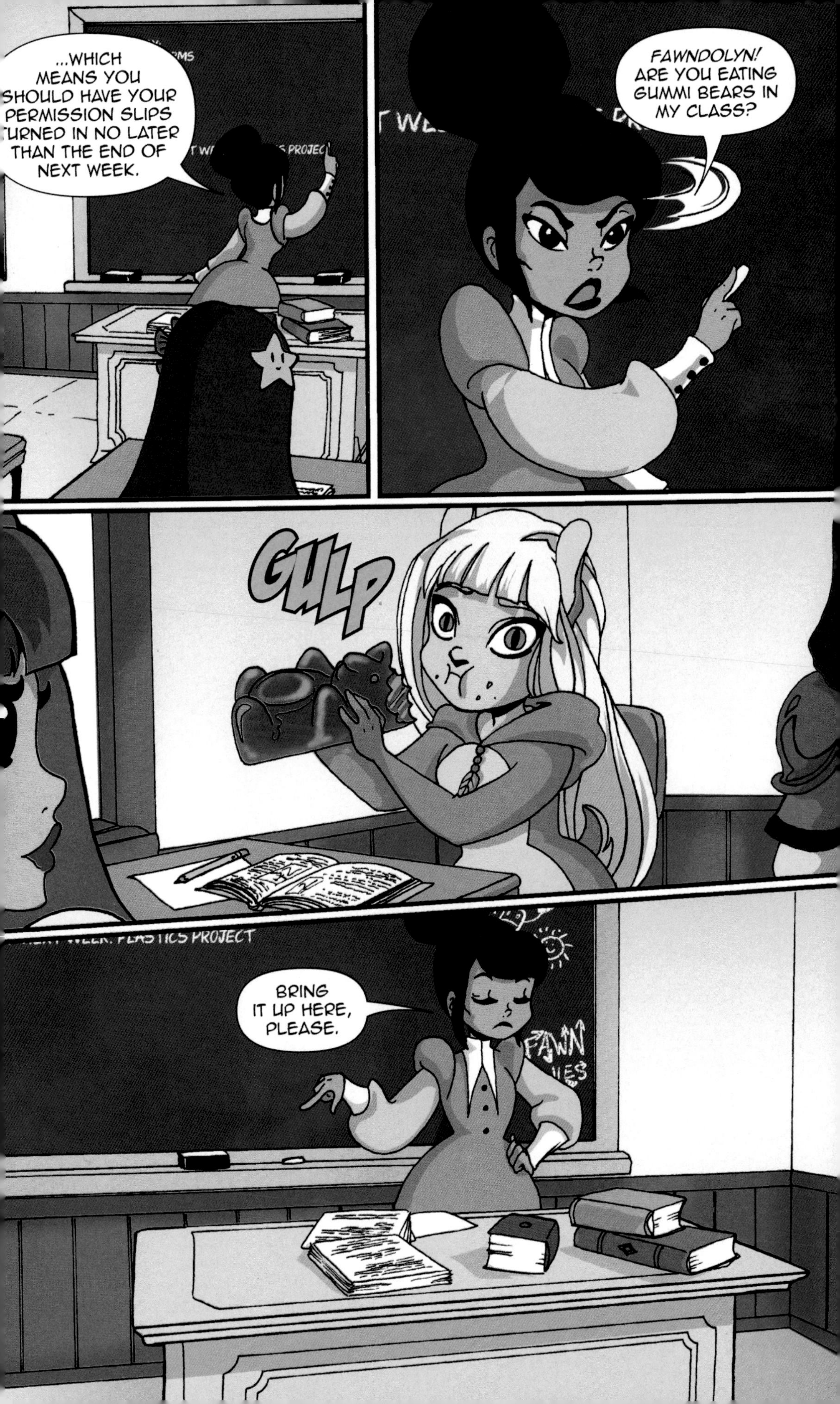
...WHICH MEANS YOU SHOULD HAVE YOUR PERMISSION SLIPS TURNED IN NO LATER THAN THE END OF NEXT WEEK.
FAWNDOLYN! ARE YOU EATING GUMMI BEARS IN MY CLASS?
GULP
PLASTICS PROJECT
BRING IT UP HERE, PLEASE.
FAWN

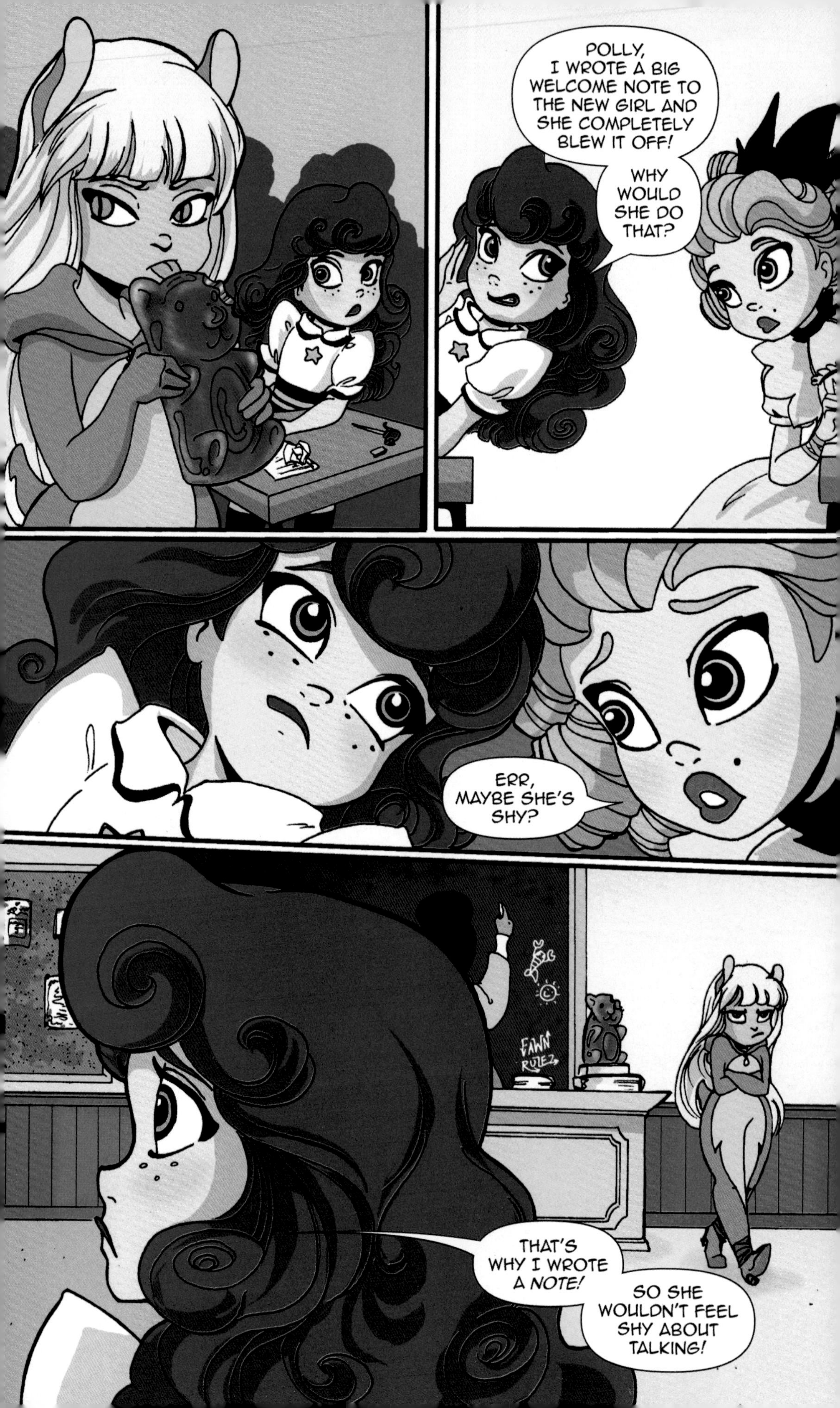
POLLY, I WROTE A BIG WELCOME NOTE TO THE NEW GIRL AND SHE COMPLETELY BLEW IT OFF!
WHY WOULD SHE DO THAT?
ERR, MAYBE SHE'S SHY?
FAWN RULEZ
THAT'S WHY I WROTE A *NOTE!*
SO SHE WOULDN'T FEEL SHY ABOUT TALKING!

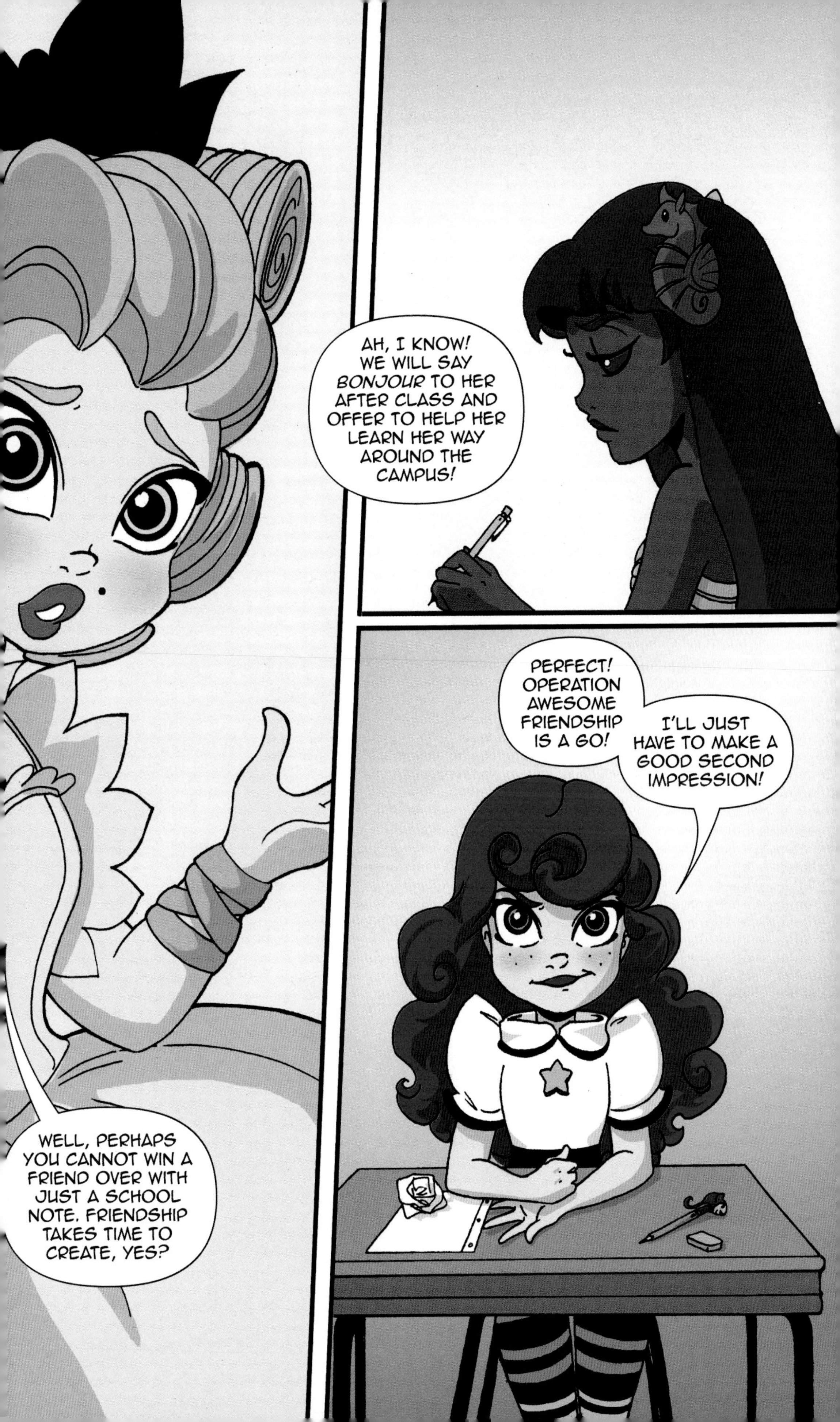
WELL, PERHAPS YOU CANNOT WIN A FRIEND OVER WITH JUST A SCHOOL NOTE. FRIENDSHIP TAKES TIME TO CREATE, YES?
AH, I KNOW! WE WILL SAY *BONJOUR* TO HER AFTER CLASS AND OFFER TO HELP HER LEARN HER WAY AROUND THE CAMPUS!
PERFECT! OPERATION AWESOME FRIENDSHIP IS A GO!
I'LL JUST HAVE TO MAKE A GOOD SECOND IMPRESSION!

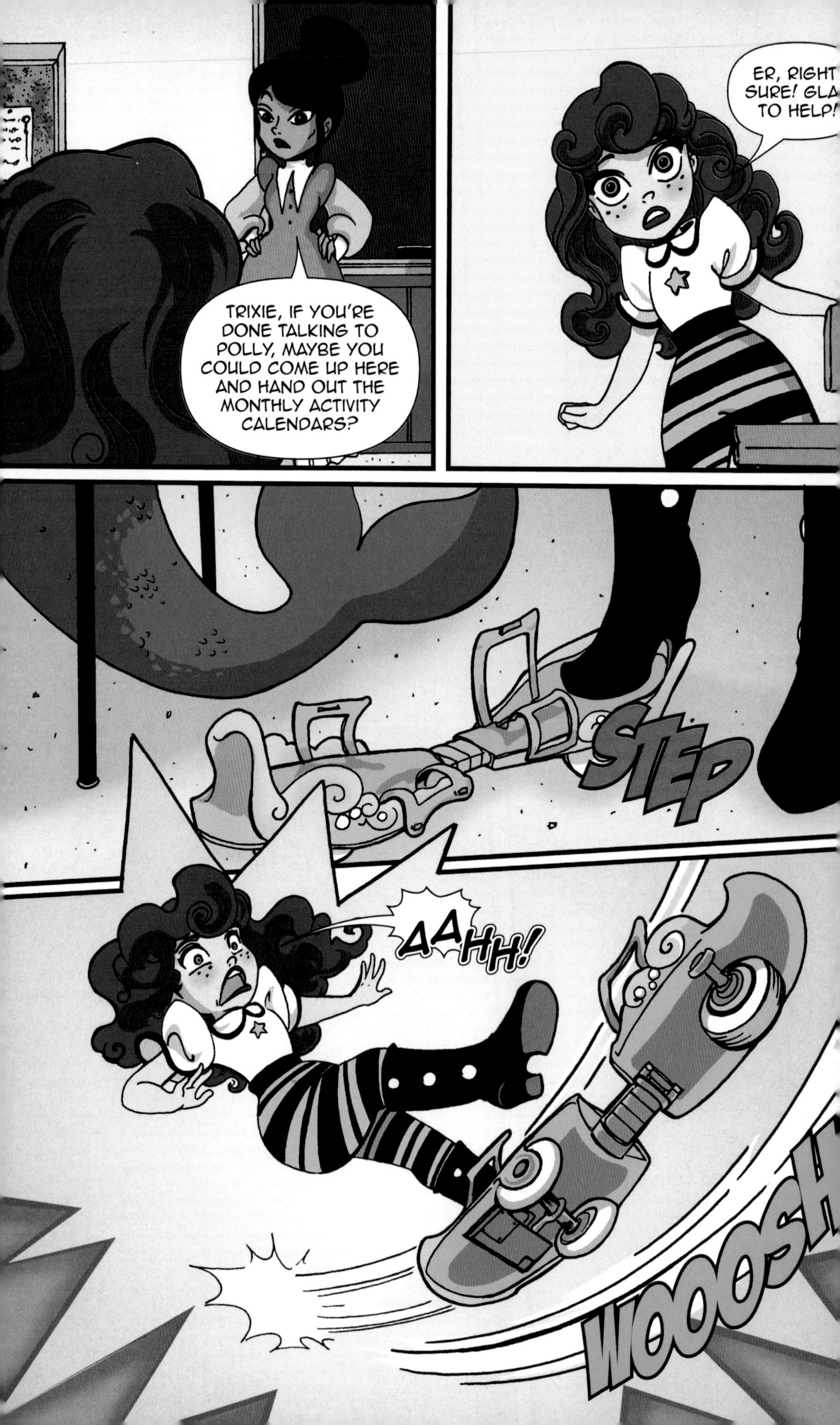
TRIXIE, IF YOU'RE DONE TALKING TO POLLY, MAYBE YOU COULD COME UP HERE AND HAND OUT THE MONTHLY ACTIVITY CALENDARS?
ER, RIGHT SURE! GLA TO HELP!
STEP
AAHH!
WOOOSH

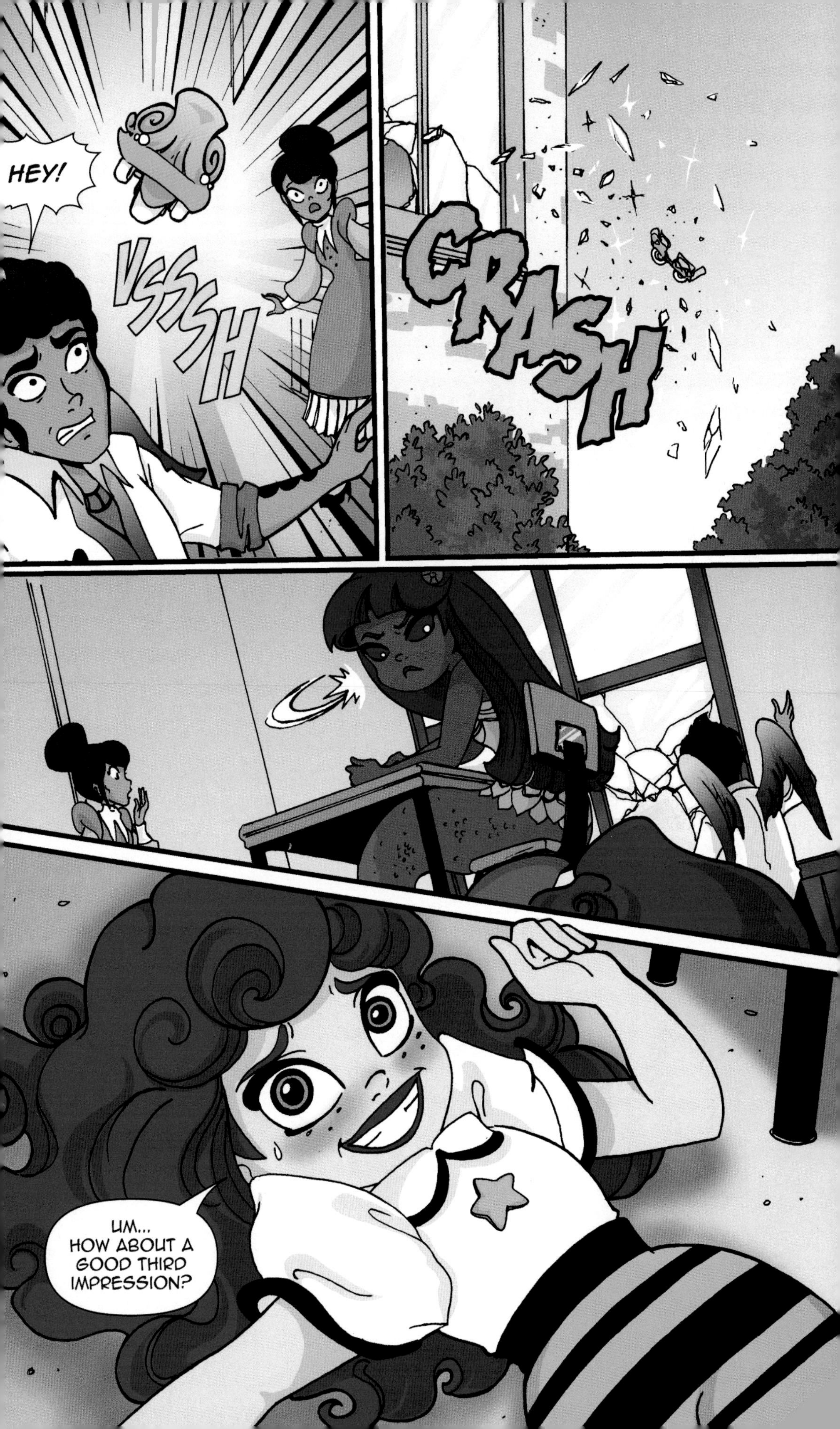
HEY!
VSSSH
CRASH
UM... HOW ABOUT A GOOD THIRD IMPRESSION?

TOYETICA
THINK OUTSIDE THE TOYBOX

DOLLINGTON ACADEMY

Trixie Tangle

Sweetina Von Bonne

Minky Mermille

Polly Fume

Unicole Safari-Sidekick

Angel Inx

Bunnard Safari-Sidekick

Dia de los Marco

Vince Charming

Nebulara, Queen of the Battle Cosmos

Becky Badluck

Dandelillian Fae

Lilly Liku

Fawndolyn Safari-Sidekick

Character Profiles

DOLLINGTON ACADEMY

Nestled inside one of many human city former vacant lots, Dollington Academy is the premiere school for young people looking to become the next big toy on the market.

With a focus on doll education, as opposed to the action figure and robot toy curriculum of rival school Mecha Tech, Dollington teaches young students everything they need to know about appealing to a human toy company. They define and hone their toy's theme, choose correct accessories, study human toy sales trends and even get a chemistry lesson in common toy plastics and polymers.

At graduation, human toy company representatives choose the graduates they want to see submit a pitch. The lucky bittle that gets chosen by a big company will have toy fame, a hefty contract and a retirement package all at once. Less lucky bittles might wind up as generic dolls, so it pays to study hard and avoid the bargain bin!

MINKY

Name: Minky Mermille
Fave food: Fiddlehead salad
Fave color: Indigo
Fave way to get someone's attention:
Impersonal sticky-note

Withdrawn, moody and brilliant at inventing, Minky's parents want her to succeed as a toy model. Although very bright, Minky is less than thrilled about her prospects as a toy, or about her two accessories, Chad and Robert (a starfish and a seahorse).

Although she doesn't need to stay in water all the time, Minky constantly drinks bottled water to stay hydrated and often sits in the school's fountain during lunch time. She sleeps in the bathtub in her dorm room. If she doesn't get a chance to return to her bowl every night, she misses out on her "scaly sleep."

ame: Polly Fume

ave color: Pink

ave food:
uit smoothies

ave way to get
omeone's attention:
urprise hug!

ixie's best friend and a
udent from France, Polly
a student with a perfume
mmick, constantly inventing
d wearing new perfume
ents that she hopes will
peal to children and toy
mpanies. Although
ented dolls are considered
assé, Polly's friends
ncourage her to pursue her
ve of perfume crafting and
ot worry too much about
r appeal for now.

olly is always cheerful and
n-loving, enjoying the
cial side of school!

POLLY

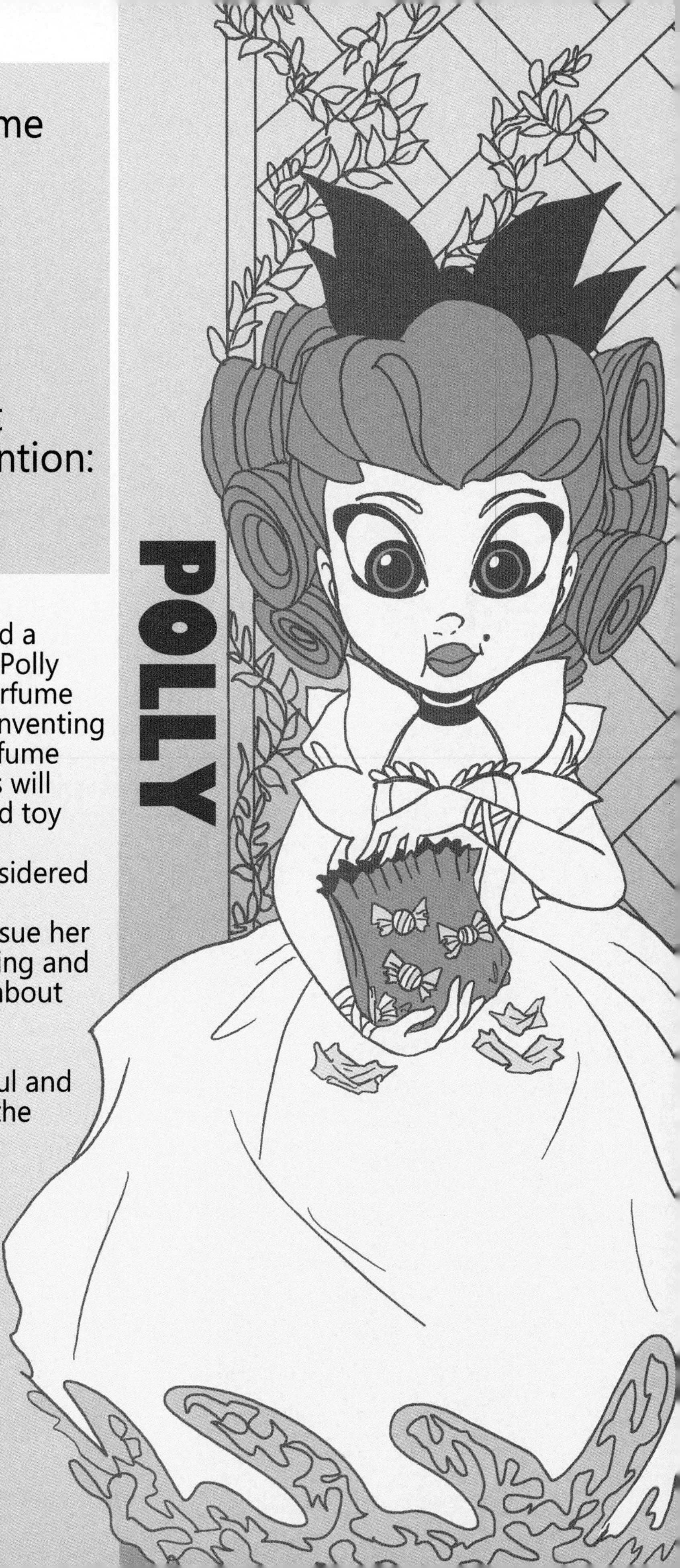

TRIXIE

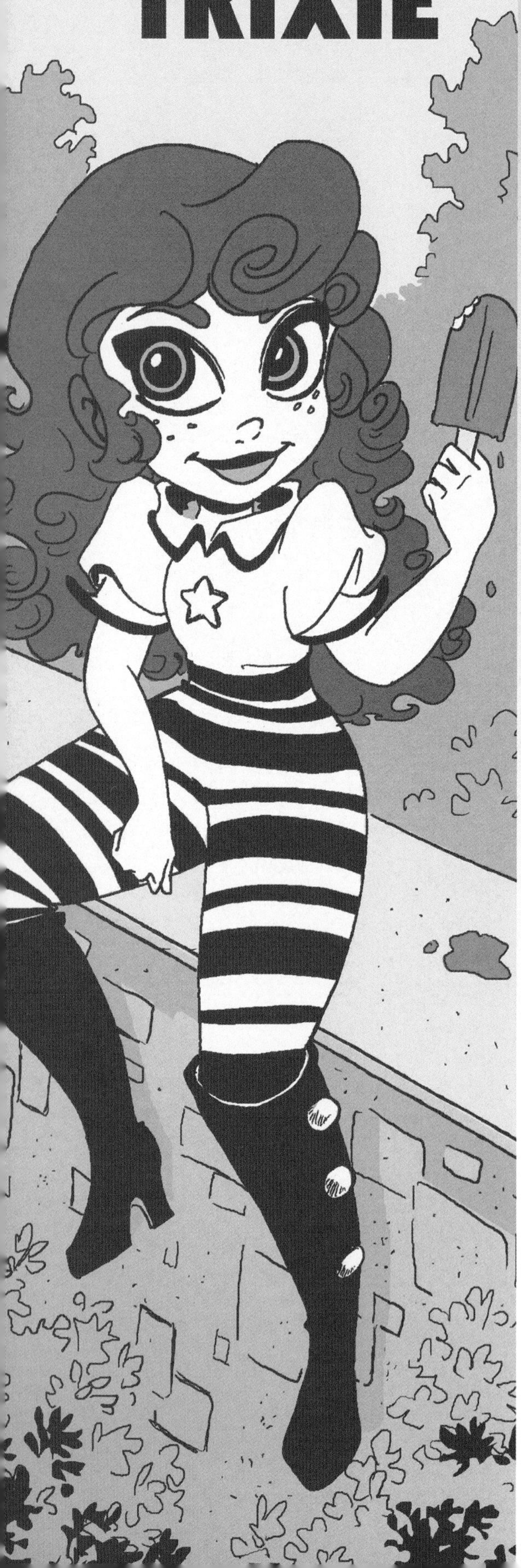

Name:
Trixie Tabitha Tangle

Fave food:
Sandwiches

Fave color:
Yellow

Fave subject:
Home Rec

Fave way to get someone's attention:
Paper airplane

Trixie Tangle is a girl who has a tough time at Dollington Academ With her red hair, striped outfit, black boots and cheering batons, she's kind of all over the map as far as "toy themes" go. What kind of doll is she supposed to be, anyway? A bee? A cheerleader? Who knows?

Trixie has a long way to go before she can live up to her successful older sister, who was the model for the popular "Traci Fitness Star doll of the 1980's.

Like practically every other girl in school, Trixie has a secret crush o the handsome Angel Inx. But wh knows if she'll ever admit it?

THE BIG KEY

PART TWO

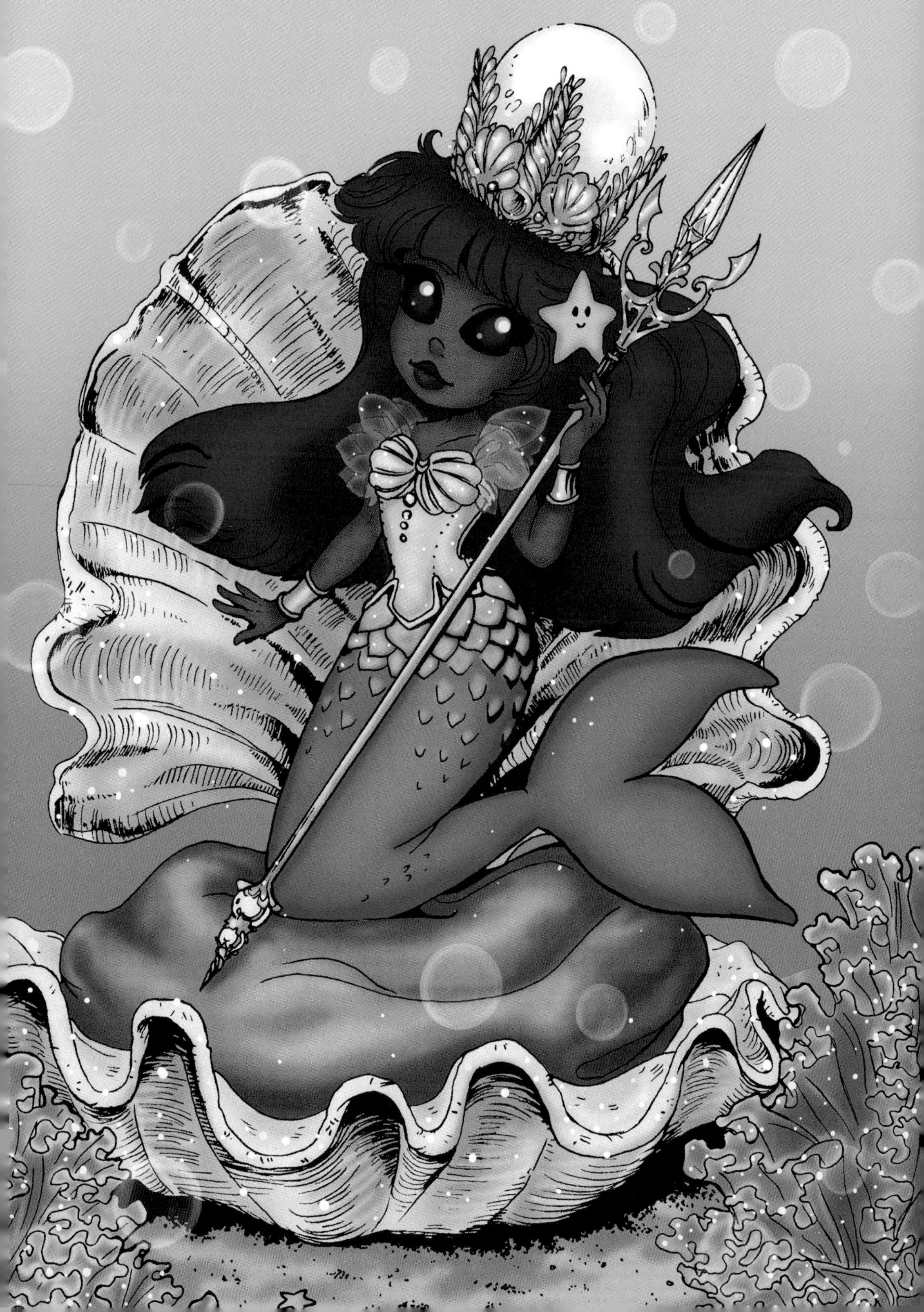

STORY AND ART BY
MARTY LEGROW

LETTERING
Justin Birch

CATERING BY
Mouseburger

Bryan Seaton: Publisher/ CEO • Shawn Gabborin: Editor In Chief • Jason Martin: Publisher-Danger Zone • Nicole D'Andria: Marketing Director/Editor
Jim Dietz: Social Media Manager • Danielle Davison: Executive Administrator • Chad Cicconi: Action Lawyer • Shawn Pryor: President of Creator Relatic

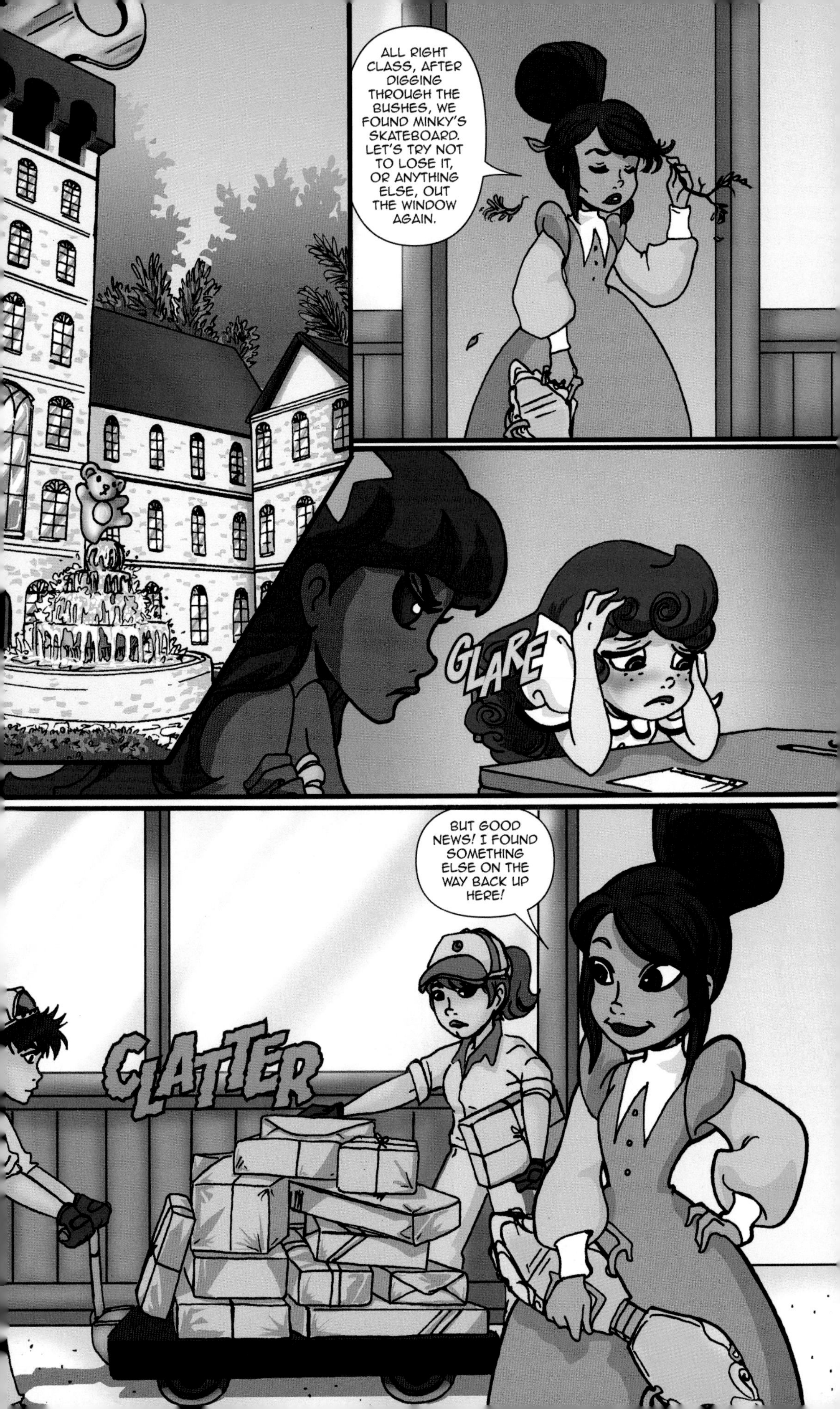
ALL RIGHT CLASS, AFTER DIGGING THROUGH THE BUSHES, WE FOUND MINKY'S SKATEBOARD. LET'S TRY NOT TO LOSE IT, OR ANYTHING ELSE, OUT THE WINDOW AGAIN.
GLARE
BUT GOOD NEWS! I FOUND SOMETHING ELSE ON THE WAY BACK UP HERE!
CLATTER

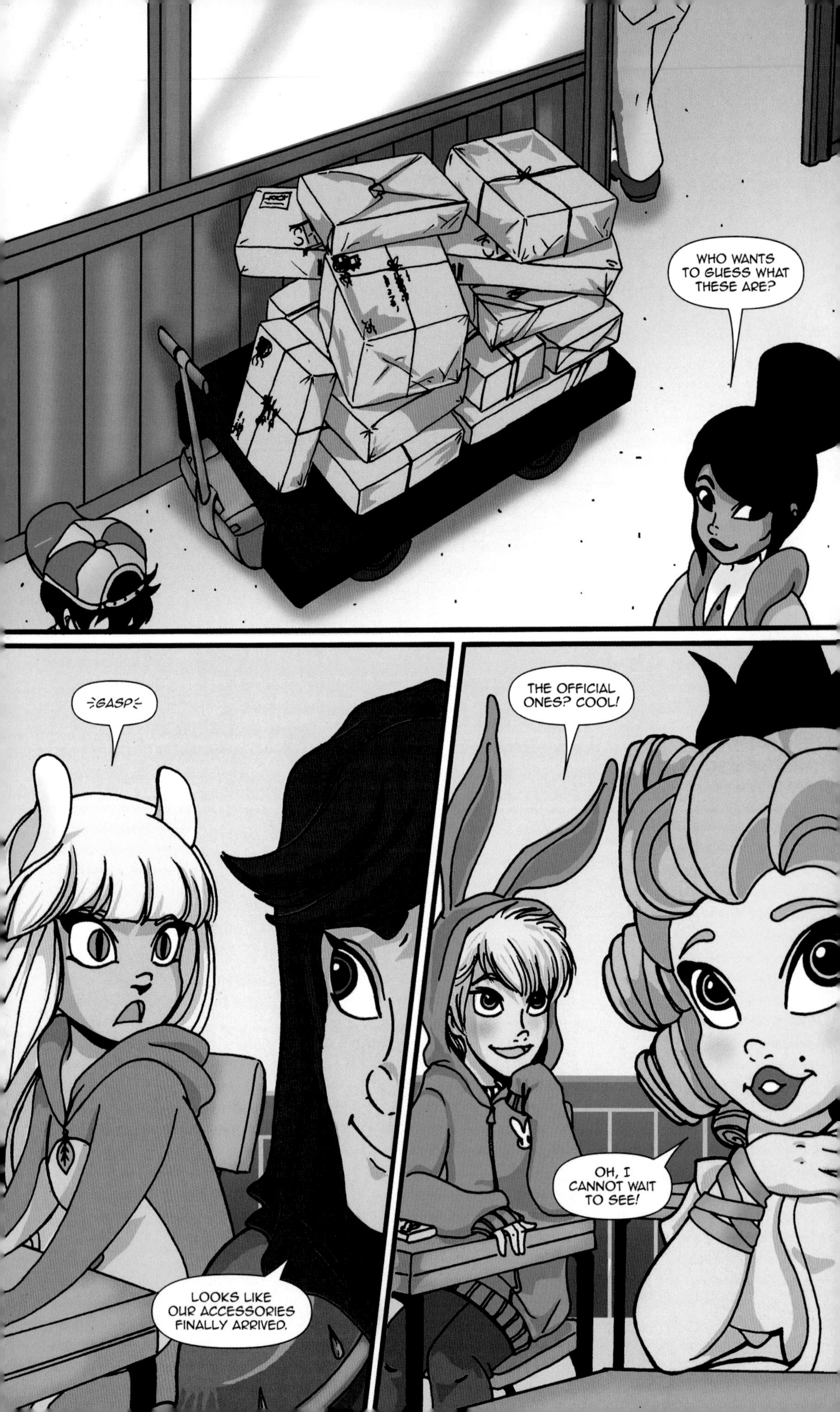
WHO WANTS TO GUESS WHAT THESE ARE?
⇉GASP⇇
LOOKS LIKE OUR ACCESSORIES FINALLY ARRIVED.
THE OFFICIAL ONES? COOL!
OH, I CANNOT WAIT TO SEE!

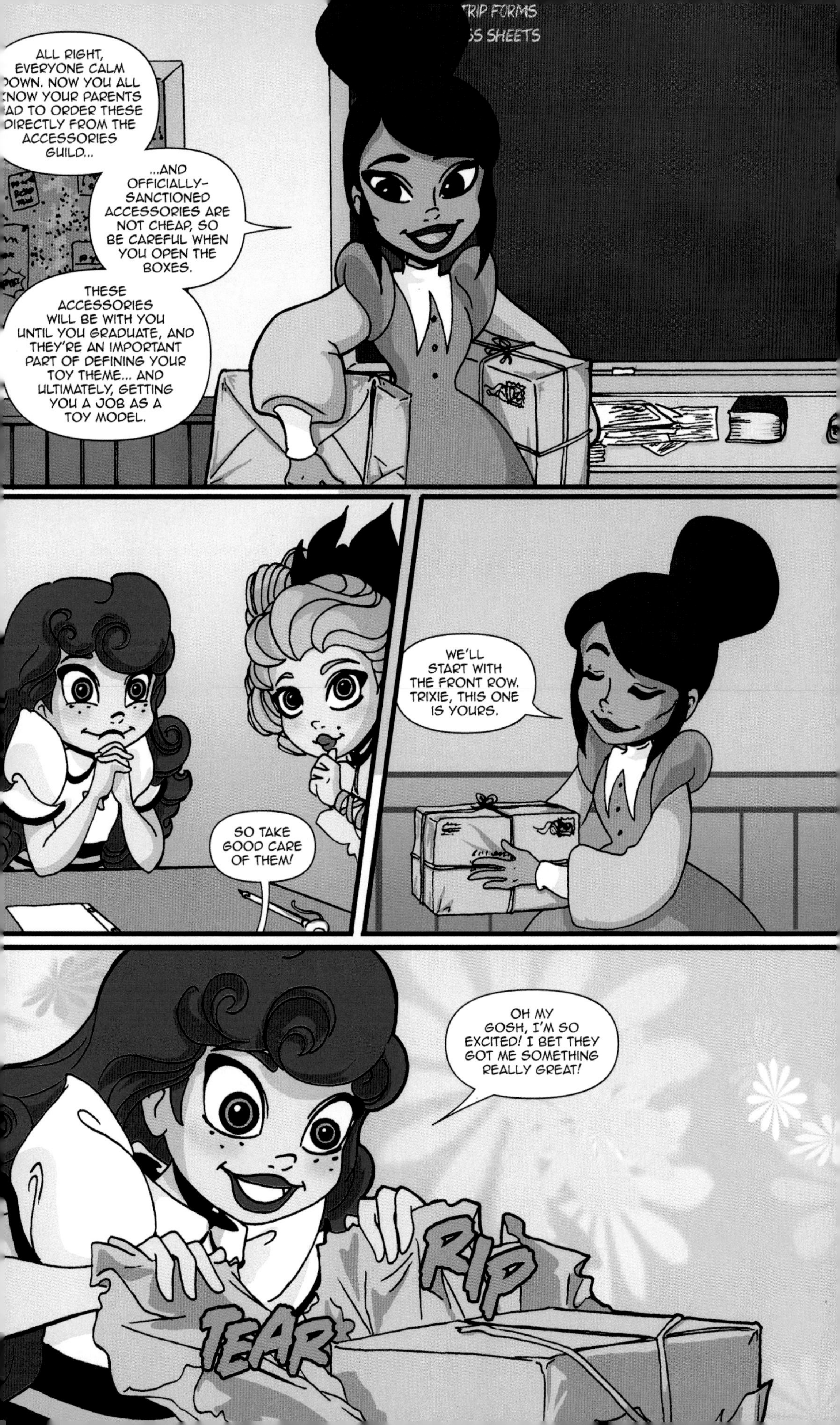

TRIP FORMS
SS SHEETS
ALL RIGHT, EVERYONE CALM DOWN. NOW YOU ALL KNOW YOUR PARENTS HAD TO ORDER THESE DIRECTLY FROM THE ACCESSORIES GUILD...
...AND OFFICIALLY-SANCTIONED ACCESSORIES ARE NOT CHEAP, SO BE CAREFUL WHEN YOU OPEN THE BOXES.
THESE ACCESSORIES WILL BE WITH YOU UNTIL YOU GRADUATE, AND THEY'RE AN IMPORTANT PART OF DEFINING YOUR TOY THEME... AND ULTIMATELY, GETTING YOU A JOB AS A TOY MODEL.
SO TAKE GOOD CARE OF THEM!
WE'LL START WITH THE FRONT ROW. TRIXIE, THIS ONE IS YOURS.
OH MY GOSH, I'M SO EXCITED! I BET THEY GOT ME SOMETHING REALLY GREAT!
RIP
TEAR

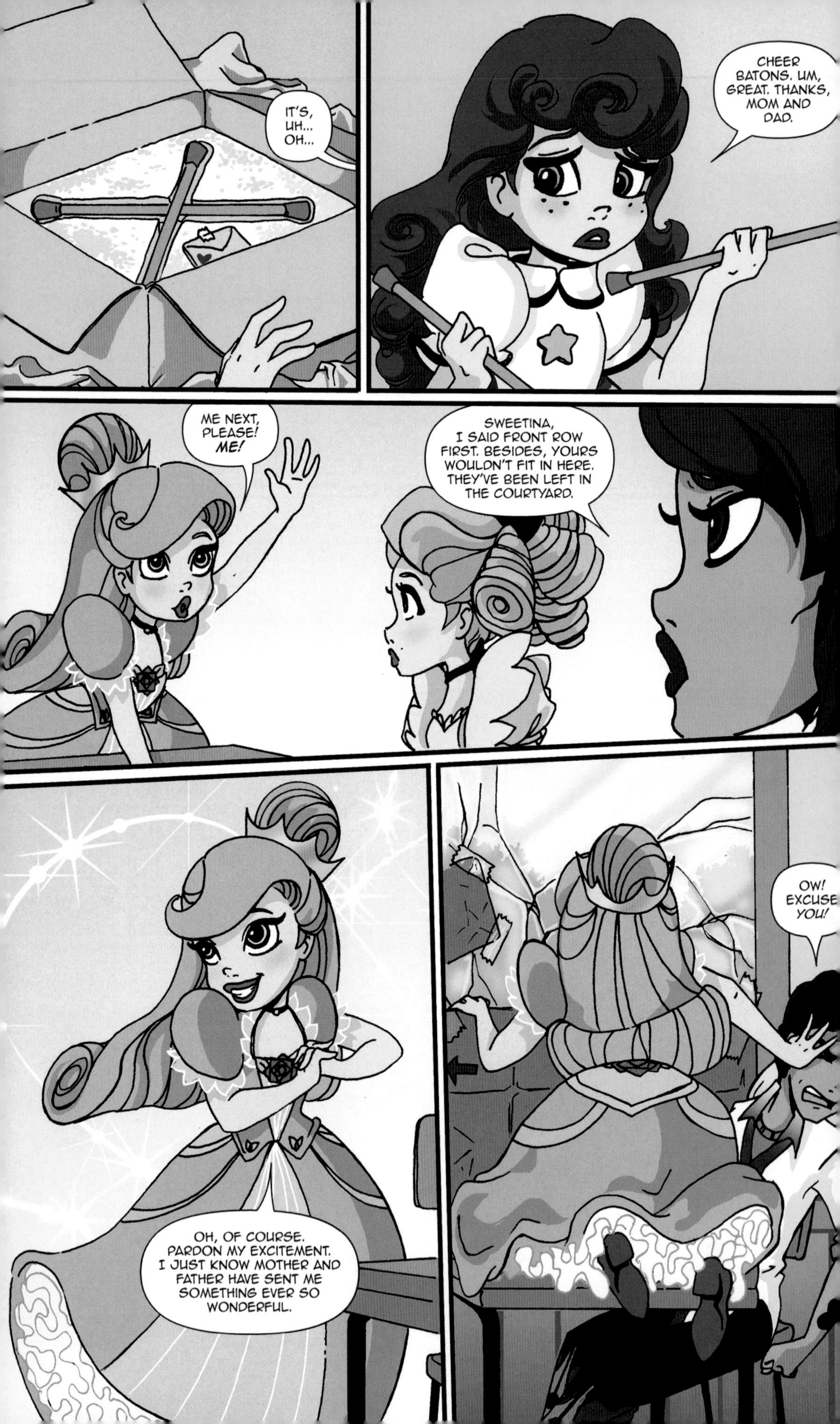
IT'S, UH... OH...
CHEER BATONS. UM, GREAT. THANKS, MOM AND DAD.
ME NEXT, PLEASE! *ME!*
SWEETINA, I SAID FRONT ROW FIRST. BESIDES, YOURS WOULDN'T FIT IN HERE. THEY'VE BEEN LEFT IN THE COURTYARD.
OH, OF COURSE. PARDON MY EXCITEMENT. I JUST KNOW MOTHER AND FATHER HAVE SENT ME SOMETHING EVER SO WONDERFUL.
OW! EXCUSE *YOU!*

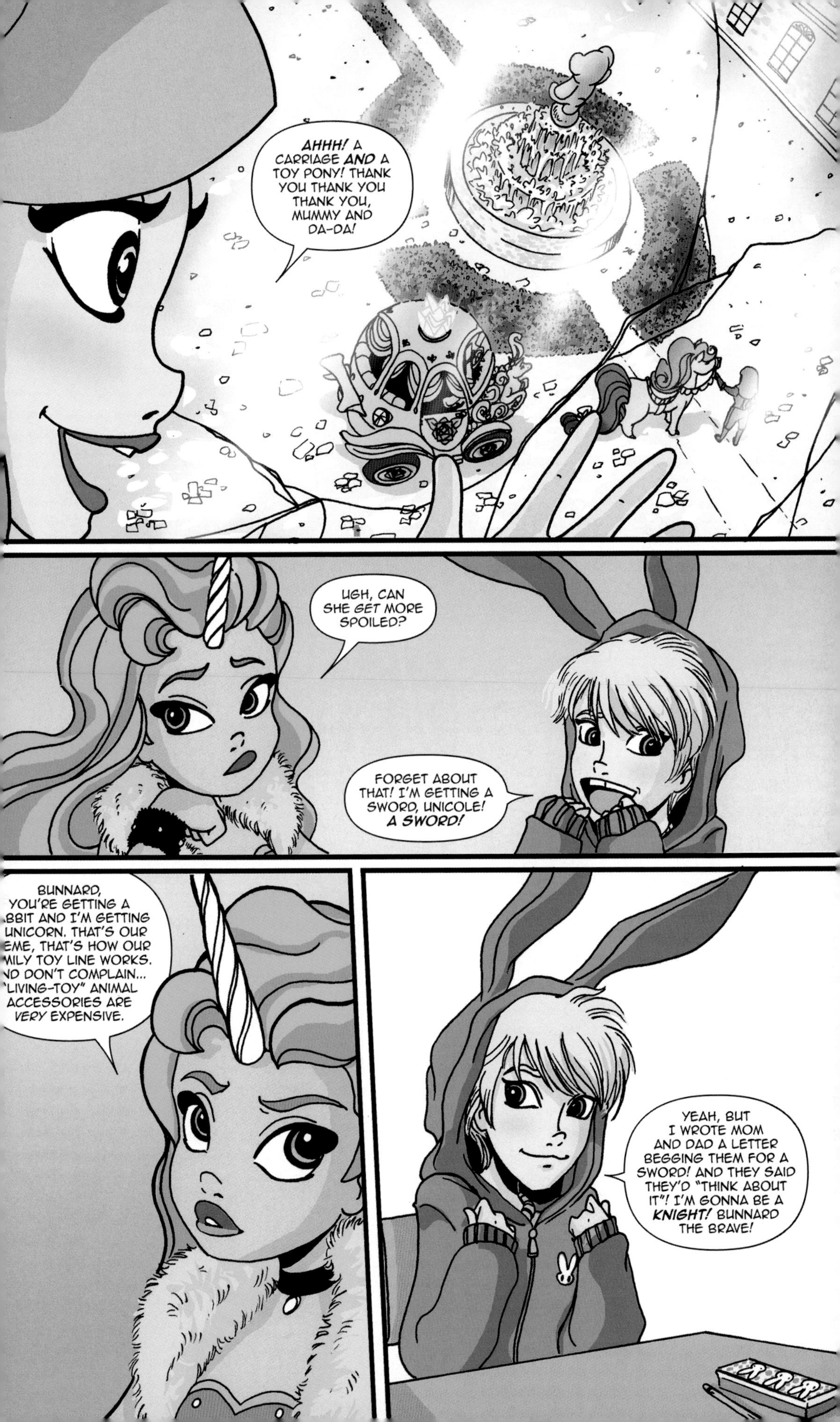

AHHH! A CARRIAGE AND A TOY PONY! THANK YOU THANK YOU THANK YOU, MUMMY AND DA-DA!
UGH, CAN SHE GET MORE SPOILED?
FORGET ABOUT THAT! I'M GETTING A SWORD, UNICOLE! A SWORD!
BUNNARD, YOU'RE GETTING A BBIT AND I'M GETTING UNICORN. THAT'S OUR EME, THAT'S HOW OUR MILY TOY LINE WORKS. ND DON'T COMPLAIN... "LIVING-TOY" ANIMAL ACCESSORIES ARE VERY EXPENSIVE.
YEAH, BUT I WROTE MOM AND DAD A LETTER BEGGING THEM FOR A SWORD! AND THEY SAID THEY'D "THINK ABOUT IT"! I'M GONNA BE A KNIGHT! BUNNARD THE BRAVE!

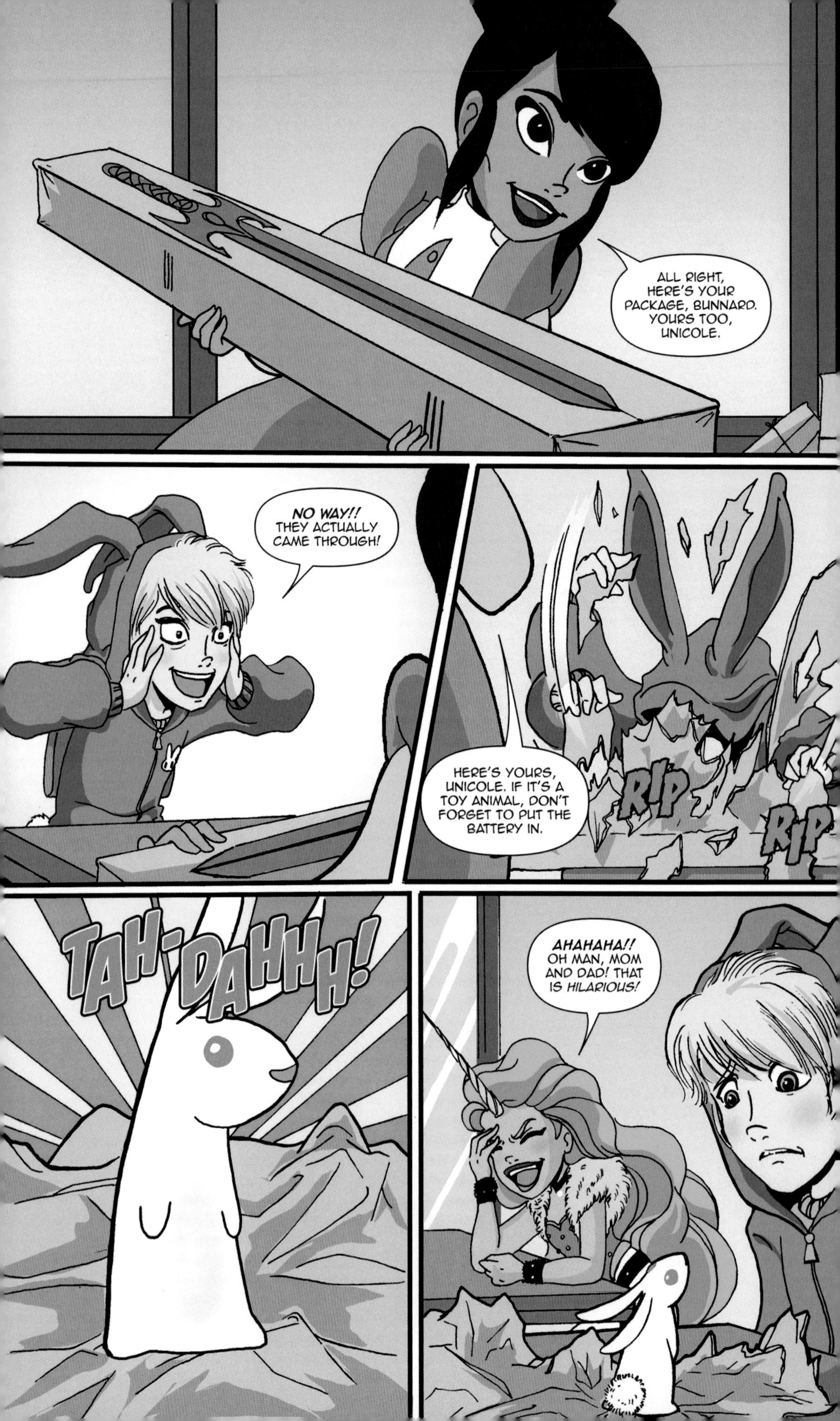

ALL RIGHT, HERE'S YOUR PACKAGE, BUNNARD. YOURS TOO, UNICOLE.
NO WAY!! THEY ACTUALLY CAME THROUGH!
HERE'S YOURS, UNICOLE. IF IT'S A TOY ANIMAL, DON'T FORGET TO PUT THE BATTERY IN.
RIP
RIP
TAH-DAHHHH!
AHAHAHA!! OH MAN, MOM AND DAD! THAT IS *HILARIOUS!*

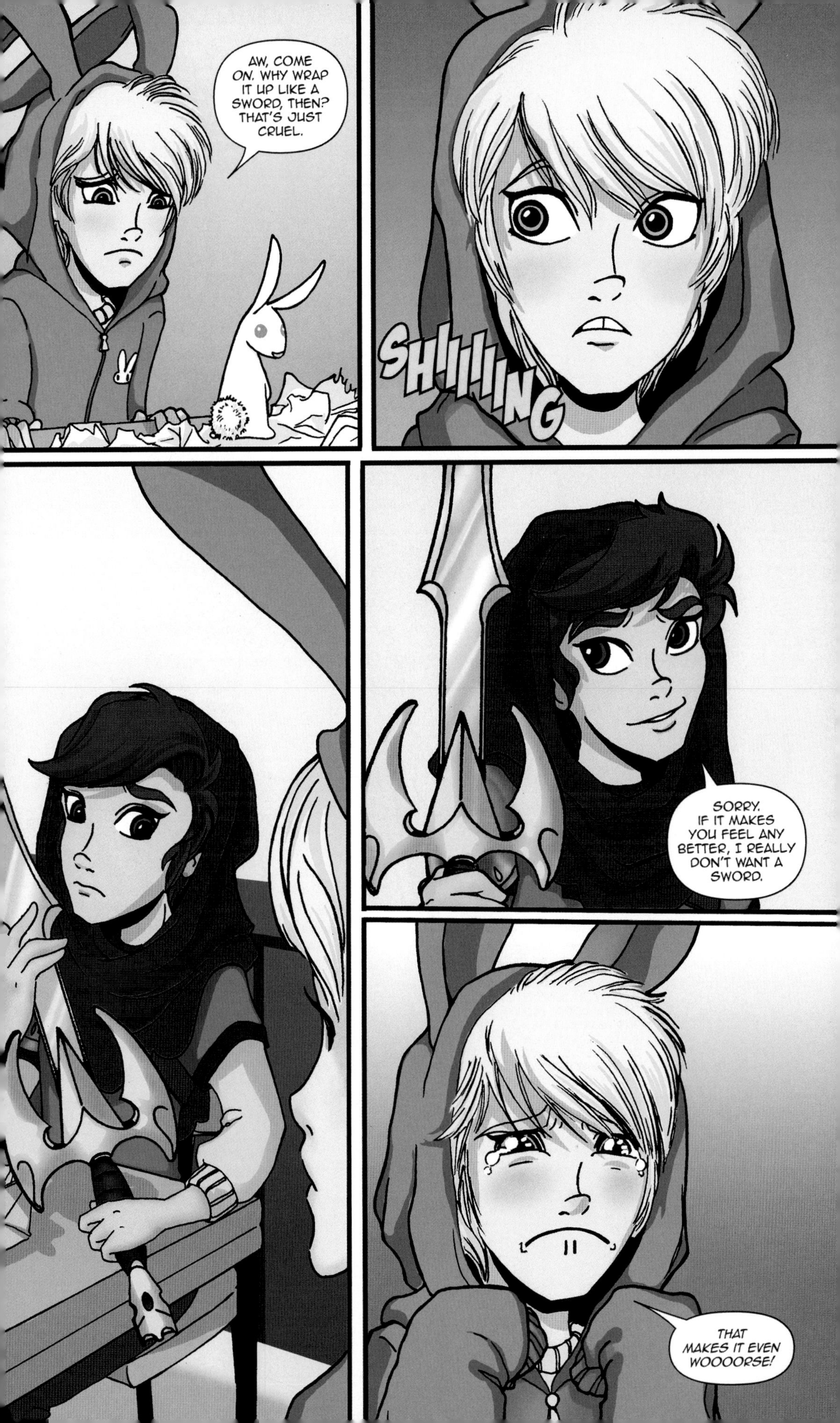
AW, COME ON. WHY WRAP IT UP LIKE A SWORD, THEN? THAT'S JUST CRUEL.
SHIIIIIING
SORRY. IF IT MAKES YOU FEEL ANY BETTER, I REALLY DON'T WANT A SWORD.
THAT MAKES IT EVEN WOOOORSE!

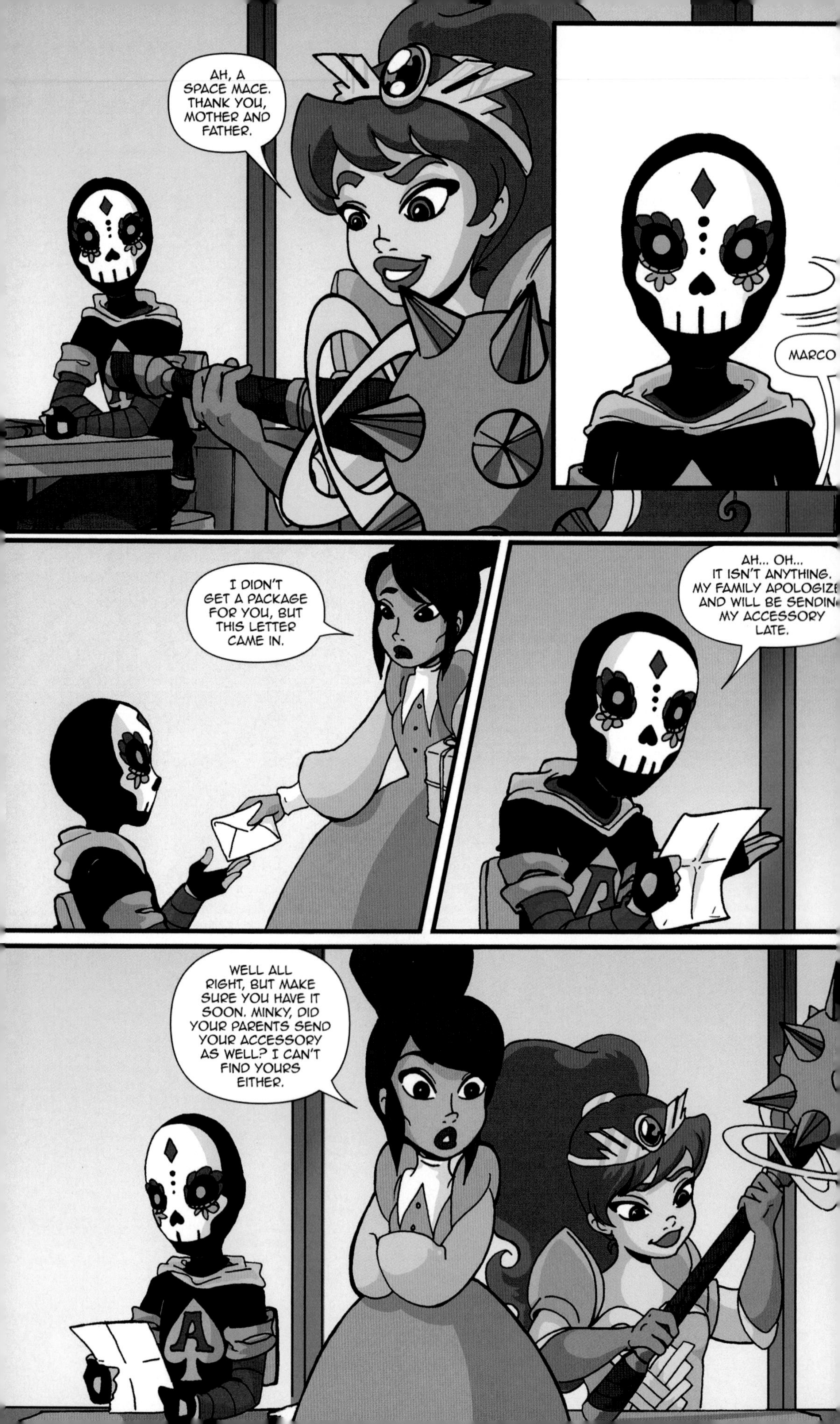
AH, A SPACE MACE. THANK YOU, MOTHER AND FATHER.
MARCO
I DIDN'T GET A PACKAGE FOR YOU, BUT THIS LETTER CAME IN.
AH... OH... IT ISN'T ANYTHING. MY FAMILY APOLOGIZE AND WILL BE SENDIN MY ACCESSORY LATE.
WELL ALL RIGHT, BUT MAKE SURE YOU HAVE IT SOON. MINKY, DID YOUR PARENTS SEND YOUR ACCESSORY AS WELL? I CAN'T FIND YOURS EITHER.

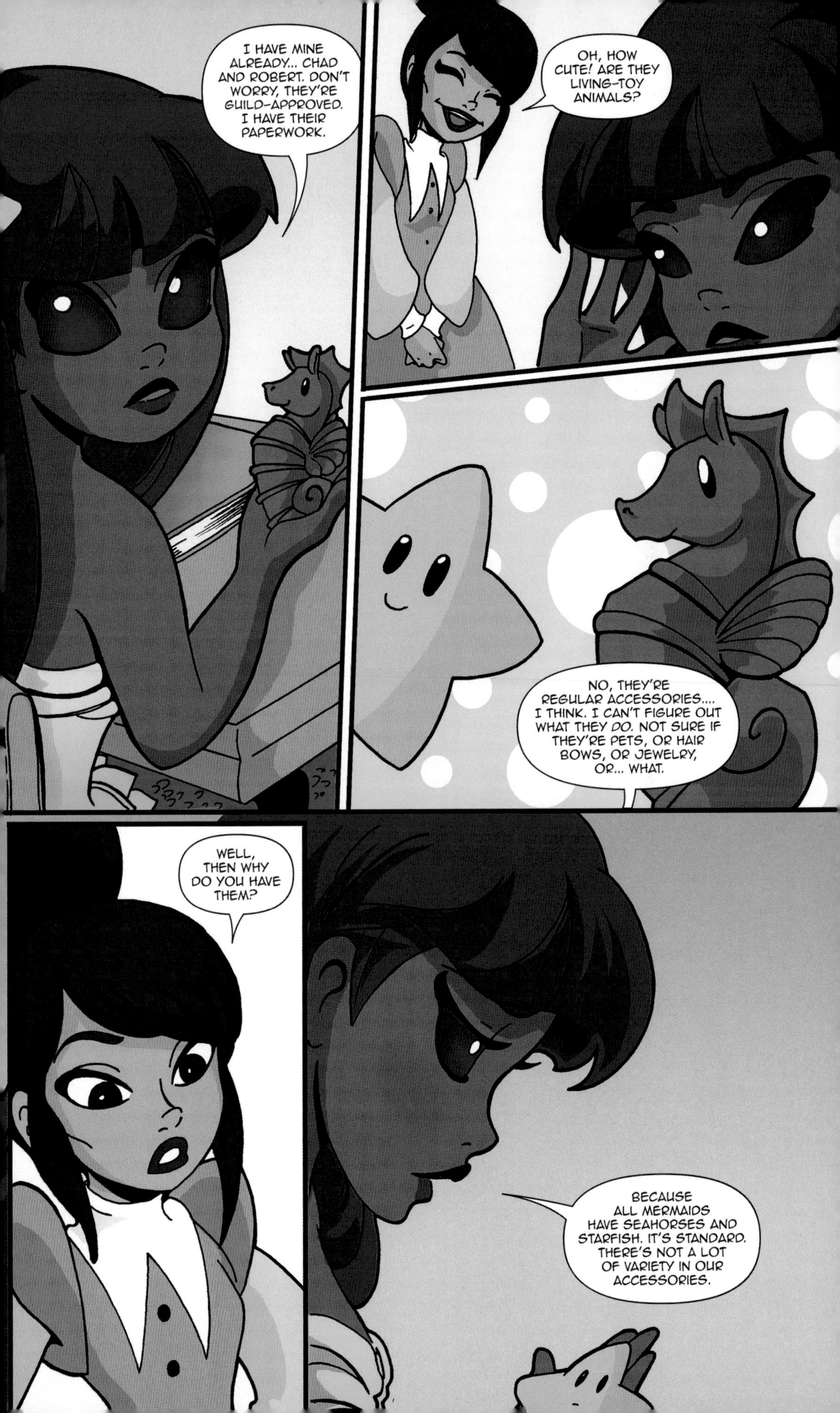
I HAVE MINE ALREADY... CHAD AND ROBERT. DON'T WORRY, THEY'RE GUILD-APPROVED. I HAVE THEIR PAPERWORK.
OH, HOW CUTE! ARE THEY LIVING-TOY ANIMALS?
NO, THEY'RE REGULAR ACCESSORIES.... I THINK. I CAN'T FIGURE OUT WHAT THEY *DO*. NOT SURE IF THEY'RE PETS, OR HAIR BOWS, OR JEWELRY, OR... WHAT.
WELL, THEN WHY DO YOU HAVE THEM?
BECAUSE ALL MERMAIDS HAVE SEAHORSES AND STARFISH. IT'S STANDARD. THERE'S NOT A LOT OF VARIETY IN OUR ACCESSORIES.

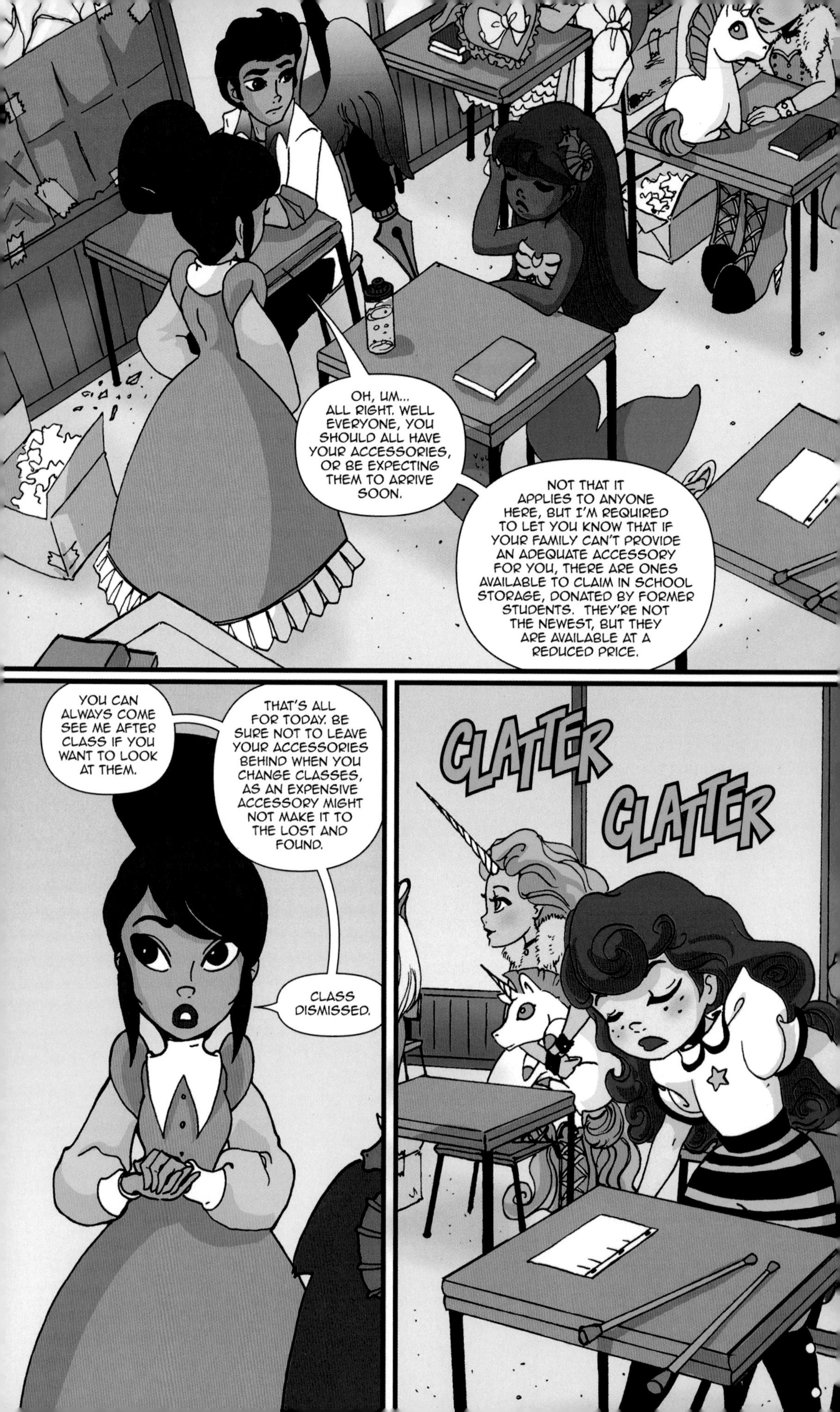
OH, UM... ALL RIGHT. WELL EVERYONE, YOU SHOULD ALL HAVE YOUR ACCESSORIES, OR BE EXPECTING THEM TO ARRIVE SOON.
NOT THAT IT APPLIES TO ANYONE HERE, BUT I'M REQUIRED TO LET YOU KNOW THAT IF YOUR FAMILY CAN'T PROVIDE AN ADEQUATE ACCESSORY FOR YOU, THERE ARE ONES AVAILABLE TO CLAIM IN SCHOOL STORAGE, DONATED BY FORMER STUDENTS. THEY'RE NOT THE NEWEST, BUT THEY ARE AVAILABLE AT A REDUCED PRICE.
YOU CAN ALWAYS COME SEE ME AFTER CLASS IF YOU WANT TO LOOK AT THEM.
THAT'S ALL FOR TODAY. BE SURE NOT TO LEAVE YOUR ACCESSORIES BEHIND WHEN YOU CHANGE CLASSES, AS AN EXPENSIVE ACCESSORY MIGHT NOT MAKE IT TO THE LOST AND FOUND.
CLASS DISMISSED.
CLATTER
CLATTER

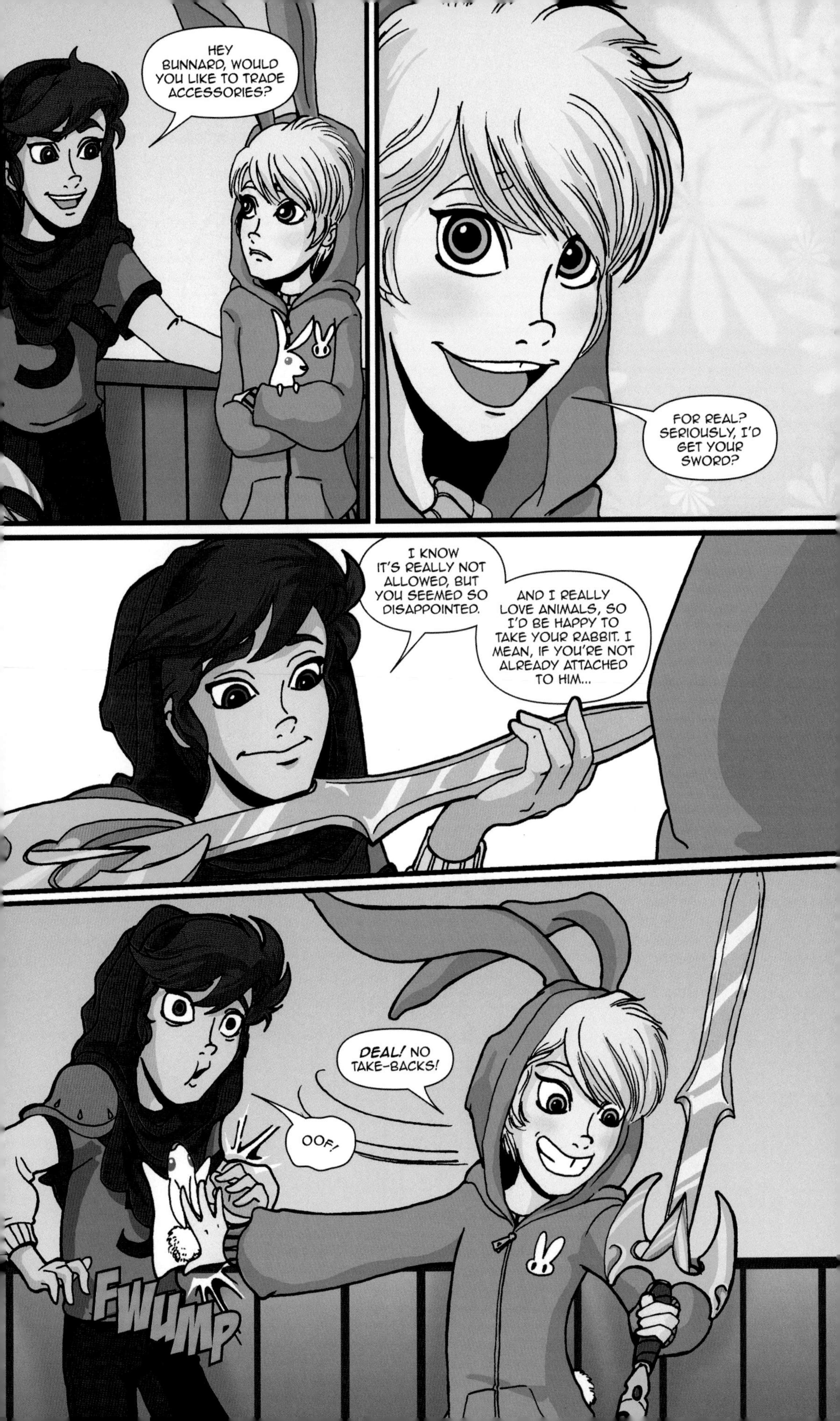
HEY BUNNARD, WOULD YOU LIKE TO TRADE ACCESSORIES?
FOR REAL? SERIOUSLY, I'D GET YOUR SWORD?
I KNOW IT'S REALLY NOT ALLOWED, BUT YOU SEEMED SO DISAPPOINTED.
AND I REALLY LOVE ANIMALS, SO I'D BE HAPPY TO TAKE YOUR RABBIT. I MEAN, IF YOU'RE NOT ALREADY ATTACHED TO HIM...
DEAL! NO TAKE-BACKS!
OOF!
FWUMP

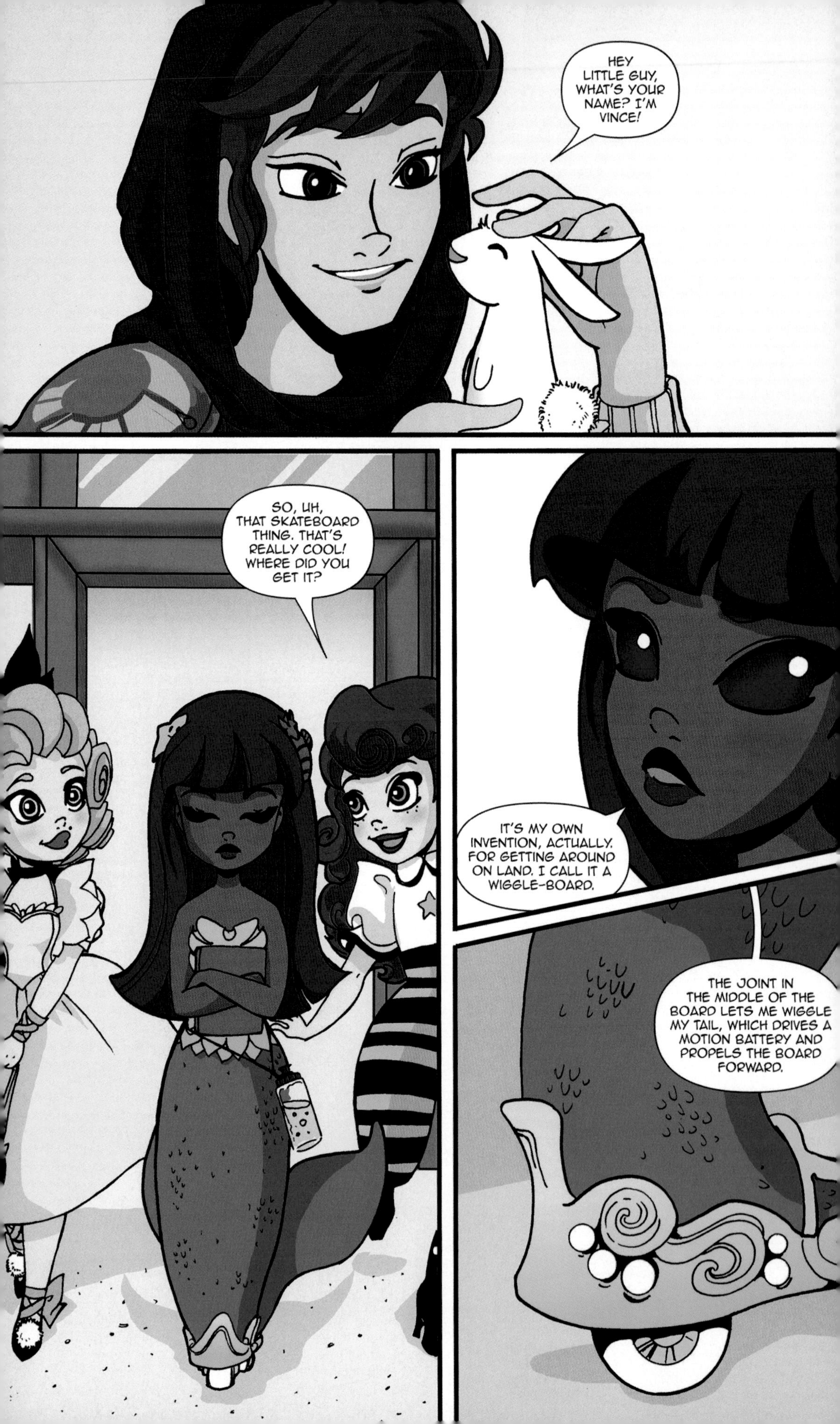
HEY LITTLE GUY, WHAT'S YOUR NAME? I'M VINCE!
SO, UH, THAT SKATEBOARD THING. THAT'S REALLY COOL! WHERE DID YOU GET IT?
IT'S MY OWN INVENTION, ACTUALLY. FOR GETTING AROUND ON LAND. I CALL IT A WIGGLE-BOARD.
THE JOINT IN THE MIDDLE OF THE BOARD LETS ME WIGGLE MY TAIL, WHICH DRIVES A MOTION BATTERY AND PROPELS THE BOARD FORWARD.

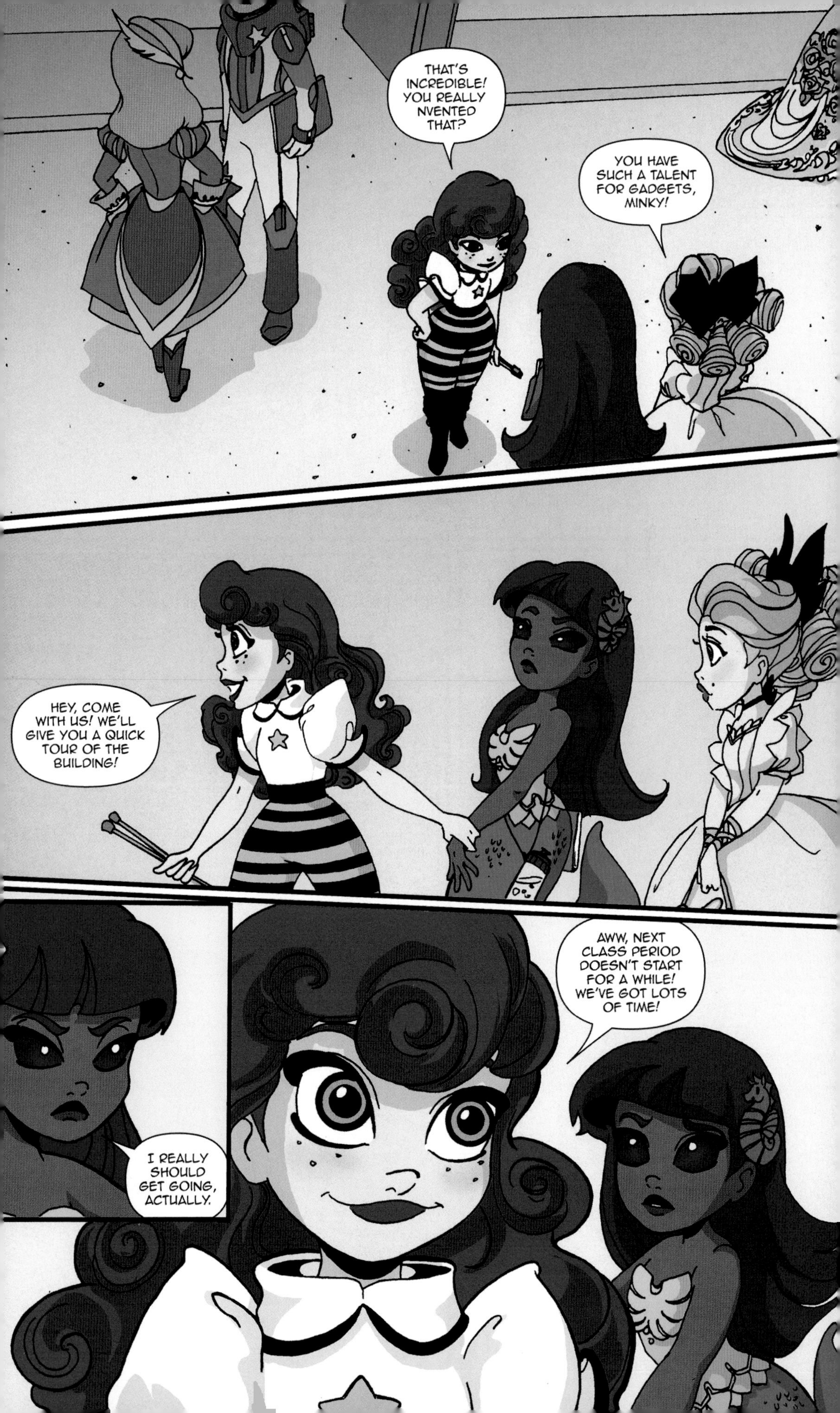
THAT'S INCREDIBLE! YOU REALLY NVENTED THAT?
YOU HAVE SUCH A TALENT FOR GADGETS, MINKY!
HEY, COME WITH US! WE'LL GIVE YOU A QUICK TOUR OF THE BUILDING!
I REALLY SHOULD GET GOING, ACTUALLY.
AWW, NEXT CLASS PERIOD DOESN'T START FOR A WHILE! WE'VE GOT LOTS OF TIME!

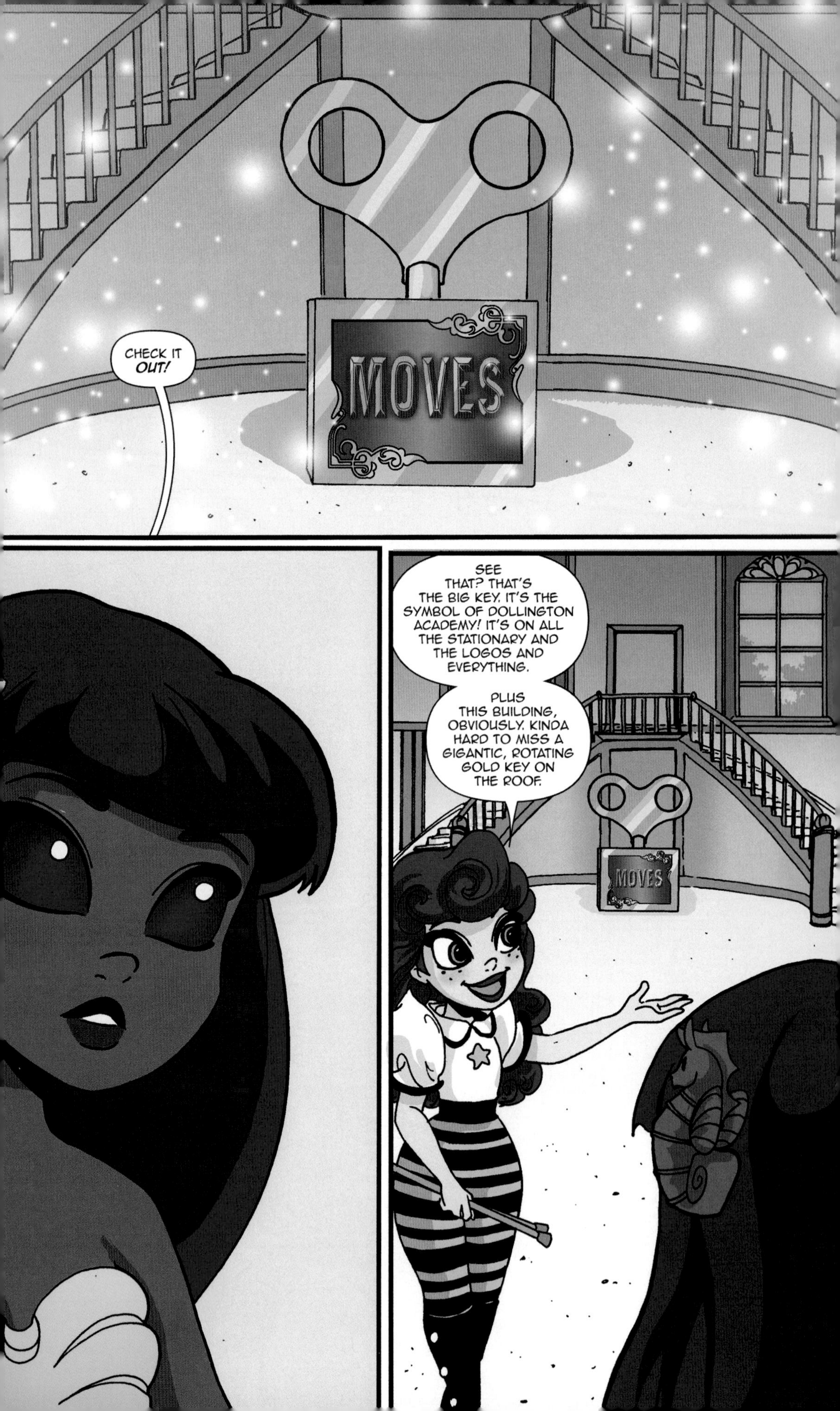
MOVES
CHECK IT OUT!
SEE THAT? THAT'S THE BIG KEY. IT'S THE SYMBOL OF DOLLINGTON ACADEMY! IT'S ON ALL THE STATIONARY AND THE LOGOS AND EVERYTHING.
PLUS THIS BUILDING, OBVIOUSLY. KINDA HARD TO MISS A GIGANTIC, ROTATING GOLD KEY ON THE ROOF.
MOVES

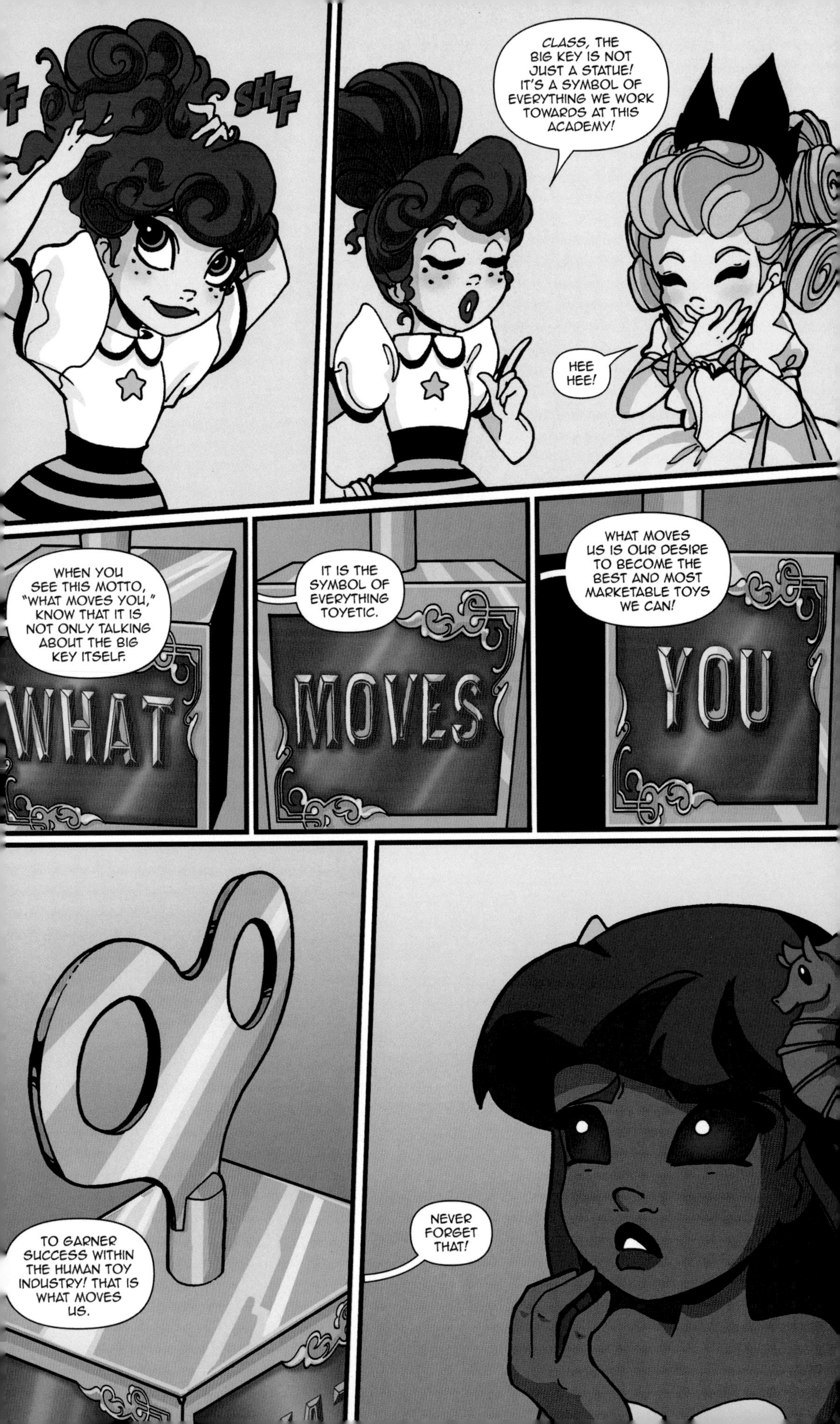
SHFF
SHFF
CLASS, THE BIG KEY IS NOT JUST A STATUE! IT'S A SYMBOL OF EVERYTHING WE WORK TOWARDS AT THIS ACADEMY!
HEE HEE!
WHEN YOU SEE THIS MOTTO, "WHAT MOVES YOU," KNOW THAT IT IS NOT ONLY TALKING ABOUT THE BIG KEY ITSELF.
WHAT
IT IS THE SYMBOL OF EVERYTHING TOYETIC.
MOVES
WHAT MOVES US IS OUR DESIRE TO BECOME THE BEST AND MOST MARKETABLE TOYS WE CAN!
YOU
TO GARNER SUCCESS WITHIN THE HUMAN TOY INDUSTRY! THAT IS WHAT MOVES US.
NEVER FORGET THAT!

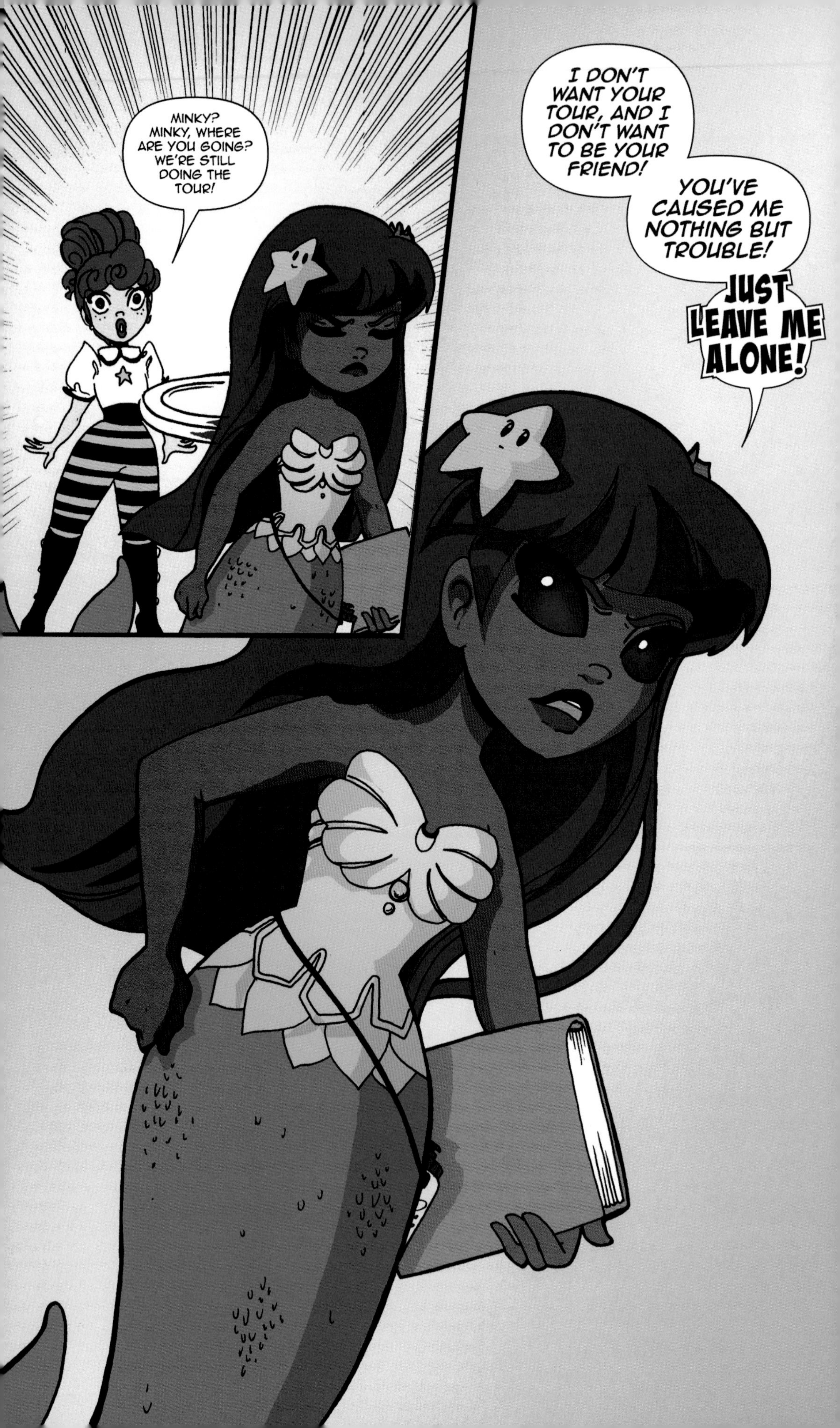
MINKY? MINKY, WHERE ARE YOU GOING? WE'RE STILL DOING THE TOUR!
I DON'T WANT YOUR TOUR, AND I DON'T WANT TO BE YOUR FRIEND!
YOU'VE CAUSED ME NOTHING BUT TROUBLE!
JUST LEAVE ME ALONE!

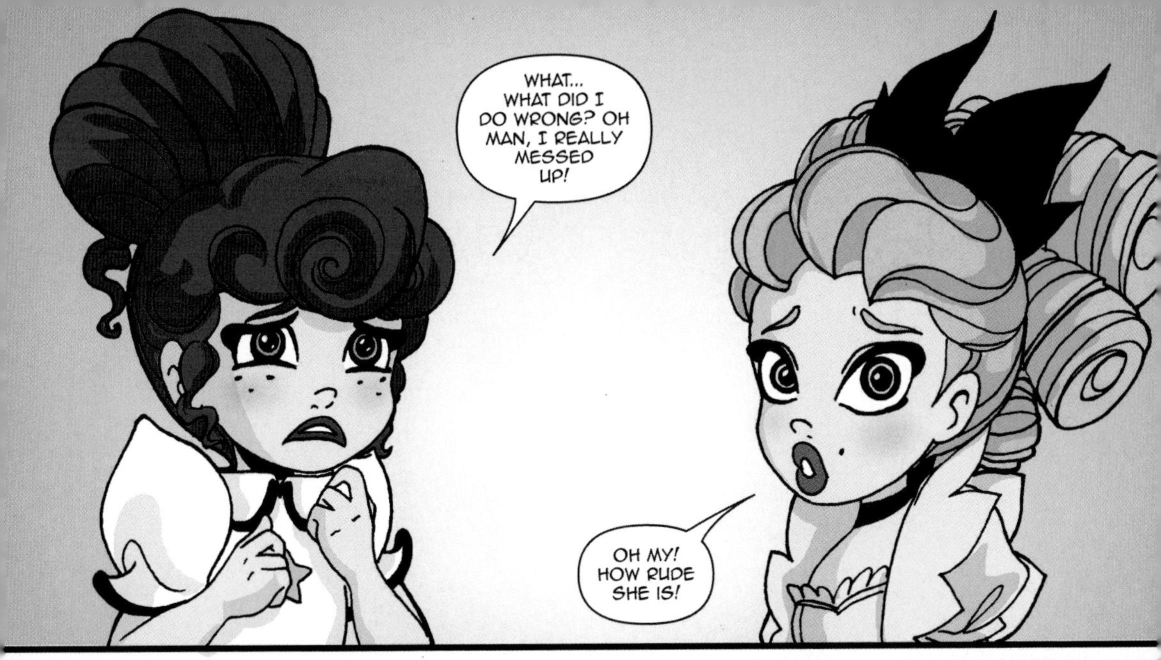
WHAT... WHAT DID I DO WRONG? OH MAN, I REALLY MESSED UP!
OH MY! HOW RUDE SHE IS!

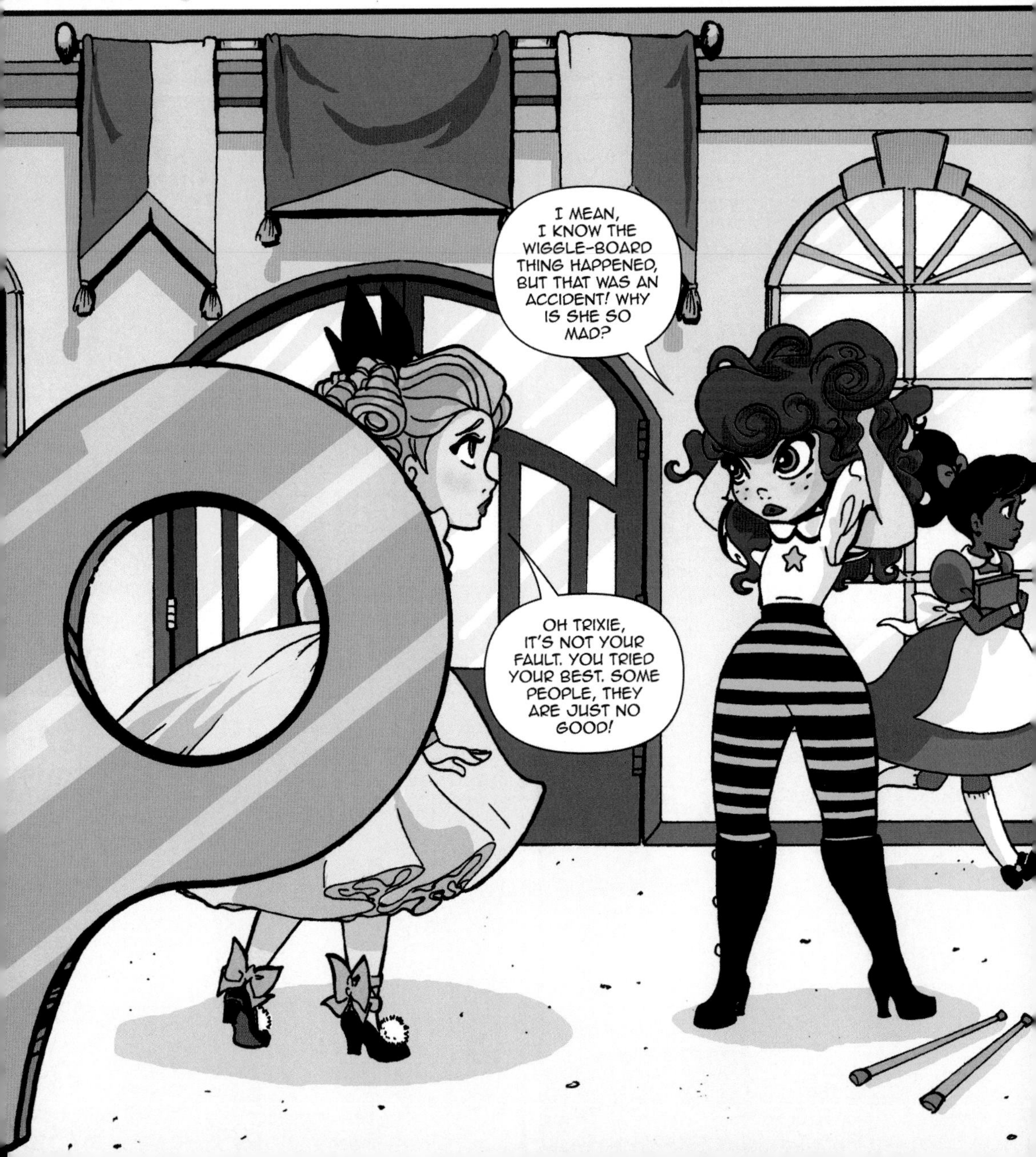
I MEAN, I KNOW THE WIGGLE-BOARD THING HAPPENED, BUT THAT WAS AN ACCIDENT! WHY IS SHE SO MAD?
OH TRIXIE, IT'S NOT YOUR FAULT. YOU TRIED YOUR BEST. SOME PEOPLE, THEY ARE JUST NO GOOD!

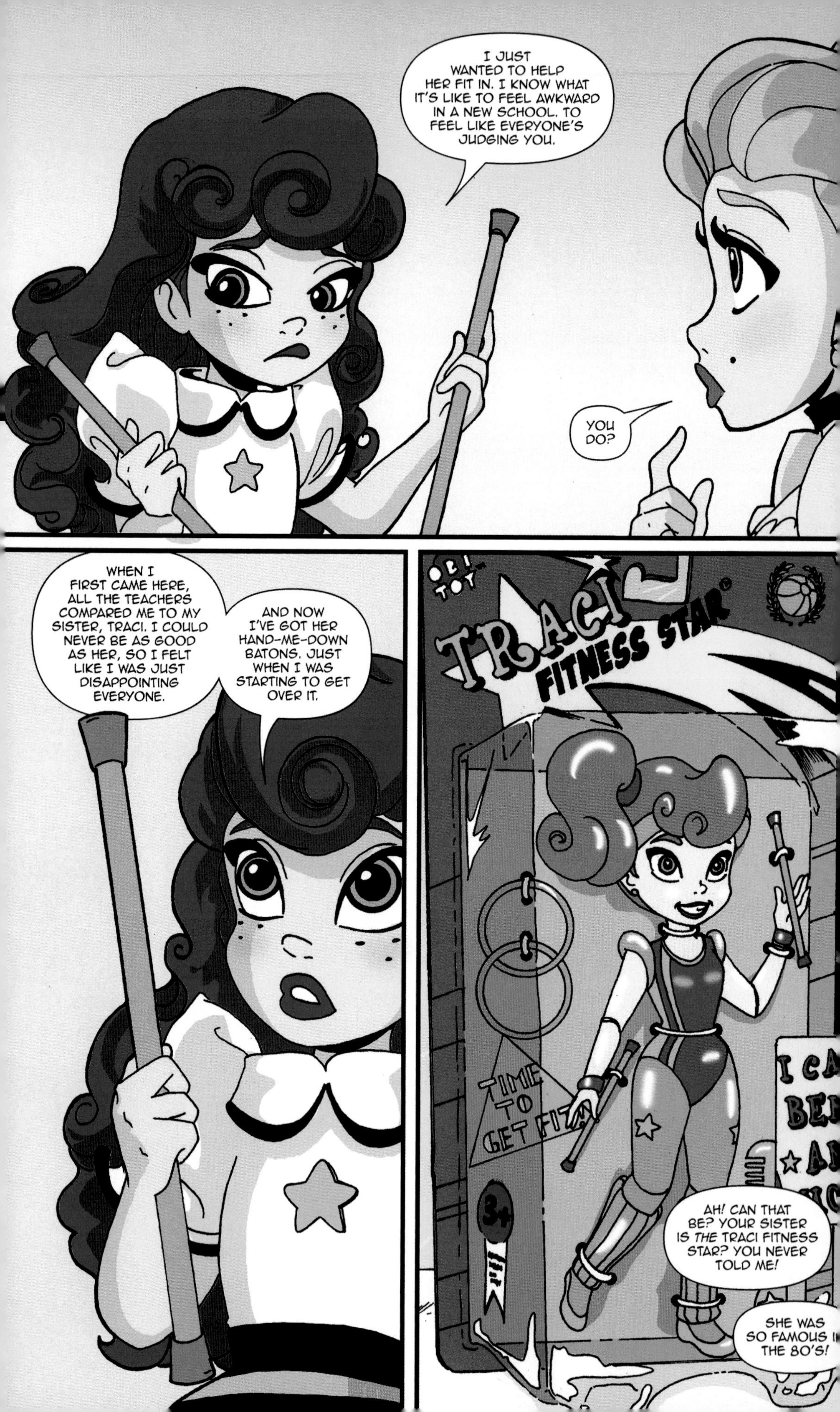
I JUST WANTED TO HELP HER FIT IN. I KNOW WHAT IT'S LIKE TO FEEL AWKWARD IN A NEW SCHOOL. TO FEEL LIKE EVERYONE'S JUDGING YOU.
YOU DO?
WHEN I FIRST CAME HERE, ALL THE TEACHERS COMPARED ME TO MY SISTER, TRACI. I COULD NEVER BE AS GOOD AS HER, SO I FELT LIKE I WAS JUST DISAPPOINTING EVERYONE.
AND NOW I'VE GOT HER HAND-ME-DOWN BATONS. JUST WHEN I WAS STARTING TO GET OVER IT.
TRACI FITNESS STAR
TIME TO GET FIT
AH! CAN THAT BE? YOUR SISTER IS *THE* TRACI FITNESS STAR? YOU NEVER TOLD ME!
SHE WAS SO FAMOUS IN THE 80'S!

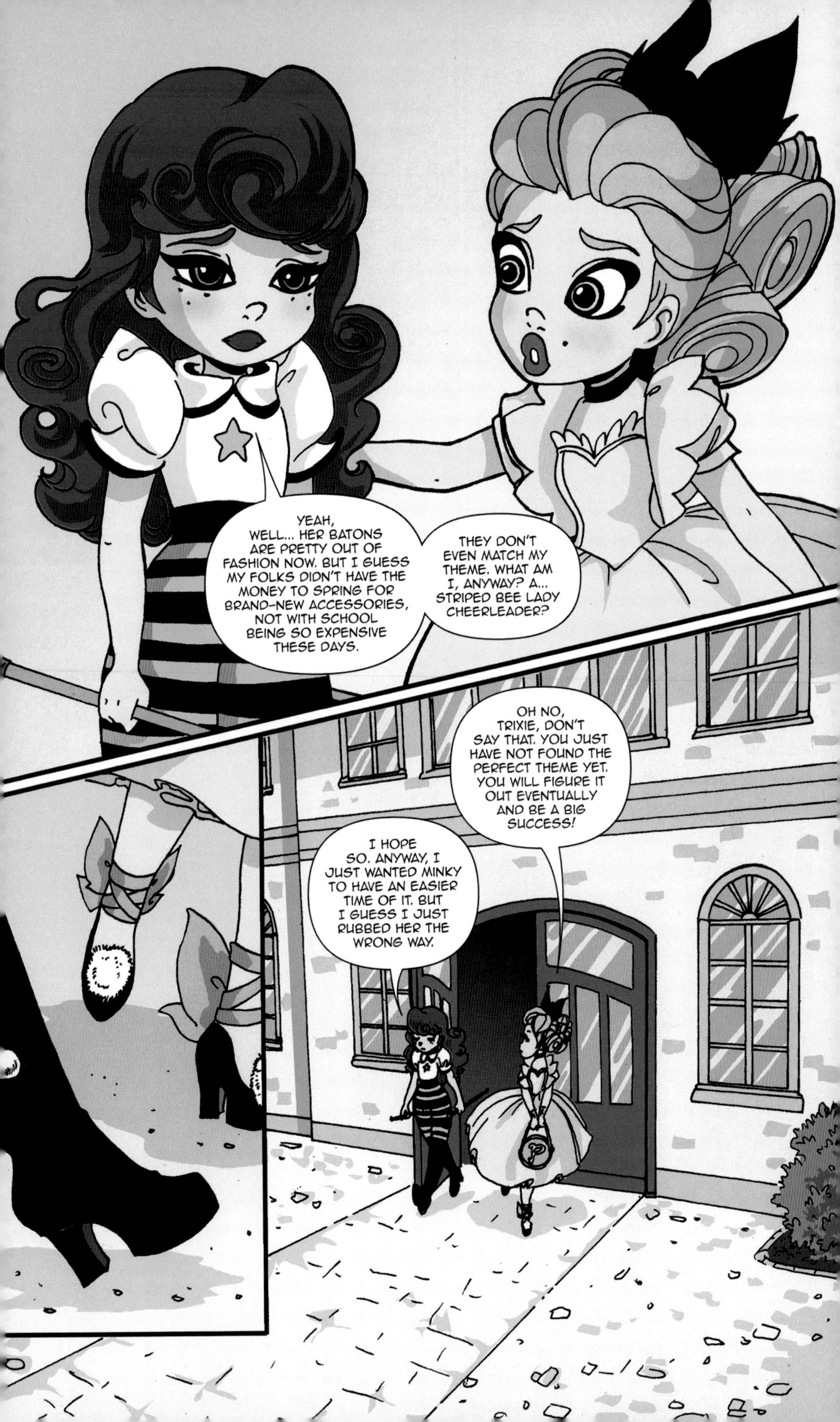
YEAH, WELL... HER BATONS ARE PRETTY OUT OF FASHION NOW. BUT I GUESS MY FOLKS DIDN'T HAVE THE MONEY TO SPRING FOR BRAND-NEW ACCESSORIES, NOT WITH SCHOOL BEING SO EXPENSIVE THESE DAYS.
THEY DON'T EVEN MATCH MY THEME. WHAT AM I, ANYWAY? A... STRIPED BEE LADY CHEERLEADER?
OH NO, TRIXIE, DON'T SAY THAT. YOU JUST HAVE NOT FOUND THE PERFECT THEME YET. YOU WILL FIGURE IT OUT EVENTUALLY AND BE A BIG SUCCESS!
I HOPE SO. ANYWAY, I JUST WANTED MINKY TO HAVE AN EASIER TIME OF IT. BUT I GUESS I JUST RUBBED HER THE WRONG WAY.

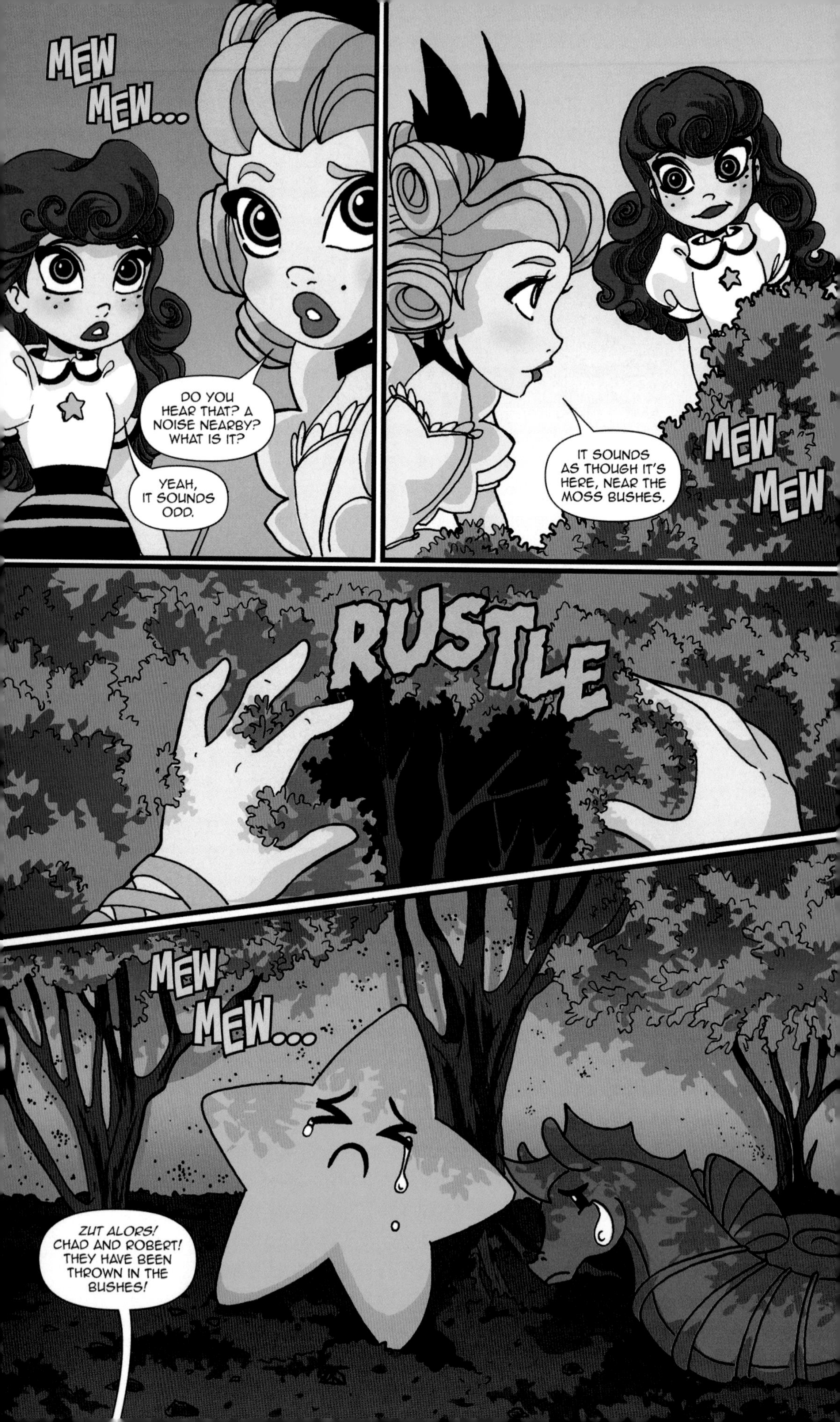
MEW MEW...
DO YOU HEAR THAT? A NOISE NEARBY? WHAT IS IT?
YEAH, IT SOUNDS ODD.
IT SOUNDS AS THOUGH IT'S HERE, NEAR THE MOSS BUSHES.
MEW MEW
RUSTLE
MEW MEW...
ZUT ALORS! CHAD AND ROBERT! THEY HAVE BEEN THROWN IN THE BUSHES!

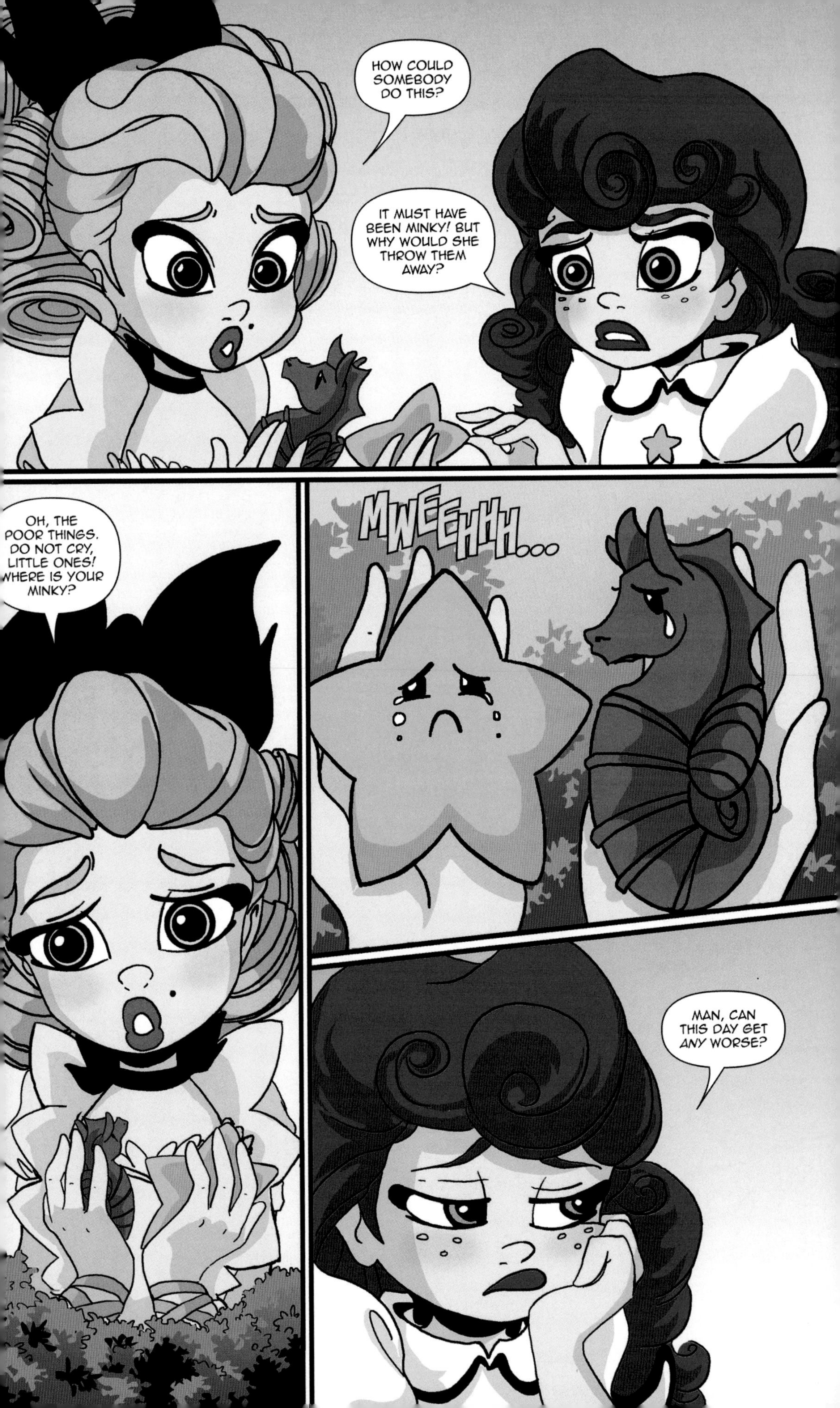

HOW COULD SOMEBODY DO THIS?
IT MUST HAVE BEEN MINKY! BUT WHY WOULD SHE THROW THEM AWAY?
OH, THE POOR THINGS. DO NOT CRY, LITTLE ONES! WHERE IS YOUR MINKY?
MWEEHHH...
MAN, CAN THIS DAY GET ANY WORSE?

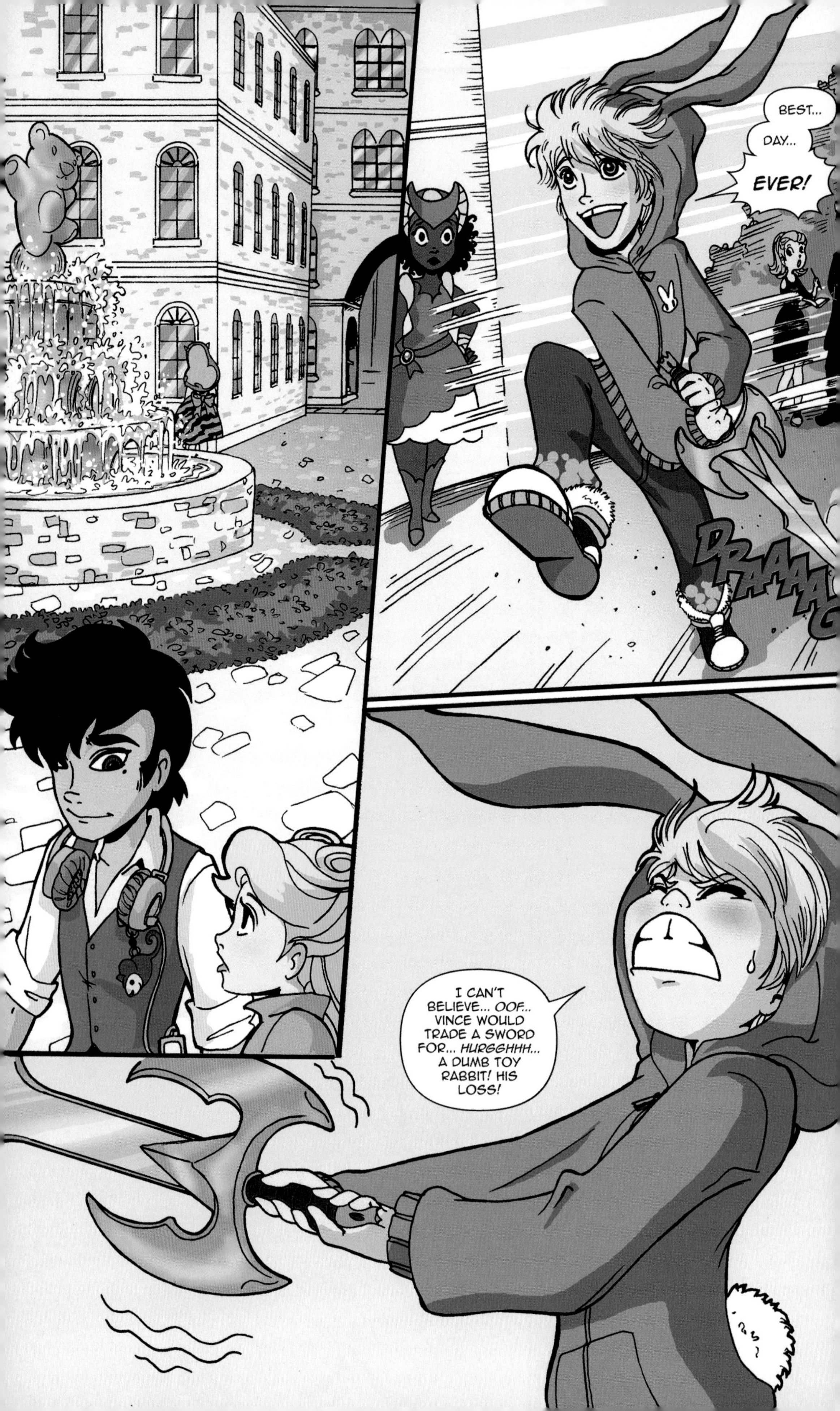
BEST...
DAY...
EVER!
DRAAAAAG
I CAN'T BELIEVE... OOF... VINCE WOULD TRADE A SWORD FOR... HURGGHHH... A DUMB TOY RABBIT! HIS LOSS!

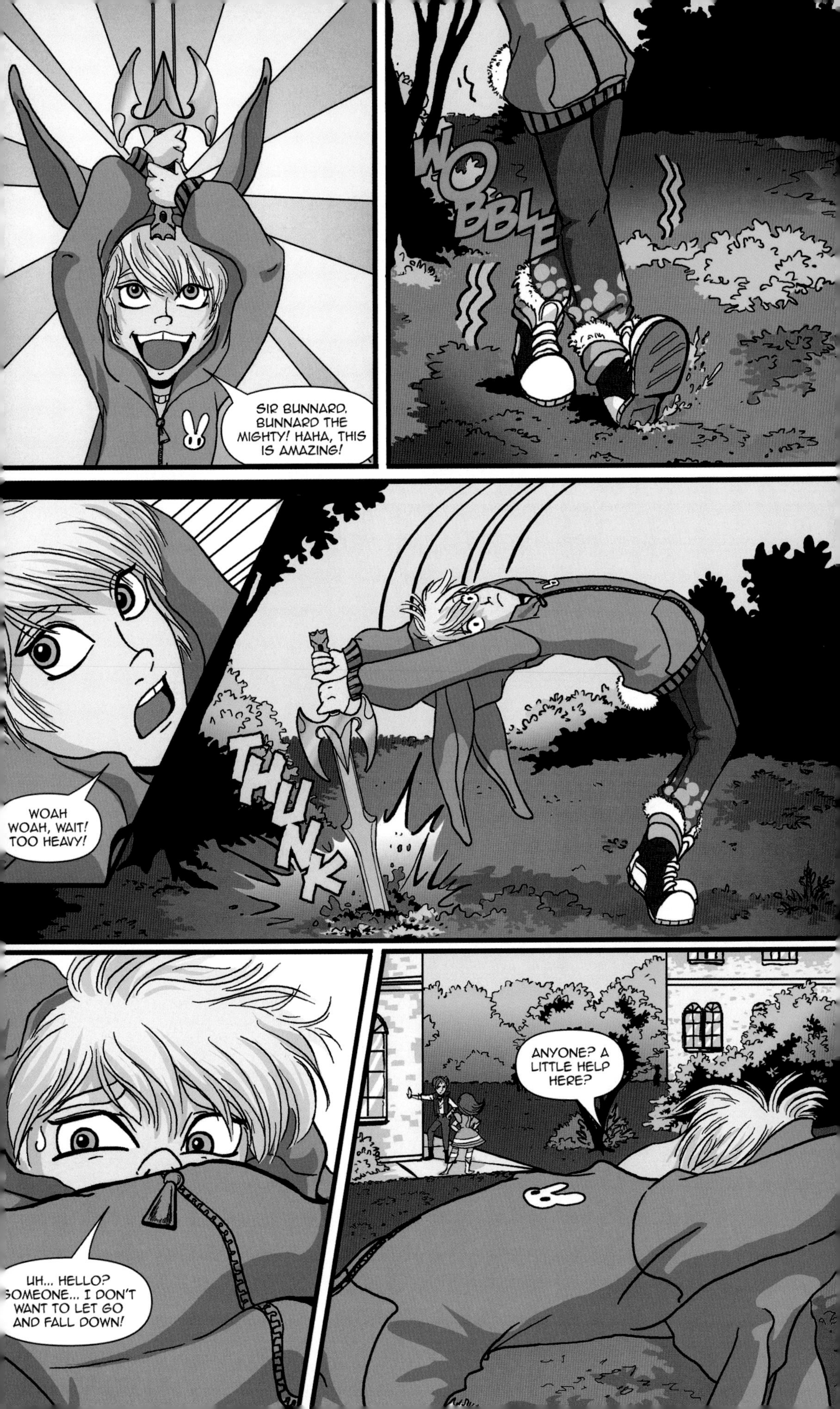
SIR BUNNARD. BUNNARD THE MIGHTY! HAHA, THIS IS AMAZING!
WOBBLE
WOAH WOAH, WAIT! TOO HEAVY!
THUNK
UH... HELLO? SOMEONE... I DON'T WANT TO LET GO AND FALL DOWN!
ANYONE? A LITTLE HELP HERE?

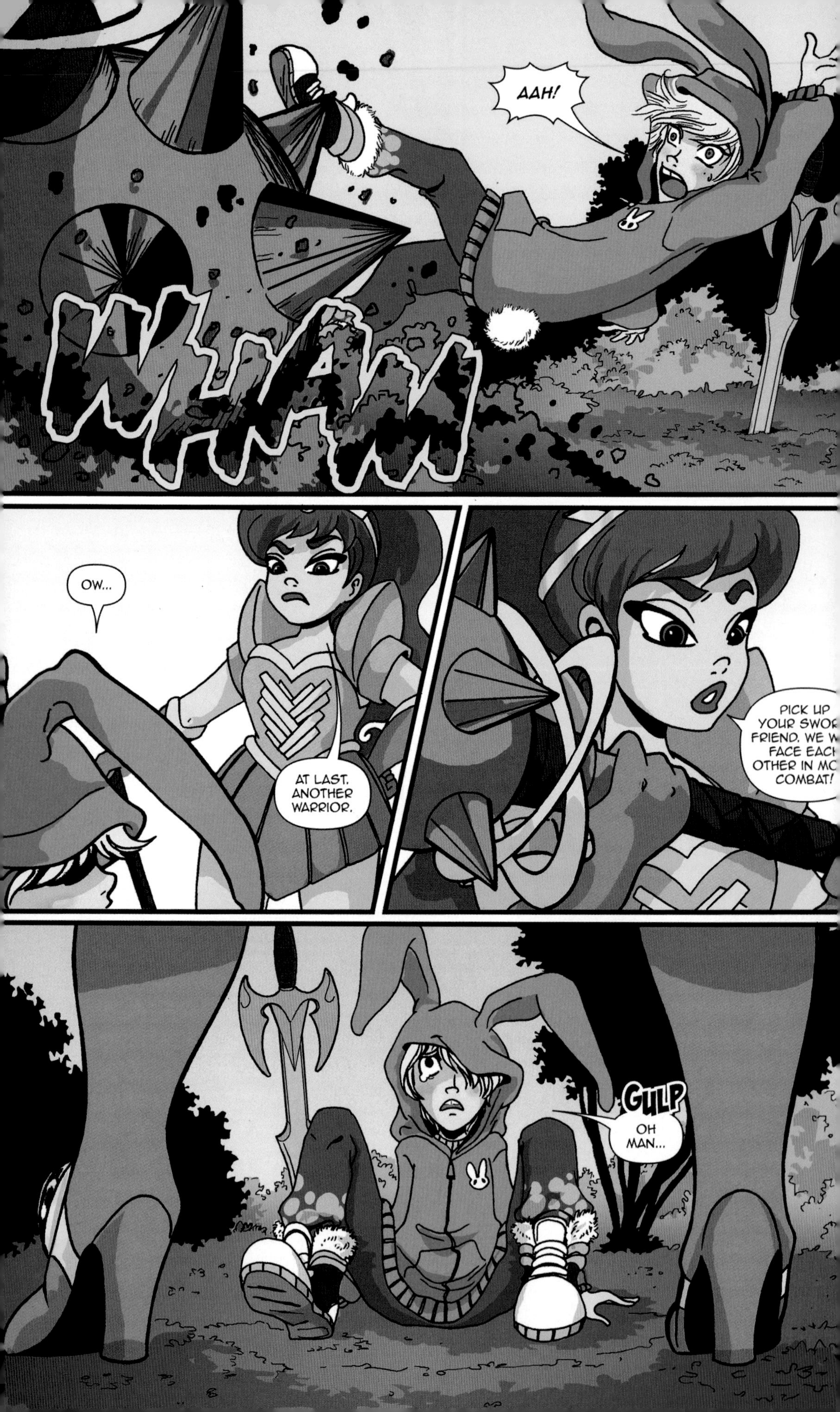
AAH!
WHAM
OW...
AT LAST. ANOTHER WARRIOR.
PICK UP YOUR SWOR FRIEND. WE W FACE EACH OTHER IN MO COMBAT!
GULP
OH MAN...

TOYETICA
THINK OUTSIDE THE TOYBOX

DOLLINGTON ACADEMY

Trixie Tangle   **Sweetina Von Bonne**   **Minky Mermille**   **Polly Fume**   **Unicole Safari-Sidekick**   **Angel Inx**   **Bunnard Safari-Sidekick**

Dia de los Marco   **Vince Charming**   **Nebulara, Queen of the Battle Cosmos**   **Becky Badluck**   **Dandelillian Fae**   **Lilly Liku**   **Fawndolyn Safari-Sidekick**

Character Profiles

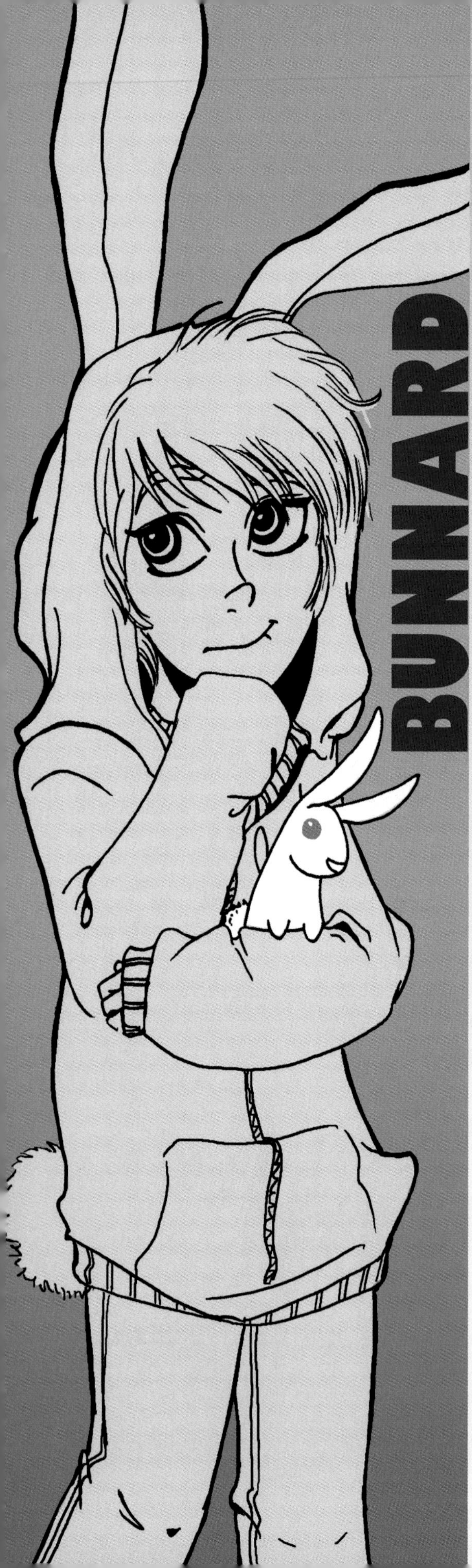
BUNNARD

Name: Bunnard
Safari-Sidekick

Fave food: Chips

Fave color:
Cornflower blue

Fave way to get someone's attention:
Sleeve-pulling

Unicole's shy little brother, Bunnarc longs to be a fierce, lion-themed gu named Lionel and model for action figures, but instead is stuck in a sweet bunny costume much more suited to his personality, as pretty much everything makes him nervou

Bunnard may seem like a cowardly little crybunny, but he tries his best to help his friends with any problen they might have...as long as it does involve spiders. Or big dogs. Or the dark. Or public speaking. Or bears or ghosts or shouting or violent sports or detentions or poisonous snakes or scraped knees or splinter or using public bathrooms or Pictur Day or that really mean guy who runs the arcade and talks too loudly or Sweetina or giant robots or skull guys or tornadoes or deep water or very shallow water that you might drown in anyway if you aren't carefi or bug bites or......

UNICOLE

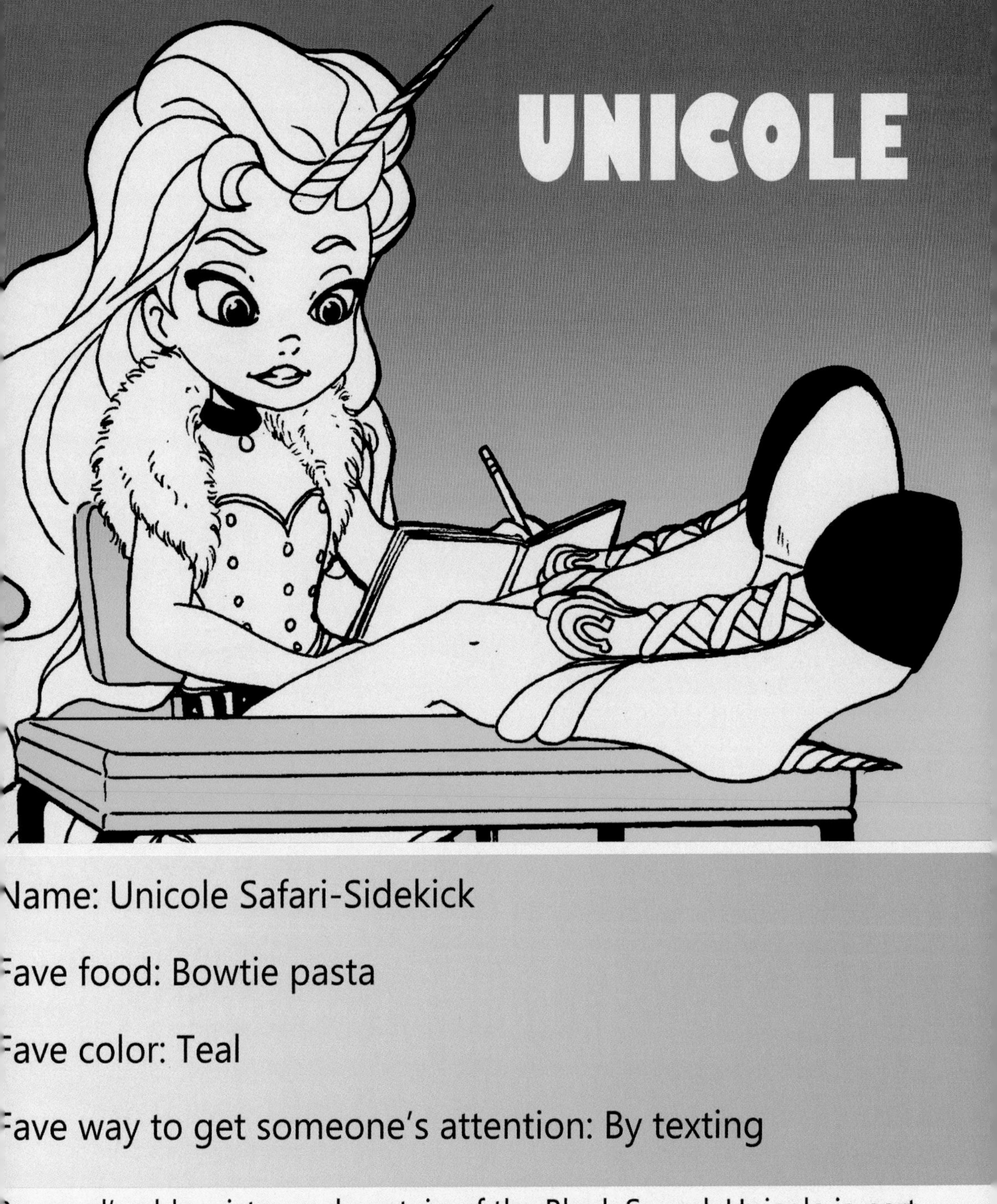

Name: Unicole Safari-Sidekick

Fave food: Bowtie pasta

Fave color: Teal

Fave way to get someone's attention: By texting

Bunnard's older sister and captain of the Block Squad, Unicole is part of the wealthy Safari-Sidekick dynasty family, named after the toy line of which their family has been the models for over 40 years. Unicole's horn and tail are not props, but real appendages she was born with, an exclusive Safari-Sidekick trait.

Unicole is a responsible student, who somehow runs every major club on campus. She's not only Block captain, but also president of the student council, the Campus Activities Board, the Honors Society, the Student Charity Organization, the Bon Bon Baker's Club, the Ultimate Frisbee League...the list goes on.

Name: Sweetina
Von Bonne

Fave color: Purple

Fave food: Cake

Fave way to get
someone's attention:
Polite shouting

Lavender-haired and perfect,
Sweetina is being eyed by toy
scouts as the hot new Princess-
themed item of the season, and
is anticipating many offers from
toy companies once she
graduates.

Her lavish background allows
her to afford only the best
accessories and clothes, all of
which she incorporates into her
product package.

Sweetina is determined to be
the school's MVT (Most
Valuable Toy) and the best at
everything, and she isn't above
resorting to scheming or tricks
to get what she wants. If you
don't want trouble, stay out of
her way.

SWEETINA

NEBULARA

Name:
Nebulara, Queen of the Battle Cosmos

Fave food:
Caramel yogurt

Fave color:
Dusty Rose

Fave way to get someone's attention:
Battle cry and a thrown mace

Nebulara is a formidable, green-skinned student who carries a "space mace" around everywhere as her accessory. Although stern and seemingly without a sense of humor, Nebulara is actually a very honorable person and easy to get along with, so long as no one mentions battles or duel challenges.

No one is sure where "The Battle Cosmos" is or if Nebulara is actually queen of it. She is very method, preferring the unusual tactic of being her toy's character at all times, even if that means claiming to be from space. When pressed about her origins, she insists her parents are "Mr. and Mrs. Of The Battle Cosmos."

The topic has been left alone at this point.

VINCE

Name: Vince Charming
Fave food: Pumpkin Bread
Fave color: Red
Fave way to get someone's attention:
Friendly slap on the back

Vince is a prince-themed student, who seems destined to be paired with a much more successful Princess doll like Sweetina and act as a companion for her. He tries not to think about it, instead devoting his time to friend sports and school, as well as volunteering with animal work.

Vince gets along with everyone at school, because he's always helpful and friendly. He plays on the Block squad as a tumbler.

THE BIG KEY

PART THREE

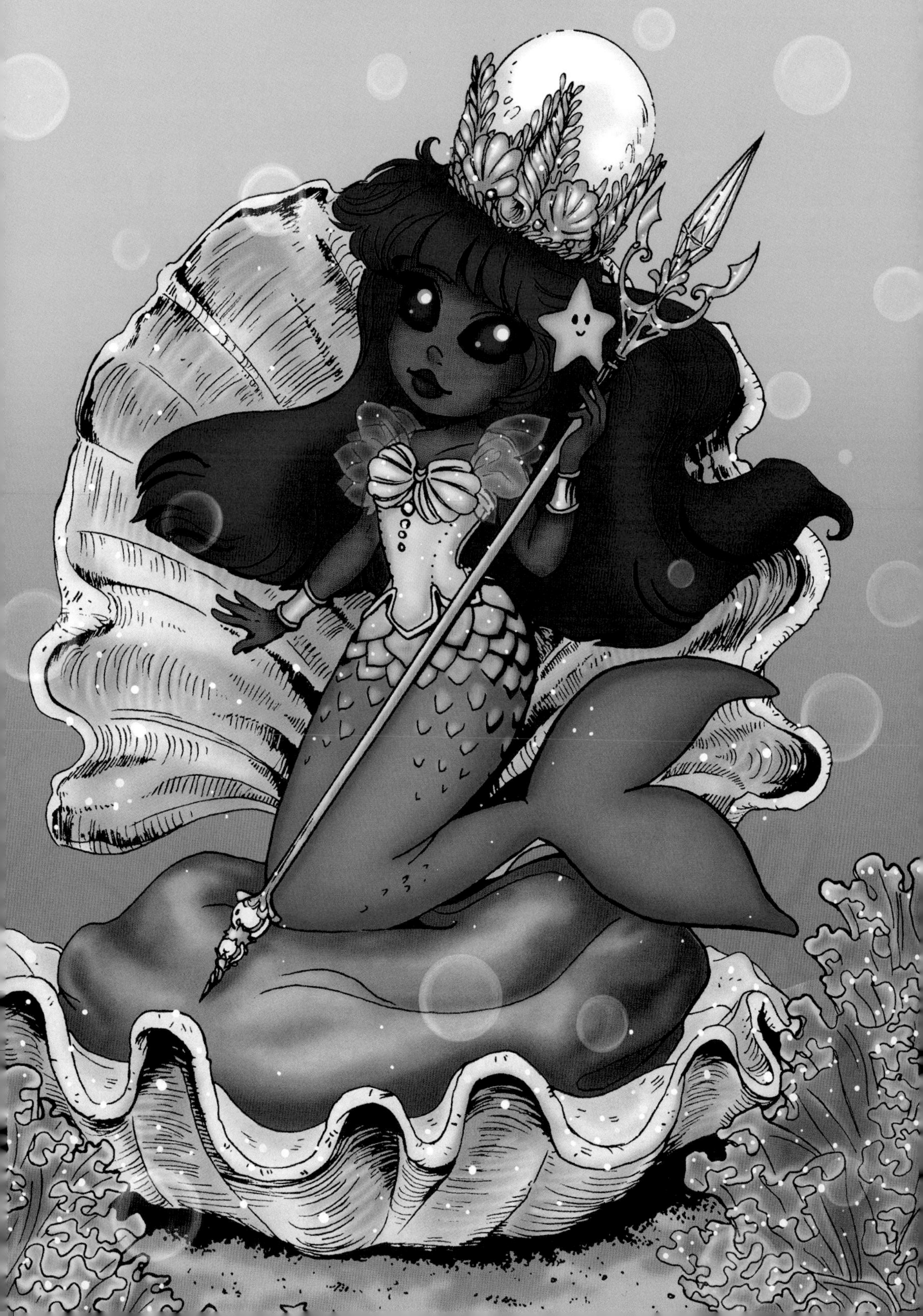

TOYETICA

3

STORY AND ART BY
MARTY LEGROW

LETTERING
Justin Birch

TODAY'S SQUIRREL THREAT
Moderate

Bryan Seaton: Publisher/ CEO • Shawn Gabborin: Editor In Chief • Jason Martin: Publisher-Danger Zone • Nicole D'Andria: Marketing Director/Editor
Jim Dietz: Social Media Manager • Danielle Davison: Executive Administrator • Chad Cicconi: Action Lawyer • Shawn Pryor: President of Creator Relatio

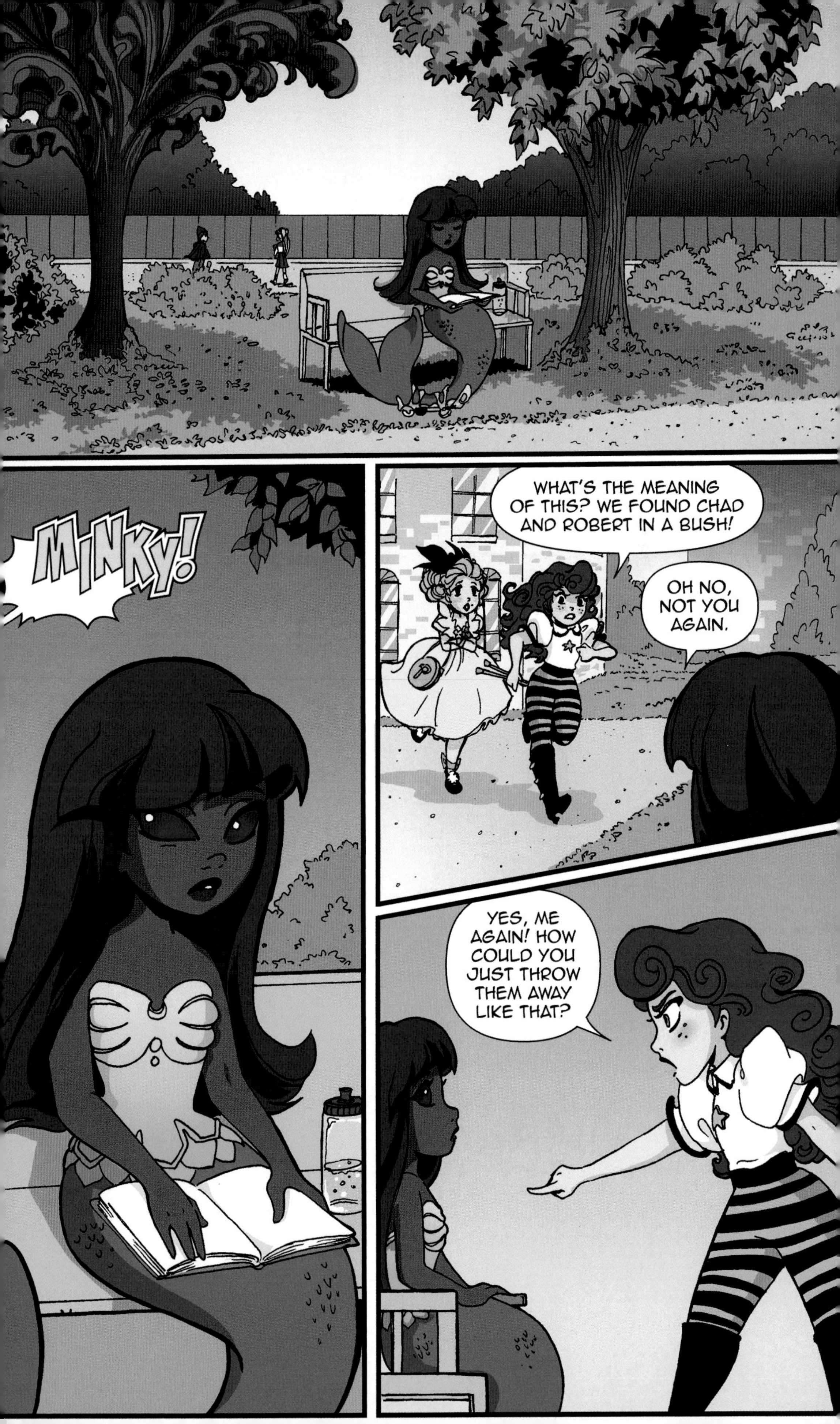
MINKY!
WHAT'S THE MEANING OF THIS? WE FOUND CHAD AND ROBERT IN A BUSH!
OH NO, NOT YOU AGAIN.
YES, ME AGAIN! HOW COULD YOU JUST THROW THEM AWAY LIKE THAT?

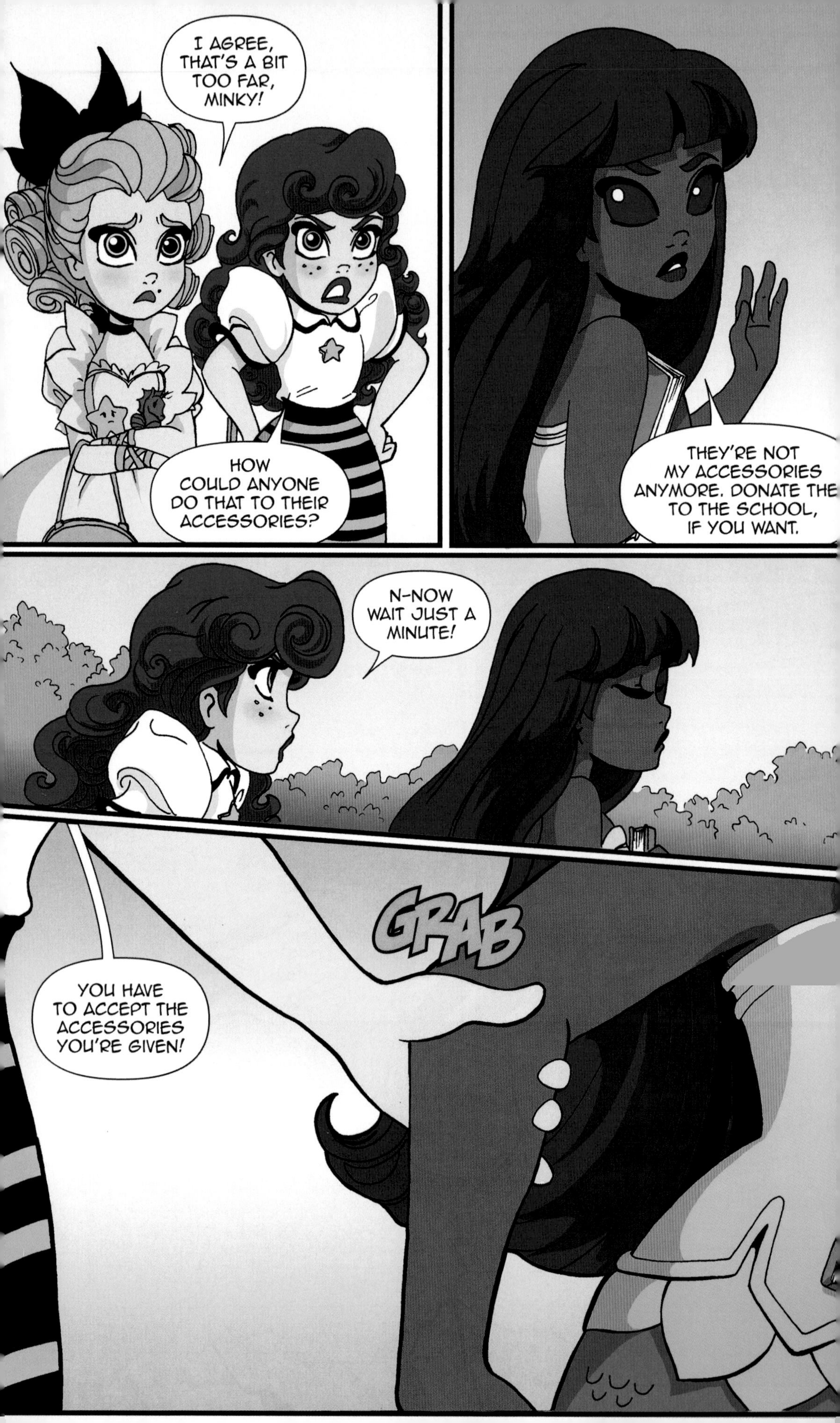
I AGREE, THAT'S A BIT TOO FAR, MINKY!
HOW COULD ANYONE DO THAT TO THEIR ACCESSORIES?
THEY'RE NOT MY ACCESSORIES ANYMORE. DONATE THE TO THE SCHOOL, IF YOU WANT.
N-NOW WAIT JUST A MINUTE!
GRAB
YOU HAVE TO ACCEPT THE ACCESSORIES YOU'RE GIVEN!

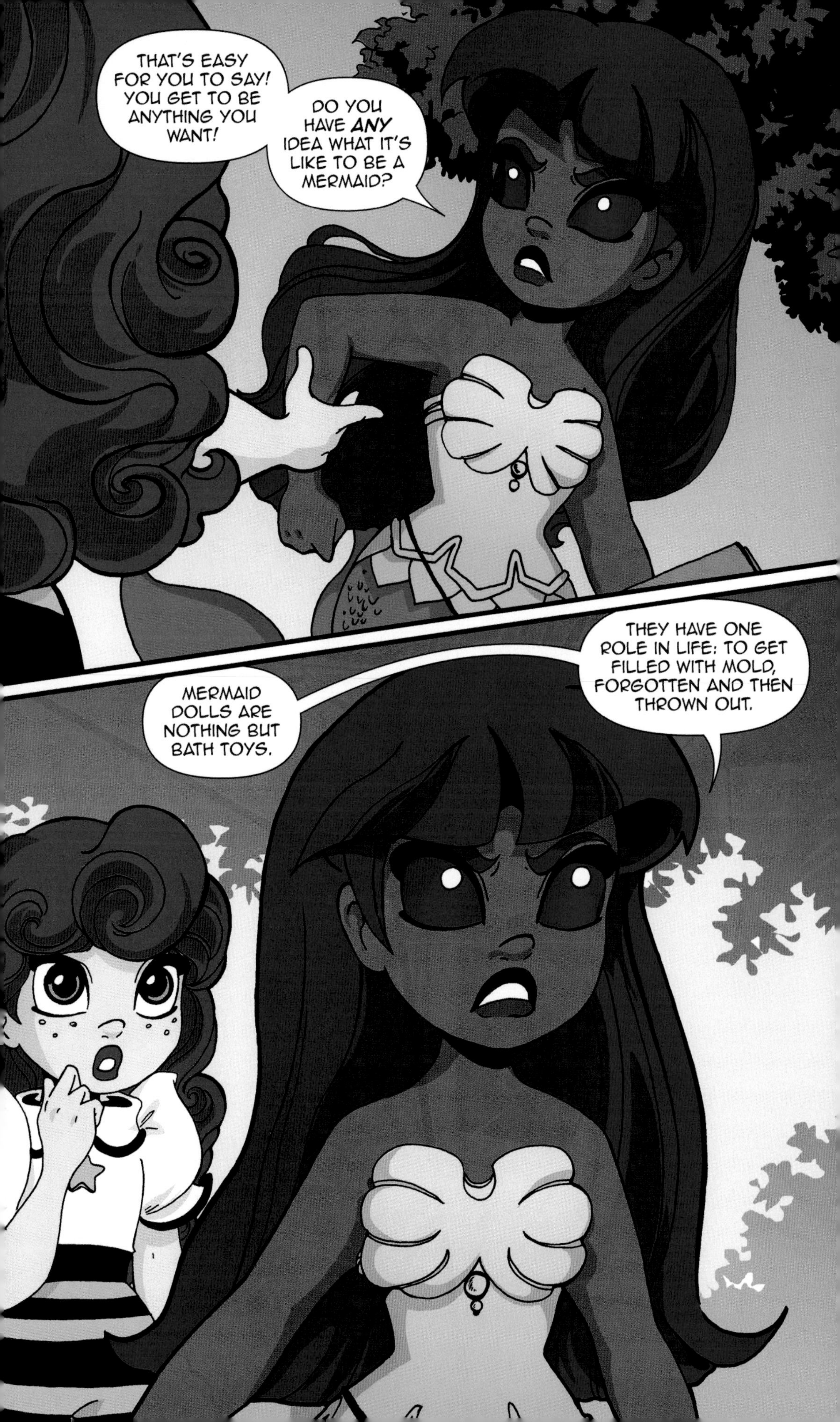
THAT'S EASY FOR YOU TO SAY! YOU GET TO BE ANYTHING YOU WANT!
DO YOU HAVE **ANY** IDEA WHAT IT'S LIKE TO BE A MERMAID?
MERMAID DOLLS ARE NOTHING BUT BATH TOYS.
THEY HAVE ONE ROLE IN LIFE: TO GET FILLED WITH MOLD, FORGOTTEN AND THEN THROWN OUT.

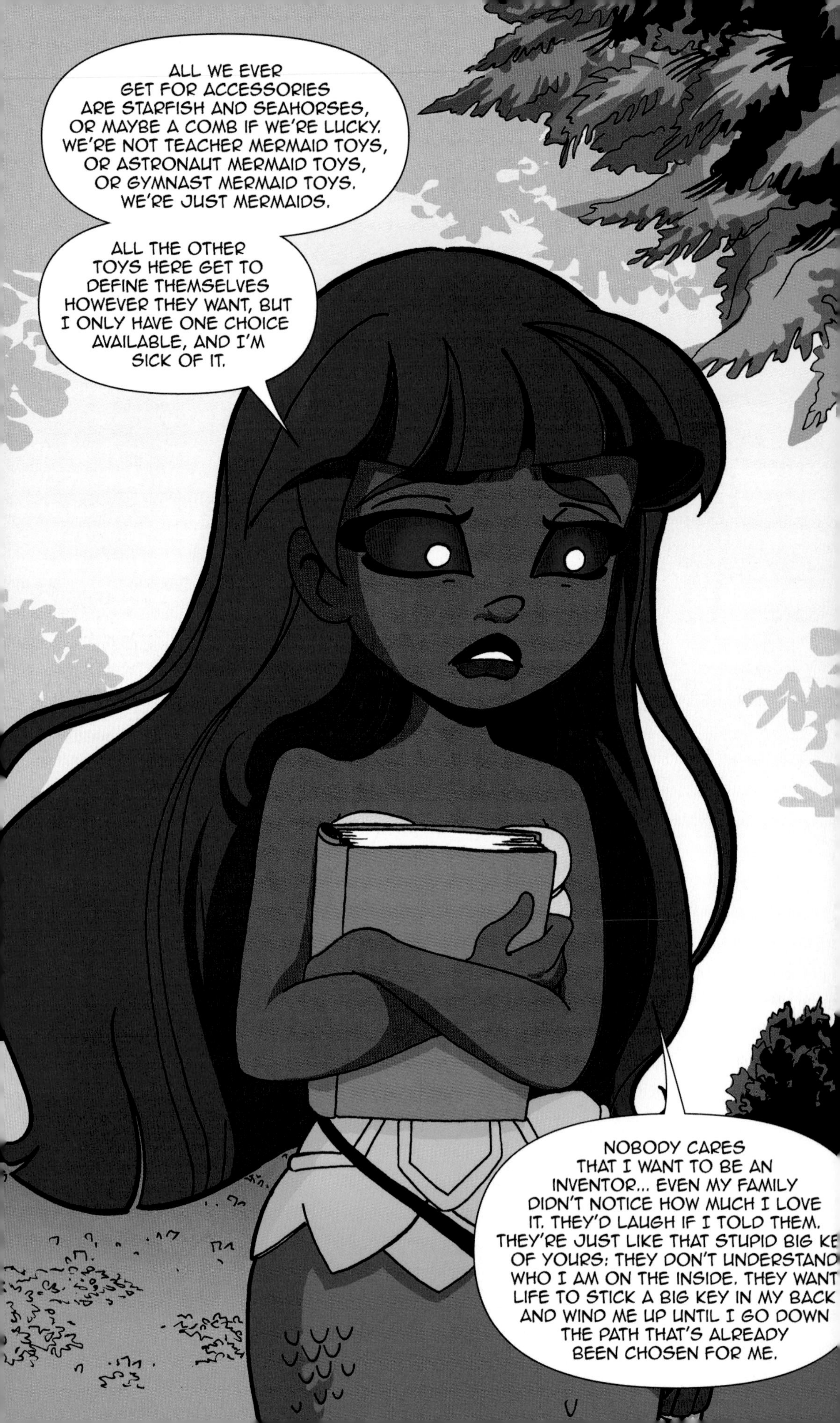
ALL WE EVER GET FOR ACCESSORIES ARE STARFISH AND SEAHORSES, OR MAYBE A COMB IF WE'RE LUCKY. WE'RE NOT TEACHER MERMAID TOYS, OR ASTRONAUT MERMAID TOYS, OR GYMNAST MERMAID TOYS. WE'RE JUST MERMAIDS.
ALL THE OTHER TOYS HERE GET TO DEFINE THEMSELVES HOWEVER THEY WANT, BUT I ONLY HAVE ONE CHOICE AVAILABLE, AND I'M SICK OF IT.
NOBODY CARES THAT I WANT TO BE AN INVENTOR... EVEN MY FAMILY DIDN'T NOTICE HOW MUCH I LOVE IT. THEY'D LAUGH IF I TOLD THEM. THEY'RE JUST LIKE THAT STUPID BIG KE OF YOURS: THEY DON'T UNDERSTAND WHO I AM ON THE INSIDE. THEY WANT LIFE TO STICK A BIG KEY IN MY BACK AND WIND ME UP UNTIL I GO DOWN THE PATH THAT'S ALREADY BEEN CHOSEN FOR ME.

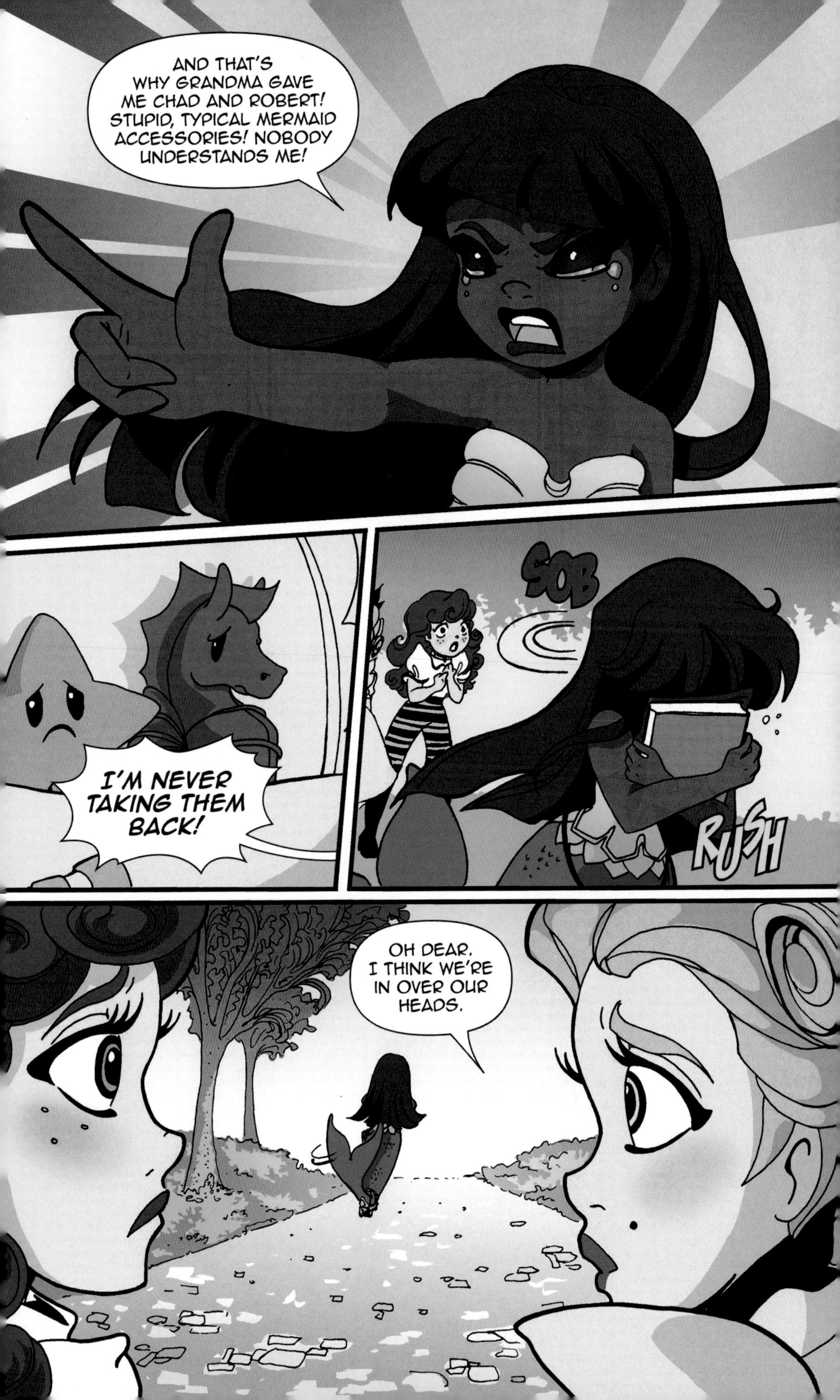
AND THAT'S WHY GRANDMA GAVE ME CHAD AND ROBERT! STUPID, TYPICAL MERMAID ACCESSORIES! NOBODY UNDERSTANDS ME!
I'M NEVER TAKING THEM BACK!
SOB
RUSH
OH DEAR. I THINK WE'RE IN OVER OUR HEADS.

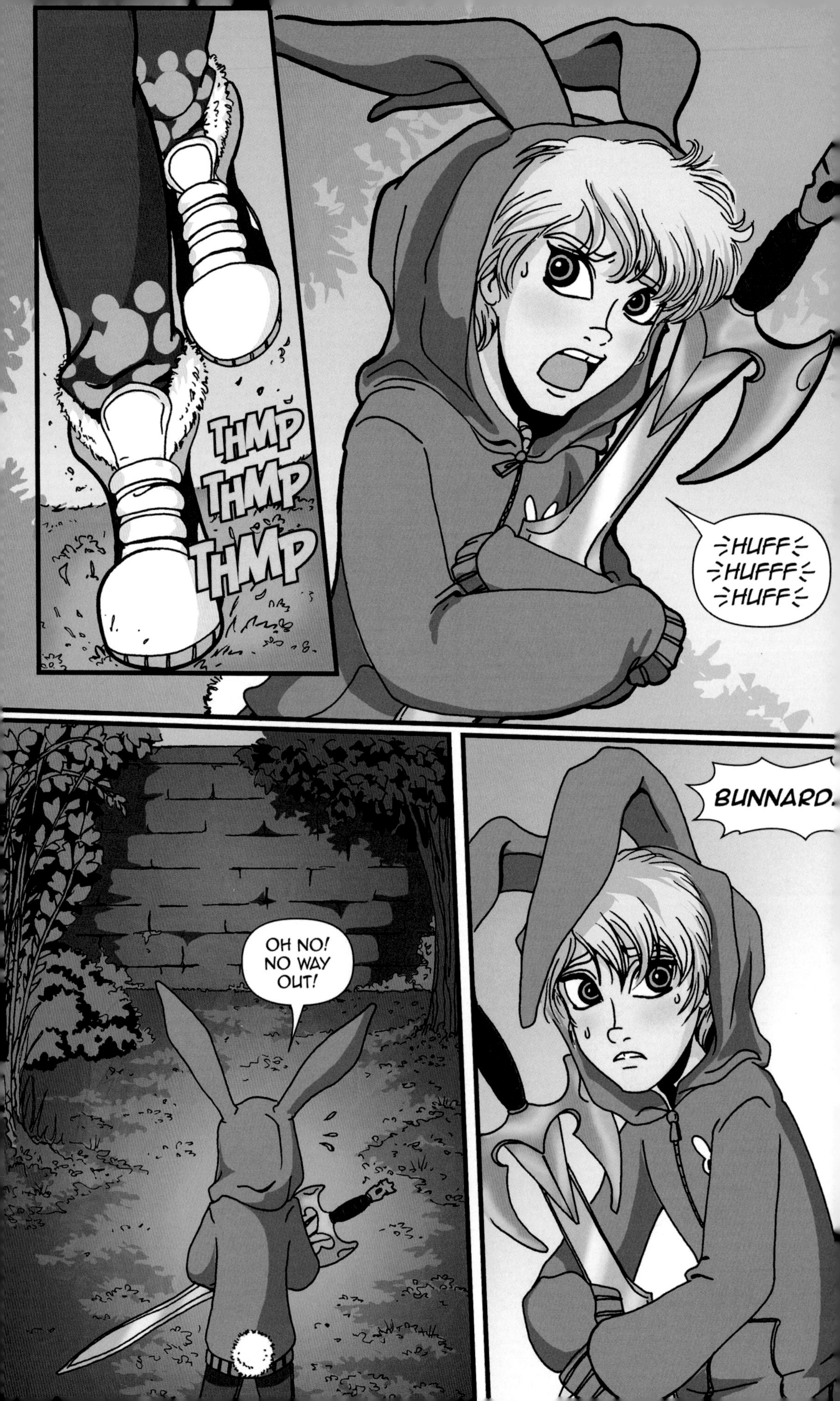
THMP
THMP
THMP
HUFF
HUFFF
HUFF
OH NO! NO WAY OUT!
BUNNARD.

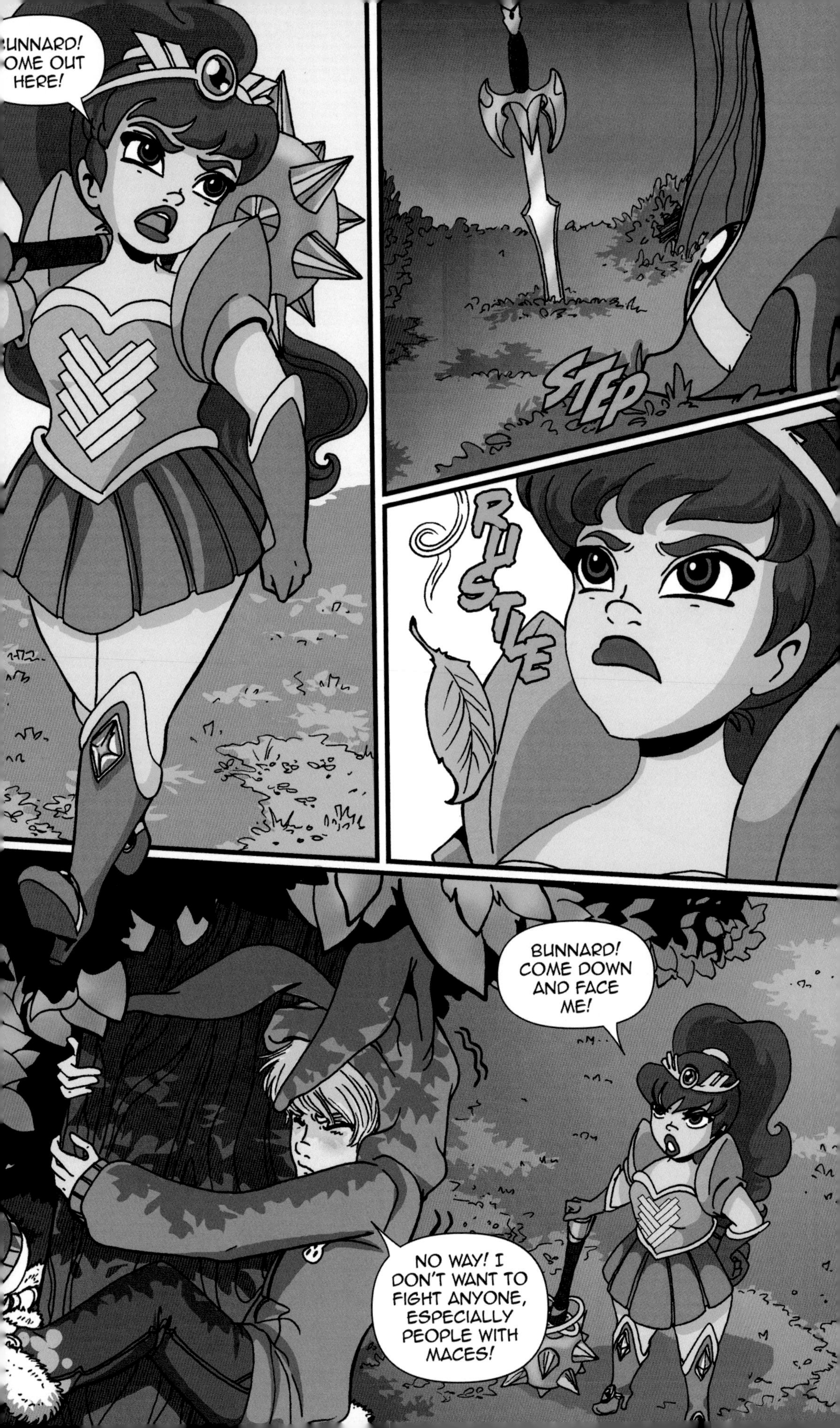
BUNNARD! COME OUT HERE!
STEP
RUSTLE
BUNNARD! COME DOWN AND FACE ME!
NO WAY! I DON'T WANT TO FIGHT ANYONE, ESPECIALLY PEOPLE WITH MACES!

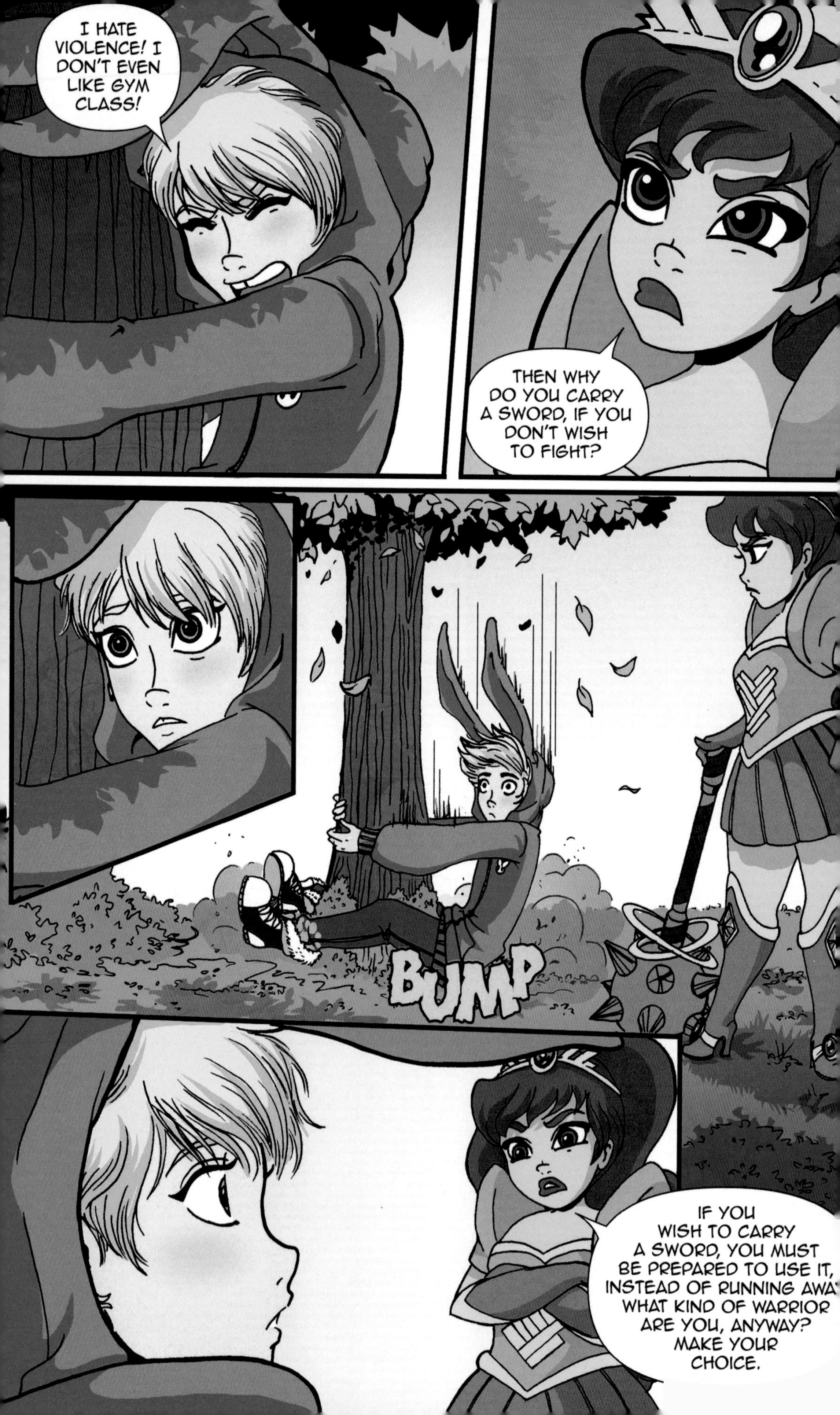
I HATE VIOLENCE! I DON'T EVEN LIKE GYM CLASS!
THEN WHY DO YOU CARRY A SWORD, IF YOU DON'T WISH TO FIGHT?
BUMP
IF YOU WISH TO CARRY A SWORD, YOU MUST BE PREPARED TO USE IT, INSTEAD OF RUNNING AWA
WHAT KIND OF WARRIOR ARE YOU, ANYWAY? MAKE YOUR CHOICE.

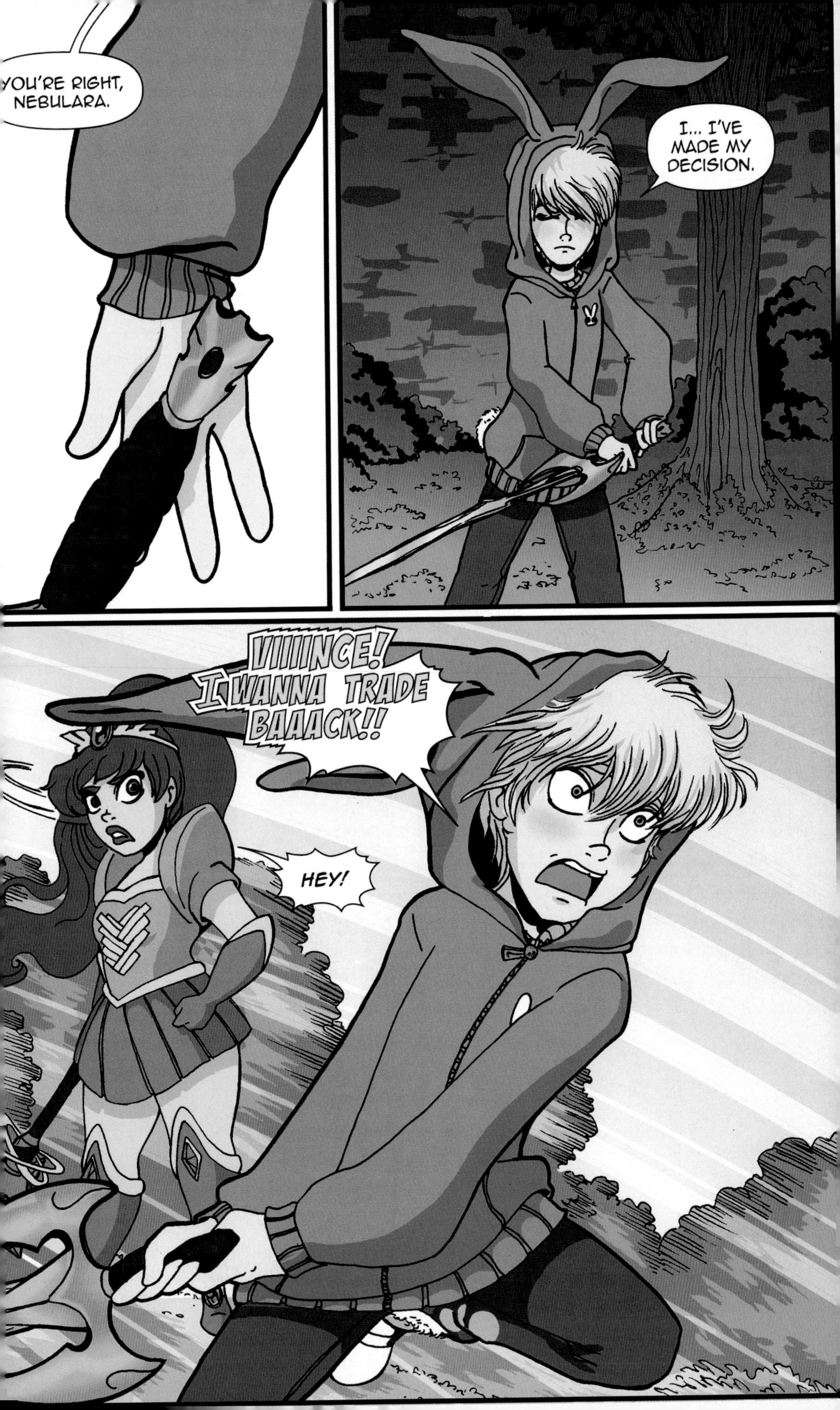
YOU'RE RIGHT, NEBULARA.
I... I'VE MADE MY DECISION.
VIIIINCE! I WANNA TRADE BAAACK!!
HEY!

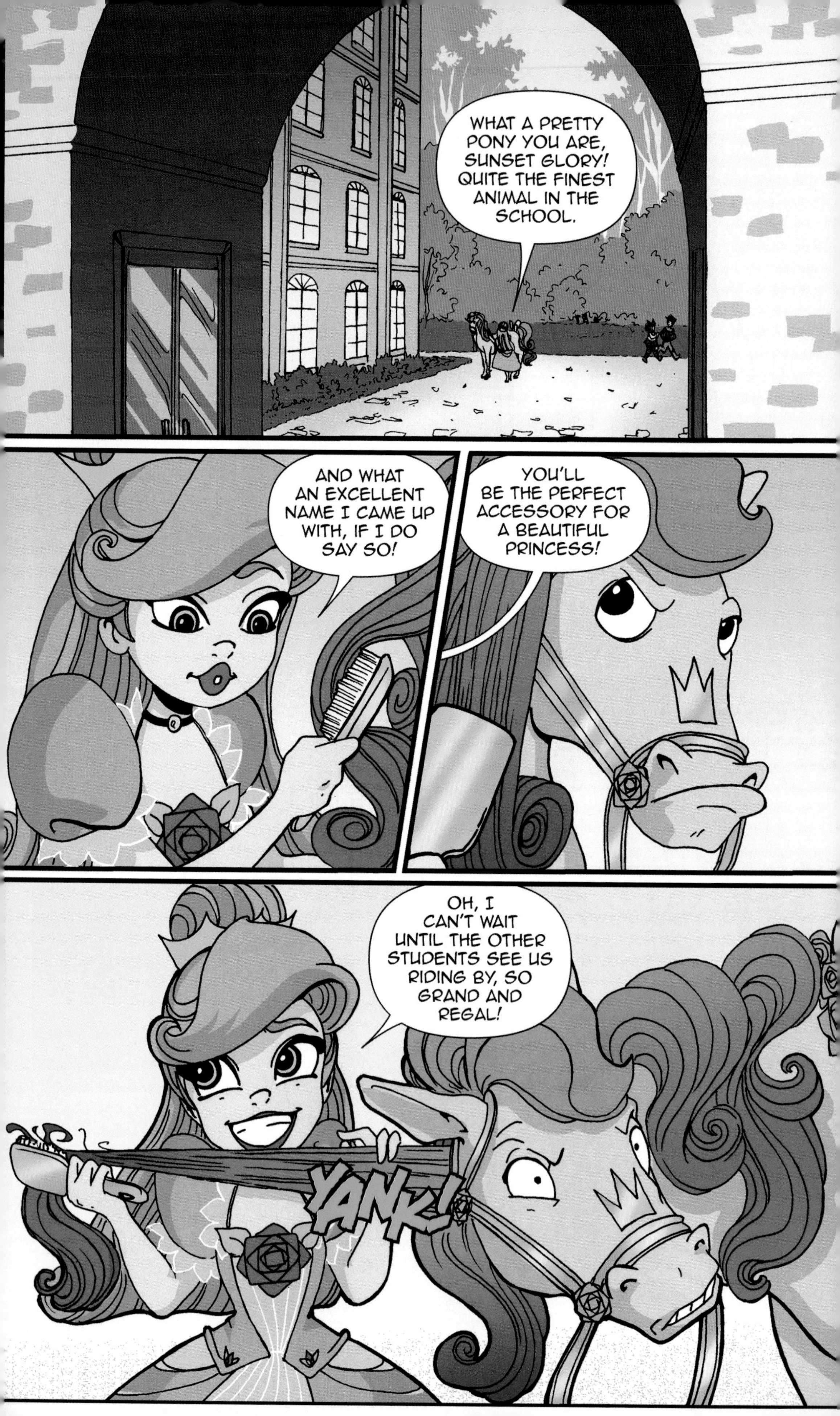
WHAT A PRETTY PONY YOU ARE, SUNSET GLORY! QUITE THE FINEST ANIMAL IN THE SCHOOL.
AND WHAT AN EXCELLENT NAME I CAME UP WITH, IF I DO SAY SO!
YOU'LL BE THE PERFECT ACCESSORY FOR A BEAUTIFUL PRINCESS!
OH, I CAN'T WAIT UNTIL THE OTHER STUDENTS SEE US RIDING BY, SO GRAND AND REGAL!
YANK!

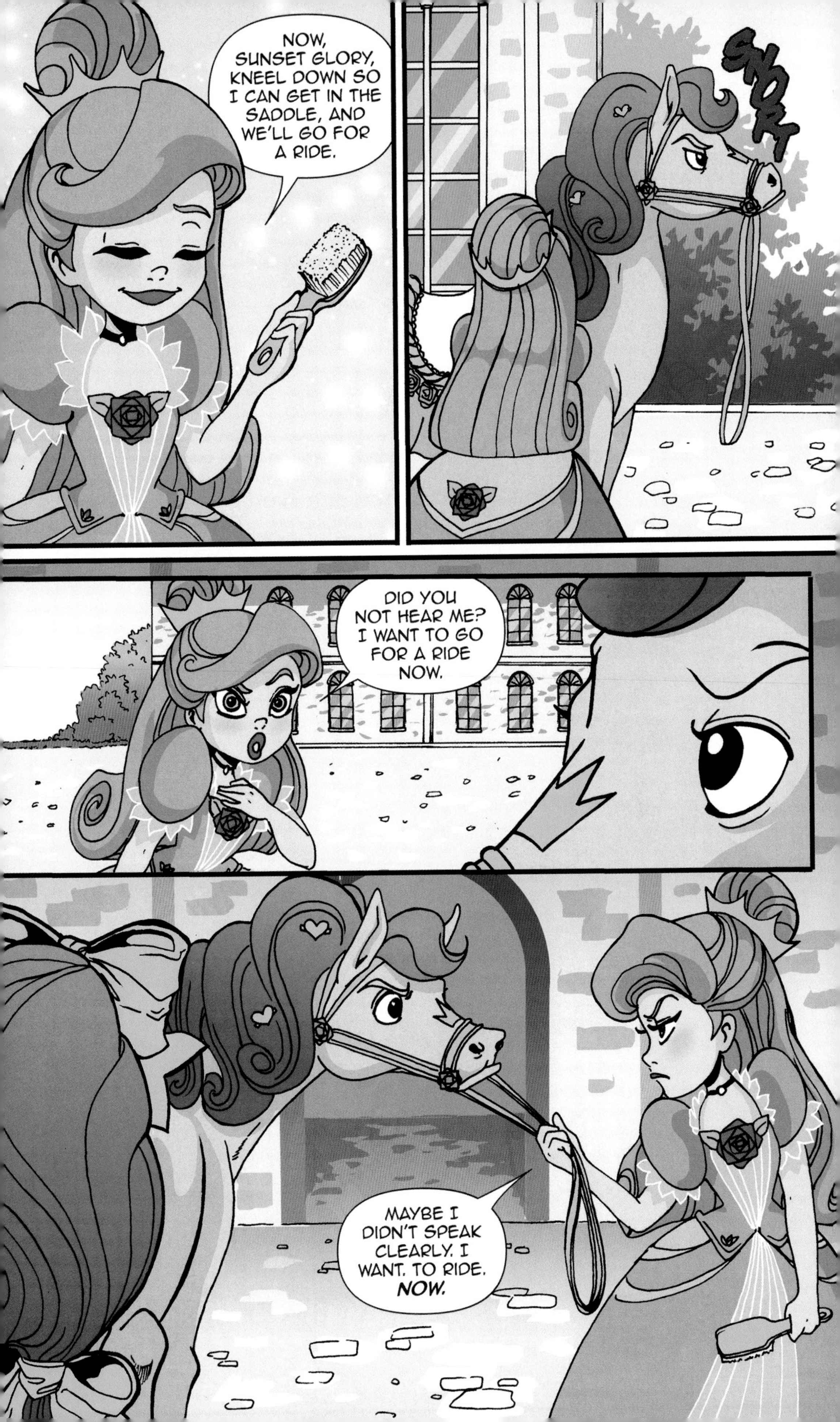

NOW, SUNSET GLORY, KNEEL DOWN SO I CAN GET IN THE SADDLE, AND WE'LL GO FOR A RIDE.
SNORT
DID YOU NOT HEAR ME? I WANT TO GO FOR A RIDE NOW.
MAYBE I DIDN'T SPEAK CLEARLY. I WANT. TO RIDE. NOW.

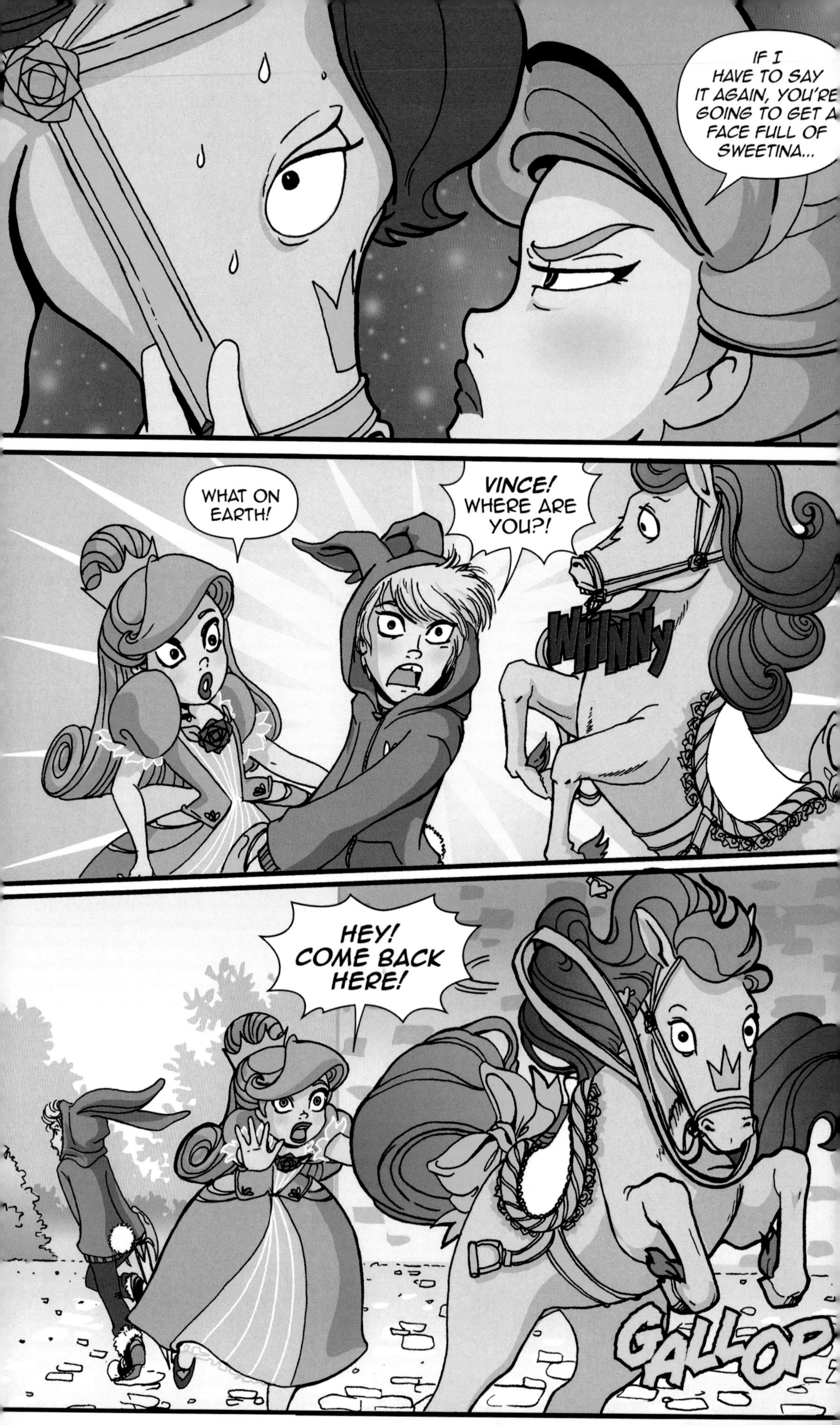
IF I HAVE TO SAY IT AGAIN, YOU'RE GOING TO GET A FACE FULL OF SWEETINA...
WHAT ON EARTH!
VINCE! WHERE ARE YOU?!
WHINNY
HEY! COME BACK HERE!
GALLOP

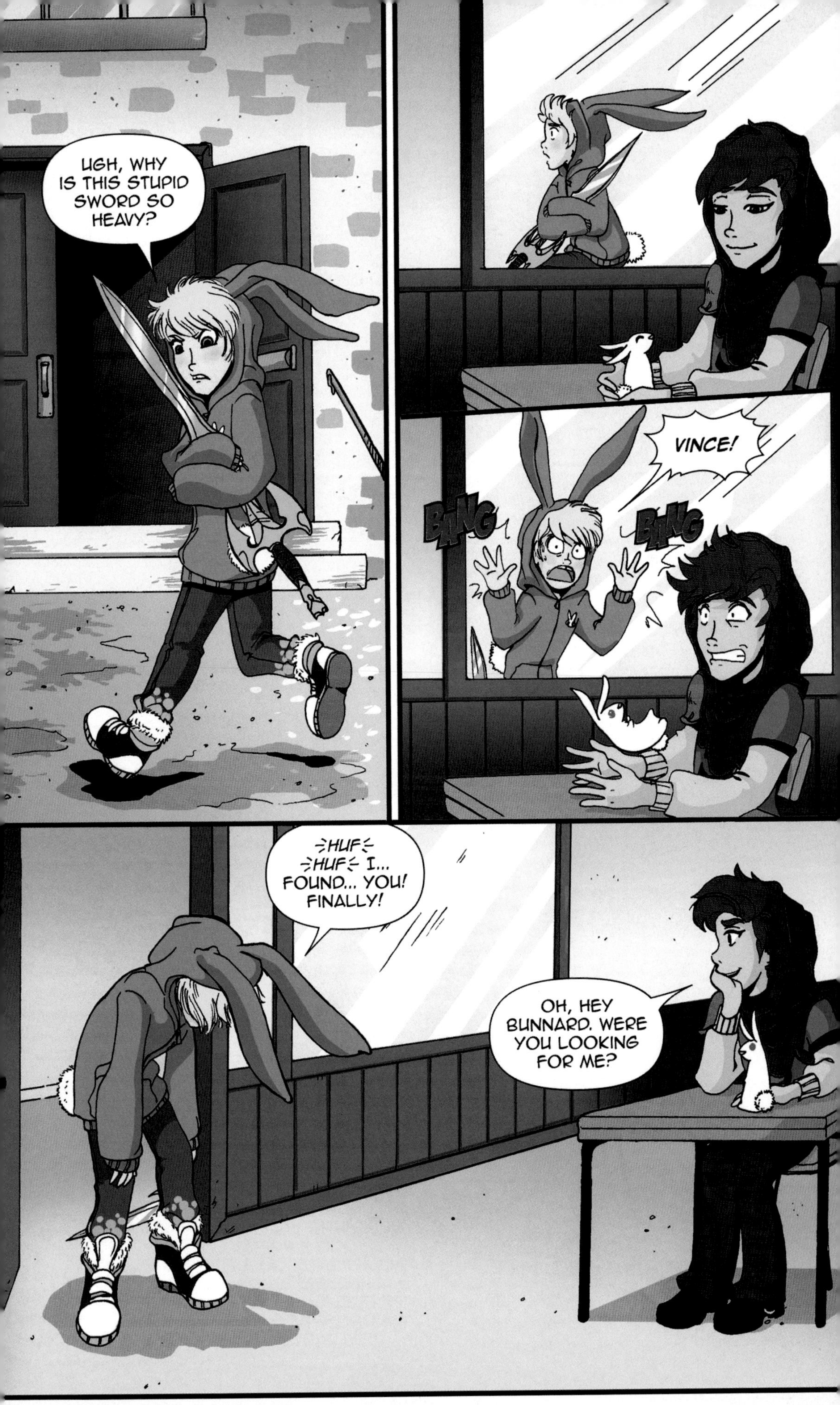
UGH, WHY IS THIS STUPID SWORD SO HEAVY?
VINCE!
BANG
BANG
HUF HUF I... FOUND... YOU! FINALLY!
OH, HEY BUNNARD. WERE YOU LOOKING FOR ME?

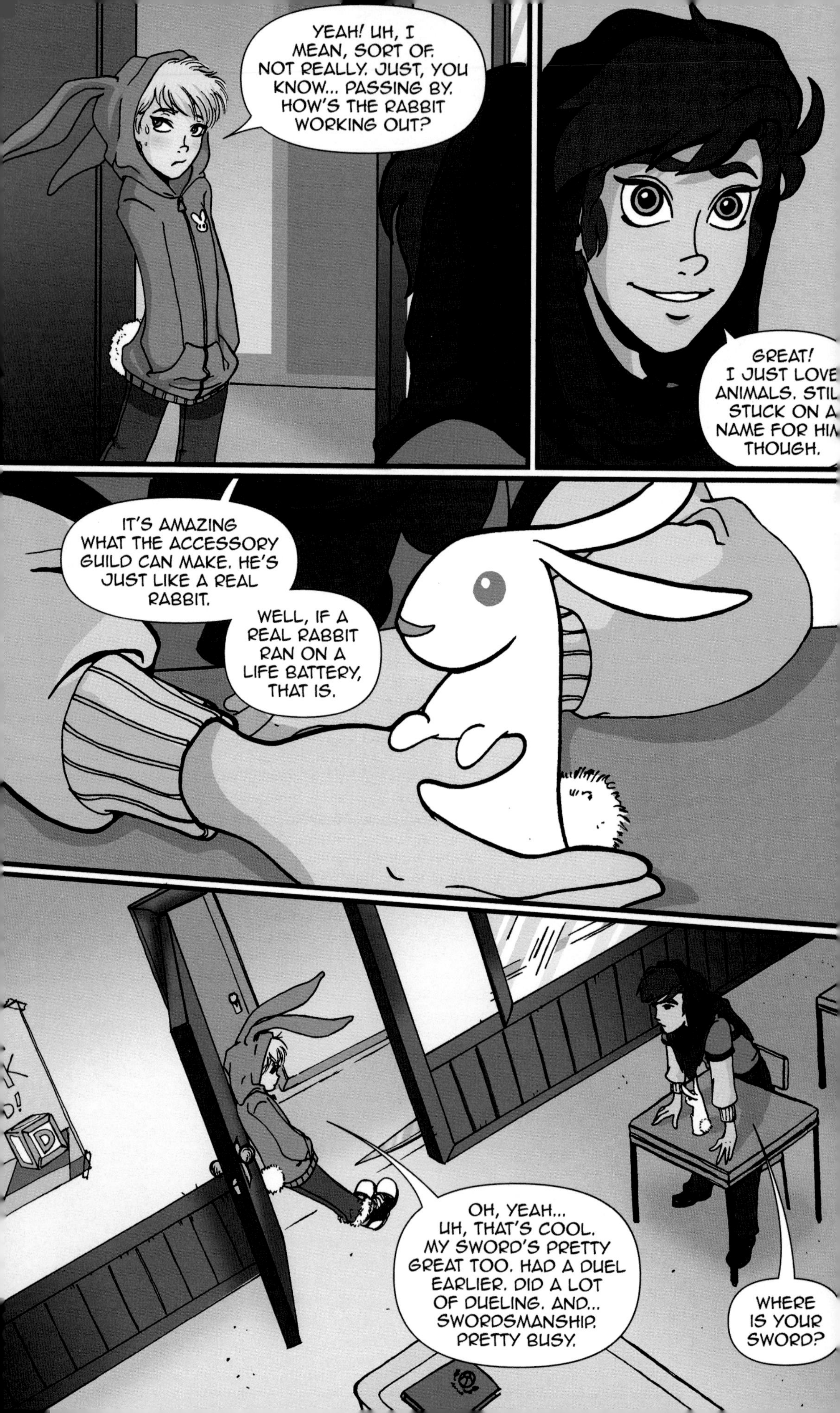
YEAH! UH, I MEAN, SORT OF. NOT REALLY. JUST, YOU KNOW... PASSING BY. HOW'S THE RABBIT WORKING OUT?
GREAT! I JUST LOVE ANIMALS. STIL STUCK ON A NAME FOR HIM THOUGH.
IT'S AMAZING WHAT THE ACCESSORY GUILD CAN MAKE. HE'S JUST LIKE A REAL RABBIT.
WELL, IF A REAL RABBIT RAN ON A LIFE BATTERY, THAT IS.
OH, YEAH... UH, THAT'S COOL. MY SWORD'S PRETTY GREAT TOO. HAD A DUEL EARLIER. DID A LOT OF DUELING. AND... SWORDSMANSHIP. PRETTY BUSY.
WHERE IS YOUR SWORD?

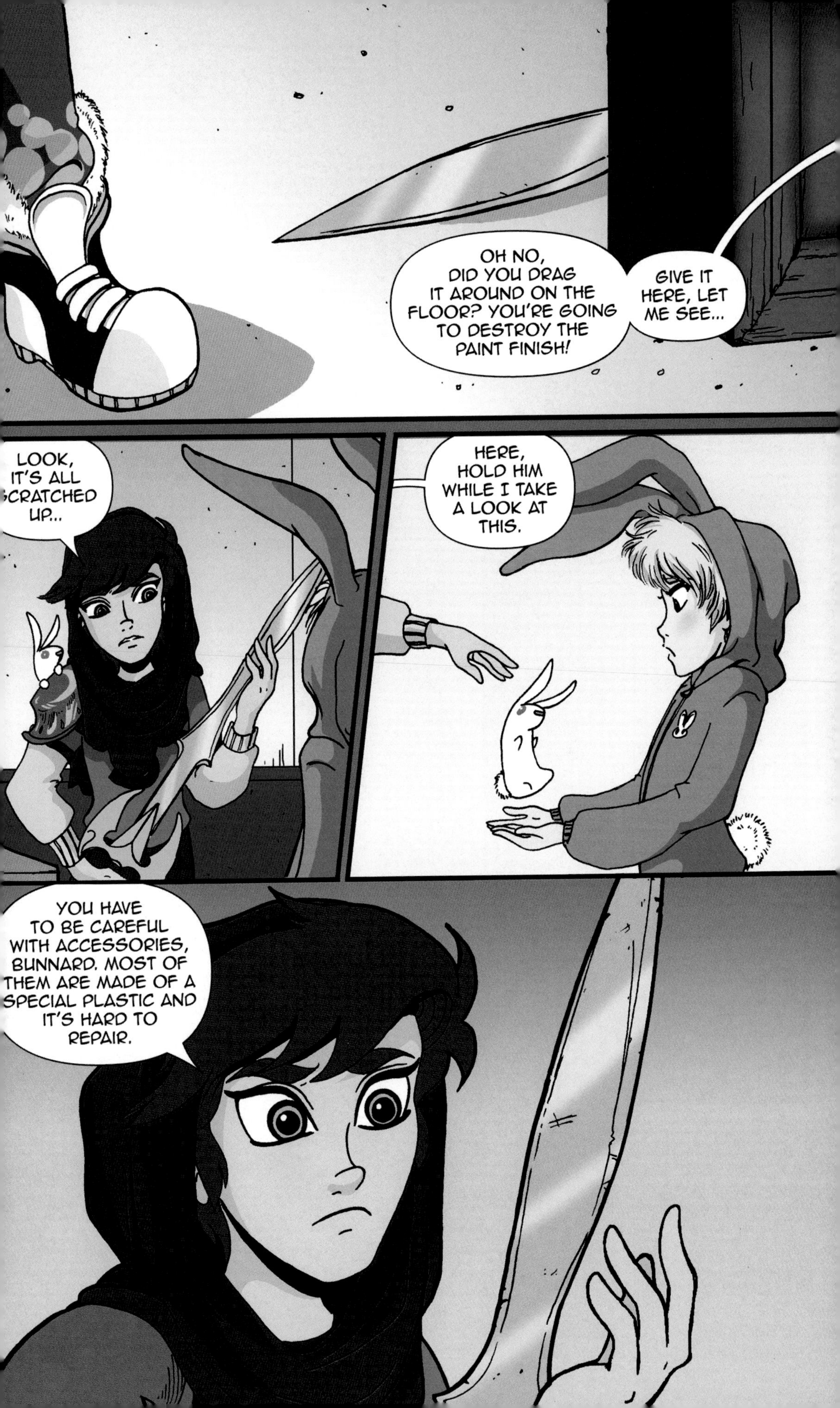
OH NO, DID YOU DRAG IT AROUND ON THE FLOOR? YOU'RE GOING TO DESTROY THE PAINT FINISH!
GIVE IT HERE, LET ME SEE...
LOOK, IT'S ALL SCRATCHED UP...
HERE, HOLD HIM WHILE I TAKE A LOOK AT THIS.
YOU HAVE TO BE CAREFUL WITH ACCESSORIES, BUNNARD. MOST OF THEM ARE MADE OF A SPECIAL PLASTIC AND IT'S HARD TO REPAIR.

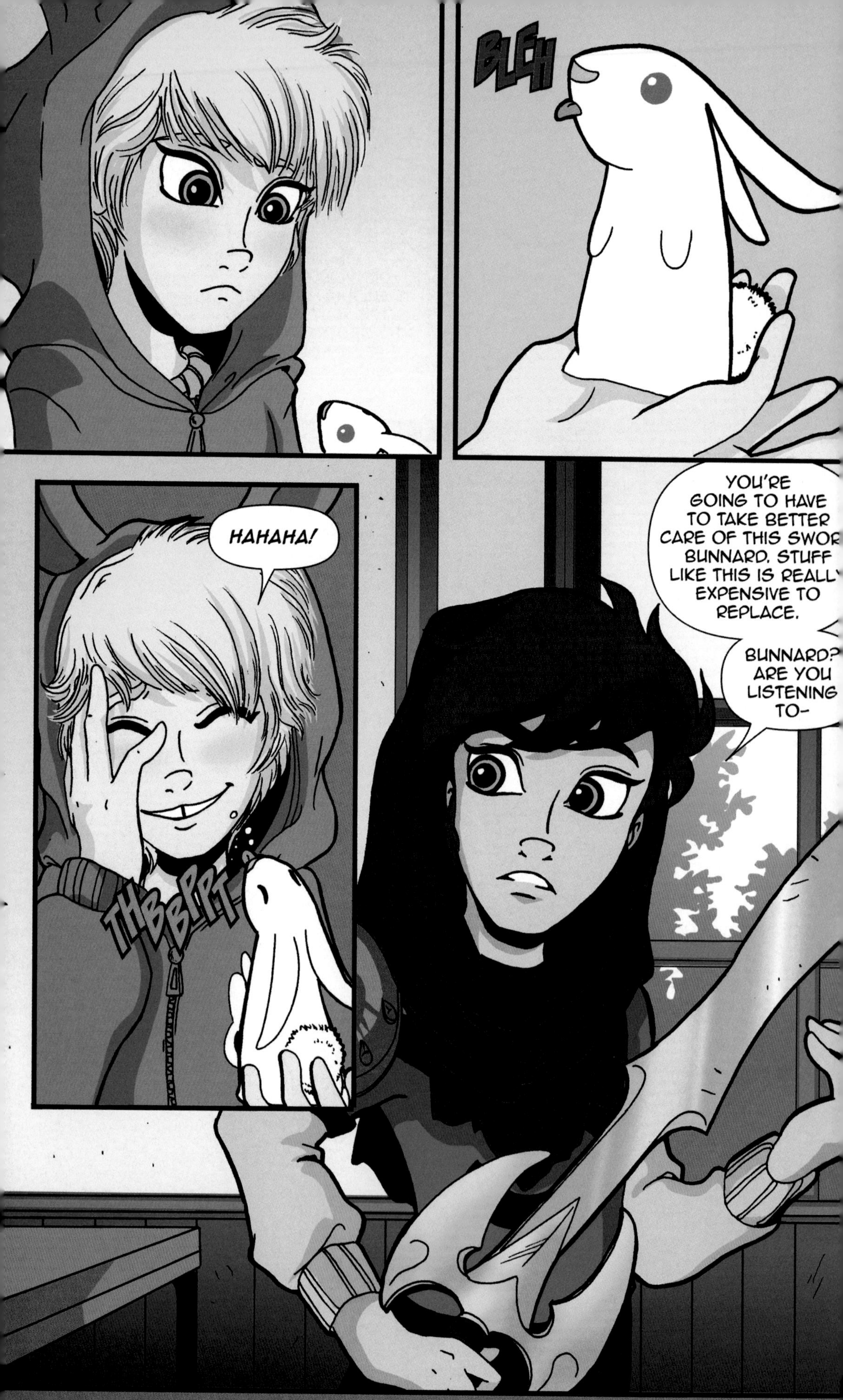
BLEH
HAHAHA!
THBBPPT
YOU'RE GOING TO HAVE TO TAKE BETTER CARE OF THIS SWOR BUNNARD. STUFF LIKE THIS IS REALL EXPENSIVE TO REPLACE.
BUNNARD? ARE YOU LISTENING TO-

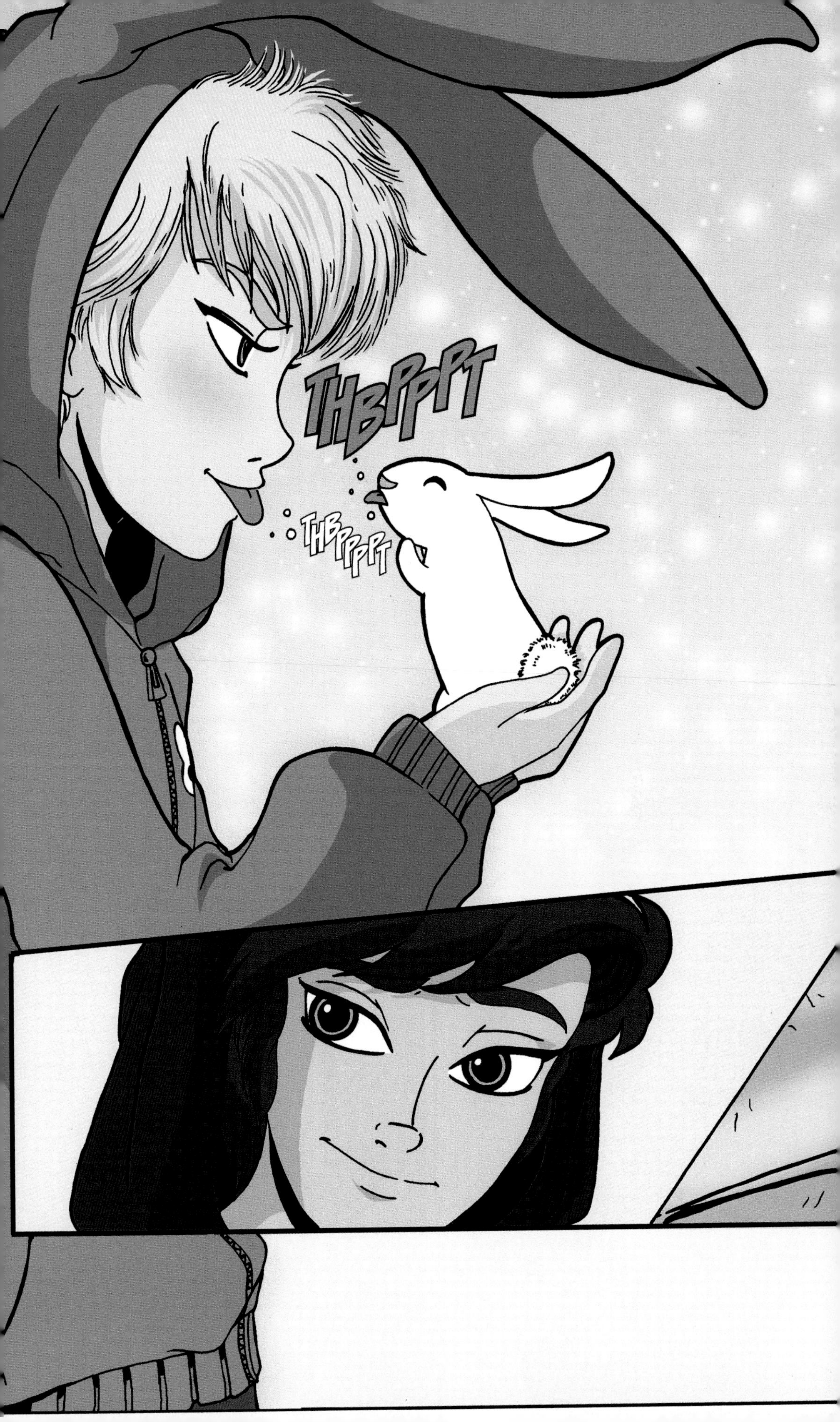
THBPPPT
THBPPPPT

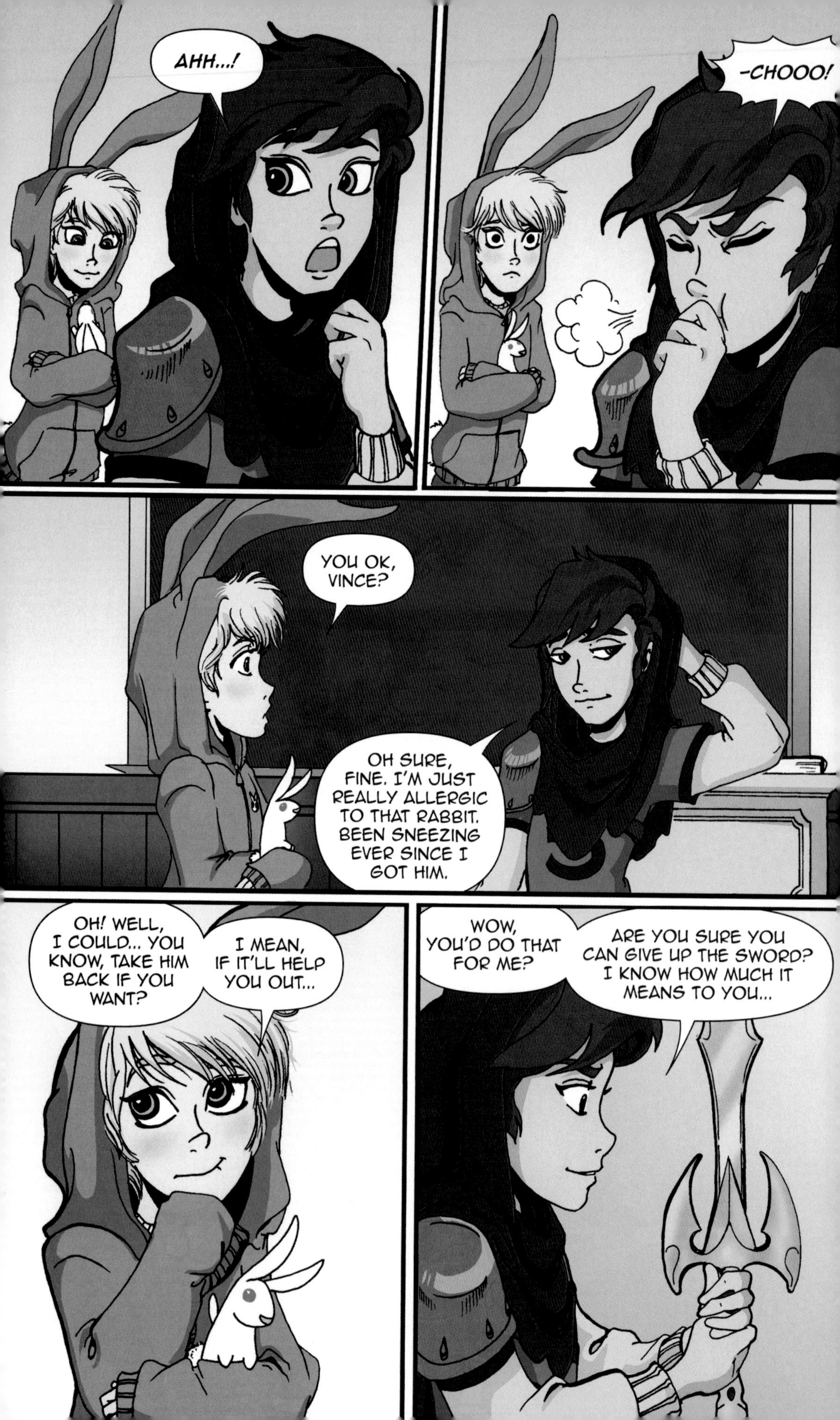
AHH...!
-CHOOO!
YOU OK, VINCE?
OH SURE, FINE. I'M JUST REALLY ALLERGIC TO THAT RABBIT. BEEN SNEEZING EVER SINCE I GOT HIM.
OH! WELL, I COULD... YOU KNOW, TAKE HIM BACK IF YOU WANT?
I MEAN, IF IT'LL HELP YOU OUT...
WOW, YOU'D DO THAT FOR ME?
ARE YOU SURE YOU CAN GIVE UP THE SWORD? I KNOW HOW MUCH IT MEANS TO YOU...

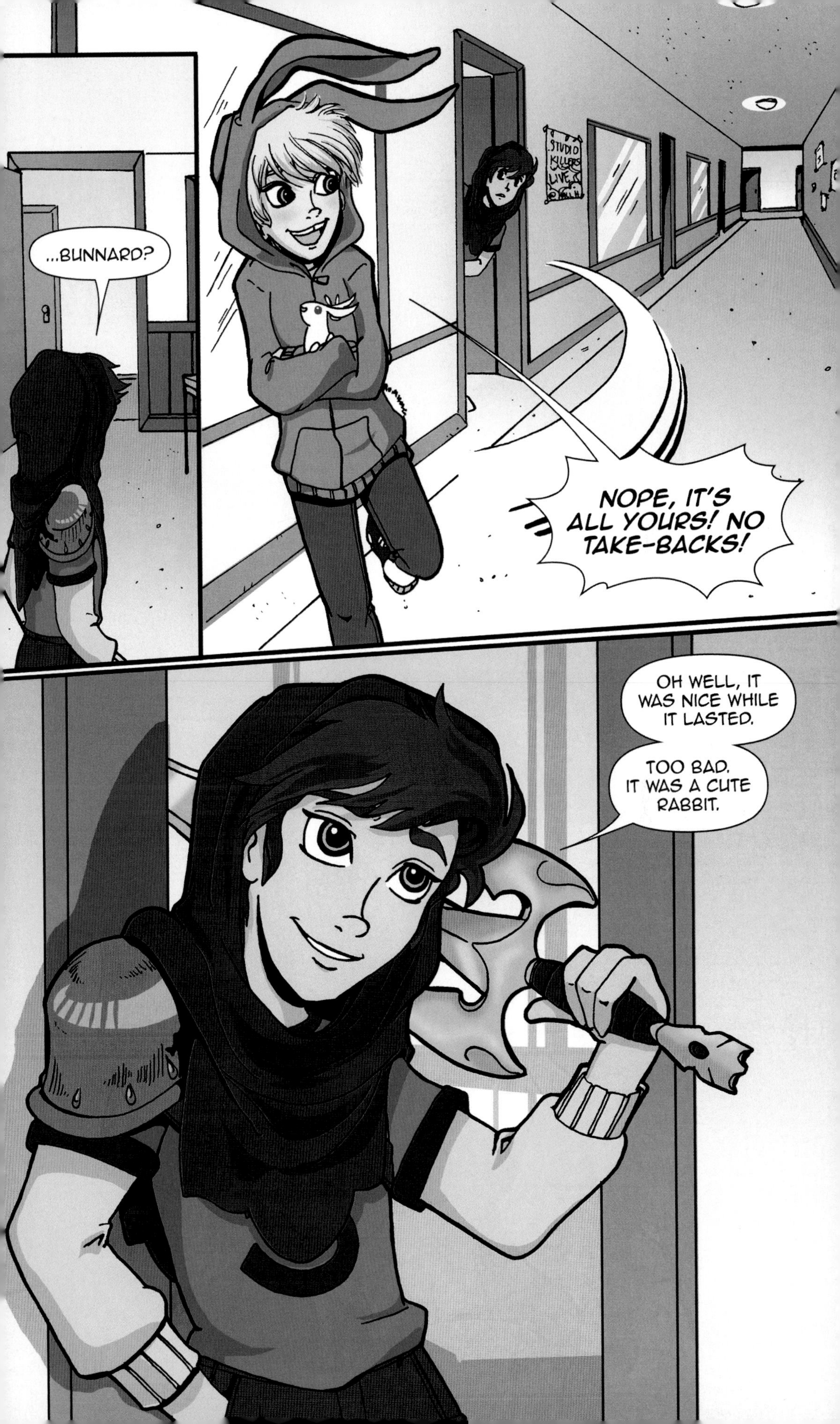
...BUNNARD?
NOPE, IT'S ALL YOURS! NO TAKE-BACKS!
OH WELL, IT WAS NICE WHILE IT LASTED.
TOO BAD. IT WAS A CUTE RABBIT.

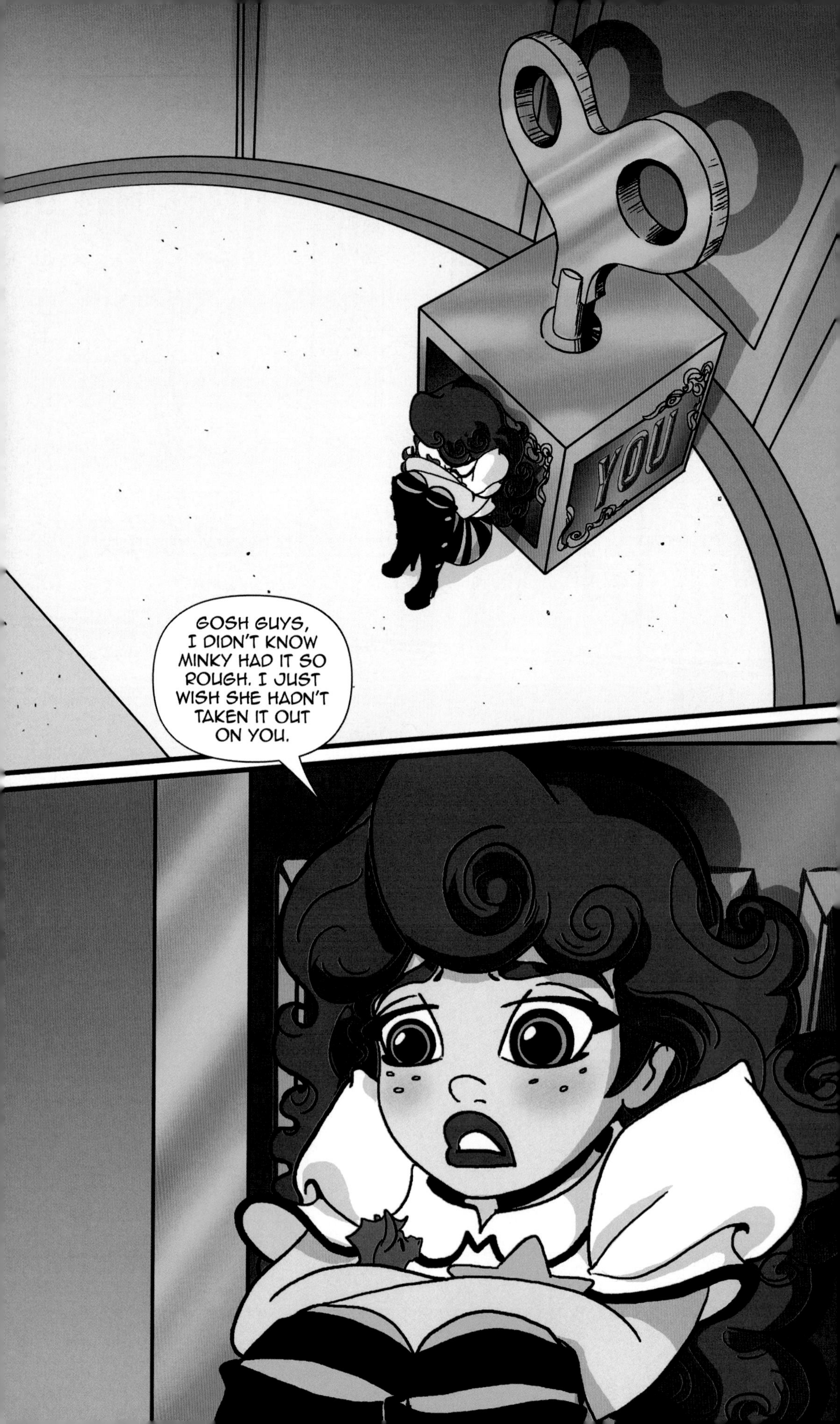
YOU
GOSH GUYS, I DIDN'T KNOW MINKY HAD IT SO ROUGH. I JUST WISH SHE HADN'T TAKEN IT OUT ON YOU.

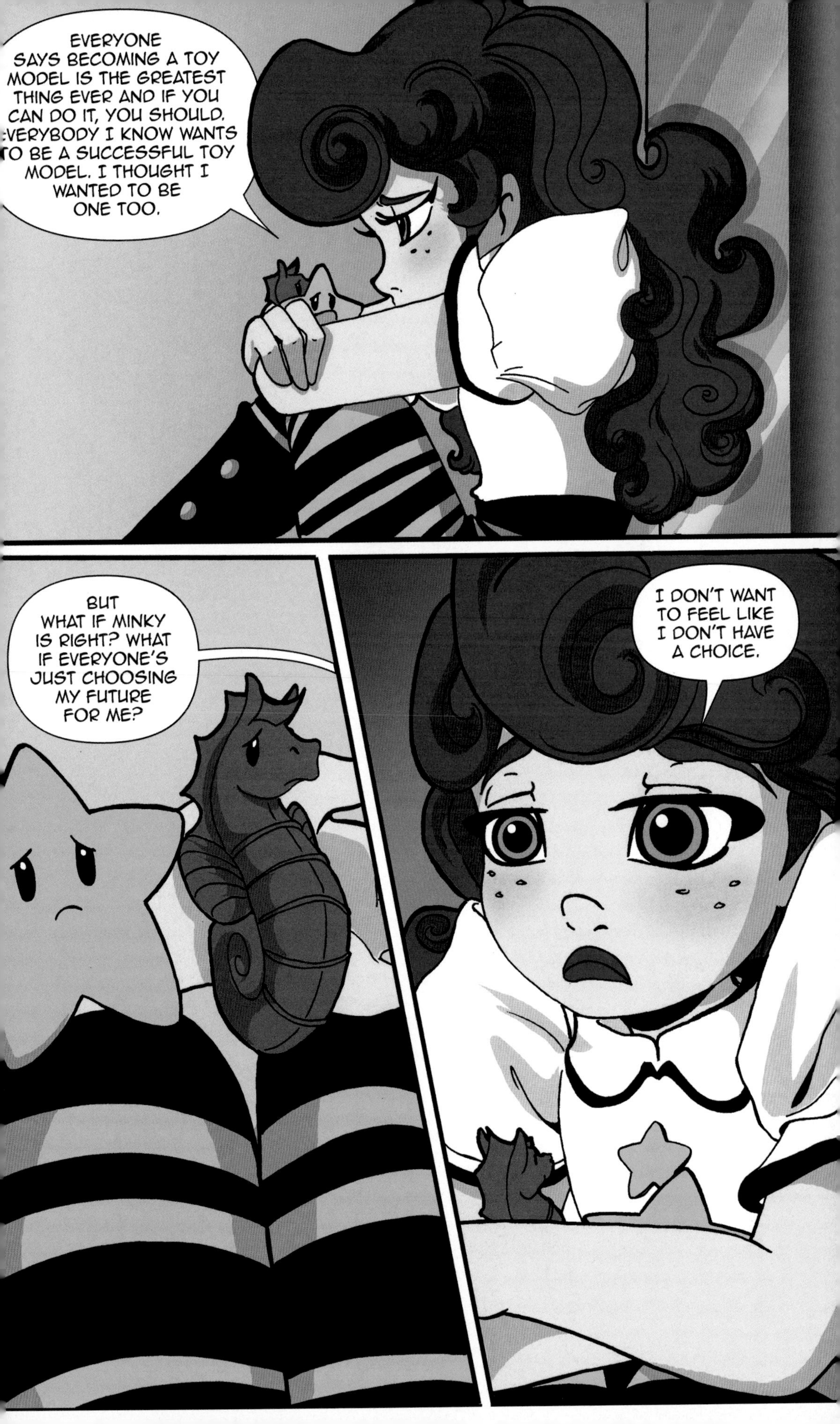
EVERYONE SAYS BECOMING A TOY MODEL IS THE GREATEST THING EVER AND IF YOU CAN DO IT, YOU SHOULD. EVERYBODY I KNOW WANTS TO BE A SUCCESSFUL TOY MODEL. I THOUGHT I WANTED TO BE ONE TOO.
BUT WHAT IF MINKY IS RIGHT? WHAT IF EVERYONE'S JUST CHOOSING MY FUTURE FOR ME?
I DON'T WANT TO FEEL LIKE I DON'T HAVE A CHOICE.

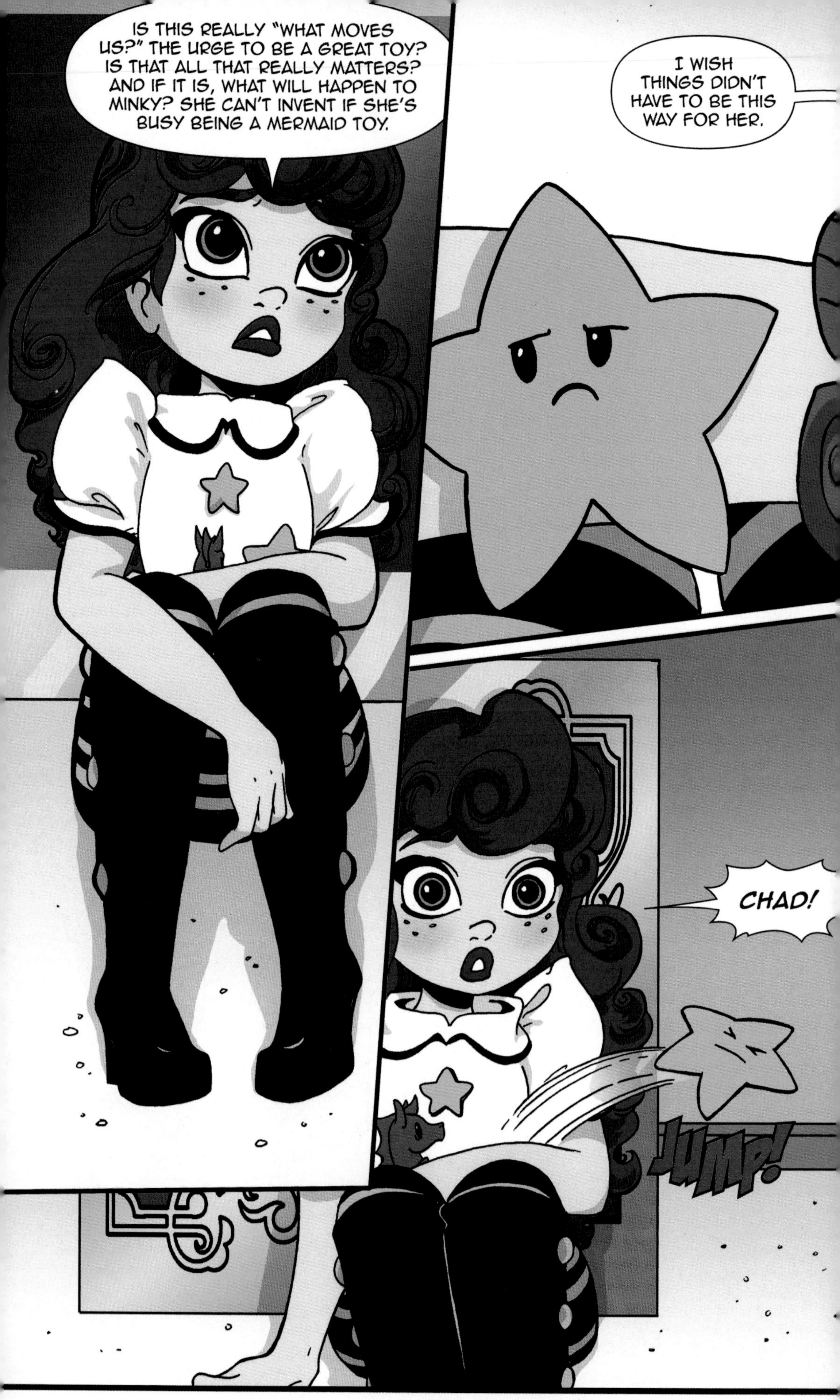
IS THIS REALLY "WHAT MOVES US?" THE URGE TO BE A GREAT TOY? IS THAT ALL THAT REALLY MATTERS? AND IF IT IS, WHAT WILL HAPPEN TO MINKY? SHE CAN'T INVENT IF SHE'S BUSY BEING A MERMAID TOY.
I WISH THINGS DIDN'T HAVE TO BE THIS WAY FOR HER.
CHAD!
JUMP!

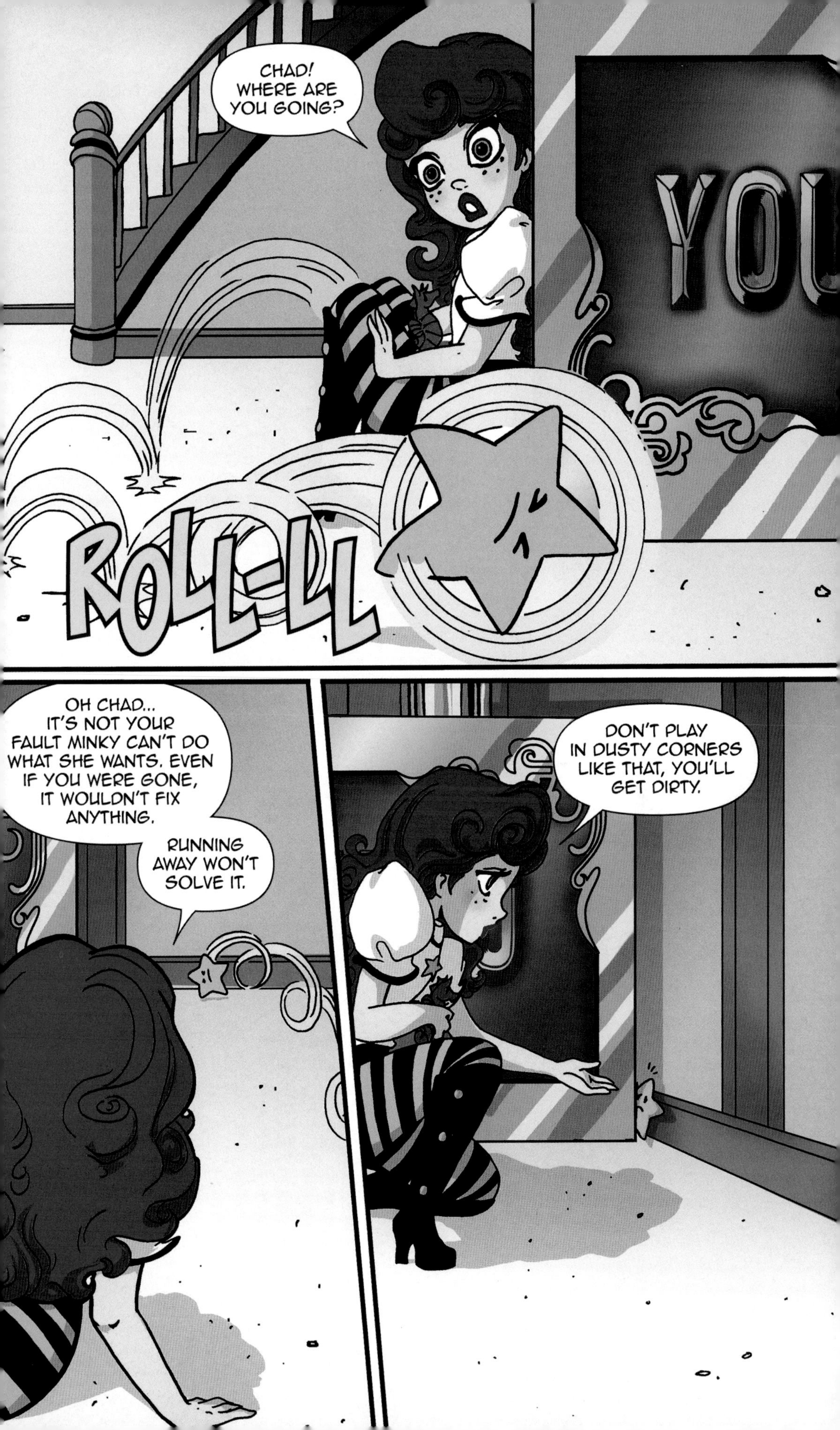
CHAD! WHERE ARE YOU GOING?
YOU
ROLL-LL
OH CHAD... IT'S NOT YOUR FAULT MINKY CAN'T DO WHAT SHE WANTS. EVEN IF YOU WERE GONE, IT WOULDN'T FIX ANYTHING.
RUNNING AWAY WON'T SOLVE IT.
DON'T PLAY IN DUSTY CORNERS LIKE THAT, YOU'LL GET DIRTY.

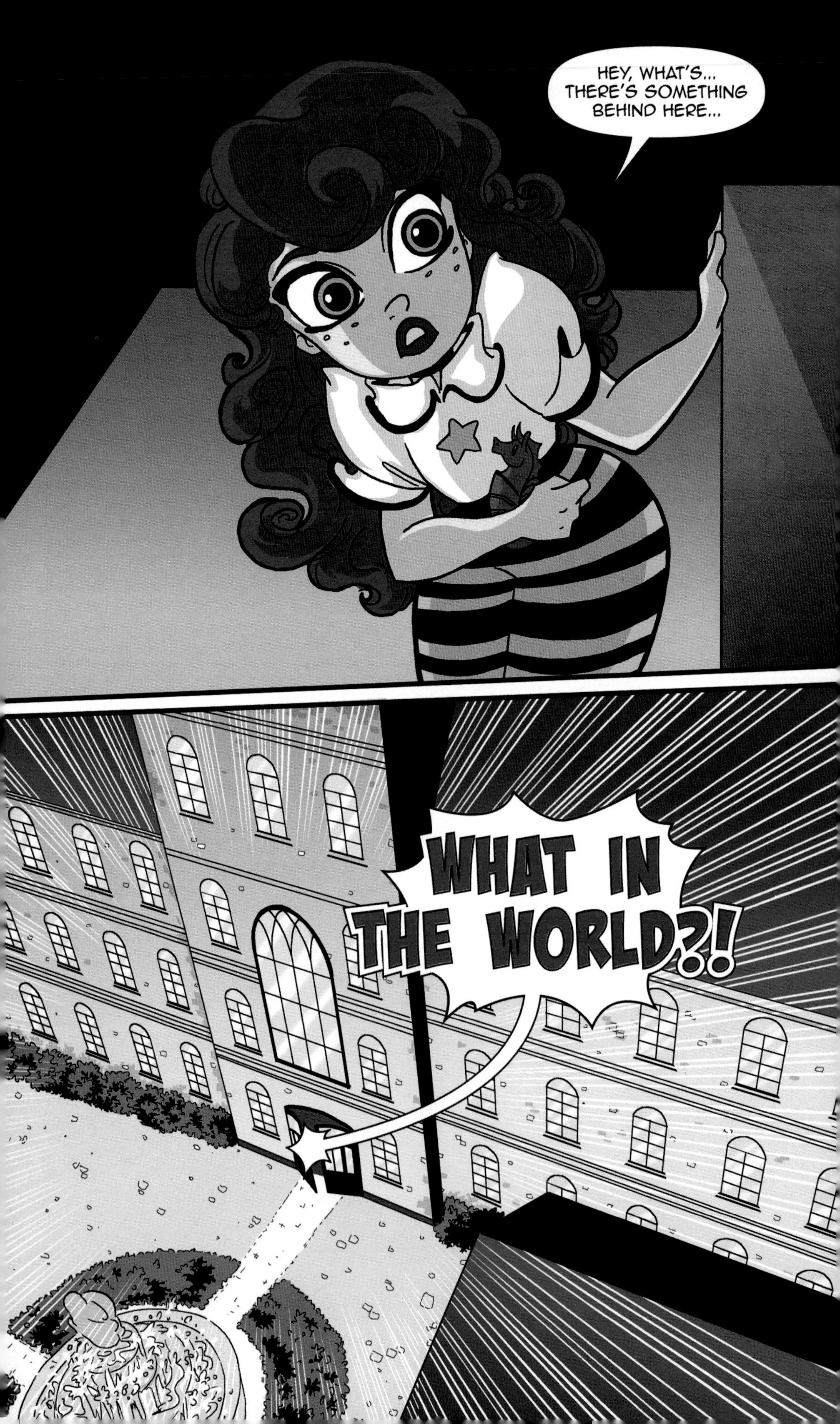
HEY, WHAT'S... THERE'S SOMETHING BEHIND HERE...
WHAT IN THE WORLD?!

TOYETICA

THINK OUTSIDE THE TOYBOX

DOLLINGTON ACADEMY

 **Trixie Tangle**

 **Sweetina Von Bonne**

 **Minky Mermille**

 **Polly Fume**

 **Unicole Safari-Sidekick**

 **Angel Inx**

 **Bunnard Safari-Sidekick**

 **Dia de los Marco**

 **Vince Charming**

 **Nebulara, Queen of the Battle Cosmos**

 **Becky Badluck**

 **Dandelillian Fae**

 **Lilly Liku**

 **Fawndolyn Safari-Sidekick**

Character Profiles

Name: Angel Inx

Fave color: Gold

Fave food: Patatas bravas

Fave way to get someone's attention:

"Why would anyone not be paying attention to me already?"

Angel is a student from Spain with ink-dipped angel wings (a fake prop for his toy theme, as he is not a member of th Safari-Sidekick line) and an "Ink and A stick-on tattoo theme. Best friend of Unicole, he knows all the most popular people and what they're doing at any given moment. He's a cool guy, always relaxed and the subject of many crushe: at the school, including one by Trixie. F considers himself the "resident artiste" of Dollington Academy. He is an incorrigible gossip hound and can often be seen texting back and forth with Unicole about happenings around the school.

Even though he's a bit egotistical, Ange is a nice guy and a truly talented artist.

ANGEL INX

Names: Becky Badluck &
Dandelillian Fae

Fave food: Whatever
Sweetina is eating

Fave color: Whatever
Sweetina likes

Fave way of getting
someone's attention:
Mockery

BECKS AND LIL

Becks and Lil are Sweetina's cohorts and best friends, following her at all times around the school. If she needs anything done behind the scenes, these two are on it in a flash.

Becky Badluck is a gothic-themed student, while Dandelillian has a fairy motif. Between them and Sweetina, they make up the popular trifecta of Most Marketable Students. But with the ever-changing trends of the human toymarket, who knows if they can stay that way?

MARCO

Name: Dia de los Marco, aka "Skull Guy"

Fave food: ???

Fave color: ???

Fave way to get someone's attention:

Silent staring

A transfer student from Mexico, Marco is never seen without his signature Day Of the Dead-style mask over his face. Marco speaks both Spanish and English fluently, when he has anything to say at all. Since he rarely talks to the other students, most people just refer to him as "Skull Guy" and avoid his unsettling mask stare. Not much is known about him and he seems to have few, if any, friends around the school. He is often seen riding his longboard around the campus.

There are rumors that he's been seen sneaking off-campus without permission and that he hangs out with a group of non-Dollington students in the local sewers. But what they do down there, no one knows.

LILLY & FAWN

ames: Lilly Liku and Fawndolyn Safari-Sidekick

ve food: Eleven

ve color: Denmark

ve way to get someone's attention: Weird wiggling

y and Fawn, who must be introduced together since they are never
art, are best friends. Lilly Liku is from Japan and her family has a long
rtnership with a famous clothing designer. Fawn is a cousin of
nnard and Unicole and a member of the Safari-Sidekick extended
mily business.

y and Fawn are always together. Their main source of personal
tertainment seems to come from mercilessly pranking rival school
echa Tech within an inch of its life. They love eating candy by the
und.

TROYBOT

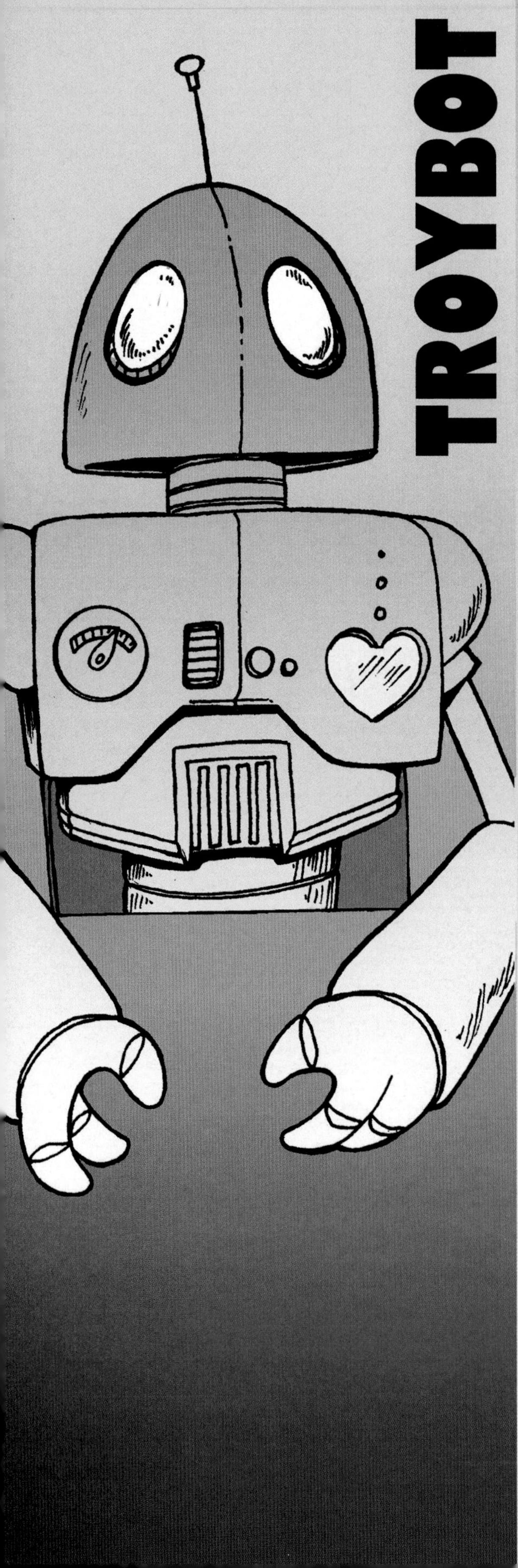

Name: Troybot, version 1.0

Fave color: none

Fave food: none

Fave way of getting someone's attention: A series of auditory solicitations

Troybot is an exchange student robot from Mecha Tech. Once built as an experiment Accessor he then mysteriously gained sentience and declared that he wanted to enroll in toy school, and was accepted.

However, his inability to understand living creatures caused much trouble at Mecha Tech, so he was transferred to Dollington, in hopes of maybe "humanizing" him a bit more.

Big,blocky and all-metal,Troybo does his best to understand the world around him, but often fai Unicole is constantly trying to recruit him to the Block team, b he sees little point in sports. His closest friend is Nebulara.

THE BIG KEY

PART FOUR

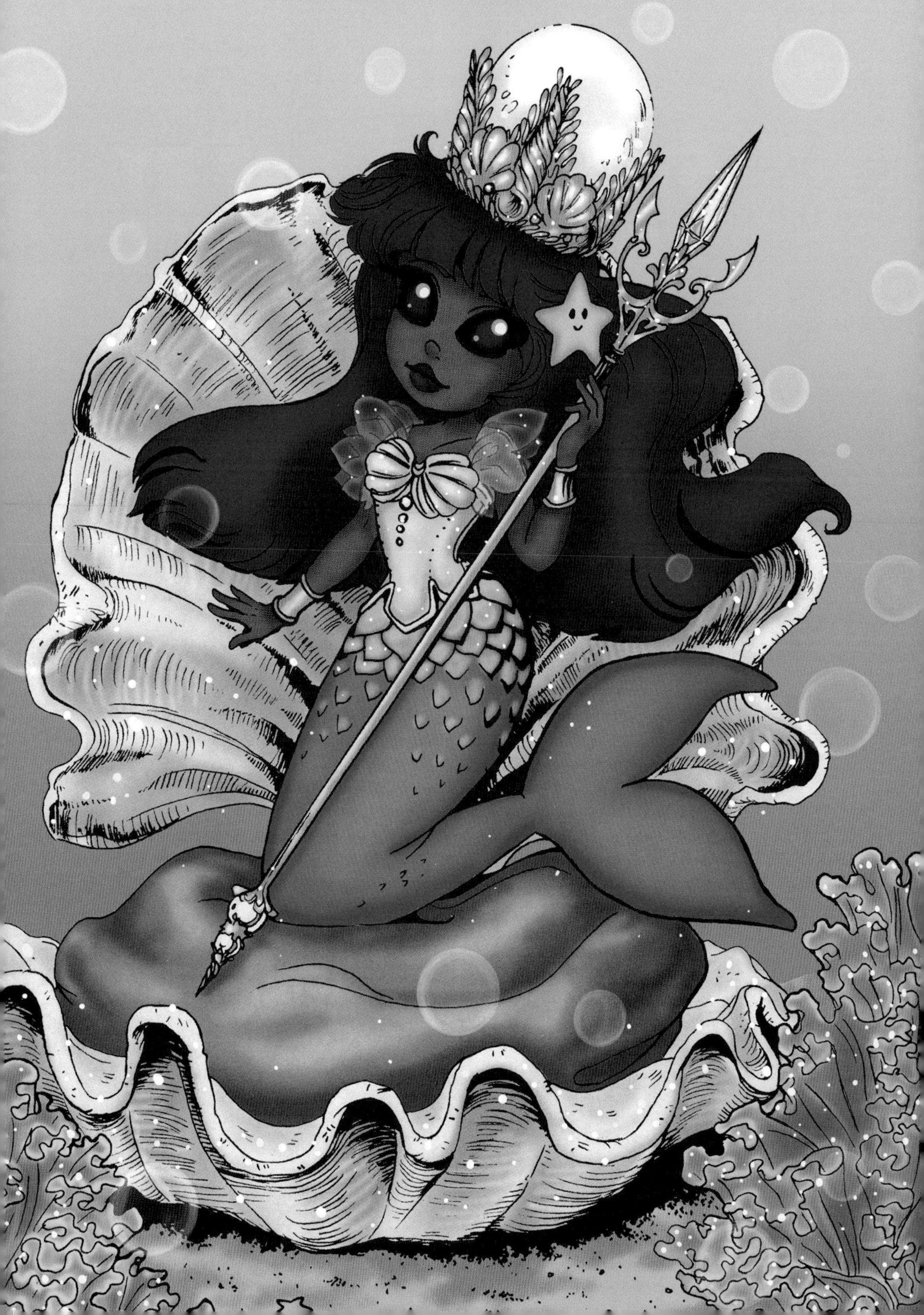

TOYETICA

4

STORY AND ART BY MARTY LEGROW

LETTERING
Justin Birch

CONGRATULATIONS
Paul and Meliss

Bryan Seaton: Publisher/ CEO • Shawn Gabborin: Editor In Chief • Jason Martin: Publisher-Danger Zone • Nicole D'Andria: Marketing Director/Editor
Danielle Davison: Executive Administrator • Chad Cicconi: Action Lawyer • Shawn Pryor: President of Creator Relations

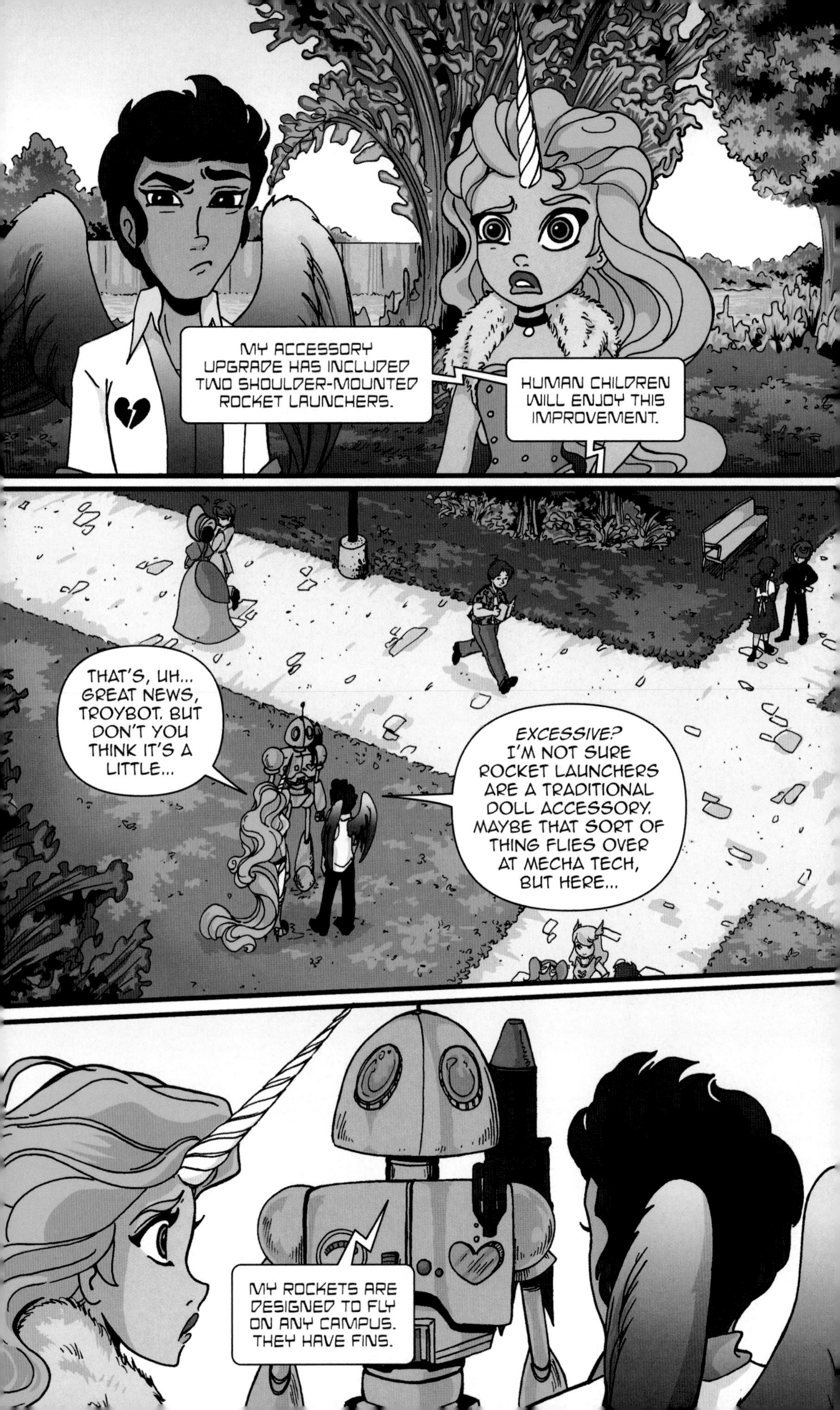
MY ACCESSORY UPGRADE HAS INCLUDED TWO SHOULDER-MOUNTED ROCKET LAUNCHERS.
HUMAN CHILDREN WILL ENJOY THIS IMPROVEMENT.
THAT'S, UH... GREAT NEWS, TROYBOT. BUT DON'T YOU THINK IT'S A LITTLE...
EXCESSIVE? I'M NOT SURE ROCKET LAUNCHERS ARE A TRADITIONAL DOLL ACCESSORY. MAYBE THAT SORT OF THING FLIES OVER AT MECHA TECH, BUT HERE...
MY ROCKETS ARE DESIGNED TO FLY ON ANY CAMPUS. THEY HAVE FINS.

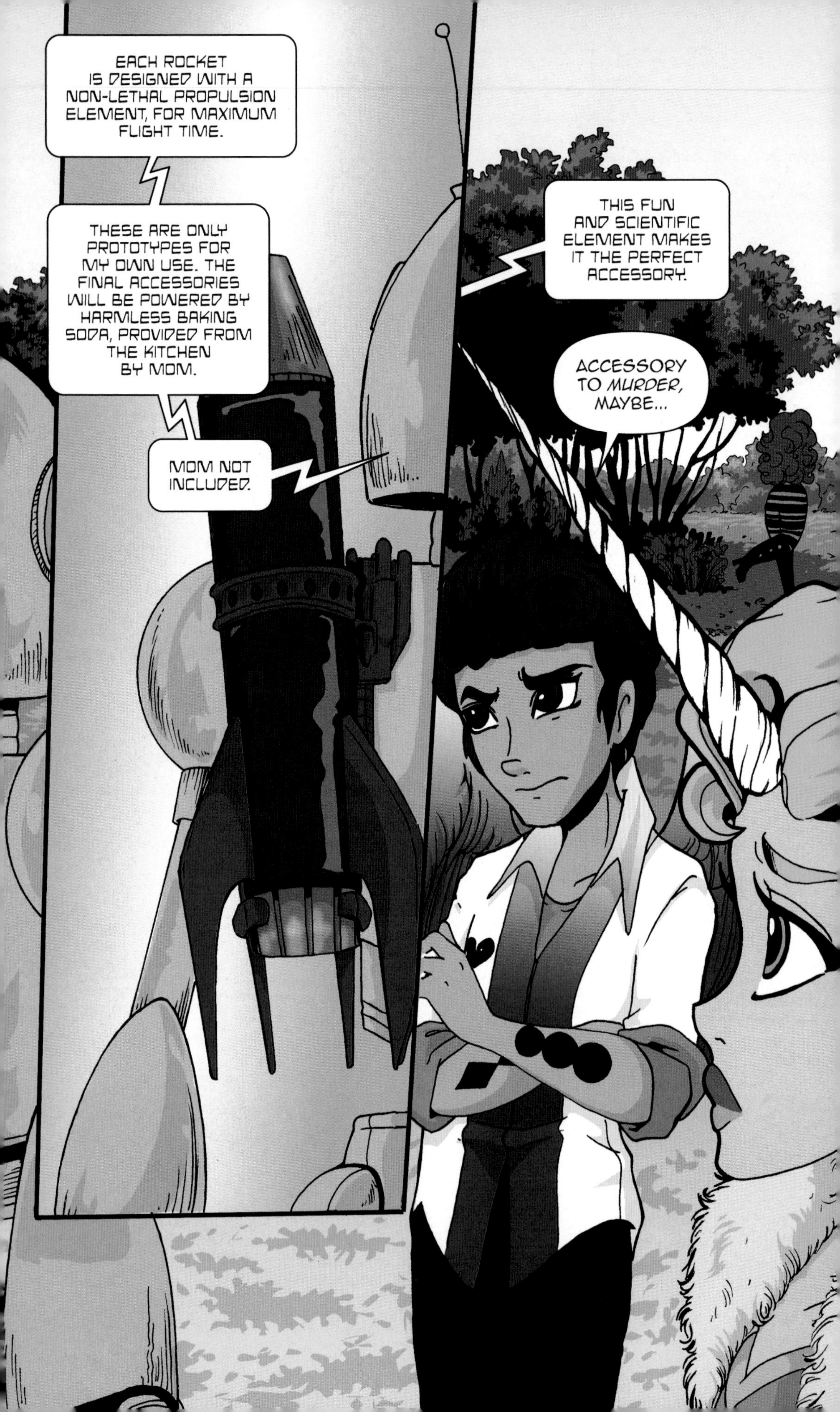
EACH ROCKET IS DESIGNED WITH A NON-LETHAL PROPULSION ELEMENT, FOR MAXIMUM FLIGHT TIME.
THESE ARE ONLY PROTOTYPES FOR MY OWN USE. THE FINAL ACCESSORIES WILL BE POWERED BY HARMLESS BAKING SODA, PROVIDED FROM THE KITCHEN BY MOM.
MOM NOT INCLUDED.
THIS FUN AND SCIENTIFIC ELEMENT MAKES IT THE PERFECT ACCESSORY.
ACCESSORY TO *MURDER*, MAYBE...

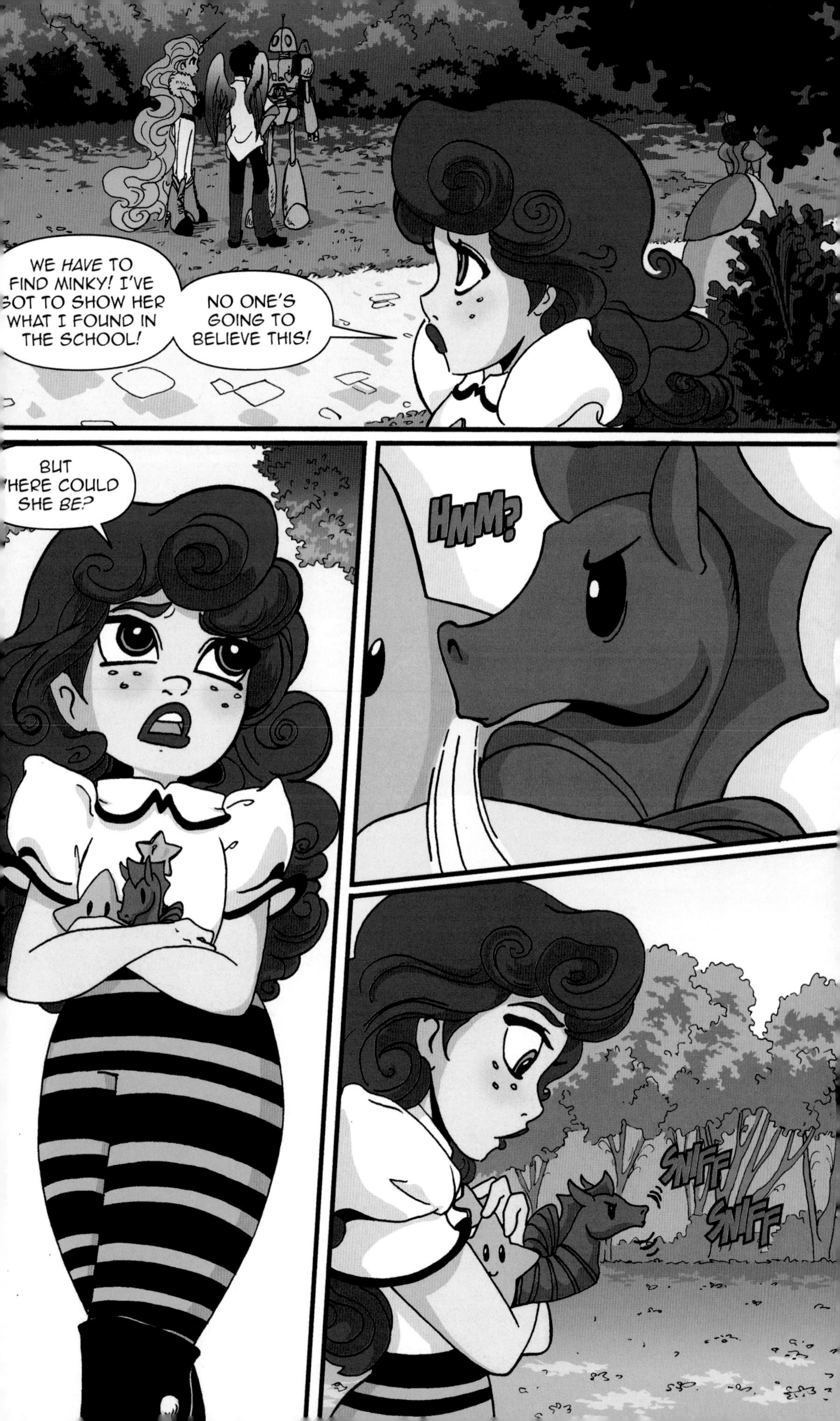
WE HAVE TO FIND MINKY! I'VE GOT TO SHOW HER WHAT I FOUND IN THE SCHOOL!
NO ONE'S GOING TO BELIEVE THIS!
BUT WHERE COULD SHE BE?
HMM?
SNIFF
SNIFF

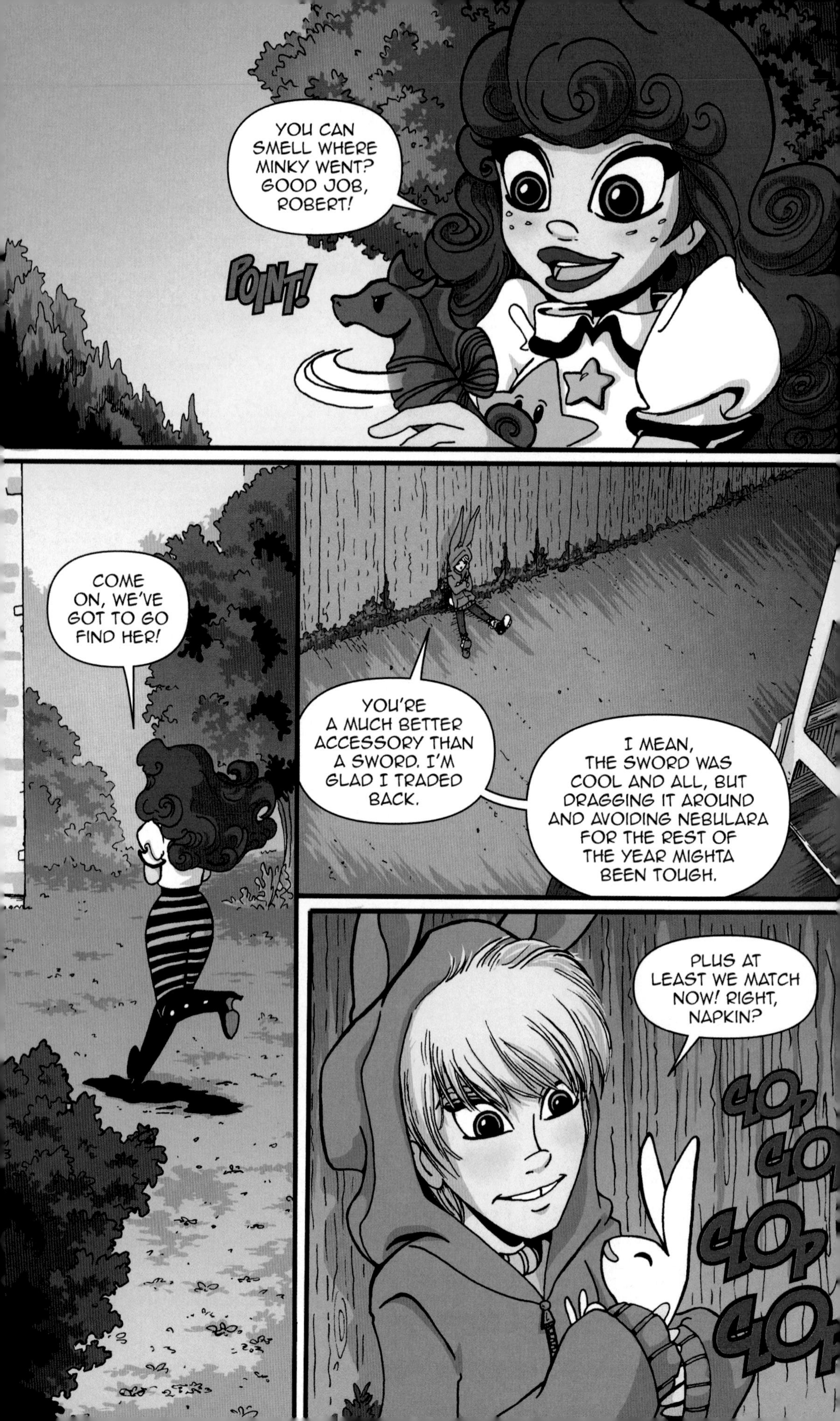
YOU CAN SMELL WHERE MINKY WENT? GOOD JOB, ROBERT!
POINT!
COME ON, WE'VE GOT TO GO FIND HER!
YOU'RE A MUCH BETTER ACCESSORY THAN A SWORD. I'M GLAD I TRADED BACK.
I MEAN, THE SWORD WAS COOL AND ALL, BUT DRAGGING IT AROUND AND AVOIDING NEBULARA FOR THE REST OF THE YEAR MIGHTA BEEN TOUGH.
PLUS AT LEAST WE MATCH NOW! RIGHT, NAPKIN?
GOP
GOP
GOP
GOP

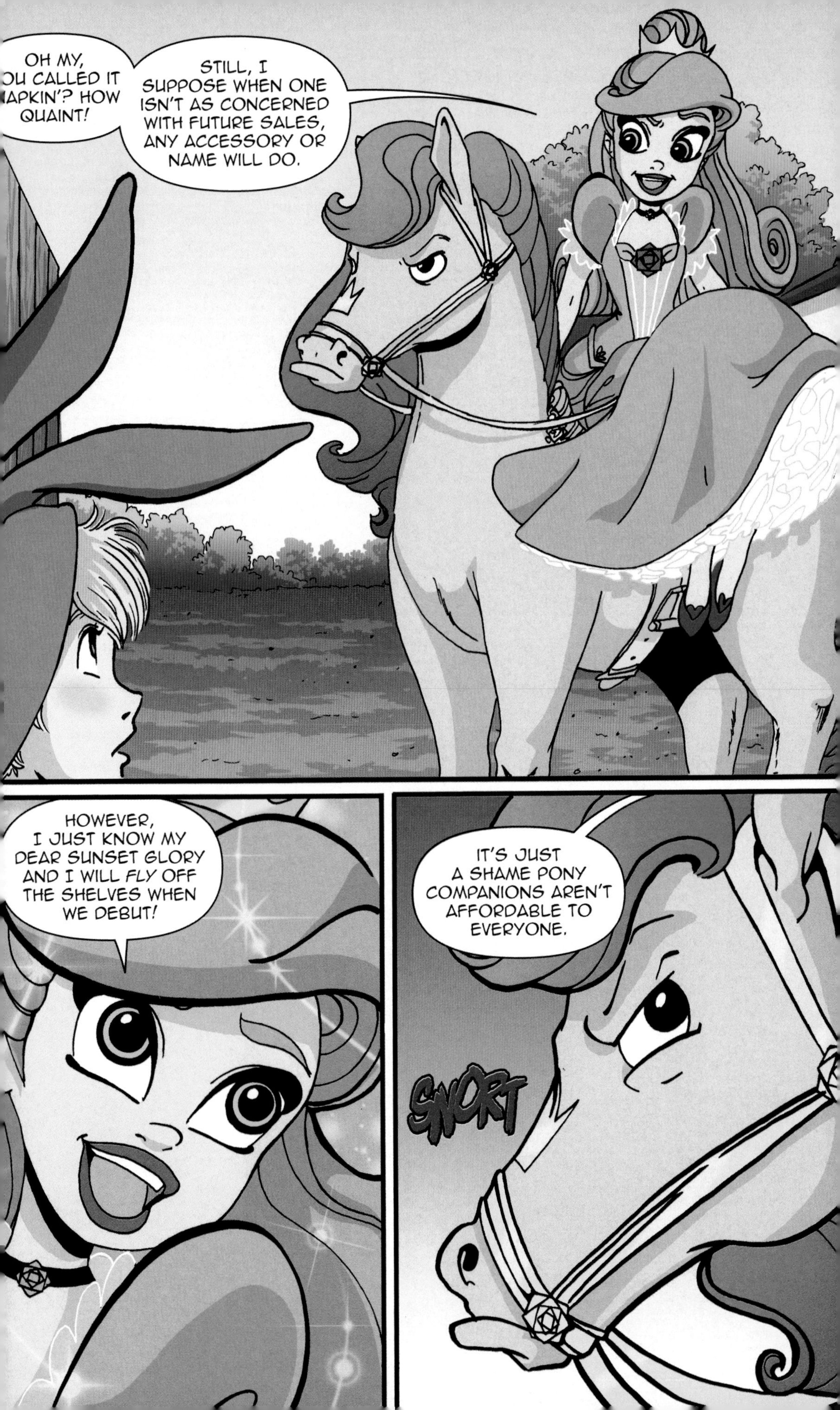
OH MY,
OU CALLED IT
APKIN'? HOW
QUAINT!
STILL, I SUPPOSE WHEN ONE ISN'T AS CONCERNED WITH FUTURE SALES, ANY ACCESSORY OR NAME WILL DO.
HOWEVER, I JUST KNOW MY DEAR SUNSET GLORY AND I WILL *FLY* OFF THE SHELVES WHEN WE DEBUT!
IT'S JUST A SHAME PONY COMPANIONS AREN'T AFFORDABLE TO EVERYONE.
SNORT

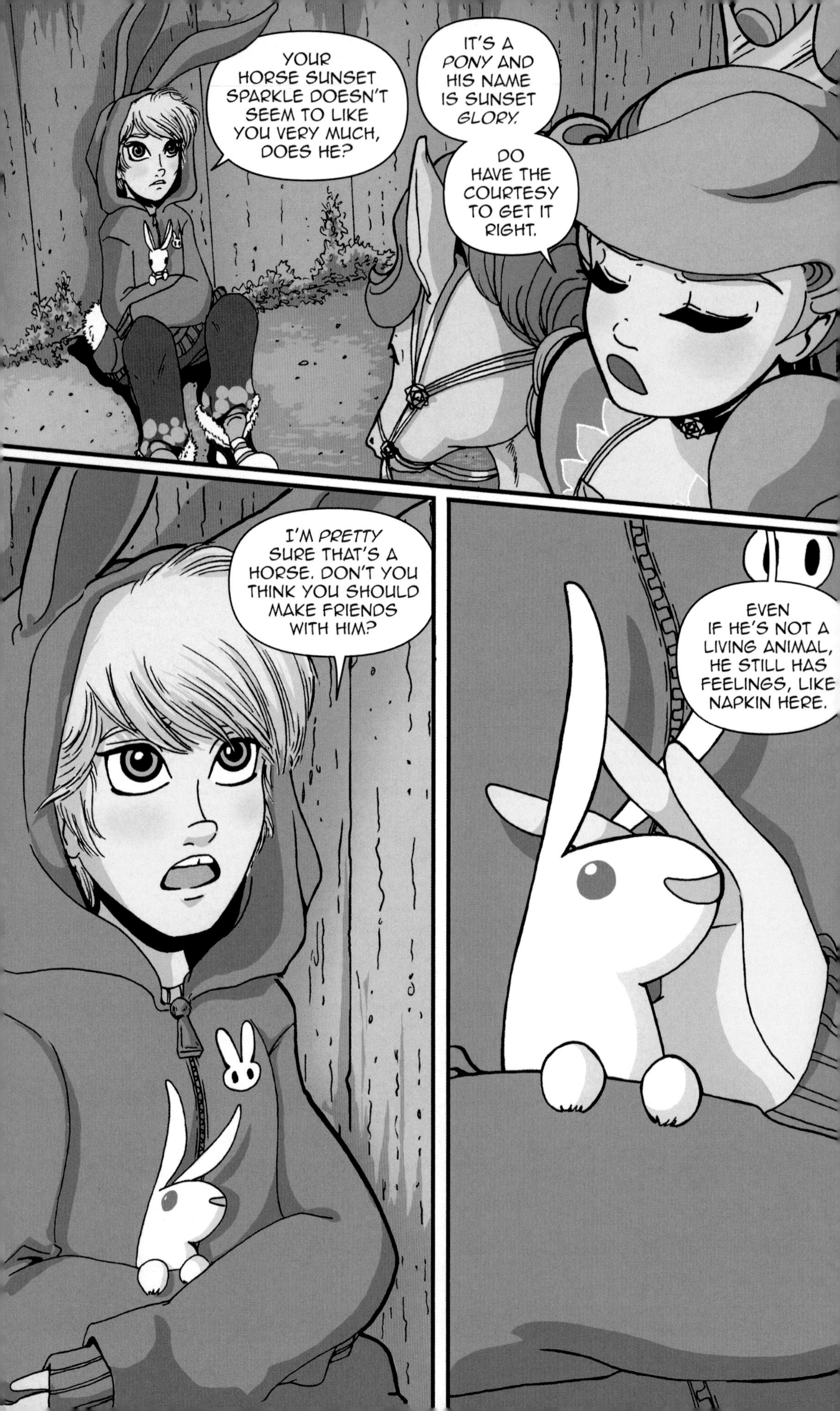
YOUR HORSE SUNSET SPARKLE DOESN'T SEEM TO LIKE YOU VERY MUCH, DOES HE?
IT'S A *PONY* AND HIS NAME IS SUNSET *GLORY.*
DO HAVE THE COURTESY TO GET IT RIGHT.
I'M *PRETTY* SURE THAT'S A HORSE. DON'T YOU THINK YOU SHOULD MAKE FRIENDS WITH HIM?
EVEN IF HE'S NOT A LIVING ANIMAL, HE STILL HAS FEELINGS, LIKE NAPKIN HERE.

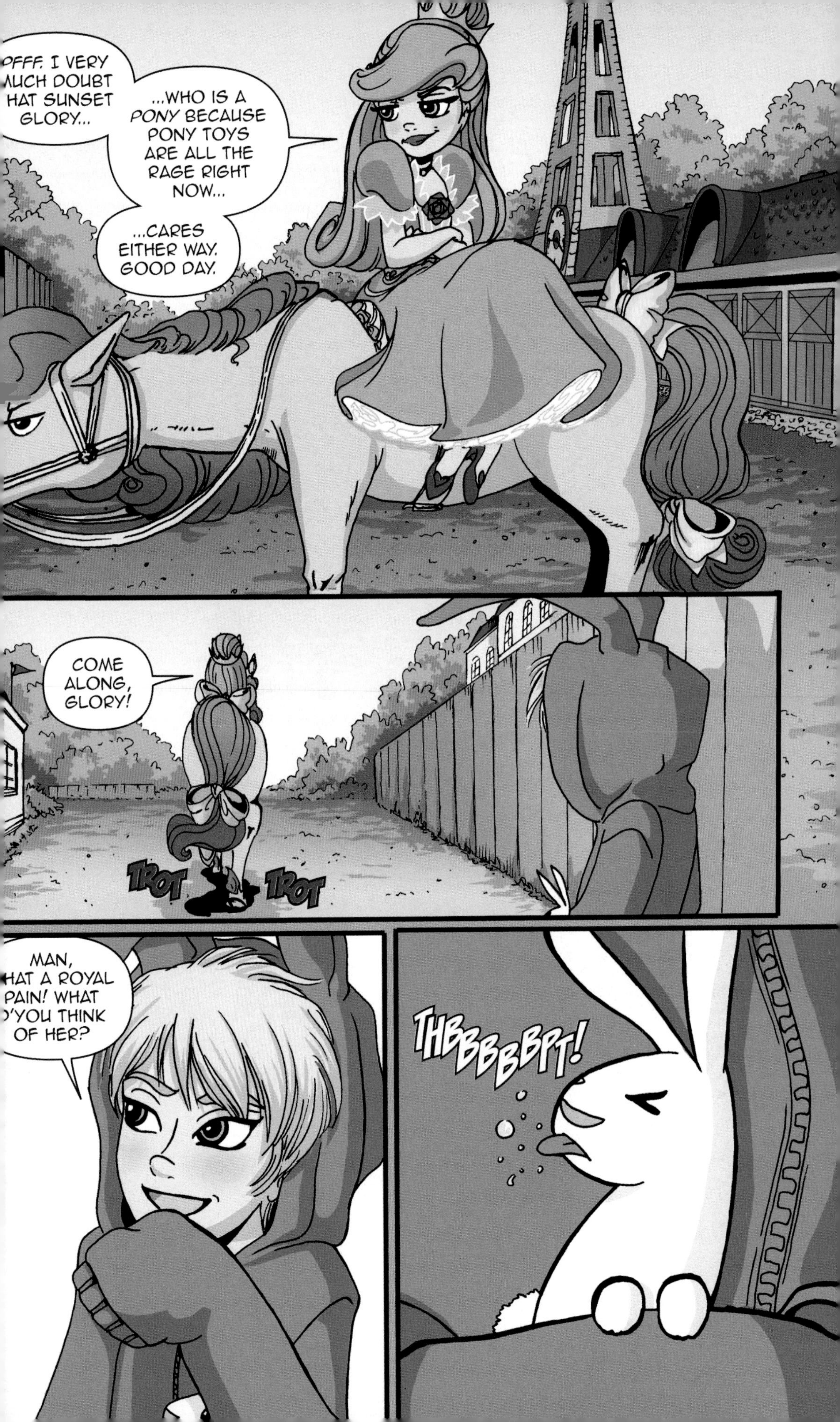
PFFF. I VERY
MUCH DOUBT
HAT SUNSET
GLORY...
...WHO IS A PONY BECAUSE PONY TOYS ARE ALL THE RAGE RIGHT NOW...
...CARES EITHER WAY. GOOD DAY.
COME ALONG, GLORY!
TROT TROT
MAN,
HAT A ROYAL
PAIN! WHAT
'YOU THINK
OF HER?
THBBBBBPT!

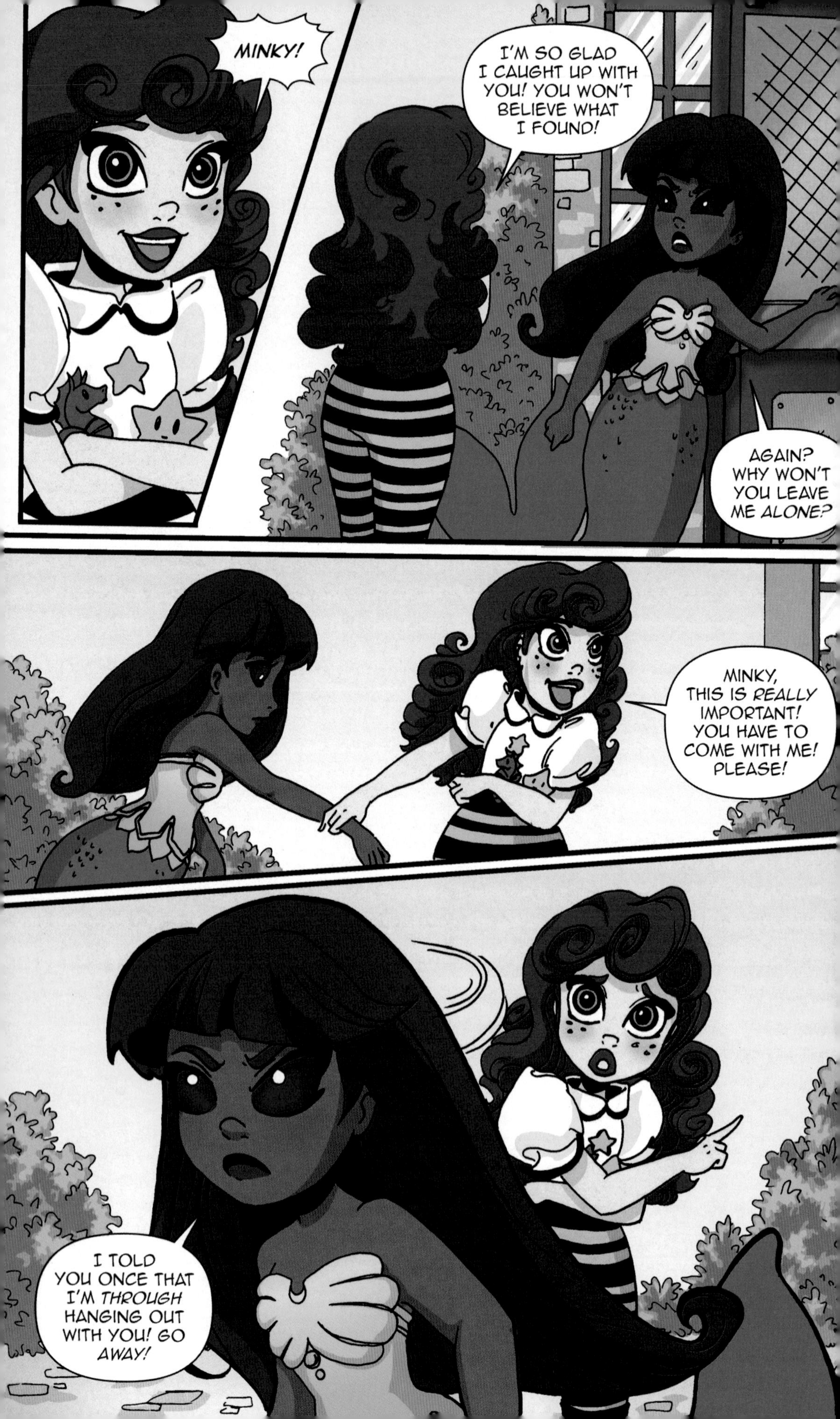
MINKY!
I'M SO GLAD I CAUGHT UP WITH YOU! YOU WON'T BELIEVE WHAT I FOUND!
AGAIN? WHY WON'T YOU LEAVE ME *ALONE*?
MINKY, THIS IS *REALLY* IMPORTANT! YOU HAVE TO COME WITH ME! PLEASE!
I TOLD YOU ONCE THAT I'M *THROUGH* HANGING OUT WITH YOU! GO *AWAY*!

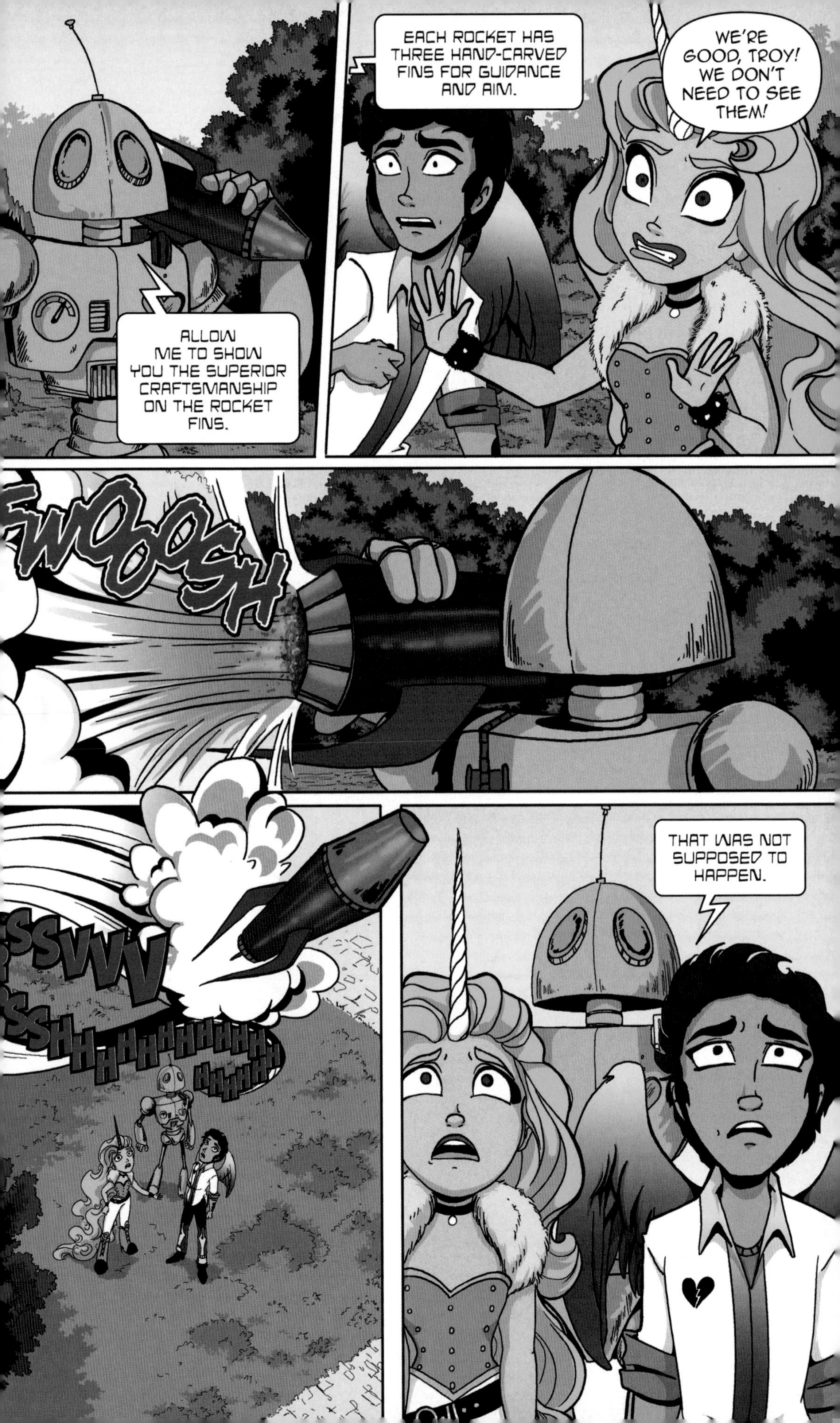
ALLOW ME TO SHOW YOU THE SUPERIOR CRAFTSMANSHIP ON THE ROCKET FINS.
EACH ROCKET HAS THREE HAND-CARVED FINS FOR GUIDANCE AND AIM.
WE'RE GOOD, TROY! WE DON'T NEED TO SEE THEM!
FWOOOSH
SSVVVV
SSHHHHHHHHHHHHHHHHH
THAT WAS NOT SUPPOSED TO HAPPEN.

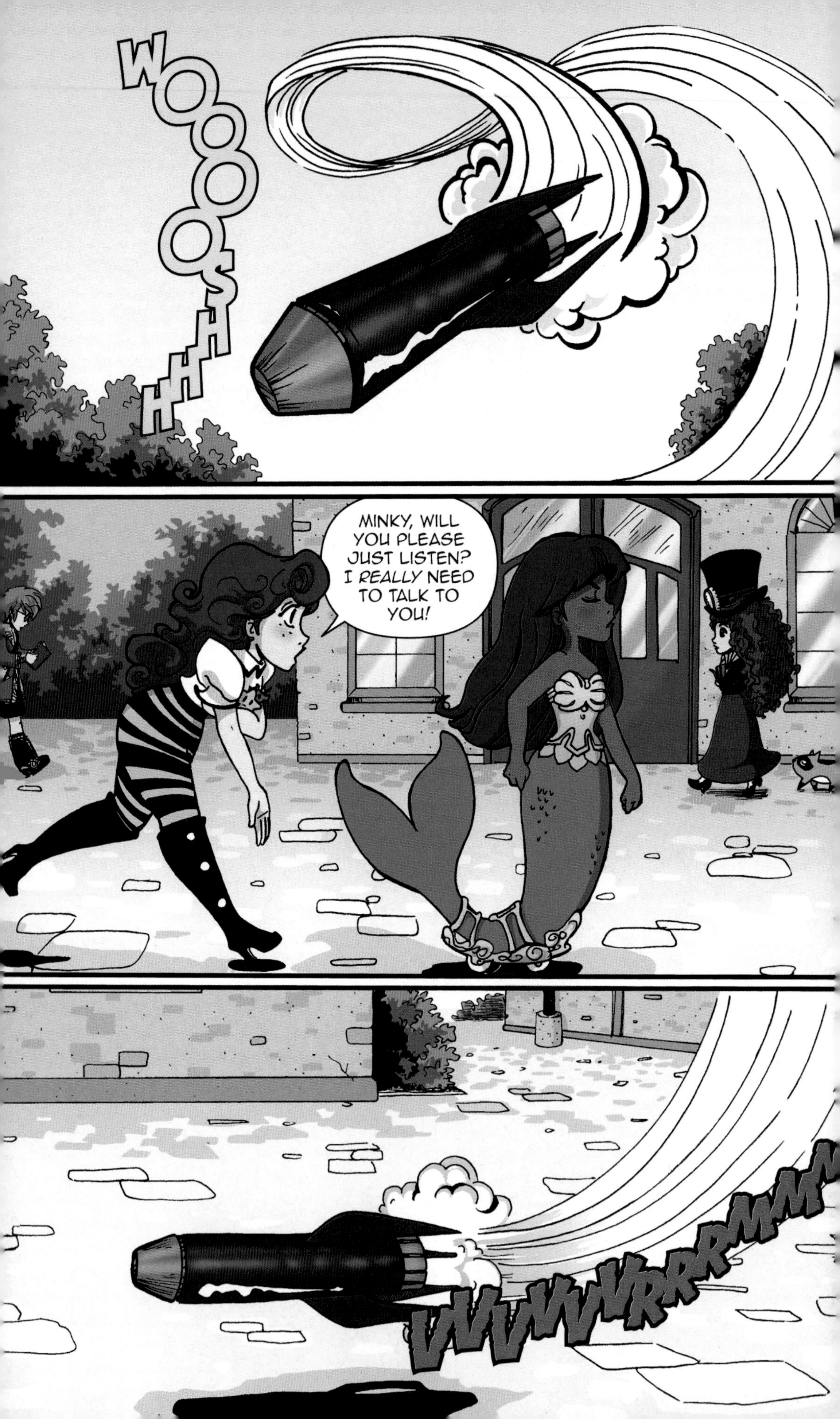
WOOOOSHHH
MINKY, WILL YOU PLEASE JUST LISTEN? I *REALLY* NEED TO TALK TO YOU!
VVVVVVRRRMMM

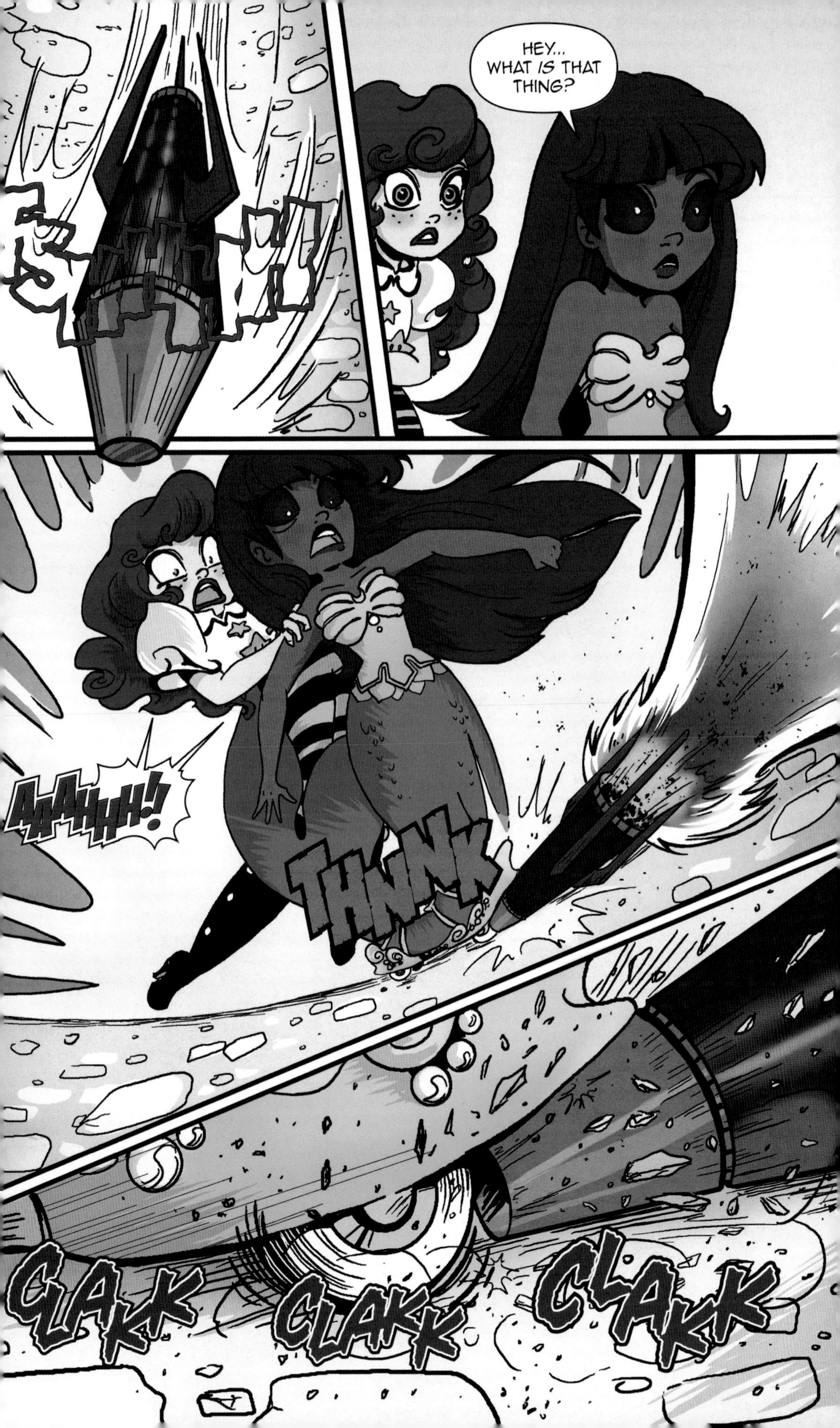
HEY... WHAT IS THAT THING?
AAAHHH!!
THNNK
CLAKK CLAKK CLAKK

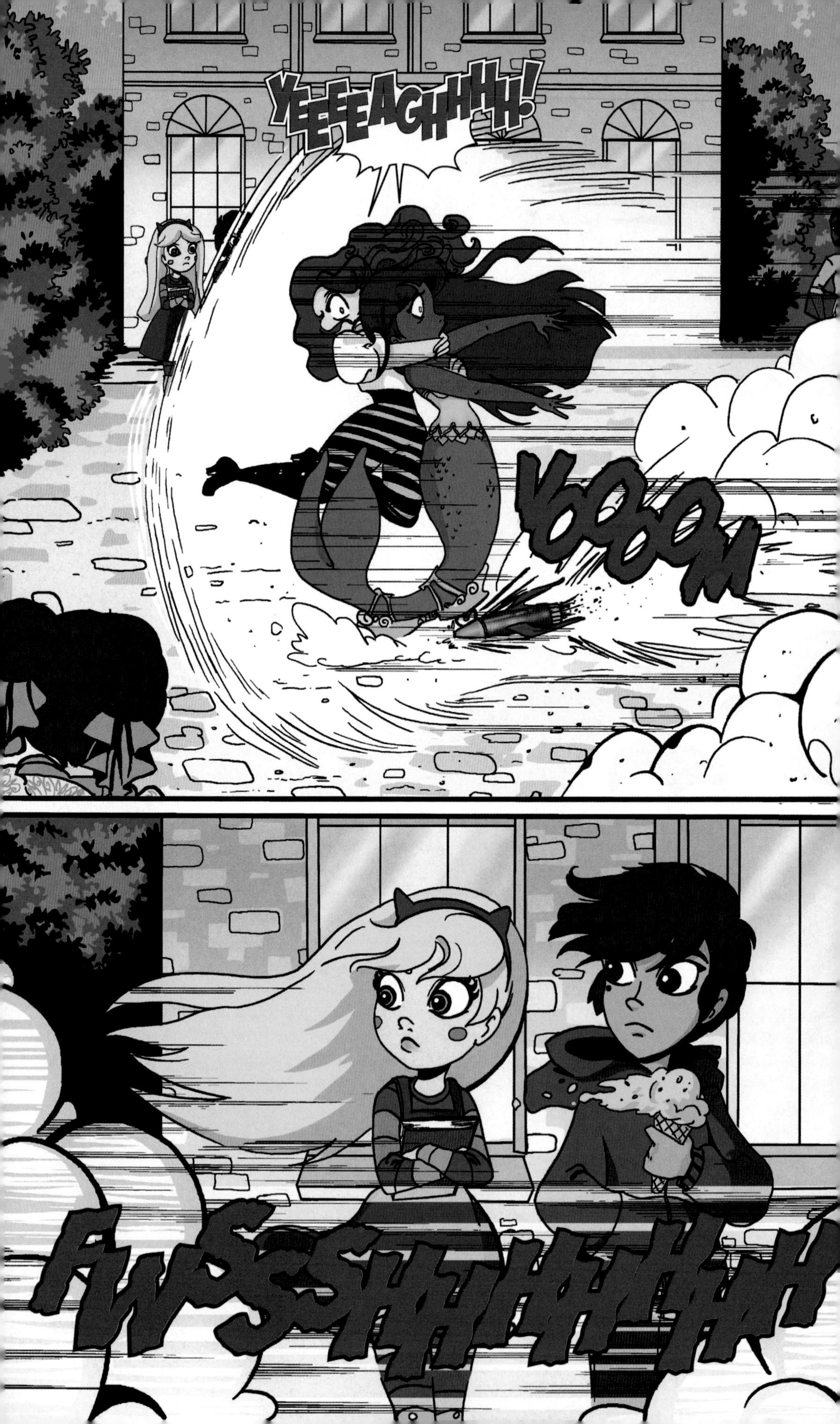
YEEEEAGHHHH!
VROOOM
FWSSHHHHHHH

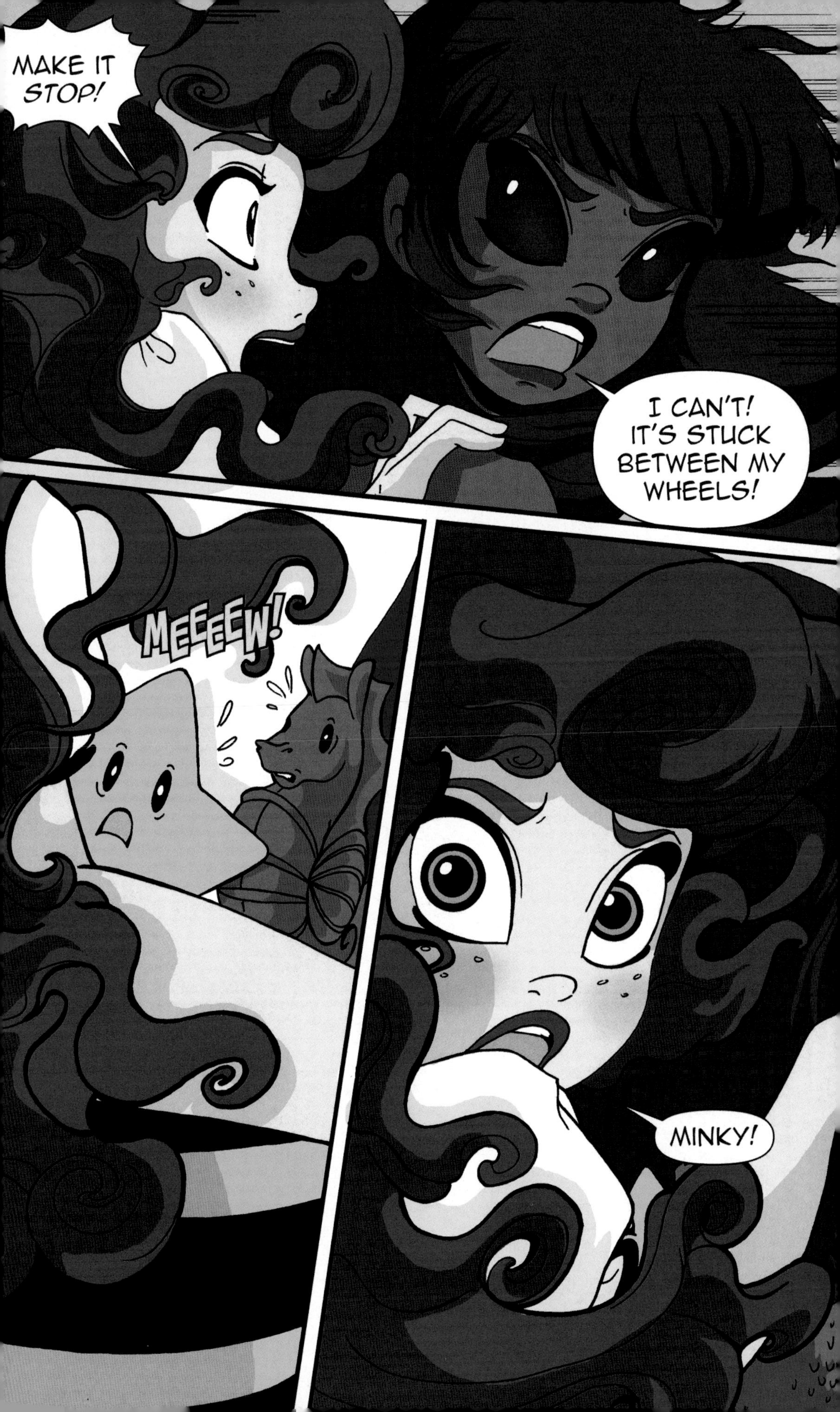
MAKE IT STOP!
I CAN'T! IT'S STUCK BETWEEN MY WHEELS!
MEEEEEW!
MINKY!

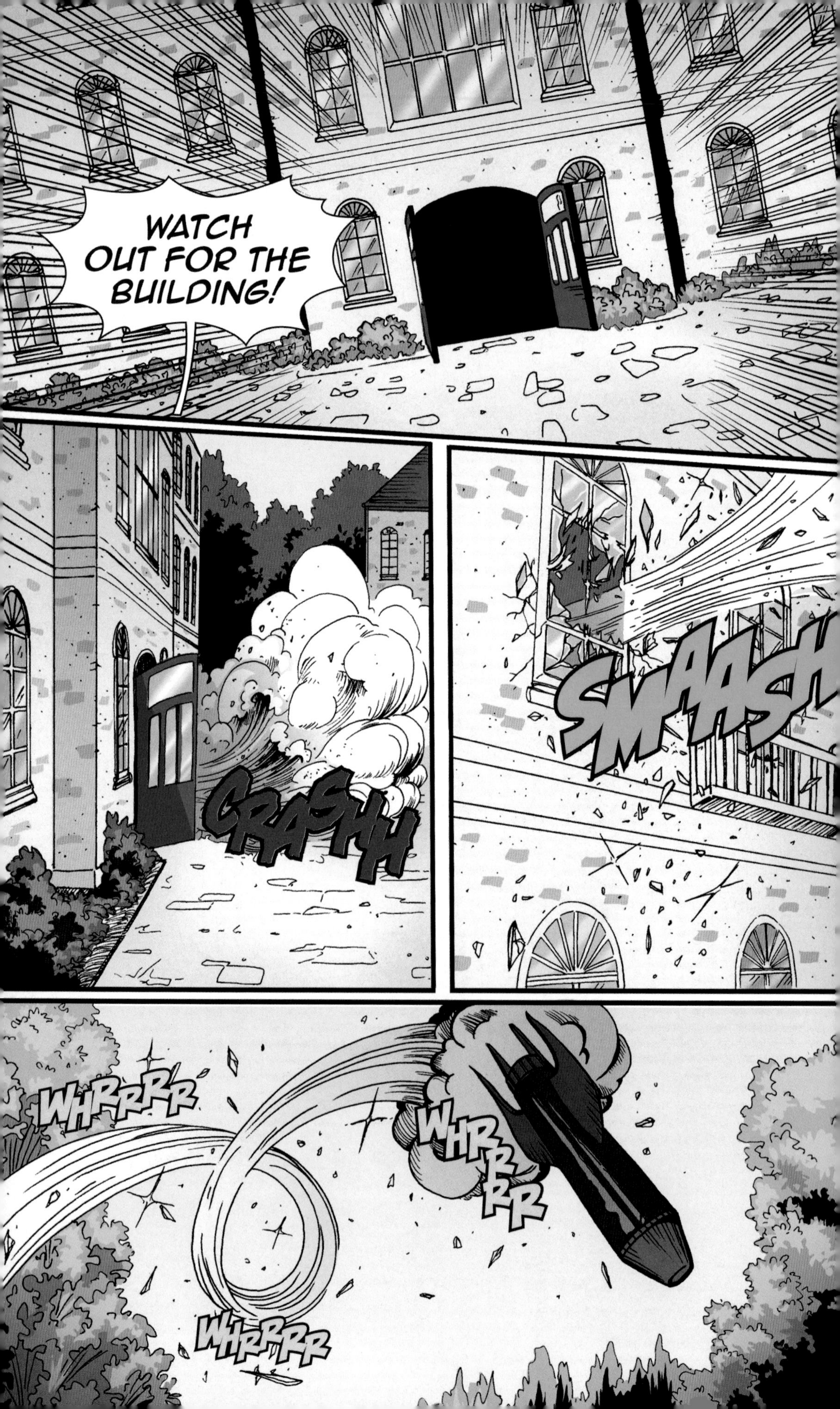
WATCH OUT FOR THE BUILDING!
CRASHH
SMAASH
WHRRRR
WHRRRR
WHRRRR

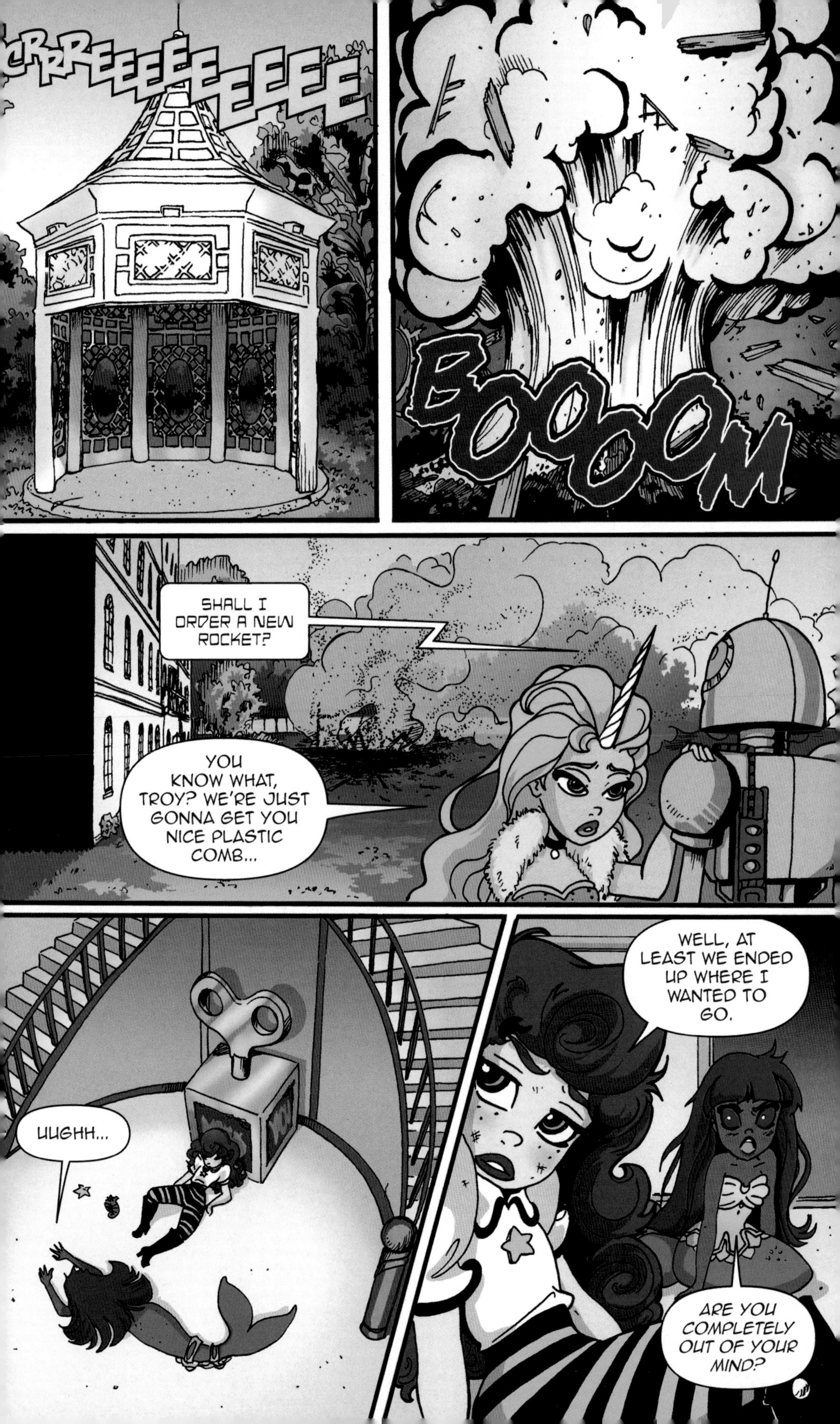
CRRREEEEEEEEEE
BOOOOOM
SHALL I ORDER A NEW ROCKET?
YOU KNOW WHAT, TROY? WE'RE JUST GONNA GET YOU NICE PLASTIC COMB...
UUGHH...
WELL, AT LEAST WE ENDED UP WHERE I WANTED TO GO.
ARE YOU COMPLETELY OUT OF YOUR MIND?

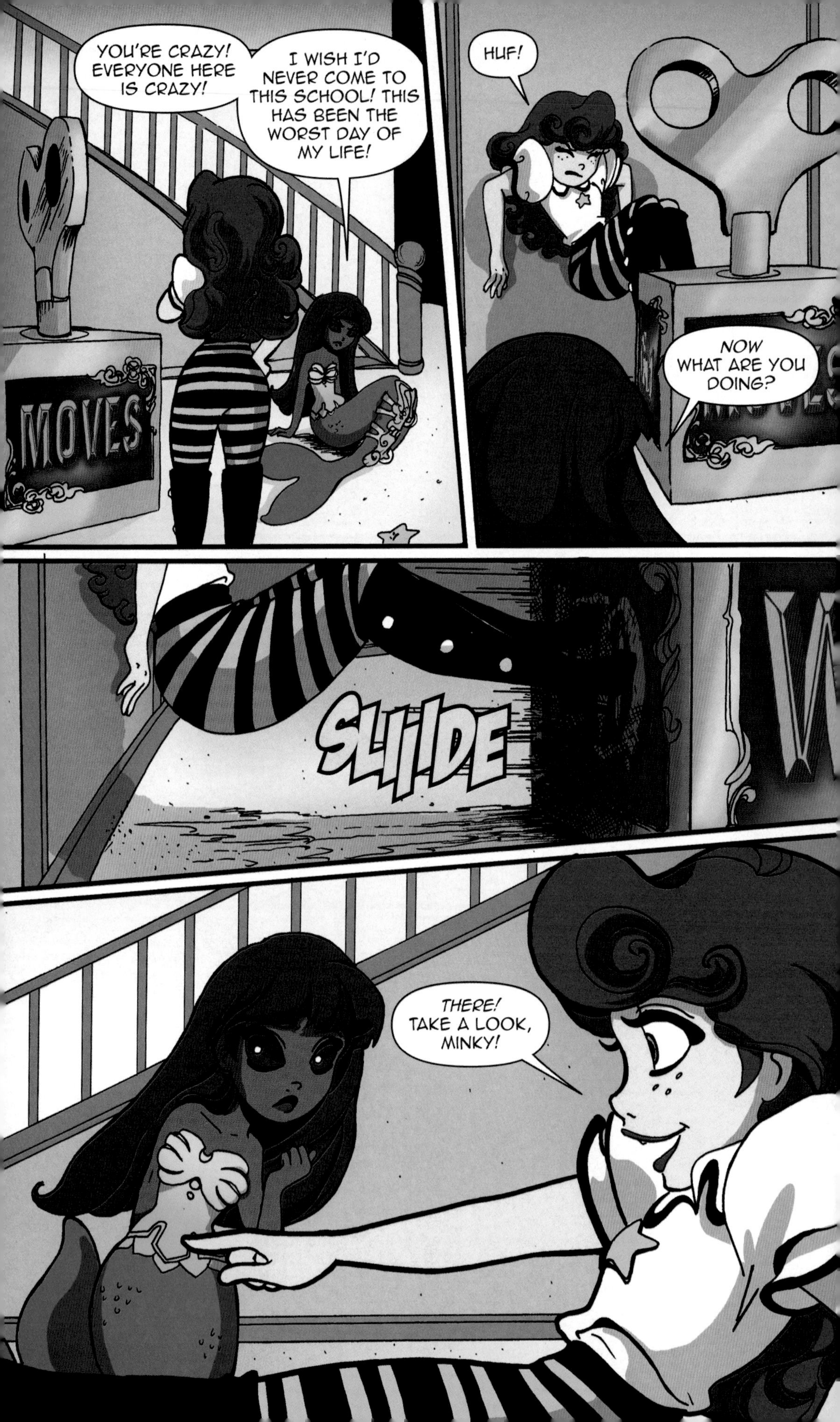
YOU'RE CRAZY! EVERYONE HERE IS CRAZY!
I WISH I'D NEVER COME TO THIS SCHOOL! THIS HAS BEEN THE WORST DAY OF MY LIFE!
MOVES
HUF!
NOW WHAT ARE YOU DOING?
SLIIDE
THERE! TAKE A LOOK, MINKY!

"FIND"?

I...I DON'T UNDERSTAND...

THIS IS WHAT I WAS TRYING TO TELL YOU...ALL THESE YEARS, WE'VE BEEN READING OUR SCHOOL MOTTO *WRONG!*

SOMEONE A LONG TIME AGO MUST HAVE PUSHED THE STATUE AGAINST THE WALL TO MAKE MORE ROOM, HIDING THE FIRST WORD ON IT. OUR MOTTO ISN'T "WHAT MOVES YOU", IT'S "*FIND* WHAT MOVES YOU"! IT'S NOT TELLING US THAT BEING TOYS IS THE ONLY THING WE SHOULD CARE ABOUT!

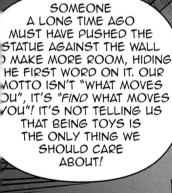

THE BIG KEY IS TELLING US THAT WE SHOULD FIND WHAT REALLY MATTERS TO US IN LIFE AND LET *THAT* MOVE US. THAT WAS THE REAL MESSAGE ALL ALONG...WE JUST FORGOT ABOUT IT.

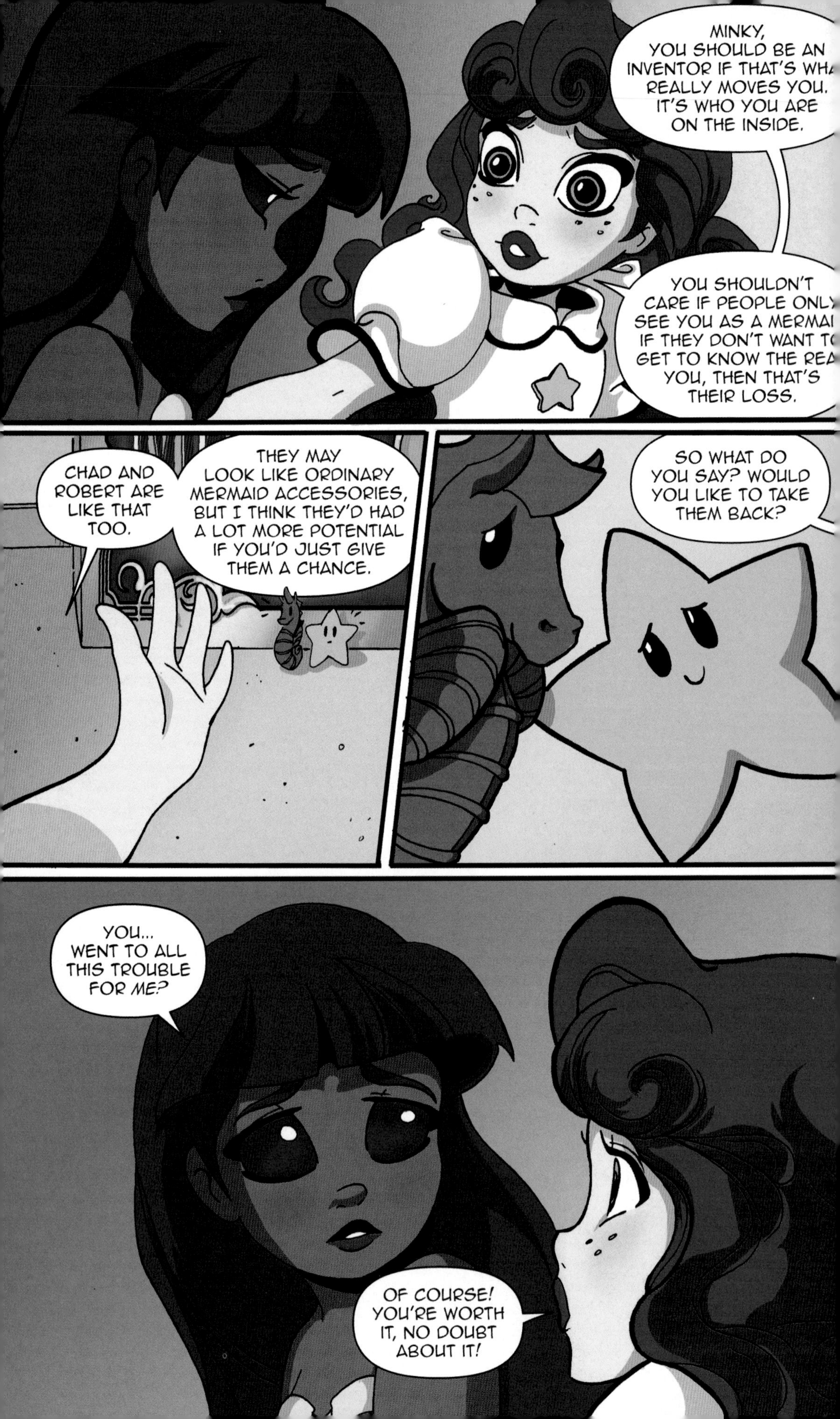
MINKY, YOU SHOULD BE AN INVENTOR IF THAT'S WHA REALLY MOVES YOU. IT'S WHO YOU ARE ON THE INSIDE.
YOU SHOULDN'T CARE IF PEOPLE ONLY SEE YOU AS A MERMAI IF THEY DON'T WANT T GET TO KNOW THE REA YOU, THEN THAT'S THEIR LOSS.
CHAD AND ROBERT ARE LIKE THAT TOO.
THEY MAY LOOK LIKE ORDINARY MERMAID ACCESSORIES, BUT I THINK THEY'D HAD A LOT MORE POTENTIAL IF YOU'D JUST GIVE THEM A CHANCE.
SO WHAT DO YOU SAY? WOULD YOU LIKE TO TAKE THEM BACK?
YOU... WENT TO ALL THIS TROUBLE FOR ME?
OF COURSE! YOU'RE WORTH IT, NO DOUBT ABOUT IT!

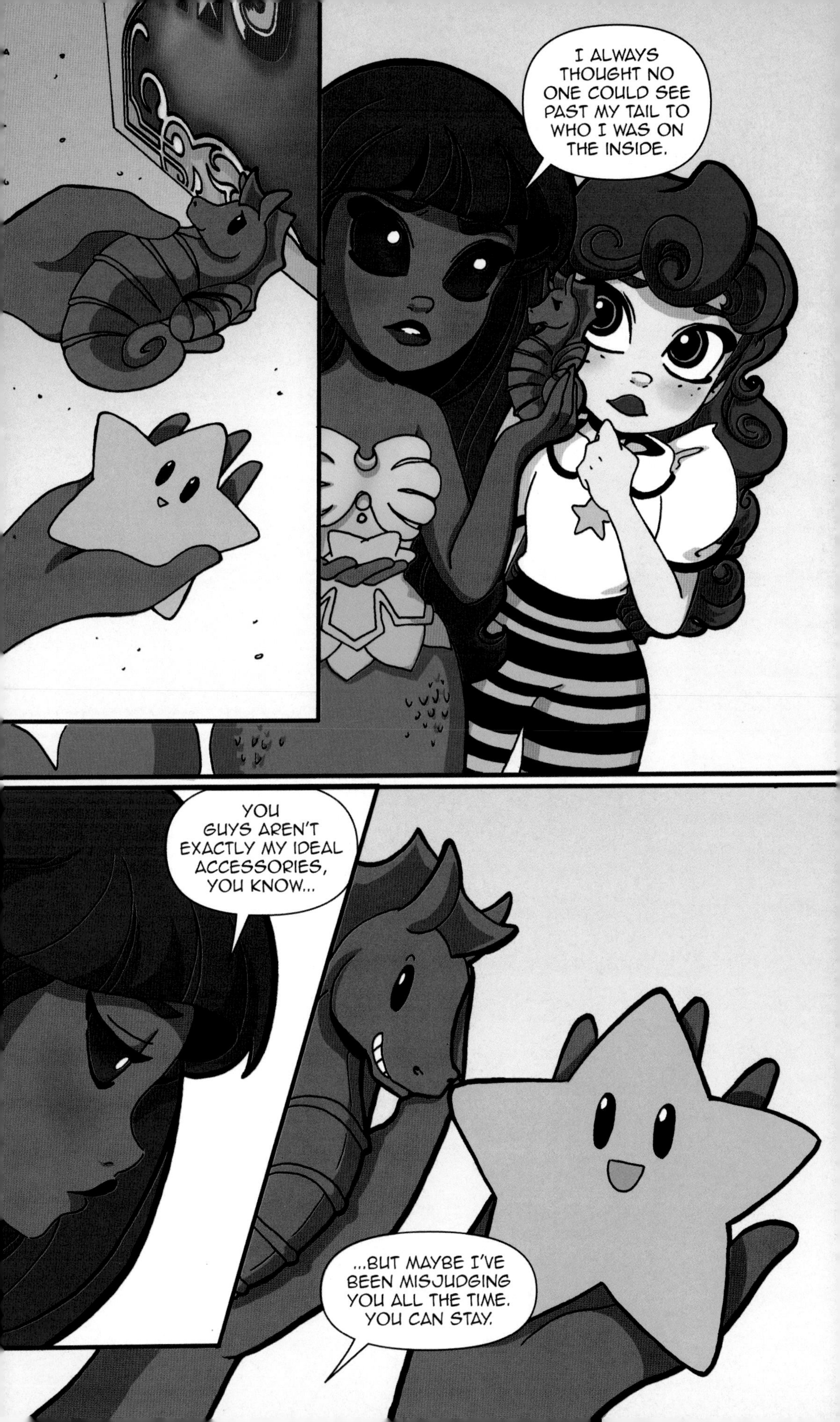
I ALWAYS THOUGHT NO ONE COULD SEE PAST MY TAIL TO WHO I WAS ON THE INSIDE.
YOU GUYS AREN'T EXACTLY MY IDEAL ACCESSORIES, YOU KNOW...
...BUT MAYBE I'VE BEEN MISJUDGING YOU ALL THE TIME. YOU CAN STAY.

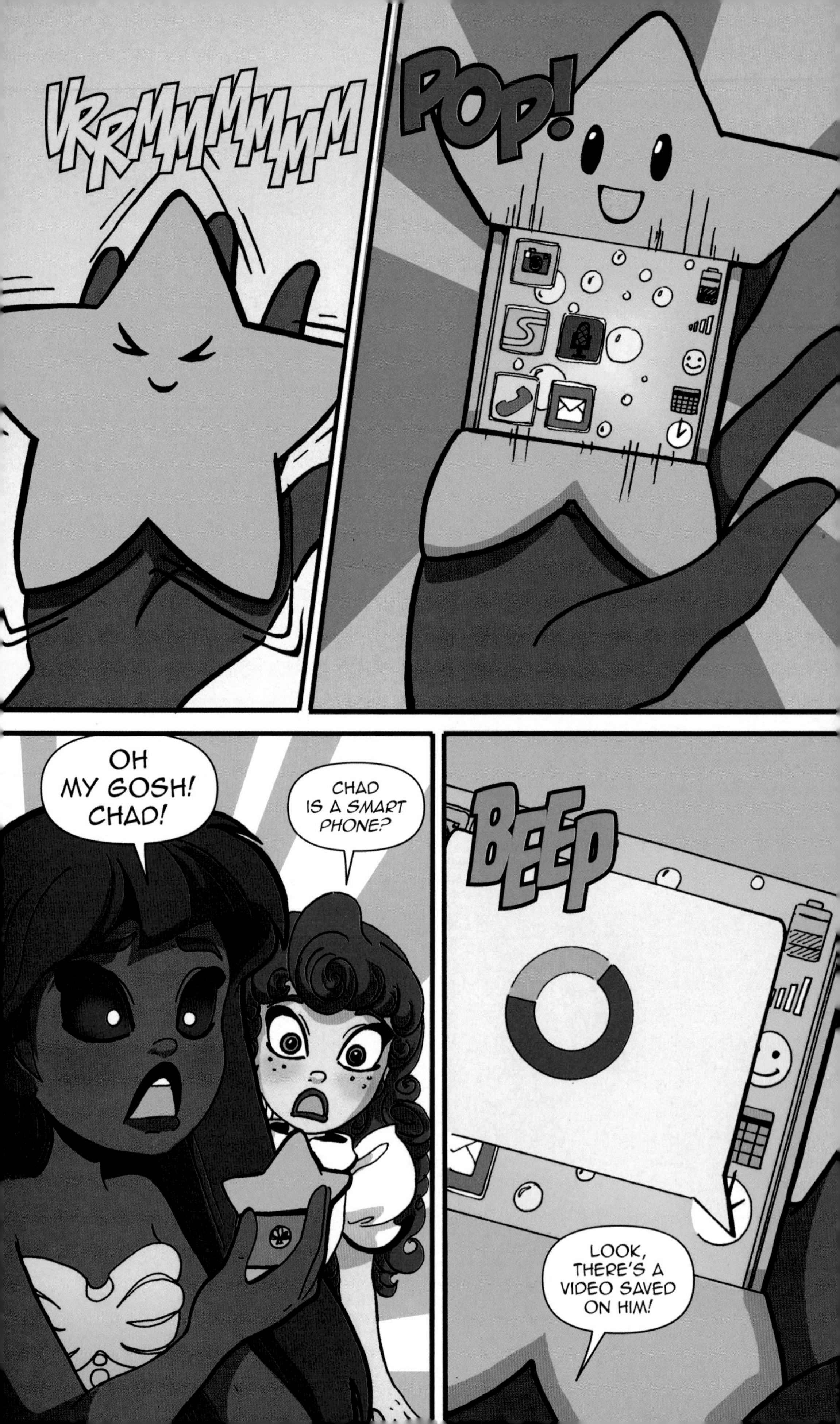
VRRMMMMMMMM
POP!
OH MY GOSH! CHAD!
CHAD IS A SMART PHONE?
BEEP
LOOK, THERE'S A VIDEO SAVED ON HIM!

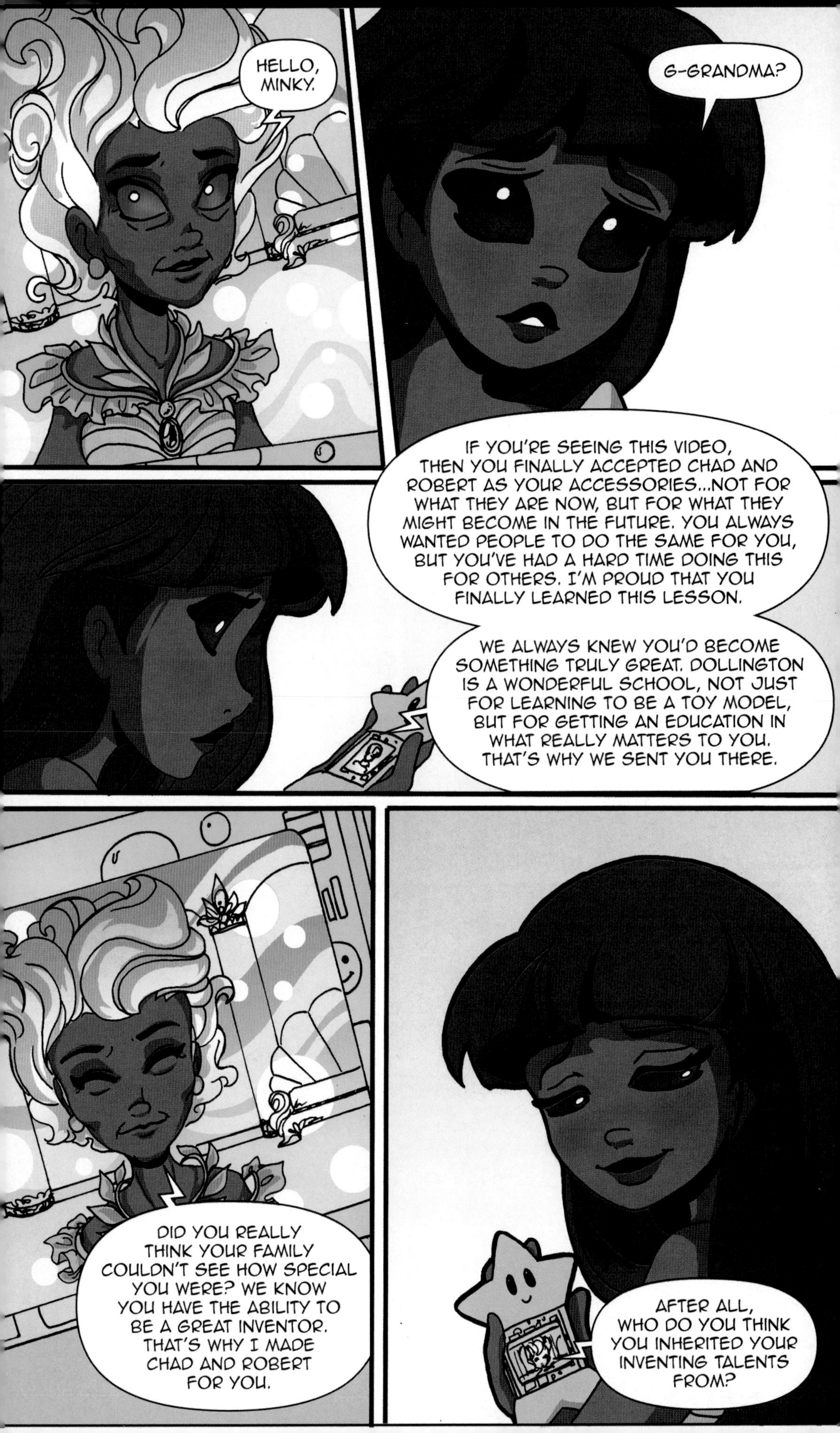
HELLO, MINKY.
G-GRANDMA?
IF YOU'RE SEEING THIS VIDEO, THEN YOU FINALLY ACCEPTED CHAD AND ROBERT AS YOUR ACCESSORIES...NOT FOR WHAT THEY ARE NOW, BUT FOR WHAT THEY MIGHT BECOME IN THE FUTURE. YOU ALWAYS WANTED PEOPLE TO DO THE SAME FOR YOU, BUT YOU'VE HAD A HARD TIME DOING THIS FOR OTHERS. I'M PROUD THAT YOU FINALLY LEARNED THIS LESSON.
WE ALWAYS KNEW YOU'D BECOME SOMETHING TRULY GREAT. DOLLINGTON IS A WONDERFUL SCHOOL, NOT JUST FOR LEARNING TO BE A TOY MODEL, BUT FOR GETTING AN EDUCATION IN WHAT REALLY MATTERS TO YOU. THAT'S WHY WE SENT YOU THERE.
DID YOU REALLY THINK YOUR FAMILY COULDN'T SEE HOW SPECIAL YOU WERE? WE KNOW YOU HAVE THE ABILITY TO BE A GREAT INVENTOR. THAT'S WHY I MADE CHAD AND ROBERT FOR YOU.
AFTER ALL, WHO DO YOU THINK YOU INHERITED YOUR INVENTING TALENTS FROM?

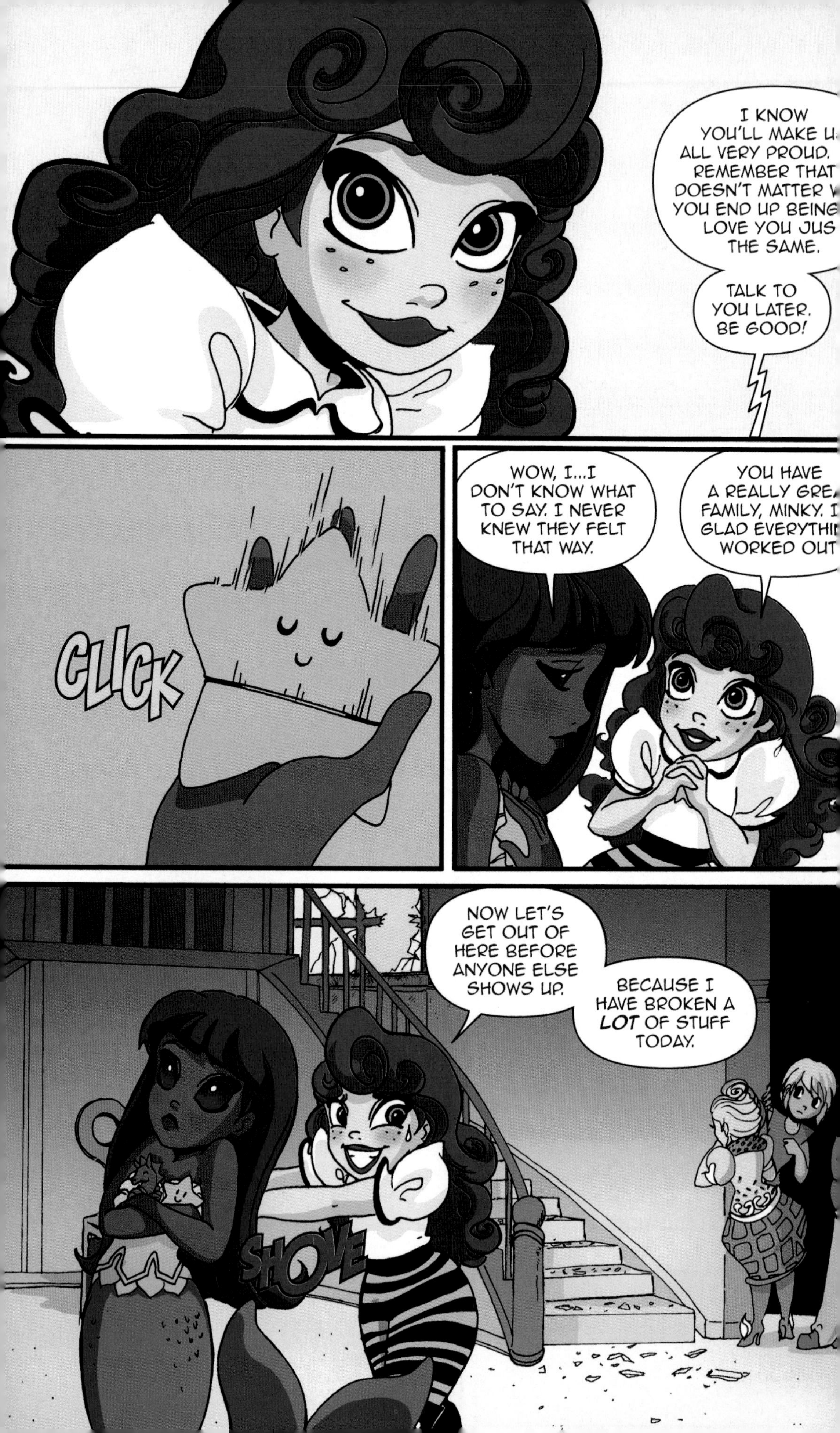
I KNOW YOU'LL MAKE U ALL VERY PROUD. REMEMBER THAT DOESN'T MATTER YOU END UP BEING LOVE YOU JUS THE SAME.
TALK TO YOU LATER. BE GOOD!
CLICK
WOW, I...I DON'T KNOW WHAT TO SAY. I NEVER KNEW THEY FELT THAT WAY.
YOU HAVE A REALLY GRE FAMILY, MINKY. I GLAD EVERYTHI WORKED OUT
NOW LET'S GET OUT OF HERE BEFORE ANYONE ELSE SHOWS UP.
BECAUSE I HAVE BROKEN A *LOT* OF STUFF TODAY.
SHOVE

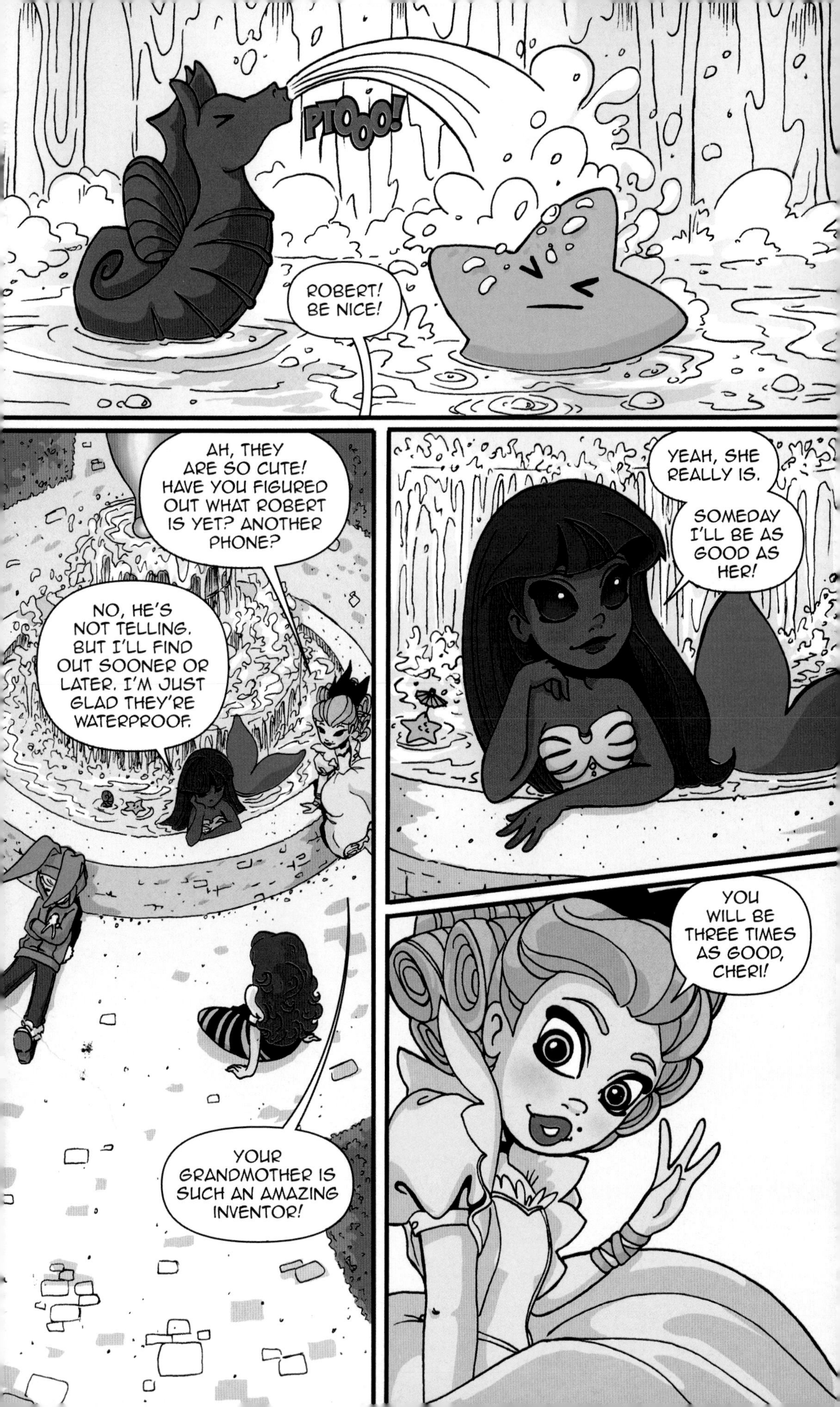
PTOOOO!
ROBERT! BE NICE!
AH, THEY ARE SO CUTE! HAVE YOU FIGURED OUT WHAT ROBERT IS YET? ANOTHER PHONE?
NO, HE'S NOT TELLING. BUT I'LL FIND OUT SOONER OR LATER. I'M JUST GLAD THEY'RE WATERPROOF.
YOUR GRANDMOTHER IS SUCH AN AMAZING INVENTOR!
YEAH, SHE REALLY IS.
SOMEDAY I'LL BE AS GOOD AS HER!
YOU WILL BE THREE TIMES AS GOOD, CHERI!

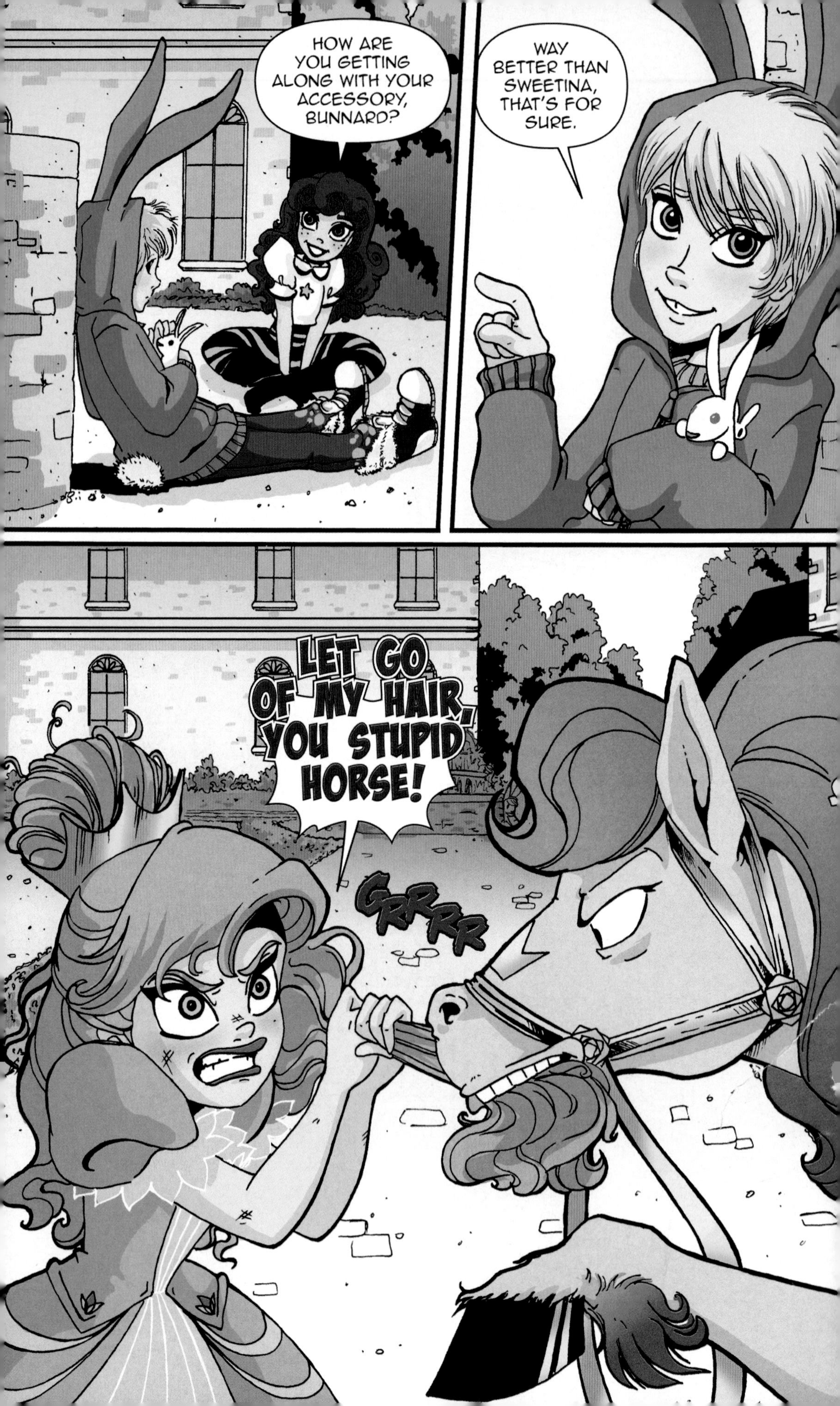
HOW ARE YOU GETTING ALONG WITH YOUR ACCESSORY, BUNNARD?
WAY BETTER THAN SWEETINA, THAT'S FOR SURE.
LET GO OF MY HAIR, YOU STUPID HORSE!
GRRRR

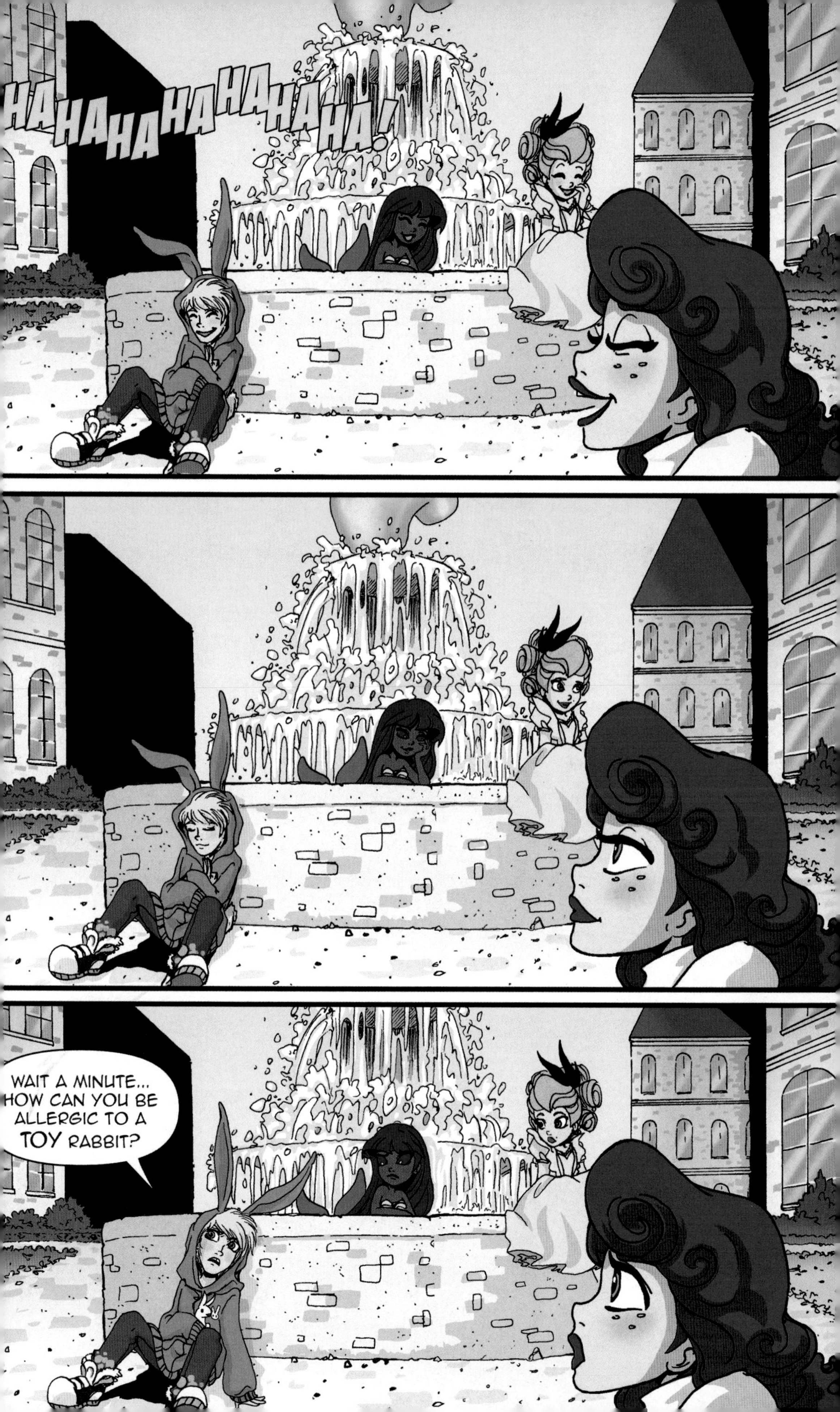
HAHAHAHAHAHAHAHA!
WAIT A MINUTE... HOW CAN YOU BE ALLERGIC TO A TOY RABBIT?

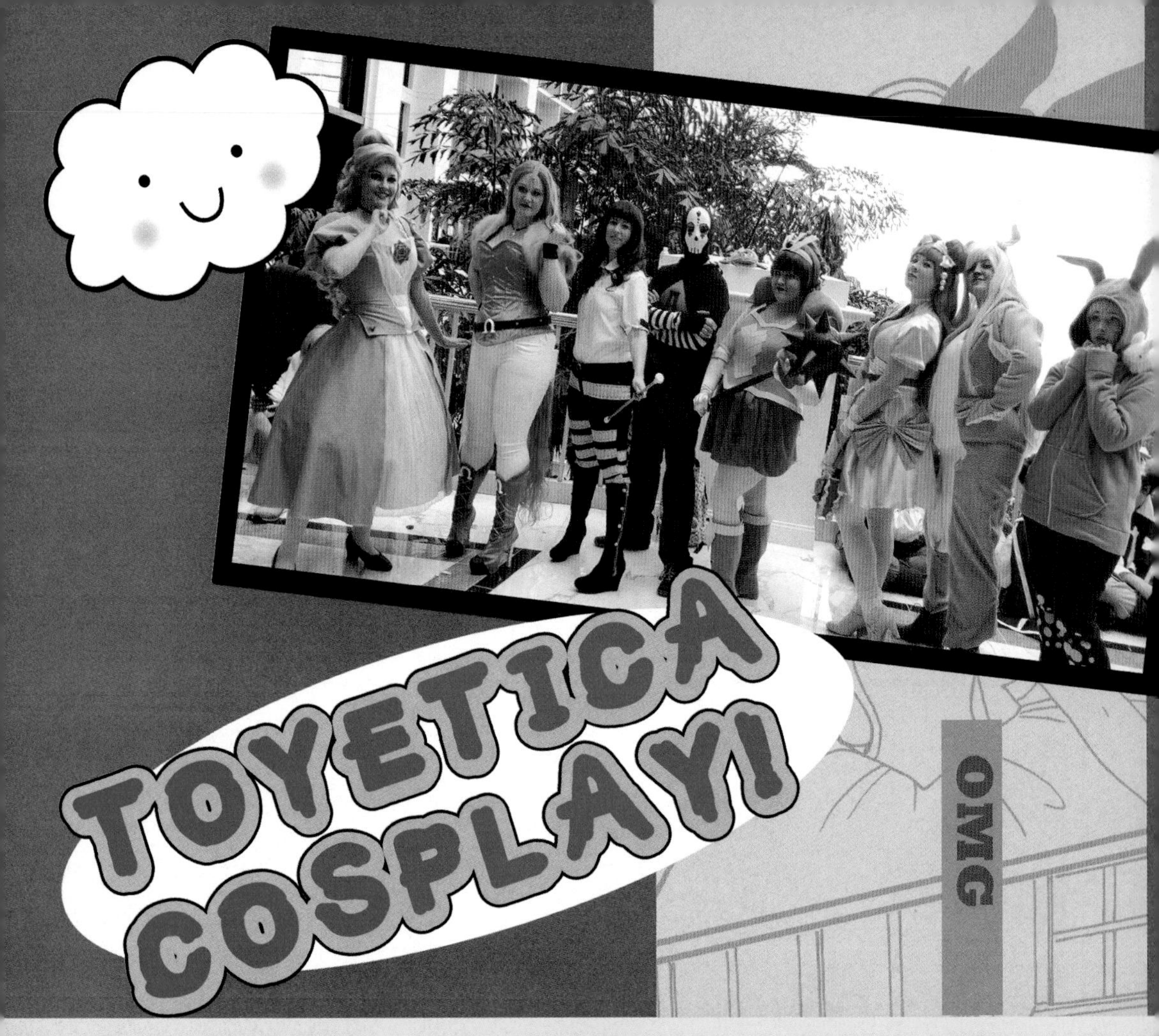

TOYETICA COSPLAY!

OMG

IT WAS A SUNNY DAY AT KATSUCON WHEN WE DECIDED TO DRESS AS OUR FAVORITE TOYETICA CHARACTERS AND GET UP TO TOTAL SHENANIGANS!

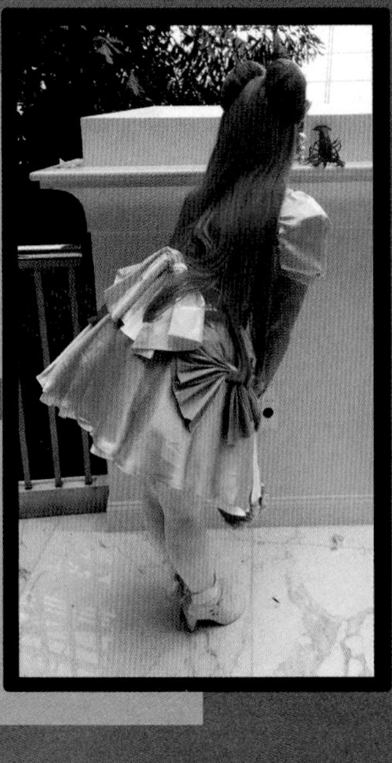

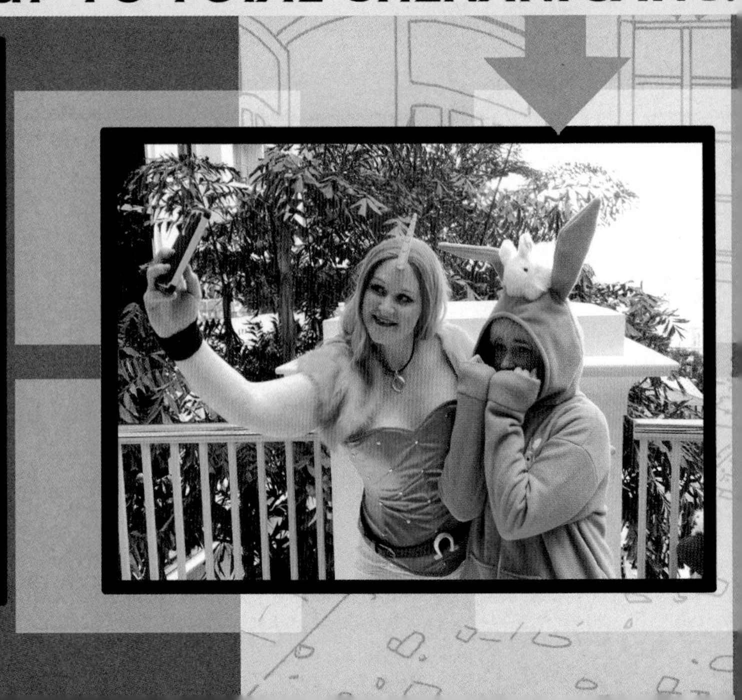

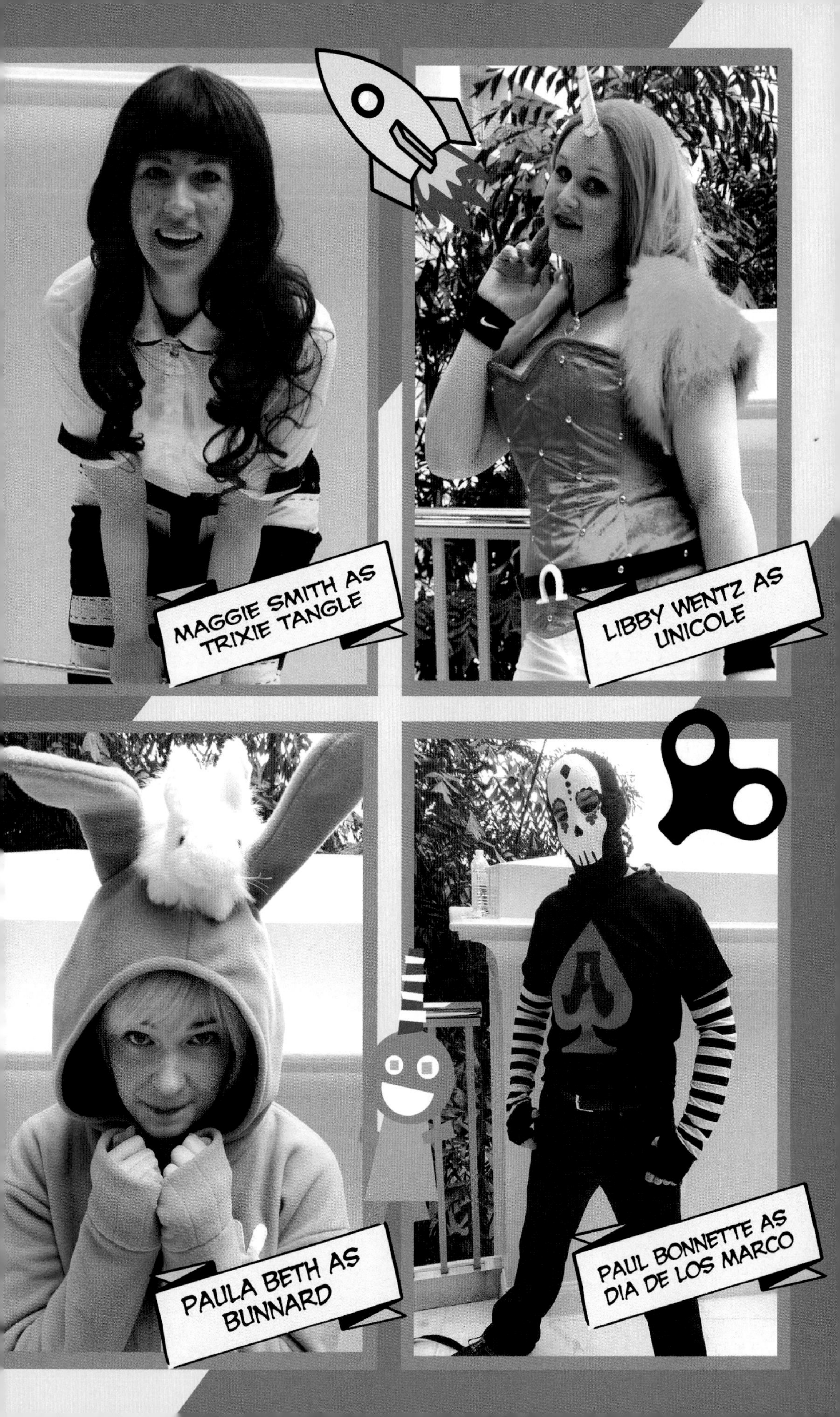
MAGGIE SMITH AS TRIXIE TANGLE
LIBBY WENTZ AS UNICOLE
PAULA BETH AS BUNNARD
PAUL BONNETTE AS DIA DE LOS MARCO

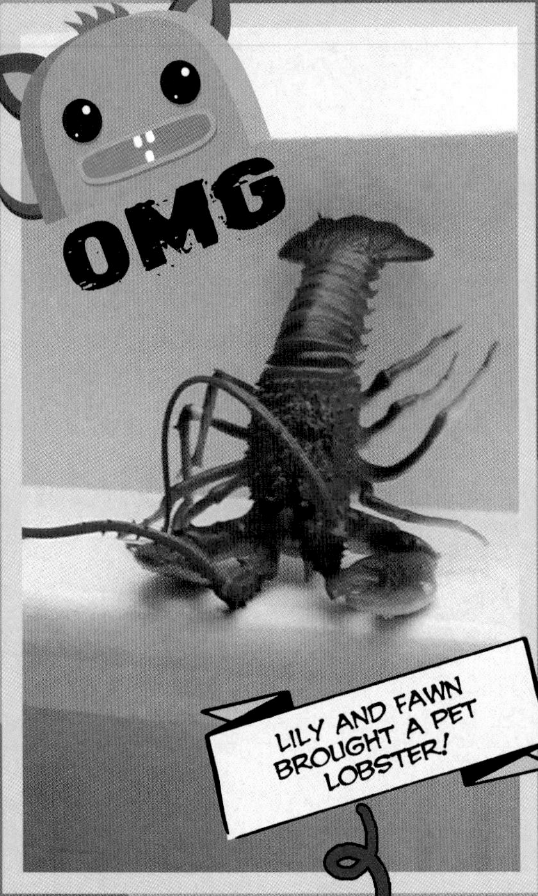
OMG

LILY AND FAWN BROUGHT A PET LOBSTER!

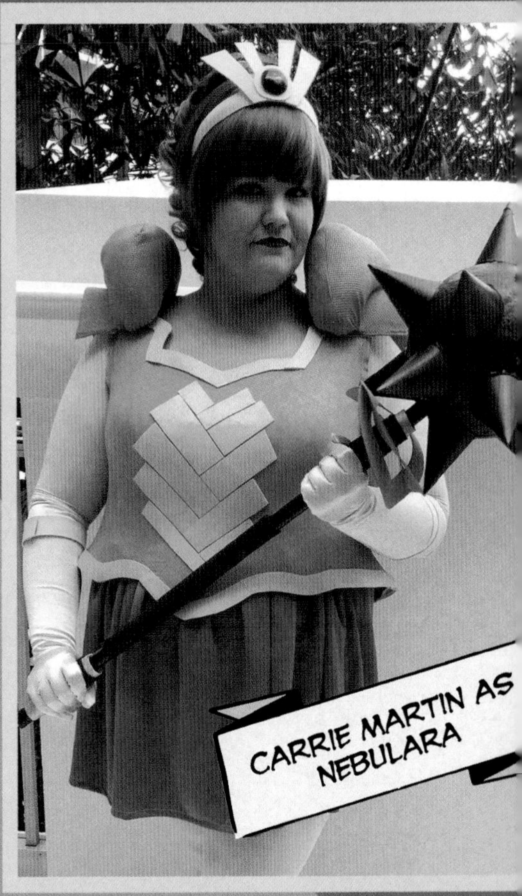

CARRIE MARTIN AS NEBULARA

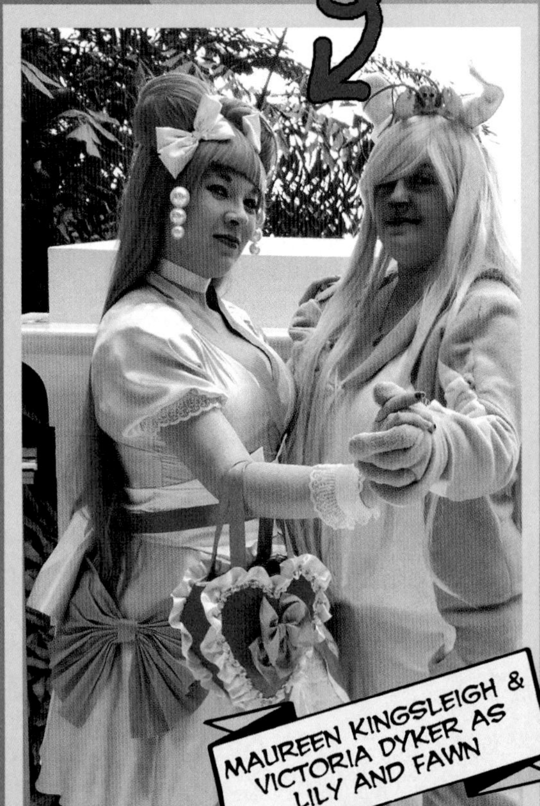

MAUREEN KINGSLEIGH & VICTORIA DYKER AS LILY AND FAWN

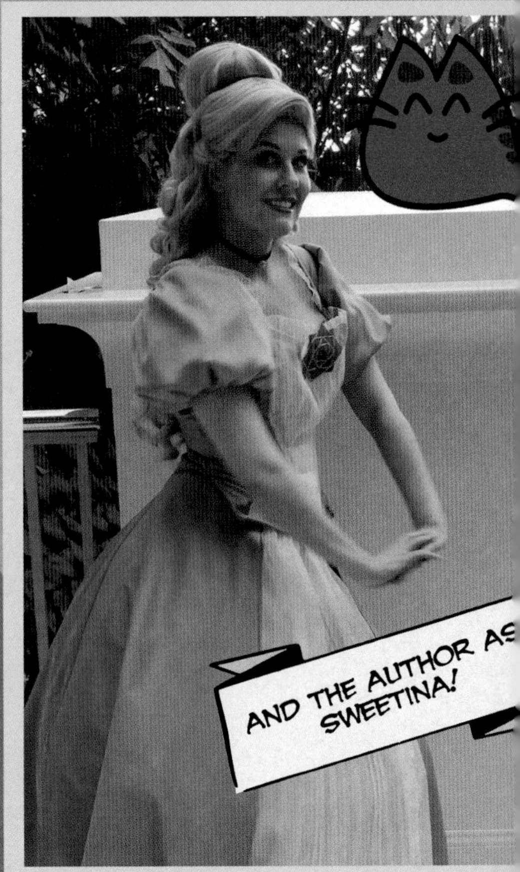

AND THE AUTHOR AS SWEETINA!

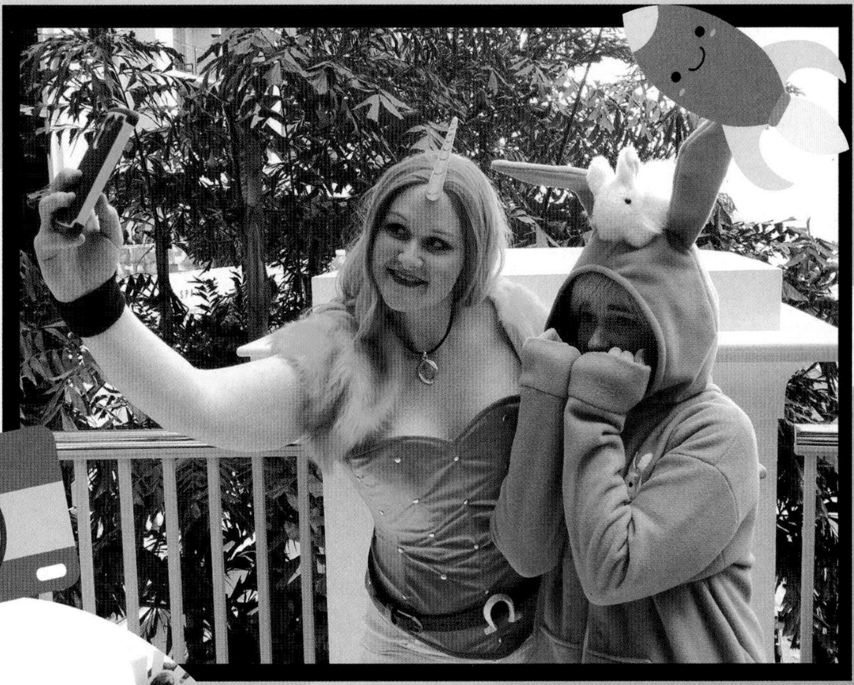

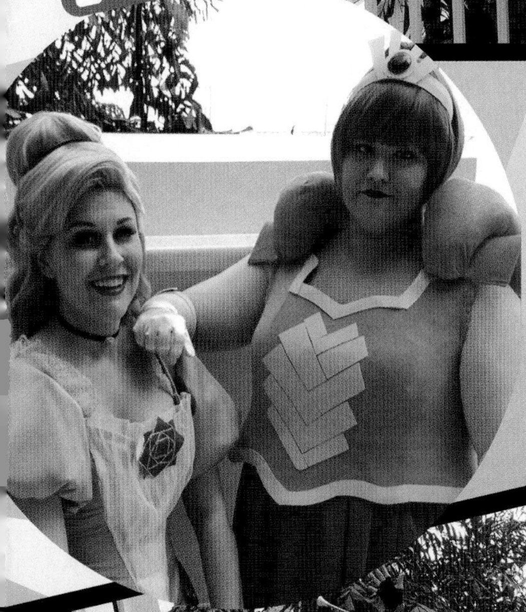

Thanks to all my friends for a wonderful fun time!

See you on the toy shelf!

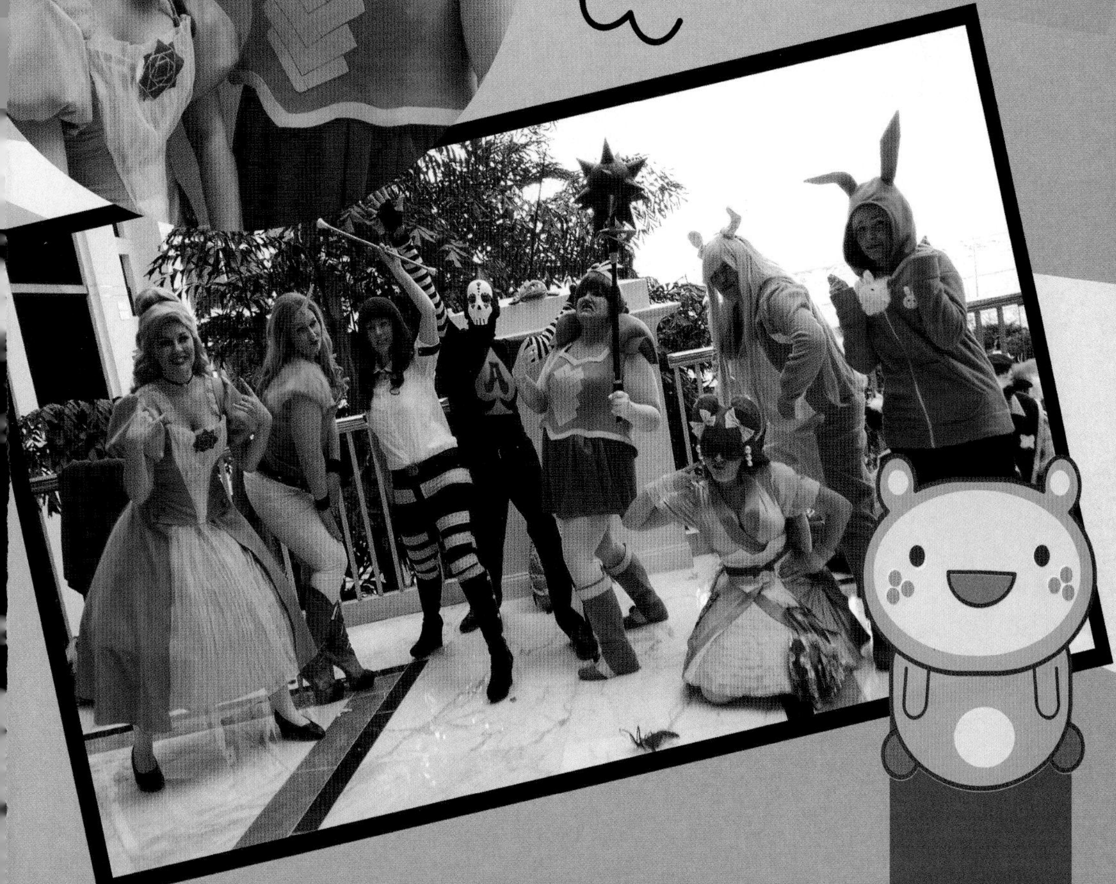

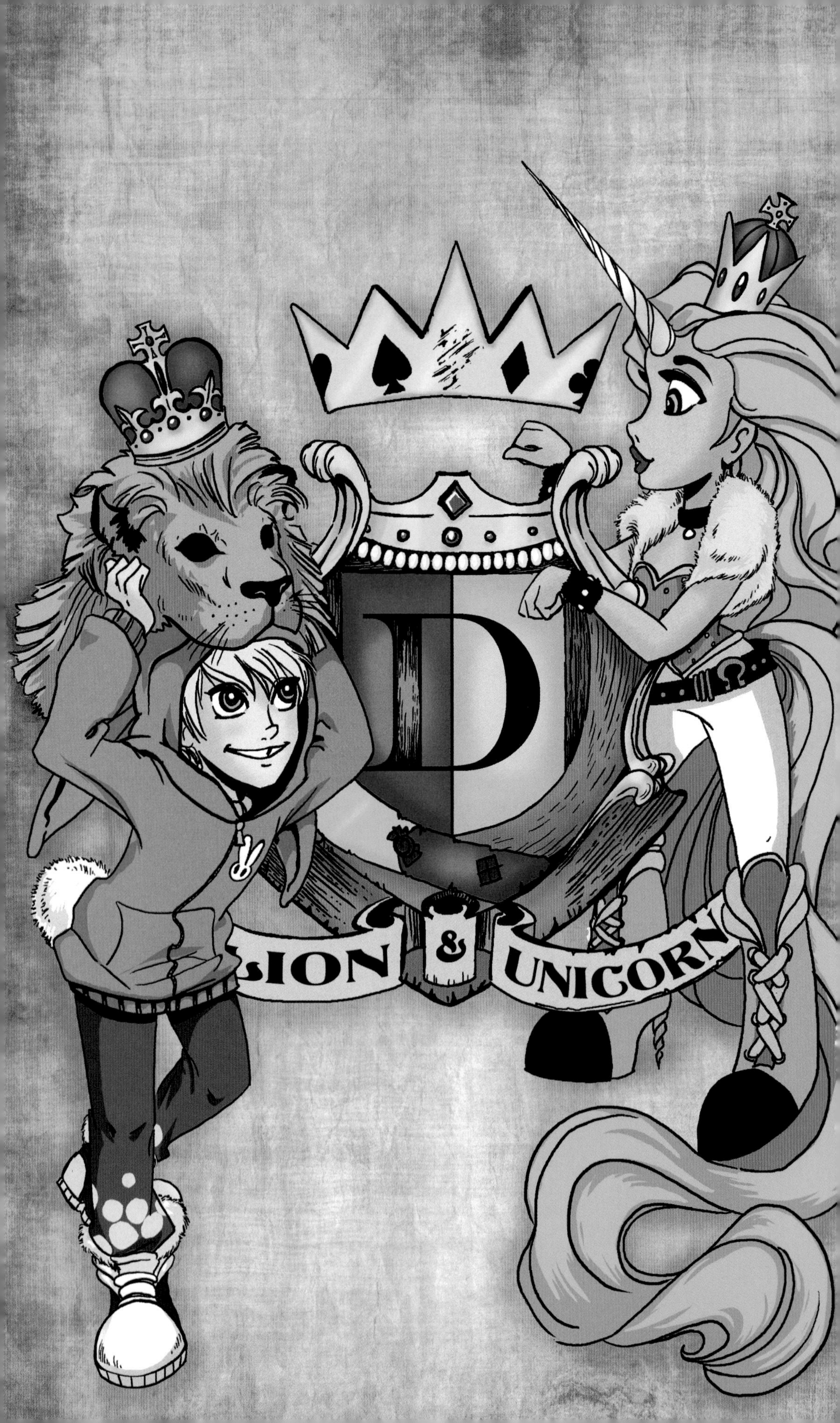
LION
&
UNICORN